# RED EMPIRE

## ALSO BY JONATHAN MABERRY

*Burn to Shine*
*The Dragon in Winter*
*Cave 13*
*Son of the Poison Rose*
*Kagen the Damned*
*Relentless*
*Ink*
*Rage*
*Deep Silence*
*Dogs of War*
*Kill Switch*
*Predator One*
*Code Zero*
*Extinction Machine*
*Assassin's Code*
*The King of the Plagues*
*The Dragon Factory*
*Patient Zero*
*Joe Ledger: Special Ops*
*Still of Night*
*Dark of Night*
*Fall of Night*
*Dead of Night*
*The Wolfman*
*NecroTek*
*The Nightsiders: The Orphan Academy*
*The Nightsiders: Vault of Shadows*
*The Sleepers War: Alpha Wave*
*The Unlearnable Truths*
*Ghostwalkers: A Deadlands Novel*
*Lost Roads*
*Broken Lands*
*Bits & Pieces*
*Fire & Ash*
*Flesh & Bone*
*Dust & Decay*
*Rot & Ruin*
*Bad Moon Rising*
*Dead Man's Song*
*Ghost Road Blues*
*Bewilderness*
*Glimpse*
*Mars One*

## ANTHOLOGIES (AS EDITOR)

*Don't Turn Out the Lights: A Tribute to Alvin Schwartz's Scary Stories to Tell in the Dark*
*Joe Ledger: Unstoppable* (with Bryan Thomas Schmidt)
*Joe Ledger: Unbreakable* (with Bryan Thomas Schmidt)
*Nights of the Living Dead* (with George A. Romero)
*V-Wars*
*V-Wars: Blood and Fire*
*V-Wars: Night Terrors*
*V-Wars: Shockwaves*
*Out of Tune Vol. 1*
*Out of Tune Vol. 2*
*The X-Files: Trust No One*
*The X-Files: The Truth Is Out There*
*The X-Files: Secret Agendas*
*Hardboiled Horror*
*Aliens: Bug Hunt*
*Aliens vs. Predators: Ultimate Prey* (with Bryan Thomas Schmidt)
*Baker Street Irregulars* (with Michael A. Ventrella)
*The Game Is Afoot: Baker Street Irregulars II* (with Michael A. Ventrella)
*Scary Out There*
*Weird Tales: 100 Years of Weird*
*Double Trouble* (with Keith R. A. DeCandido)
*The Good, the Bad, and the Uncanny: Tales of a Very Weird West*
*Weird Tales: Best of the Early Years 1923–25* (with Justin Criado)
*Weird Tales: Best of the Early Years 1926–27* (with Kaye Lynne Booth)

# JONATHAN MABERRY

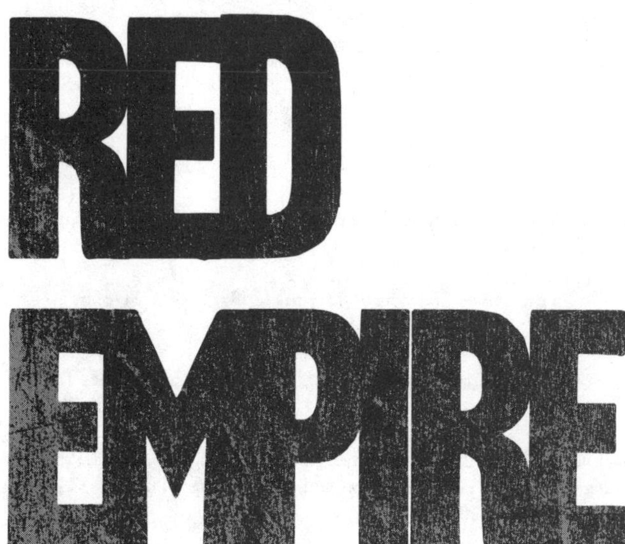

# RED EMPIRE

## A JOE LEDGER AND ROGUE TEAM INTERNATIONAL NOVEL

ST. MARTIN'S GRIFFIN
NEW YORK

This is a work of fiction. All of the names, characters, organizations, places, and events portrayed in this work are either products of the author's imagination or used fictitiously.

First published in the United States by St. Martin's Griffin, an imprint of St. Martin's Publishing Group

*EU Representative:* Macmillan Publishers Ireland Ltd, 1st Floor, The Liffey Trust Centre, 117–126 Sheriff Street Upper, Dublin 1, D01 YC43



www.stmartins.com

The Library of Congress Cataloging-in-Publication Data is available upon request.

ISBN 978-1-250-89268-3 (trade paperback)
ISBN 978-1-250-89269-0 (ebook)



First Edition: 2026

10 9 8 7 6 5 4 3 2 1

**This one is for Chad Stahelski.**
**Director of the John Wick films. Fellow martial artist, fellow pop-culture nerd.**
**Colleague and friend.**

**And, as always, for Sara Jo.**

# PROLOGUE

> **"Where there is mystery, it is generally suspected there must also be evil."**
>
> **—GEORGE GORDON, LORD BYRON**

The world keeps trying to kill me.

It's taken some pretty serious shots and as the months and years pass, it hasn't lost any of its enthusiasm. Or its deviousness.

I keep sucking air, though. Each time I somehow manage to pick myself up, and either slap off the dirt and stagger back to the fight, or someone medevacs me to an aid station or a trauma hospital and the doctors do their magic to ensure that I have another season to run.

You know that saying how a bone is stronger in the place where it broke? And the thing from Nietzsche everyone and his brother always quotes—about the things that don't kill you making you stronger? Yeah, a lot of that is true.

I'm stronger than I used to be. Less physically vulnerable. Not that I have superpowers. Bullets don't bounce off my skin the way they do with Superman, and I don't have Iron Man's armor. I don't have spider-sense or adamantium bones. No, I'm stronger because each time I survive a fight, I learn from it. I become less trusting, less naïve.

Colder.

Harder.

It takes more to kill me because as time goes on it becomes easier for me to take the first shot, and to make sure that shot is the last one fired.

This is part of the cost of war. A true warrior takes up his sword and shield because his ideals drive him to do it, and his love of family and flag puts steel into his arms and an unbreakable determination into his heart.

I was like that.

That love, that passion, makes you dangerous at first, but it also bares your breast to arrows other than those fired by your enemy. The glow of idealism makes it easier for the sniper in the bushes to take aim.

And so you get harder. There's no other path to survival.

You shove that idealism down into the dark, you turn the dials on passion down because you don't want to draw the shooter's aim. It casts you into a kind of darkness. A predatory darkness. In those shadows you change from someone defending the weak—the prey—to someone who is as much a predator as the enemy.

Your motives and justifications may be better, cleaner, but your methods are not. While fighting monsters you risk becoming one. Nietzsche warned about that, too.

And yet . . .

And yet. There is a line in the psychological sand that any person fears to cross, and yet which pulls us toward it. Loss. Grief. Call it what you want.

On this side of the line, you feel the full horror of a love lost. A friend, a brother-in-arms, a son or daughter. A lover. Someone who means the world to you. You will burn down heaven to protect them. You believe—truly believe—that you would march into hell to keep them safe. No matter what happens to you.

You take those risks because you believe that after all of the gun smoke clears, and if you're still alive, then you and the person you love will have a life together afterward. Both of you the same as you were before. You believe that even while the world and the war try to make you a monster.

But when the person you love is taken and the war goes on . . . ?

Damn.

That's where the real monsters are made. When you have nothing left to love and the enemy still stands before you, grinning at your pain, feeding on your loss. In those moments, the grief can kill you. It can drive you to a final act of passion in which you throw everything away. You attack without skill or art, merely with fury. And you die without balancing any cosmic scales, without inflicting punishment. Maybe you spend the rest of eternity in your own private hell, feeling your loss and realizing your defeat.

Or . . .

Or you *don't* give in to the passion of hate.

Instead, you let that hate grow cold, and in the secret dark places of your soul you crouch over that unsavory meal and feed upon it. You become a monster dining on the manna of the pit. On cold, cold hate. Knowing that with each bite you are less of the person who once loved. You are less of the person who, had you and your love survived, would have reclaimed joy and innocence and optimism.

That version of you wouldn't know this dark and rapacious thing.

Because it is the monster that survives. It's the monster that *can* survive.

I loved twice in my life before I fell for the love of my life. But the two previous times the love was just as strong. Different in unique ways, but powerful and real. And both times the universe used my happiness as the light by which to take aim.

The first time was Helen. My first love, when I was fourteen and the world was filled with light and magic. Four older teenage boys trapped us in a deserted field and taught us about darkness and their own brand of sorcery. They beat me nearly to death, and while I lay there, bleeding and almost dead, I saw what they did to Helen.

Her heart continued to beat after that, after hospitals and surgeries and counseling. But she was dead. Years later when I found her at her place, the empty bottle of drain cleaner lying where it had fallen from her hand, I felt the darkness begin to take root in the soil of my soul. Flowers of hate have blossomed since.

A few years ago, I fell in love again. A woman named Grace Courtland. A fellow soldier, a fellow warrior against real darkness. A woman who saved the world. The actual world. And died doing it. I held her as she left me. I breathed in her last breath as all of the heat left her through a hole an assassin's bullet had punched into the world.

More recently, a murderous little man delivered a brightly wrapped gift to my family on Christmas Eve. They were all there—my brother, Sean, his wife and their kids, my dad. Even the family dog. All of them gathered around to open the present.

Maybe they were still smiling when the bomb went off. Maybe their last living thought was the fun of a surprise gift and the joyful spirit of the season. I hope so. God, how I hope that was what filled their minds instead of horror, fear, and terror.

I have to hold on to that belief. Without it I would lose myself. As I did once. As I did after that big bang. The darkness inside consumed me for a while. It owned me, body and soul, and as its agent I went hunting for the bad guys and did things to them.

I beat the darkness, but that's like beating the Devil. You win a battle, but the war goes on, and the enemy is patient and relentless.

My friends and colleagues tell me that I've made a great recovery since then. That I'm my old self again. That I look *happy*. Which is all the proof I'd ever need of that philosophic belief that we each exist in our own reality, each separated inside an envelope of a completely separate dream.

I will never be my *old* self again.

How could I be? The blast took them but it ruined me. I'm soiled and scarred and alien to myself in many important ways.

And happy?

Sure, I can laugh. So do hyenas, and it means about as much.

My enemies don't think I'm a happy guy. When they look into my eyes, they see the truth that my friends can't see.

They see what I've *really* become.

I know this because I see the fear in their eyes when I kill them. I used to be a nice man. The world used to be a place of sunshine and magic.

Monsters, though, don't thrive in the light.

# THE WAR IS THE WAR

# PART 1

**"Do not tell secrets to those whose faith and silence you have not already tested."**

—QUEEN ELIZABETH I

**"Whenever I had anything and saw a fellow being suffering,**
**I was more anxious to relieve him than to benefit myself.**
**And this is one of the true secrets of my being a poor man to this day."**

—DAVY CROCKETT

# CHAPTER 1

## CEDAR HILL CEMETERY
## BROOKLYN PARK, MARYLAND

I remember a poem a girlfriend wrote when we were in college. When she was eleven, her entire family died in a car accident. At the time, she was the only person I ever knew who had no living relatives.

She wrote this fragment of verse . . .

*Do not threaten me with death,*
*For . . . everyone I ever loved is down there*
*in the kingdom of shadows.*

At the time, I thought it was the saddest thing I ever read, mainly because I was so close with my whole family.

Now, like her . . . I was the last living person to whom I was related by blood.

Do I fear the grave?

Or would dying be like going home, where I am welcome and loved?

# CHAPTER 2

## CEDAR HILL CEMETERY
## BROOKLYN PARK, MARYLAND

I sat for a long time on a little folding stool I'd brought with me.

The tombstones stood in a neat row, arranged with the obsessive tidiness afforded to the dead. Some late-winter frost clung to the ground, and the March sky was a cold blue dome. No clouds at all. The north exhaled a chilly wind and I turned up the collar of my jacket. A thermos of coffee stood by my left foot, and Ghost—my big, white shepherd—lay dozing by my right.

As had become my habit, I placed the stool precisely in the middle of the row of stones, adding my own selection to the geometry of the place. Mom was on my left, my heart side. Dad was on my right because he had always been about right and wrong—first as a cop then as mayor of Baltimore.

My body had healed from the injuries I received in Pennsylvania during the Burn to Shine case. Mostly, anyway. There were echoes of pain from wounds to flesh and bone, and to my psyche. At this rate, by the time I retired from field work I would be composed of ninety percent scar tissue and the rest caffeine. My mind was a haunted house.

When I arrived at the cemetery, I saw that someone had been there recently and placed stones on their marble markers. We're not Jewish, but that's a nice tradition. More lasting than flowers. Stones don't die, so there was no amplification of death. Few things are more depressing than seeing withered flowers on a loved one's grave. And plastic flowers get dusty and that creates its own disappointing image.

The stones stood there, patiently waiting out the uncountable moments of eternity. If one of the bioweapons me and mine fight so hard to stop ever gets off the chain and wipes humanity off the board, those rocks—and the tombstones themselves—would remain. Chunks of marble or granite that would endure even after centuries of weather and neglect caused skyscrapers to collapse and weeds cracked apart every road and street. They would be fixed points even as Mother Nature, in all of her patient cruelty, took back the world we had taken from her. And all of those billions of dead would become compost to turn an overdeveloped planet into an endless green forest.

Weirdly, that thought gave me a measure of peace.

"I wish you were here, Pop," I said softly. "There are so many things I need to tell you. To *ask* you."

The breeze gusted for a moment, ruffling Ghost's fur. He shivered, though I couldn't tell if it was the cold or his dreams. My own dreams had been bad for a while now. More than either my best friend and sometime shrink, Rudy, or my lover, Junie, knew. Though it was clear they were aware that I was dealing with something. They offered to listen. They wanted to be there for me, but I wasn't ready to let them in.

"Something happened," I told my father's ghost. "I had a case—a bad one—in Israel. The one I told you about. We labeled it as Cave 13, but there was a lot more to it than ever went into the after-action report."

A few dry leaves skittered past.

"Thing is, I saw ghosts. Yours. Sean's. Grace, too." I continued. "And it was Grace who told me something that is really scrambling my eggs. It's making my head spin and I don't know what to do."

Somewhere, in one of the bushy pine trees behind a mausoleum I heard a crow cawing. I looked that way but didn't see him.

"Pop . . . Grace told me the names of the teenagers who attacked Helen and me. Yeah, I know how that sounds. How could Grace know their names when I never did? How could anyone? The cops got no DNA matches and neither Helen nor I knew them. The police sketches were so vague they might as well have been store mannequins. It's nuts. But Grace's ghost told me the names."

I took a sip of coffee from the cup I'd been cradling between my palms. It was tepid, but I drank it anyway.

"The thing is . . . I think she really *was* there. Grace, I mean. And I think those names are legit. Don't ask me how any of that is possible because—shit—my life's become a string of one impossible thing after another."

I swear I could almost hear Pop's laugh.

Ghost groaned in his sleep.

"What do I do about it, Pop?" I begged. "Do I give those names to Bug and let him turn MindReader loose to find them? If so, if he does find them . . . what then? I can't arrest them. I mean, sure, if I had proof. Maryland doesn't have a statute of limitations for felony sexual assault. But I *don't* have proof. All I have is names. So . . . what do I do? Go find them and take them out one at a time into the woods and kill them? That's what I *want* to do. Or could I take them and beat the shit out of them like they did to us? Stomp them until they're ruined and leave them broken and bloody? Is that justice? Does that do anything for Helen? Or for me? Or anyone?"

I sighed, finished the last of the coffee, and set it down.

"What if they're sorry for what they did? What if they were whacked out of their minds on crack or something stronger? What if that was their only crime and they found a way back to being human beings? That's not rationalization, Pop. It's just a what-if. And . . . what if they're married now? What if they have wives and kids? Is it justice to out them as monsters even though I have no proof? Or would that be its own kind of abuse to lay that kind of thing on the people who love them?"

A cloud shadow fell past me onto my dad's tombstone.

Except it wasn't a cloud. I looked up at the sky. Totally clear.

Then a voice said, "Oh, I think you should hunt them down and kill them. Make it hurt. Make it messy."

I jumped off the stool, spun fast, and had my pistol out in a heartbeat. Ghost sprang awake and began barking wildly. An old man stood directly behind where I was sitting. He was medium height, skinny, wearing baggy clothes that were soiled and stained.

## CHAPTER 3

### CEDAR HILL CEMETERY
### BROOKLYN PARK, MARYLAND

"The fuck?" I snarled.

Ghost jumped and yelped. Dogs are hard to sneak up on, but mine didn't have a clue. That scared him and it definitely jolted me.

The man looked up at me and smiled. It was not a nice smile. He had a lot of white teeth and they were very wet and oddly sharp. His skin was sallow and sickly-looking, and marked by deep lines. Some of those lines looked like scars but most looked like evidence of great age. He studied me with eyes that were an unpleasant mix of the wrong shades of green and brown. The fact that I held a big automatic thirty inches from his face did not seem to bother him at all.

"You should find those boys—those *men*—and do everything to them they did to you," he said. "And make it hurt ten times as much. That's what you should do."

"Who the hell are you?" I said.

He ignored the question. "I wonder . . . are you strong enough to do that to the men who used to be those boys? Do you have the stones for it? Hmmm . . . maybe not. You're one of those macho types who believes in the fiction of your own mythology."

I told Ghost to be quiet. He stopped barking but stood his ground, muzzle wrinkling with silent snarls.

"Not going to ask again," I said. "Who are you and why are you here?"

"Oh, I'm no one. Soon I'll be no one at all. As for why I'm here? Actually, I come here a lot, son. It's one of my favorite places. The conversation here is surprisingly lively given the . . . ah . . . well. Given the fact everyone is bones in boxes. But they get chatty once you get them started."

Ghost began to growl.

"Best keep your dog still or you'll need to dig another grave. Though . . . I wonder . . . do they let you bury dogs here? Interesting question." He laughed until he began to cough. Deep, racking coughs. He pulled out a soiled handkerchief and dabbed his lips, looked at the cloth, sighed, and tucked it away. I saw that there were bright red stains on it.

"Okay, asshole," I snapped. "That's enough. Turn around and put your hands on your head. Lace your fingers. Do it right now."

"Or what, Joe?" he asked.

That stopped me.

"How do you know my name?" I demanded. "Who are you?"

"Well, hell, son, I know your name, your age, your height and weight. I know what beer you like to drink and what team you root for and what position you like to fuck your woman in. I know lots of things."

I held the Sig Sauer in my right and reached for him with my left. But he stepped back, lithe and quick as a dancer despite how sickly he looked. I nearly shot him. Swear to God, I almost did, even though he was unarmed, older than me, frail, and half my size.

I didn't, though.

Nor did I try for another grab. There was something weird about him. Something so out of focus that I wondered if I was having some kind of psychic fracture. Like maybe the Darkness was trying to come back and own me. Or maybe the hallucinogens to which I was exposed back in the Israel case were causing a flashback.

Ghost kept growling and I let him. Felt like growling, too.

The man now stood ten feet away, smiling with obvious amusement. Then I suddenly understood. I pointed the pistol directly at his heart.

"Your face is different, but you're *him*," I said. "Aren't you?"

"And who would that be?"

"You're Nicodemus."

# CHAPTER 4

## CEDAR HILL CEMETERY
## BROOKLYN PARK, MARYLAND

My comment brightened his smile even more. He even gave me a small, comical bow.

"You should win a prize for knowing that answer," said Nicodemus. "You're quick. But then again, St. Germain always did hire the clever ones. He surrounds himself with the best killers. Always has."

"I shot your ugly ass. How are you standing here? And how did you get a new face that fast?" I was pretty freaked out, to tell the truth. It wasn't that many months ago when I'd encountered him in his Mr. October disguise during the Burn to Shine case in Pine Deep. He looked totally different.

"Yes," he said. "You shot me. Sadly, it didn't take."

"What's that supposed to mean?"

But he only smiled.

"And you're a good ten inches shorter. How?"

"Special shoes," he said, then laughed at his own joke. "After all this time I thought you would have some insight into who and what I am."

"I don't give a fuck," I lied. But I wasn't in the mood for his mind games. "Get down on your knees.Do it now or so help me God—"

"No," he said sharply. "Do not swear by God. Not your god or any god. You don't know what that even means. Any real faith you once had has leaked away like piss down your pant leg."

My finger ached to slip inside the trigger guard. I tried to look around without making it obvious. There were cars in the lot and some people in the distance, but no one seemed to be looking our way. Even so, they were potential witnesses.

"What are you doing here, asshole? What do you want?"

He began to answer, then coughed again. His strange eyes had the wet, glassy look people get when they know the symptoms people see are nothing compared to the truth of what they feel. I saw that look in my mother's eyes in the days leading up to her death from cancer. It was weird how much it humanized him and—God help me—I felt a flicker of sympathy for him. Go make sense of that, all things considered.

When he could talk, he wiped his mouth and gave me a devious little smirk. "I'd have knocked on your front door if you were home. And, no, I'm not talking about the front door of your old family place in Robinwood. The one Santoro blew up and sent nearly everyone you love to this green and quiet place. No sir. Not there. If I was up to traveling, I might have visited where you *live.* Not saying I'd storm the castle, but in happier days it might have been fun to drop by with some *koulourakia* and coffee."

That chilled the air a few extra degrees. Rogue Team International was headquartered on Omfori Island in Greece. No one was supposed to know about it. And the crack about storming the castle was intentional and specific. The island had been a volcano a long time ago, and all of RTI's facilities were built beneath the ground in a series of caves left over from when it was active. Squatting atop this—no joke—secret lair in a hollowed-out volcano was a castle that Church bought and had transported to the island and reassembled brick-by-brick. That castle had once been owned by Francis II Rákóczi, a Hungarian nobleman from the early eighteenth century who had been the Prince of Transylvania from 1704 to 1711.

I kept my reactions to his words off my face, aware that he was watching me sort through his words for the little thorns he so carefully placed. I kept looking at him looking at me. Maybe it was the sunlight half-blinding me, but I swear the color of his eyes changed. The green and brown tones began to swirl, obscuring the black pupil and white sclera.

Ghost yelped and pissed on the ground. He stood his ground and bared his teeth, but he was terrified. So was I.

"Why *am* I here?" mused the terrible little man. "I'm the bringer of news and tidings."

"Yeah, I bet."

"First off, I want to give you a message and ask that you deliver it to your master. To the *creature* you call Mr. Church." He shook his head. "Stupid name. All full of a feeble attempt at irony. Mr. Church, Dr. Pope, the Sexton, the Deacon, John Temple, Andrew Cross . . . how many others? All in an attempt to put another coat of whitewash on who he really is. On *what* he really is. The bastard son of a Bastard Knight. But *I* know his truth. Yessiree Bob. I know who and—more to the point—*what* he is when no one else is around."

"You're so full of shit."

"Am I?" Nicodemus's tongue darted out, quick as a serpent's, and licked a stray drop of blood off his lower lip. "Tell you what, my friend, you repeat to Mr. *Church* exactly what I say, and you watch *his* eyes. Look past those tinted lenses and see his real eyes. Then tell me if I'm full of shit."

There was thunder in the east. That made no sense because it was winter and the sky was clear.

The sound made Nicodemus chuckle. He pretended to look alarmed. "Ooooooo . . . there's a storm coming. Could be a bad one."

I almost said something to contradict him because the five-day forecast had zero percent chance of rain. But that was a trap and I didn't need his ridicule. He looked briefly disappointed.

"Yeah, yeah, storm coming," I said. "Big whoop."

"It'll be a big storm, too. Big and red and black and oh boy is it going to change the landscape of the world as you know it."

"Yawn," I said, saying the actual word.

"You don't believe me?"

"For someone who claims to know so much about everything, you waste a lot of damn time being all spooky and cryptic and shit. Maybe that works for the tourists, Sparky, but vague threats don't do a whole lot for me."

He contrived to look wounded. "Oh, you're no fun at all. Didn't you ever read Batman comics when you were a somewhat less psychopathic child? The Joker and the Riddler were always dropping clues about looming threats and half the fun was seeing how long it would take Batman to suss it out."

"I'm not Batman, you're sure as shit not the Joker, and this isn't Comic-Con," I said. "Though, to give you props, you cosplay a total dickhead pretty well."

He laughed at that, then screwed up his face as if pondering something of great importance. "Hmmm, what can I tell you that might spark insight in a Neanderthal's brain?" He shot me a quick look. "You weren't born on a Saturday, by any chance?"

I didn't answer.

"Ah. You *were*. I peeked. There are people who would find that very interesting. Some of them would want to be your friends. Some of them would want to tear your throat out and look in your eyes as you bled out."

"That means nothing," I said. But in truth it actually did. It rang a bell from a case a few years back, but as Nicodemus was *part* of that case, I took it as him trying to be clever.

"It should mean something to you," he said, miffed. He took out his soiled handkerchief and dabbed at sweat that glistened on his face despite the cold. "Or, at least to someone smarter. Perhaps Circe O'Tree . . . ?"

"Whatever."

"You're not as much fun as I hoped," he pouted.

"Imagine how little I care."

"You will care," he said. "You should. Your whole world is about to change. It'll be epic. Lakes of blood. Rivers of it. And I wouldn't be at all surprised to see death carts in the streets."

"Yeah, yeah, same bullshit, different day." I shook my head. "As I recall, Nicodemus, you've messed with us a bunch of times and each and every time we handed you your sorry ass. You like everyone to think you're the Big Bad and get all freaked out. It's a cool shtick, but it's played out. You try and pretend you're the mover and shaker, but you always hide behind the *real* players. Hugo Vox and the Seven Kings, the Red Order, the Tariqa, the Red Knights, Zephyr Bain, Harcourt Bolton . . . Hell, I could go on. Lately it's been a bunch of can't-get-laid wannabe militia assholes. As track records go, yours is embarrassing. As I see it, you're batting a thousand in the loser's league. I mean, are you even *trying* to win?"

"Win? *Win?*" He laughed at that. A soft, mocking, unpleasant little laugh. "What makes you think I'm trying to *win* anything?"

"So . . . what then? You saying you're a professional loser? Ah, got it."

"Trust me when I say that chaos is a lot more entertaining than either winning or losing," he said. "And here I thought you were intelligent enough to grasp that concept. How disappointing to know you're incapable of the subtler aspects of big-picture conceptualization."

"And you're a jackass who thinks being cryptic will make people think you're either smart or scary. That's pretty disappointing, too, sport."

Nicodemus coughed again, deeper and more destructively, and spat a gob of glistening red phlegm onto the ground between us. Then he lowered his voice and said, "Listen now, boy. Listen and hear me."

"Save it, dickless. I don't want to hear anything you have to say."

"Yes," he said, and now there was a growl in his voice. "You do."

The gun felt so heavy in my hand. My wrist and fingers ached. Beside me, Ghost was whimpering quietly.

"Tell your lord and master this," said Nicodemus, and leaned toward me. Almost close enough to touch. "Tell him that he *owes* me and the debt has come due. Tell him that and, as I said, watch his eyes. If you look closely enough . . . yeah, you'll see."

"How about I cuff you and take you to see him face-to-face?"

He looked as if he was seriously considering that, but ultimately shook his head. "No, you have other matters requiring your attention."

I caught movement out of the corners of both eyes. I looked left and right and saw men walking toward me through the rows of mausoleums, tombstones, and crypts. Six of them. Big men with scowling faces.

The strange little man bowed again and began to turn, then stopped and gave me another of his wicked smiles. "You'll hear from me again, Colonel," he said. "And you'll know when it's my call, I guarantee that."

Nicodemus turned and walked away as the six men closed in on me.

# CHAPTER 5

## CEDAR HILL CEMETERY
## BROOKLYN PARK, MARYLAND

I could have shot the evil little bastard.

I should have.

So, why didn't I? It wasn't because he looked so sick. It wasn't because I was afraid of him. It wasn't anything I could name.

I honestly couldn't tell you.

# INTERLUDE 1

## THE GRAND EXPERIMENT
## HOUSE OF SAFETY AND PRAYER
## BERGAMO, ITALY
## AUGUST 9, 290 CE

The old man tapped on the door three times, waited for a moment, then tapped again. Then he quickly hurried away. The door remained closed and no one inquired through it of whoever knocked.

He walked completely around the long block, moving quietly and without apparent haste. Stopping here to smell flowers, and there to give a coin to a beggar woman who huddled against a wall with a baby suckling at her breast. All the time the old man was covertly looking around and behind him to make sure no one was following. Only when he was positive that he was unobserved did he return to the door. It was of rough-cut boards, banded by iron, and hung with an idol of Lar—a Roman guardian deity, symbol of protection for a conservative household. However, carved very subtly into the wood, well above where the eye would casually fall, was a tiny outline of a fish. It was so skillfully worked into the grain of the wood that you had to know it was there, and know how to find it, in order to see it at all.

"Please, God," murmured the man, and he knocked again. Three knocks, a pause, three more.

This time the door was opened, though only an inch. A shadow moved inside.

"What do you want?"

*"Intereō,"* said the old man. *"Me adiuvāre potes?"*

*I'm lost. Can you help me?*

The door opened and a younger man stuck his head and shoulders out, looked up and down the street, and then pulled the older man roughly inside. The door closed quickly but without sound.

Before the traveler could speak a word, a hand was clamped over his mouth by a third man—much bigger and very strong—and the sharp blade of a knife was pressed against throat-flesh. Cold, sharp. The room was only dimly lit by faint spillage from a shuttered lamp, but it was clear there were several people there. Bits of lamplight gleamed on the edges and points of knives and daggers.

"Who sent you?" asked the big man. "Answer wrong and your family will never find enough of you to bury. Do you understand? Yes? Good, now who sent you?"

"I was directed here by a fisherman," said the old man.

There was utter silence in the room.

"And what was the fisherman's name?"

"His name is Petrus," said the old man, "and he fishes without nets."

"Lucius," said the man who'd opened the door, "let him go. But search him."

The big man, Lucius, withdrew the knife, but held it in his hand, low at his side, while he used his other to pat the old man's clothing, searching for hidden weapons.

"He is unarmed, Marcus."

The smaller man nodded. He signaled to one of the other people to unshield the lamp, and warm golden light washed the room. Marcus was in his thirties, slender but fit, with very short curly hair and intense dark eyes. He wore a simple tunic and was barefoot.

"Tell me your name, traveler," he said in a flat tone still filled with caution.

"I am Felix of Pistoia," said the old man. "I am a grain merchant and am in the city on a selling trip."

"You have the correct passwords," said Marcus. "Who gave them to you?"

"A man of my acquaintance."

"Which man? And of which town? Which church?"

"His name is Rusticus," said Felix. "A wealthy man from here in Bergamo. We walked for three days together, for he was searching for another man, Firmus, also of this town. Firmus had been taken by the soldiers because he would not pray to Roman gods on a Christian feast day. The soldiers bound Firmus and beat him cruelly, but still he would not pray to false gods. Rusticus heard that Firmus was being taken to the court, to be interviewed by the judge, Anolinus, and it was the wish of Rusticus to be tried as well. To show solidarity with his fellow Christian. Before we came upon the soldiers escorting Rusticus, Firmus told me to stray from the road and hide, but when it was safe to come here to this house."

Marcus narrowed his eyes. "Firmus and Rusticus *were* tried," he said. "They were tortured for days. When they would not renounce Christ, they were beaten with clubs and beheaded."

The room was quiet except for a single, wretched sob from the watching people. A woman. And those around her laid gentle hands on her shoulders and spoke soft words of comfort to her.

"Yes," said Felix, "I heard about the deaths of those two good men. And that is why I have come here. Firmus was afraid that Anolinus would not be satisfied with the deaths of two of our brothers. Emperor Maximian is Satan on Earth, or a demon set loose upon the flocks of Christ Jesus."

"The crimes of Anolinus and Maximian are known to God," Marcus assured him, taking him by both hands. The old man gripped his in return. "The Lord's wrath will be very great and . . ." His words trailed off and he suddenly sought to release the traveler—however, the old man held tight.

Felix studied the smaller man. "Is something wrong, brother?"

"Your . . . your hands," gasped Marcus. "They are as hot as flame. Are you unwell?"

Felix smiled. "I have never felt better."

Marcus winced. "Please, brother, let me go. Your skin is so hot. I . . . I think you're burning me."

And as he said it there was a smell in the air.

It was the aroma of cooking meat.

Marcus jerked at the hold. "Owww . . . oww! Let me go, I beg you."

The other people gasped as smoke curled up from where Felix held Marcus. Then the big man, Lucius, stepped in and closed his powerful hands around the old traveler's wrists.

"Let him go, brother," he roared. "Can't you see that you're hurting him?"

He pulled at Felix's thin wrists, but it was like pulling on bands of iron. And hot iron at that. Lucius hissed in pain and nearly let go, but his friend was in agony now.

"Let him go, damn you."

Others closed in and began pulling at Felix, trying with combined strength to dislodge him. Marcus was screaming now and melting flesh ran like tallow and dripped to the floor.

"God in heaven save me from this demon!" he wailed.

Felix's smile grew and grew.

"Demon you name me," he said, and his voice was different now. More of a hissing rasp, as if a reptile had been given the power of human speech. "No . . . not a demon."

There was a cracking sound as the bones in Marcus's hands snapped.

Lucius drew his dagger and slashed at the old man's wrists. Blood welled, black as ink from the wounds, and suddenly everyone recoiled. Steam rose from that black blood.

"Satan," breathed Lucius, staggering backward, his knife falling from his hand, the steel blackened and bent.

"No," said the traveler, "not him, either. Though I thank you for the compliment."

With a terrifying whoosh of gas and a flash of bright sparks, Marcus burst into flame. In the space of a heartbeat his entire body was wreathed in yellow fire. He opened his mouth to scream but inhaled more fire. His eyes flared as bright as torches and exploded in his sockets. The gathered Christians stumbled backward, screaming, weeping, throwing prayers at the ceiling.

Felix finally released Marcus, whose body lingered there, a torch in the shape of a man, before he crumpled into a heap of burning meat. The Christians rushed past their dead leader and the horrific *thing* that had come among them. Felix flung open the door and they crowded out into the street.

Where a squad of Roman soldiers waited in a half-circle, their glittering spears ready for a red harvest. It was not a fight. Not even with Lucius, who towered over the tallest soldier. The spears were thirsty and they drank deep. The bodies fell as the house caught fire and flames clawed up to the roof and fed. Within moments everything was burning.

Then there was movement in the doorway. The soldiers recoiled, leveling their spears once again.

"Wait," cried their *optio centuriae,* raising his sword. He was a seasoned soldier who had been handpicked for this detail. Even so, he felt his mouth go dry as he waited for what he knew would happen. He licked his lips and took a small—a very small—step forward.

The shapes inside the doorway changed. Not because a shadow moved, but because the flame itself moved. Part of it seemed to detach itself from the howling conflagration, to retain a specific form instead of the wriggling pillars of fire that rose from the wooden floor and furnishings. Behind him, the *optio centuriae* heard his men gasping, muttering prayers to Stata *Mater*—the goddess who offered protection from fire—and Deverra, who protected the devout against evil. One voice called out to Jupiter himself.

And then something came out of that dying house.

It was not one of the Christians running for safety. It was not one of them staggering out of the place as he died.

No.

This figure walked out slowly. Without haste. Without screams or flailing. Merely walked. Flames coiled and twisted around his body like ten thousand red and orange snakes. But then they faded, burning out to become wisps of smoke that rose like steam from the flanks of a horse on a cold morning. Until they were all gone and a man stood in the street. He looked around at the corpses and the blood. A smile grew on his mouth, twisting his lips, making them writhe, revealing very white teeth that seemed unnaturally long and sharp.

But it was his eyes that made the *optio centuriae* and his soldiers recoil. When the flames disappeared, they were a medium brown. Normal, almost kindly. As the last flame vanished, though, the color seemed to change. The healthy brown swirled as if it were paint in a pot. Other colors appeared. The purple-green of rotting vegetation.

The darker purples of bruises. And the unhealthy brown-yellow of poison frogs from a forgotten swamp. Those colors swirled and swirled about that smiling mouth. One by one the soldiers sank to their knees and raised their shields to cover their faces. Kneeling in respect. In fear.

In horror.

"Beautiful," murmured the old man.

Though he no longer looked old. The fire seemed to have burned away the years. He stood before the living and the dead, naked, his body unburned, his cock erect, his muscles trembling as if from the climax of a deeply erotic experience.

And those eyes.

Those swirling, ugly, unnatural eyes.

"Beautiful," he said again.

# CHAPTER 6

## CEDAR HILL CEMETERY
## BROOKLYN PARK, MARYLAND

The six men began spreading out as they closed in. On some level I knew that this was as much about distracting me from reporting in as it was for whatever ass-kicking he had planned for me.

I studied the situation very quickly and thoroughly. None of the six guys had weapons in their hands, but as they approached I could see telltale bulges under their coats. Not sure what their play was. Maybe a comprehensive beating—though with a trained combat dog and my own unresolved rage issues I kind of liked my odds.

Beside me, Ghost was still trembling, but visibly recovering from the effect Nicodemus had on him. On both of us. He gave me a look that was equal parts embarrassment, insecurity, and anger. He was every bit as pissed off as I was, but we were both confused on a profound level.

"Yeah, fuzz-monster, I felt it, too," I told him. "Maybe later you can bite his balls."

That earned me a couple of wags.

The closest of the six men was fifty yards away. My car was eighty yards from my family's graves, and a direct path would take me between two of these guys. The closer they got, the more they spread out, trying to form a ring around me to eliminate sightlines on all of them at once.

So I moved, too.

I clicked my tongue for Ghost and we slanted away fast, edging toward a series of tall, blocky mausoleums. As soon as I began to move, they quickened their pace. Shouting threats or warnings at them didn't feel like a useful play, so instead I changed the battlefield to something more useful for one against six.

"Ghost," I said quietly, "field and play."

The command snapped him back to the moment, and his body language changed from scared dog to hunting wolf. He was gone in a flash. The order was to get outside the ring of opponents and make a big circle that was still within earshot. If the opportunity came for a safe line of attack he would take it, but only if he saw or heard me act first. We'd spent a lot of hours on his training, and he knew how to work an obstacle-rich environment. He vanished behind a monument. Two of the men turned toward him as if undecided if they should follow or ignore.

That gave me even more of a chance to bolt for cover. I broke and ran into the heart of the cemetery where the houses of the dead waited to protect me. The bad guys yelled and gave chase.

As soon as I ducked behind cover, I tapped my earbud, switching on the comms to Phoenix House, headquarters of Rogue Team International. It was 10:30 on a cold morning in Maryland but 8:30 at night on Omfori Island in Greece. The call was answered right away.

"Station," said a familiar voice.

"Outlaw to Grendel," I said, using the call sign for our chief of operations, Scott Wilson.

"Go for Grendel."

I told him where I was and that I was being hunted by six assailants. Scott—never my biggest fan—was nonetheless clannish. I may have been "an American thug," as he once described me, but I was *his* thug.

"And you're sure it was Nicodemus?"

"Very."

"Do whatever you need to do to exfil safely, Outlaw. Police have been notified and are en route."

"Tell them not to shoot the guy with the dog."

"Copy that," he said dryly.

I did a quick lean-and-look and saw that Nicodemus's men had their guns out now.

Swell.

# CHAPTER 7

## CEDAR HILL CEMETERY
## BROOKLYN PARK, MARYLAND

One of them, a burly fellow with huge shoulders and a face like an eroded wall, raised his empty left fist and the others stopped.

He alone kept advancing, walking slowly. He lowered the hand to point at me.

"Blasphemer," he yelled.

I had to smile. The day was getting more surreal and when things get this wacky there is an element of comedy. Not actually funny, but so absurd one has to laugh.

Ghost, less amused, growled.

That caused Big Shoulders to slow his approach. He turned to stare at Ghost, who peered cautiously out from his hiding place. The guy gave my dog a good five-count, then looked over to where I'd knelt behind a tombstone. He was frowning with uncertainty.

"I . . . do not understand."

"It's called a *dog*," I said slowly. "*Canis familiaris*. Ringing any bells? Also goes by fuzz-monster and fluffer-nutter."

The look he gave me is the kind reserved for the very insane or deeply weird. Fair call.

"Who are you and what do you want?" I asked, keeping my voice conversational.

Big Shoulders' expression tightened, becoming hard, showing anger. Strange lights danced in his eyes. Not swirly colors like what I saw in Nicodemus's eyes. This was more like the too-bright passionate ferocity you see in the more out-there revival tent preachers. The ones who fondle snakes and speak in tongues. The pointing left hand fell away and he raised his gun and fired.

I saw it coming and ducked fast behind a monument near where Ghost was hiding. I lunged out, grabbed my dog, and pulled him over to me.

Bullets hit the stone three inches from my favorite head. Small chips stung my cheeks. Then they all opened up on me, driving me farther back into the cemetery with a hail of bullets. I hunched down and covered my head as rounds punched bigger chips of marble from the monuments. The fusillade wasn't well aimed, but there was a lot of it. I scuttled sideways to the opposite corner of the tomb, leaned out and shot Big Shoulders, and watched him stagger.

Stagger. Not fall. Had to be body armor under his winter coat. Good stuff, too.

Shit.

He stumbled sideways behind a tree and immediately returned fire. But I wasn't there. As soon as I'd shot, I whirled and ran to a different crypt and hid behind it. This one had a low stone wall around it anchored by four pillars atop which were angels, each playing a different instrument—harp, horn, violin, and flute. Another pair of the attackers was running fast toward where I'd been. I made myself as small and skinny as I could behind one column. The distance was still about fifty yards, which is the maximum range for a handgun. I didn't want to waste bullets, so I let them get ten steps closer and then I fired.

My first bullet took a brawny red-haired man in the left eyebrow and the hollow-point blew an apple-sized chunk out of the back of his head. Redhead's legs ran two more steps even as his body lost all tension and he puddled down.

All five of the other men zeroed on me and blew through full magazines trying to catch me with direct fire or ricochets—a barrage, clearly intended to pin me in place and end it all right there. I had to flatten out and crawl like a salamander for cover. I spindle-rolled behind more headstones, then shimmied up to a nice vantage point. One of them tried to use a tall tombstone as a shooting blind, but even as he raised his weapon, a big white missile slammed into him.

*Ghost.*

He is one hundred and five pounds of muscle and he's real damn fast. The big white shepherd bore the man down even as he snapped his jaws shut around the poor bastard's throat. Blood geysered up hot and red, and the man's scream rose high and wet and then ended with a terminal abruptness.

I pivoted and ran again, leaping the low stone wall and diving behind a large decorative shrub. I tucked, rolled like Captain Kirk on those old episodes of *Star Trek,* and came up into a kneeling position, firing as soon as I raised my gun. The first round caught an attacker high on the chest, and though it jolted him, his vest kept him alive.

For half a second.

I put the next round through his upper lip.

Three down.

The fight seemed to be going my way, but there was something weird about it. These guys were heavily armed and wearing some kind of high-end body armor, but if they had police or military training it wasn't evident. At six-to-one odds, I should have been dead. So should Ghost. And yet I was gaining the upper hand.

This went through my mind fast, but there was no time to pause and analyze. Maybe they'd thought I'd be unarmed. Maybe they hadn't seen the Sig Sauer in my hand when I faced Nicodemus. That might account for the first part of this shit show, but if so, then they were more than a step slow getting to first base.

Not that I wanted to see them level up. To quote the Dalai Lama, oh *fuck* no.

One of them snapped off shots in Ghost's direction, but the fur-monster was already gone. His orders were to take out anyone he could approach from behind. Standing there and bragging about it wasn't part of the training, and so he was gone, running fast and smart between marble headstones and monuments. The bullets just hit stone or trees.

I got to my feet and ran for better cover. Bullets chased me across an open patch.

Chased. *Not* led.

This was every bit as weird as it was deadly.

I jagged left and went low, hitting the ground and sliding a few feet on my side across frozen ground while firing up at the closest man. He must have seen me and started to turn, so my first two shots hit his side and then his gun arm, punching a red hole through the meat of his forearm and the biceps behind. Then I shot him in the side of the head before he could even scream, then rolled under a bush as his friends turned to try and kill the killer.

As I came out of my roll, I dropped the nearly spent magazine and swapped in a full one. Then I rose up and jagged right, snapping off two shots to draw their focus. Both of them turned toward me but split apart to take cover. The closest one dropped into a squat behind a headstone cut to look like an open Bible—big, wide, and solid. I had no clean shot, and so wheeled around and fired at his buddy. He faded to one side, anticipating my aim, and that lean put him right in the direct path of Ghost's silent attack run. As my dog tore into him, I swung back to the first guy, Big Shoulders, who spun around as his friend screamed.

I dropped him with one through the thigh and a second in the belly, below the natural hem of body armor. He collapsed and lay there screaming.

Ghost killed the other one. He was messy about it, too. Maybe making up for how he soiled himself when facing Nicodemus. He ripped the gunman to pieces, and I let him, because I was moving then, checking the downed men.

Six against one, or six against two, counting Ghost. We should not have won, and definitely not this easily. I mean, yes, they were trying to kill me and nearly managed it, but if they'd had better training then I might as well have dug my own grave next to my family.

And yet . . .

There were sirens in the far distance. I almost laughed. They'd have never been able to save my ass in time, and I had no real interest in answering ten thousand questions. I hurried with slapping the pockets of the dead shooters. I found extra magazines, billfolds with cash, and nothing else. No cell phones or wallets.

Then I knelt beside Big Shoulders. The leg wound wasn't bad, and I wasn't trying for a kill shot when I parked one in his gut. But as I looked at him it was obvious that my bullet had punched through and clipped his spine. His legs were totally limp. His face was gray with pain and sweat boiled from his pores despite the cold. Even so, he tried to grab his pistol, which lay nearby; I swatted it away.

"You're shot to shit," I said. "I can get a top medical team here, get you airlifted to the best spinal surgery center on the East Coast. Or I can let you bleed out, shitting in your pants because you're dead from the waist down. Your call, but I know which door I'd pick."

"God will strike you down," he said between gritted teeth.

"Looks to me like God isn't taking requests right now. Not yours, anyway. Not that freak Nicodemus, either."

"You are the one they call God's Left Hand," he spat. "You are an apostate of hell."

"No, I'm an Orioles fan from Baltimore. And I'm offering you the best deal you'll ever get. Tell me who you are and why you and your butt-buddies tried to kill me and my dog."

"False dog," he snarled.

I said, "Um, what, now . . . ?"

He sneered at me. "Did you paint him? Did you dye him white to try and pass?"

"Pass? Is this some kind of racism against dog color, 'cause otherwise you lost me 'round that last turn."

The sirens were getting louder. Still far off, but time was melting away.

His hands were shaking very badly and he tried to claw a knife from a belt sheath. I let him get it halfway out, then took it away from him. Gently. I glanced at the blade, which was etched with a symbol of the cross with a circlet of thorns around the crosspiece. That rang a bell, so I took his wrist and pushed his sleeve up. And there it was.

He had a small tattoo of a cross just above his wristwatch. These words were inked into his flesh. Arched over the top of the cross was:

***Ad extirpanda***

Below the cross:

***Exurge D Et Judica Causam Tuam***

I recognized that tattoo and it sent a chill rippling through me. It was the motto of the Holy Inquisition. These guys were—no joke—vampire hunters. I'd encountered some of them in Iran years back.

Suddenly, other things that Nicodemus said began to make a very unpleasant kind of sense. My nerves, already frayed, began to burn like melting wires. I opened the flaps of his sports coat and saw that he had a sharpened piece of hardwood doweling and a rubber mallet snugged into holsters on his belt. I patted him down and found vials of garlic oil and small pouches of garlic powder.

I said, "Well, kiss my ass. You clowns are Sabbatarians?" He glared at me, which was all the answer I needed. I pointed to Ghost. "He's not dyed, dumbass. He's really a white shepherd."

His mouths formed the words *Fetch dog*.

"Sure," I said. "He's a fetch dog. One of the good guys. And whatever lies Nicodemus told you about me are bullshit. Christ, don't you guys ever getting tired of being fooled? You were cannon fodder in Iran and now you're circling the drain because you believed the least trustworthy person on planet Earth. I'm not the bad guy."

"Then . . . why do you bow to the accursed one who drank the devil's blood . . . ?" His voice was fading, but the question was clear. It was only meaning and context that were missing.

"The Devil's blood? The hell's that supposed to mean? What are you idiots even *doing* here? Why come after me? If anything, we're more or less on the same side. Maybe you didn't get the memo, but we're both against the Red Knights and the Red Order."

Doubt flickered in the man's eyes and he mumbled something that sounded like *"Stregoni . . . benefici . . . ?"* There was a rising inflection as if he was asking me something, or maybe still struggling with whatever kind of bad guy he thought I was.

"Beneficial witches?" I asked. "What's that supposed to mean?"

Big Shoulders stared at me in stubborn silence. Then I realized his gaze went straight through me and through the headstones around me and through the sky itself. He settled slowly back as his broken body leaked his life into the frozen dirt.

I sat back on my heels for a moment, then took the stake, hammer, oil, and powder and stuffed them into my coat pockets.

"Ghost," I snapped as I rose. "*Car.* Go!"

We ran like sons of bitches and were gone before the cops rolled screaming into the cemetery.

# CHAPTER 8

## IN MOTION

## BROOKLYN PARK, MARYLAND

The call was answered on the second ring. The person who answered said, "Line?"

"Clear," said the small man.

A pause. "Is it done?"

"It is."

"Is he alive or dead?"

"Alive."

"Good," said the man on the other end of the call.

"Yes," agreed Nicodemus. "It'll be so much more fun this way."

He ended the call and started his car. Instead of driving, he sat there, leaned back, and laughed out loud for a long time. The laughter turned into another coughing fit and he coughed and coughed and coughed until the dashboard and the inside of the windshield was spattered with red.

Even so, he never stopped smiling.

# INTERLUDE 2

## THE GRAND EXPERIMENT

## NICOMEDIA, BITHYNIA

## (MODERN IZMIT, TURKEY)

## CHRISTMAS DAY, 304 CE

"This is an easy choice," said the Emperor Maximian to the dozens of men and women who knelt before him. They huddled together in a rough circle formed by walls of gleaming spear points. "Renounce the false prophet. Renounce this so-called Christ and none of you will be harmed. Not a scratch or a bruise."

The Christians were already bruised and bloody. Many were swathed in stained bandages. One man clutched the stump of his right wrist to his chest—the rags binding it were black with infection. A woman clutched a bundle to her breast, and though she rocked and cooed to it, the baby within the rags was utterly still.

The church was large but not ornate, and its few decorations had been torn down and trod upon. The rough-hewn statues of Jesus of Nazareth had been chopped from the walls and urinated on by every soldier in the room. Even Maximian had emptied his bladder on the face of the upstart messiah. Three of his men had been ordered to defecate on the altar and had done so to the rough jokes and rude laughter of their fellows.

The gathered Christians were reported to be the elders of the church, the heretics who evangelized and proselytized with such zeal that the number of converts in the region had swelled to nearly twenty thousand. They had been brazen about it, and so openly disrespectful. Even after Maximian's great victories these Christians would not so much as sacrifice a chicken at any of the idols or temples of the Roman gods. And so far, no amount of threats or beatings—not even dismemberments and gang rapes—would coerce them into admitting that this Christ was nothing more than a false hope.

"Are you fools?" he demanded, amazed at the suicidal stubbornness of these people. "Just say the words. My men are witnesses. Renounce this Christ and you can walk out of here. You and the others."

Over the last weeks the emperor's soldiers had systematically rounded up thousands of Christians. Perhaps not all twenty thousand, but enough so that the town's small circus was crammed, and so were the jails and stockades. Feeding them was a threat to the town's budget, and Maximian certainly wasn't going to authorize a wagon train of grain, dried meat, and salt for these bastards.

Maximian walked along the front of the group of kneeling heretics. "Well?" he demanded. "Is there no one here with enough courage to even speak?"

The room was silent except for some broken sobs.

The door opened and an old man walked in, flanked by two soldiers. He was small and thin, his face heavily lined and his head shaved, leaving only a rime of white stubble. He wore a simple robe of stained gray, with a cracked leather belt around his hips from which dangled a heavy purse and a sheathed dagger. The man carried a staff but did not lean on it or appear to need it. His stride was powerful.

"Hail, Augustus Maximian," said the old man in a strong but odd voice. It was cracked and oily, as if a Nile crocodile had learned to speak.

Maximian felt his heart jump in his chest. Not for joy, but in dread. He did not like this man. No one he knew did. But they all feared him.

Oh yes, everyone who knew Nicodemus the Traveler feared him.

Nicodemus of Tarshish, he was called, though as far as Maximian knew, there was no Tarshish except in ancient legends of the Phoenicians. Why a man would claim to come from a dead and vanished country was one of the many mysteries surrounding Nicodemus, and hardly the strangest thing about him. Rumors ran wild, with some claiming the man was a thousand years old, or ten thousand. Or that he was from a long line of sorcerers, all of whom took the name of Nicodemus. And there were other rumors—that he was descended from a Hebrew Pharisee who had known Jesus of Nazareth and even brought myrrh and aloe to the so-called messiah's tomb. All stories. None of which could be true, of course.

Unless they were.

Maximian managed a smile, though, because he did not want his men—or the heathens on the floor—to know that the great emperor of Rome was afraid of anyone.

"Greetings, friend Nicodemus," he said with false warmth. "I hadn't heard you were in town."

The little man stopped in front of the bigger, broader former soldier. "I often return to Nicodemia," said Nicodemus.

"Is . . . your family from here? I ask because of the similarities of your name . . ."

"From here?" Nicodemus shook his head and smiled thinly. "No. Not from here."

When he offered no further explanation, Maximian said, "What brings you to our presence this afternoon?"

Nicodemus turned and gestured to the kneeling Christians. "I have been following current events. When I heard that so many of these . . . *people* . . . had been rounded up by your soldiers, I hurried to arrive before it was all over."

"Over? What do you mean?"

"Why . . ." said Nicodemus, drawing it out, "the burning, of course."

Maximian frowned. "What . . . *burning*?"

The old man turned to face him and for just a moment there was something strange about Nicodemus's eyes. The flat brown seemed to swirl, to take on other colors—a jaundiced yellow and mushroom white and bile green. Swirling and swirling, obscuring pupil and whites. Maximian recoiled but caught himself. His mouth went dry as dust and the air in his lungs was suddenly too hot.

Then the strangeness was gone, leaving him feeling weak and sick.

". . . burning . . ." murmured the emperor. He did not know—*could* not know—that for a few broken moments his own eyes had swirled with the same complexity of ugly colors.

Nicodemus of Tarshish stood watching him. Smiling his reptilian smile.

"Yes," said Maximian in a voice more like his own. Cold, full of command. "Yes, burning."

He turned and beckoned to the centurion overseeing the roundup of Christians. The man hurried over and bowed.

"These people are heretics and traitors," said the emperor. "Burn them."

The centurion blinked. "Sire . . . ?"

"Burn them all."

"All of them?"

"Yes," said Maximian. "These fools. The ones in the circus. All of them."

The centurion took a half step closer and lowered his voice. "Sire, there are nearly twenty thousand Christians in the—"

"*All* of them," said the emperor. "Burn them all."

Nicodemus the Traveler leaned on his staff and smiled.

# CHAPTER 9

## LONG JOHN SILVER'S RESTAURANT
## 5501 RITCHIE HIGHWAY
## BROOKLYN PARK, MARYLAND

I took the Governor Ritchie Highway north to Walton Avenue, then spent the next fifteen minutes taking random turns through neighborhoods and commercial districts, doubling back, making three lefts to come up behind where I'd been. Looking for a tail and not finding one.

While I drove, I tapped my earbud and told Scott Wilson, the chief of operations at RTI, to put Church on the line.

"He is rather busy at the moment," said Wilson, sounding more waspish than usual.

"It wasn't a request," I told him. "Get him now."

A moment later I heard Church's distinctive New England drawl. "Outlaw, I thought you were taking some R and R in Maryland."

"Yeah, that turned out just swell," I said. "Lovely to see the old hometown. Good for the soul."

"So it seems. Are you safe?"

"Relatively speaking," I said. "I'm checking my backtrail. So far it looks clean. I have some new intel for you, but I need to pull over and run an anteater over the car before we have any meaningful chat."

Anteaters were proprietary tech obtained for RTI field teams from one of Church's "friends in the industry." He seems to have friends in every industry, and that works just fine for me.

"Do that and call me back," said Church, and he disconnected.

Always a Chatty Cathy, that guy. But it was okay because it gave me a chance to think things through before I spoke to him again.

I hated to admit it, even to myself, but Nicodemus had succeeded in turning dials on me. It's never clear how much he actually knows and how much he pretends to know. Never a comfort either way, and certainly not without some deep insight into what his motivations are. We've fought him time and again, and I'm no closer to understanding him.

*What makes you think I'm trying to win anything?*

Yeah, all of my instincts—especially those of the Cop inside my head—felt that this wasn't some offhand bit of obfuscation. It felt like a *telling* remark.

Even so. What the actual fuck?

I found a Long John Silver's and pulled into the far corner of their lot and parked beside a dumpster. There was a full field kit in the trunk and I opened it to remove several key items. First, though, I took off my jacket and shirt and pulled on an undergarment that was barely thicker than flannel but was a special blend of Kevlar, spider silk, and graphene tubing. Stuff that will stop anything short of a high-velocity rifle round while diffusing much of the foot-pounds of impact. It'll even turn most blades. Call it a security blanket for an overgrown kid playing James Bond.

After I put my clothes back on, I took three magazines and replaced the one in my gun and slotted the other two into my shoulder rig. Then I removed the anteater, which looks like a TV remote, and spent the next five minutes sweeping the entire car, inside and out. The little green light on the display never wavered. No bugs, active or passive.

That's comforting, to be sure, but on the other hand, if I'd found any sneaky gizmos then they might be useful in tracking them back to their source, or to a vendor whose sales records would have no protection from Bug and MindReader. But there was nothing, and again that surprised me. If Nicodemus had wanted me dead, he could have managed it. If those six Sabbatarian thugs had come at me with automatic rifles, or if they had put a bomb under my car. Et cetera. Lots of things they could have done, and yet they'd come at me in a way that was as clumsy as it was dangerous. Nicodemus knows what my skill level is, or what it has to be for me to lead one of Church's field teams. He has the resources to hire a medium-size army.

The stake, hammer, and garlic went into a clear plastic evidence bag. Not sure what forensics could be lifted from it, but it's always worth a try. That stuff went into a concealed compartment over the wheel well.

Last thing I put on was a thin and flexible piece of plastic that was actually a sophisticated and combat-durable tactical computer. These tac-coms are premarket and bleeding-edge. Once it was on, it autosynced to my comms unit.

I looked at Ghost. "Now I feel like a real Inspector Gadget superspy."

He sat there, his big brown eyes flicking from me to the drive-through at the Long John Silver's. The message was clear—fighting is over, now it is time to pander to the fur-monster's obsession with greasy fast food.

We did the drive-through experience and I dutifully bought him a fish and shrimp platter, with hush puppies and waffle fries. He dropped into the footwell and began eating in that weirdly delicate way he has . . . slowly, one piece at a time. He also does it by themes—fish, fries, shrimp, hush puppies. I got a Pepsi. Stomach wasn't ready for solid food.

Then I found a nice quiet corner of the parking lot and killed the engine.

## CHAPTER 10

### LONG JOHN SILVER'S RESTAURANT
### 5501 RITCHIE HIGHWAY
### BROOKLYN PARK, MARYLAND

Church listened to everything that happened, waiting until I was finished before speaking.

"He sounded unwell?"

"He sounded like he was dying," I said. "Coughing up blood. Looked feverish and older than he's been described by you, Top, and Rudy."

"Now isn't that interesting?"

"Yeah, I figured you wouldn't be all torn up over it."

"And he sent Sabbatarians after you?" mused Church.

"Yeah. Maybe he's dying and that was a going-away present. But at least this time those jackasses didn't try to poison me with garlic powder or drive a stake through my heart."

"Take the win," he said.

"Mind you, though . . . they did *bring* their complete Junior Van Helsing kits with them. I took some samples for the lab."

"Good. What are your overall impressions of what happened?" Church asked.

I laughed. "Where to start? I've been trying to unpack everything that spooky jackass said. Different points keep sticking out and are maybe beginning to make sense."

"Be specific."

"He mentioned Greek pastries and joked about storming the castle. Has to mean he knows where RTI is located and that we have Dracula's castle overtop of it."

"Not Dracula's castle," he said under his breath and with weary patience.

"Whatever," I said. "Oh, point is, he *knows,* which means we're vulnerable."

"I will take all appropriate actions," Church assured me.

"Yeah, let's not forget that some of our former playmates knew we had a field office in Baltimore and they blew that halfway to orbit."

"I'm unlikely to forget."

The destruction of the Warehouse in Baltimore claimed the lives of 169 DMS staff members. People I knew and liked and worked with. People who had become family to me in the way people on the front lines of a war can *be* family.

I said, "And who the hell is the 'accursed one who drank the blood of Satan' or whatever?"

"No one comes to mind," he said. Was there a brief pause before he answered? Was he thinking about the Warehouse, too, or did that question trigger something else? Either way, he said nothing else and waited for me to continue.

"And why would they nickname *me* the Left Hand of God?" I demanded. "I mean, cool name if I was a biker in, say, 1968. But how's that even fit their skewed view of who I am? Or am I overthinking it and they just had the wrong cat?"

"We have no idea what disinformation was fed to them by Nicodemus."

"Yeah," I said. "There's that. And maybe that's where all of the biblical name-calling came from. Even so, there's other weird shit in what he said."

"Such as the offhand remark about you playing *fetch* with Ghost?" Church ventured. "Yes, I thought so, too. Nicodemus was setting the stage for the appearance of the Sabbatarians. Ghost is a white dog, and to people of certain cultural and superstitious beliefs, such animals are referred to as Fetch Dogs. Vampires are supposed to fear large white dogs because they are supposed to be able to sniff out evil and lead monster hunters to the lairs of vampires and so forth."

"I remember," I said. "When I ran into the Sabbatarian hit team in Iran, they were surprised that I was in the company of a white dog. This time they thought I took Ghost to the salon for a dye job. These cats are pretty close to the most clueless villains we've ever come up against."

"Sadly, there's not a lot of competition for least efficient murderers. Be glad."

"Right. Yay, lucky me. You want to make any guesses as to why Nicodemus sicced them on me today?"

"Not yet."

"Look, boss, during the Iran gig, Nicodemus was still playing his *Father* Nicodemus role. We know he was acting as advisor to the Scriptor, the head of the Red Order. Either in partnership with Hugo Vox or as a solo act. Did we ever lock down that he was advising the Sabbatarians, too?"

"He was, Outlaw," said Church. "He was playing on all sides of that little war. Lilith thinks he was even pretending to be an imam to exert influence over the Tariqa. And possibly even the Red Knights. Some of that intel was gathered by Arklight and shared after you moved on to other cases. It's in a briefing file, though, in case any of those groups became active again. I'll send the file to your tac-com."

"Good. Once I get somewhere quiet, I'll review it. Hey, have you ever heard the phrase *stregoni benefici*? Roughly translates as beneficial sorcerer. That mean anything to you?"

"Interesting. Your translation is accurate, but the contextual connotation is different. In medieval times it meant *Beneficial Vampire.* A more accurate label would have been *Vampiro Benefico,* but education was less precise back then. And in Romania they were known as Vampirii Lui Dumnezeu—the Vampires of God."

"Yeah, but what's that mean? A good guy vampire? Was that what the Sabbatarian was asking before he died?"

"It's possible."

"*What's* possible? I still don't know what he meant."

"The *stregoni benefici* were rumored to be a splinter group of the Upierczy who rebelled against the Red Order and rejected the subjugation of the Red Knights. The folklore holds that these were vampires captured by warrior monks and then *reeducated* so they once more embraced Jesus Christ and therefore became loyal to the pope. Those same legends suggest they were used as assassins for the Church, but there is no proof to substantiate this. It's all rumors, and they have faded out over the years."

"That Sabbatarian must have thought there was more to it than rumors from hundreds of years back."

"He was dying at the time," Church reminded me. "It's hard to know how lucid he was at the end."

"I guess," I said doubtfully. There was something about the look on the man's face as he asked that question of me.

Church interrupted my reverie. "Repeat that part about Nicodemus's message to me."

I closed my eyes so I could see the words painted on the inside wall of my mind. "He said, *'Tell him that he* owes *me and the debt has come due.'"*

"That is also quite interesting," mused Church.

"I thought so," I agreed. "He said that I should watch your eyes when I told you. Which, of course, I can't do."

"Well . . . that wouldn't be particularly instructive anyway."

Was there another slightest pause before he said that? Or was I just in paranoid gear? Hard to say.

"Oh, and he said that I would hear from him again, and would know when it's his call," I said. "And truth to tell, boss, I've got a whole bunch of questions."

"Feel free. We're on a private channel with active scramblers," Church reminded me.

"Okay, first, why does this asshole have such a hard-on for you?"

There was another slight pause before he said, "It is fair to say that both the DMS and RTI have greatly interfered with his plans. One can assume a certain degree of frustration and resentment."

"I mentioned that, but he laughed it off and made some comment about chaos. Like he wasn't trying to win and instead grooves on just stirring shit up."

"That is not an entirely inaccurate assessment."

"Meaning . . . ?"

"At the risk of losing all credibility with you, Outlaw," he said, "there is a movie line Bug likes to quote. From one of the many *Batman* films, I believe."

"Let me guess. Alfred talking to Bruce Wayne suggesting that the Joker does what he does because, like some people, he just wants to watch the world burn."

"That would be it, yes."

"I soooo want to bust you for making a pop-culture reference," I said.

"If you want to end this call, then by all means."

"Kind of funny that Nicodemus *also* made a Batman reference."

"Yes," said Church. "Hilarious."

I laughed. He didn't. We moved on. I said, "Is the takeaway here that Nicodemus is motivated more by chaos than by accomplishments?"

"That has been his pattern. More than once in the past he has described himself as a 'chaos trickster.'"

"What, like Loki? God of mischief?"

"Or so he would like people to believe. It would hardly be the first time we've faced someone who has delusions of supernatural grandeur."

"Yeah, the Goddess comes to mind."

That was the contrived identity used by Hugo Vox's mother. She made outrageous claims of divinity while using legions of social media hackers to rewrite everything from Wikipedia to the computer records of major universities to edit herself into history. She was, as far as I know, the first person to use AI for deepfake videos.

I said, "With Nicodemus, is it runaway ego or a polished strategy of deception?"

"Likely both."

"Yet," I said, "when we first dealt with him—the DMS, I mean—he was cooling his heels in a supermax prison in Pennsylvania and had been there for years. How's that fit into his pathology?"

"Your guess would be as good as mine," admitted Church. "There is a great deal about the person who calls himself Nicodemus that I still do not understand."

"A lot of people think you're psychic."

"A lot of people would be wrong." He paused. "Though, admittedly, clairvoyance would be useful. As would telepathy. But I possess neither talent."

"Does Nicodemus? He seems to know a lot. Like the location of Phoenix House, which is giving me that itch between my shoulder blades like someone's out in the weeds with a scope on me."

"The source of his information has always puzzled and alarmed me, Outlaw," Church said. "However, there are quite a lot of ways for criminals to obtain sensitive data. A person who thrives on chaos would go out of his way to seek out useful details and then use that intel strategically. That has worked for him many times, and even against us. But to be clear, Colonel, he is not omniscient. We learned that during the *Sea of Hope* matter because he made predictions about you that appeared to possess knowledge he could not possibly have. Yet, in retrospect, it's clear he was being fed information in real time, likely from Hugo Vox or someone else involved with the Seven Kings. One or more of the inmates, possibly, and very likely one or more persons working at the prison. And he has had a lot of time to build a network of intelligence gatherers. We saw that last year with the Burn to Shine matter. The effect of this gameplaying is to unnerve us and sell the belief that Nicodemus is possessed of supernatural abilities."

"You're saying he's not, though . . . right?"

"I'm saying that whatever he is, he's not infallible."

"Sure, okay . . . but he is always planning something, though. That is a given, right?"

Church said, "Except for those rare times when he goes completely off the radar, he is usually involved in actions, large and small, that hammer cracks in the status quo. He is happiest when there is conflict."

"Have to say, though, boss . . . he looked really sick. Maybe he *is* dying and he's setting things up to be one hell of a going-away party."

"Let's both hope you're wrong about that, Outlaw."

# INTERLUDE 3

## THE GRAND EXPERIMENT

## VILLAGE OF MONTAILLOU, FRANCE

## DECEMBER 26, 1236 CE

"But Father . . . you *cannot* die!"

Benoit LaRoque clung to the withered hand that had once been powerful. He held it as tightly as he dared, but even in his passion he was careful. His father's skin was like dried paper, and the bones beneath felt like those of a frail bird—hollow and brittle.

The old knight looked at his son with patience and love.

"Death comes to all of God's creatures," said Sir Giles in a voice that was a cruel imitation of the strength and power it once possessed. Benoit leaned close to hear every word. "I do not fear the grave, for I am upheld by the love of our lord and savior."

Benoit had to bite back the savage retort that sprang to his lips. Death was no blessing, and if this was God's hand, then the Almighty was cruel.

Aloud, the young man said, "It is not your time to go, Father. So many people depend on you. The entire Red Order waits upon you for guidance and direction in this terrible war."

"The war," echoed Sir Giles bitterly. "The war was being fought long before I was even born, and by better men. That crusade will continue long after both of us, my son, are dust. Such is the nature of the Holy Agreement."

"The Holy Agreement . . ." said Benoit, almost hissing the words. He shook his head. "It is sinful. Surely this cannot be the will of God."

"Hush!" chastised the old knight. "You are young and such things may seem strange to you. Stranger still, since in public we must needs decry the Saracens and yet in private we call them allies. And yet . . . that alliance is both sanctioned and blessed by the Holy Father in Rome."

"But it's madness, Father. We are at war with the Muhammadans. They are infidels. How can we call them allies when they slaughter our pilgrims? They burn our churches."

"As we burn theirs," wheezed Sir Giles.

"It makes no—"

"Hush, boy, and listen to me. I have so little time left and there is much to tell you. Please, if you love me and love God, you will listen."

It took much for young Benoit to rein in his anger. There was such heat, such hurt and hatred in his heart. And there was so much fear. He closed his eyes, took several slow and very deep breaths, then nodded.

"I will listen and I will hear you, Father."

A tear broke from the corner of the old knight's eye. He squeezed Benoit's hand with as much strength as he could manage. It was fierce in intent but weak in execution.

He said, "I am the Scriptor of the Red Order. I have done many things that could be seen as sins—and perhaps they are, though that is for Jesus to decide. What I have done, I swear on my sacred honor, has been done to protect the faith and the Church and our people."

Sir Giles paused to cough and Benoit waited him out, using a cloth to dab at the droplets of blood around his father's mouth.

"When the Holy Agreement was made, the first Scriptor, Sir Guy LaRoque, the cornerstone of our family line, and his counterpart within the infidels, Ibrahim al Asiri, included in the Holy Agreement the promise to record all actions taken to do what they believed—what I *still* believe—is God's work. These acts—you may call them crimes or sins, my son, but you will understand in time—were written down in the Book of Shadows. This book is written in a language created by Sir Guy and Ibrahim, with help from their priest and advisor, Father Nicodemus. Like the Tariqa and the Scriptor, there is a Father Nicodemus appointed in each generation. They created a language using several ingenious codes. Without knowing the key, the language is meaningless. Should that book ever fall into unsanctioned hands, it would appear to be something written in some foreign land. It includes artwork intended to deceive casual eyes. Pictures of the stars, of fruits and vegetables that do not actually exist. Other things, too. Immodest images of women and more. The effect is that the book does not appear to be what it is, and that is a secret the Tariqa and the Scriptor must guard with their lives. With their honor and their faith in the divine."

He looked at his son with caution and fear, but with love and hope.

"There is a second book, my boy. The *Scriptor's Diary*. Its existence has been a secret kept only within our family. Not even the other members of the Ordo Ruber know of it, and it tells the *whole* truth of how the LaRoque family have fought God's war, and at what cost. It is a fearsome thing to read and requires courage. You must learn to read that language in order to read and study *both* books, my boy," he said, his voice growing weaker each time he spoke. "You will learn the special history and the horror, but that is the price we are asked to pay by our faith and our God."

"How . . . how can I learn that language? How could I read such books?"

"The code key," said Sir Giles. "Father Nicodemus will come soon. He has been sent for to administer my last rites and take my confession so that I may enter heaven and be judged by the Almighty and his Blessed Son. But he will stay and guide you. He will be your teacher and your advisor, and in him you can place your total trust."

"He frightens me, Father. He always has," protested Benoit. "Have you seen his eyes? They are demon eyes. The colors change with his moods."

"He is appointed by the pope and blessed by God," said Sir Giles sternly, a splinter of his old steel coming briefly into his voice. "You may trust him in all things. Promise this to me."

Benoit summoned his strength of will and, though his heart rebelled at every word, gave his promise. The lie was hard for him—telling an untruth to his dying father. But Sir Giles raised Benoit's hand and kissed it with such gentleness and gratitude that it came close to breaking the boy's heart.

"My will has been written and witnessed these many years," said the old knight. "When I am gone, you will be the lord of the LaRoque house. Since your mother waits for me in God's kingdom, your infant brother, Henri, can go to my sister in Toulouse, where he can be raised and educated, where he will be loved and protected. For you, my son, the road ahead will require much. All of my lands and holdings will be yours, with the towns and villages and their incomes. There are holdings abroad as well—in England and Spain, and in the Holy Land. You will want for nothing, for my treasury overflows. But all of this come with the burden and honor of being Scriptor."

Benoit bowed his head to acknowledge both the gifts and the burden.

Then Sir Giles clutched at him, pulling him closer still.

"And now, my son, I must tell you about weapons you will use to wage our war on behalf of heaven."

"Weapons? I have my own sword and—"

"No, Benoit. I do not speak of earthly arms, but of creatures who have been taken in by Father Nicodemus and my brothers in the Red Order. Creatures who have accepted Jesus into their hearts and will do for Christendom what swords and spears cannot. Listen, lad, and I will tell you of the Upierczy."

## CHAPTER 11

### LONG JOHN SILVER'S RESTAURANT
### 5501 RITCHIE HIGHWAY
### BROOKLYN PARK, MARYLAND

"You make him sound like some kind of vampire," I said after some thought. "Feeding off stress and hysteria."

Church considered that. "Circe might make a case for him being something akin to an essential vampire—one that feeds off of psychic energy, thoughts, feelings, and so on. That is something psychiatrists have been studying for years as a form of pernicious charisma amplified by a kind of empathy that lacks benevolence. Rudy insists that Nicodemus is a self-aware sociopath. In either case, neither believe Nicodemus is in any way supernatural."

"That's slim comfort," I said, "but I'll take it. So, why come for me, though? Why give me a message for you and then try to have me whacked?"

"As you described it to me," said Church, "the Sabbatarians were not top of their class. Despite their numbers and a record of shocking violence, they really struggle to keep the mission of the Inquisition alive. They seem to be habitual victims of either bad intel or piss-poor judgment. In either case, they blunder around and accomplish little. If anything, *they* are better agents of chaos than Nicodemus."

"Even an idiot is dangerous if he has a gun."

"Of course. But," he added, "their lack of efficiency and unchecked aggression make them useful *tools* of someone hoping to cultivate chaos."

"There's that," I conceded. Then said, "How good's our file on them? On what they've done in the past? What they're up to now?"

"Arklight has more of that information than we do. I'll make a call and see if we can get the full dossier. For the moment, Outlaw, we are probably correct in the assessment that they are used by Nicodemus to provide chaos and distraction. Their actions have always been erratic, sloppy, and inefficient. They tend to respond in knee-jerk ways and approach their problem-solving with broad strokes. Very useful if you want to slow down an enemy—as happened today—while allowing the overall game to continue."

"Nicodemus hired the Sabbatarians just to let *me* put *them* down while he waltzed off?"

"It is hardly the first time he's done something along those lines. He would likely find that amusing."

"Ha fucking ha."

"And he would take some pleasure in your discomfiture."

"That seems like a small win."

"It's still a win, Outlaw," said Church. "Those men forced you into action that gave him ample time to make a clean and certain exit."

"I could have shot him in the back."

"Could you?" asked Church. "Would you, in fact, have ever shot an unarmed man in the back? No need to answer, because it doesn't fit the profile of either the Modern Man or the Cop."

That stung. Church is one of the few people who know about the depth and complexity of my psychological makeup. The trauma of what happened to Helen and me left me fractured. Broken into pieces. At first that manifested with dozens of fragmented personalities. Countless hours of therapy, much of it with Rudy, resulted in the roaring crowd being shaved down to three distinct subpersonalities. The Modern Man is that part of me who is nonviolent, civilized, optimistic, and—for want of a better word—normal. He has taken a real beating ever since I joined up with Church.

The second aspect is the Cop, and that's really my core personality, the one I lean into most of the time. That's the patient, informed, empathetic investigator, and I'm at my best when he's driving the car.

The third aspect is the Warrior, whom I more often view as the Killer. That is a less evolved side of me—brutal, extremely violent, and willing to do virtually anything if it results in taking the bad guys down. When he's let out to play then, yeah, shooting someone in the back is not at all unlikely.

Was Church implying that Nicodemus knows this about me? Looking back on it, I think a case could be made.

"I think he was just messing with me," I said. "But my gut tells me it runs deeper than that. And there's something I want to ask about your relationship with him."

Church said nothing.

"When we first ran into him during the King of Plagues case, you didn't seem to know him. But later on it became clear that you knew each other from previous encounters. Care to make sense of that?"

"When the name Nicodemus came up during that case, Outlaw," said Church, his voice giving nothing away, "it was not immediately evident to me that *Nicodemus* was the same person I had encountered before under other names. To my knowledge, it was the first instance of him using that alias in any way that directly overlapped with the Department of Military Sciences."

"Sure, but later on I got the impression that he *had* used the name Nicodemus before."

"In other circumstances, yes," said Church. "Though quite a long time ago. Well before your involvement with my organizations. Before, in fact, the formation of the DMS. So, as unusual as the name was, it was not immediately clear that the Nicodemus we encountered while fighting the Seven Kings was the same person who was involved in those older cases."

"So," I said, "he switches names just like you do . . . ?"

"As do many people in our line of work," Church observed.

"Which means he *has* been a player in your games before."

"Yes," he said.

"Under what names?"

"Many."

"Such as?"

"Does it matter?" he asked, and for the first time I hear a note of reserve in his voice.

"When someone goes out of their way to find me at the graves of my family, then tries to kill me . . . ? Yeah. It matters. So please stop dodging the damn question."

This time the pause was so long I had to check to make sure my comms were still working. Eventually he said, "You know about some of those names. Most recently he took the identity of Kuga and Mr. Sunday. Before that he was John the Revelator. But, over the years he has gone by names ranging from the mundane—like James Smith—to those of a more theatrical nature including, but not limited to, Elegga, Juha, Anansi, Coyote, Renart the Fox, Caliban, Simon Fog, Flagg, Kappa, Mbeku, John of the Cross, Yaw, Păcală, Mr. Krampus, Cin-an-ev, Baron Samedi, Talihsin, and Nanabozho. I could go on."

"Jesus. How long have you known this asshole?"

"Under one aspect or another," said Church wearily, "I have known him as long as I have fought this war."

"And how long is that?" I asked.

"Long enough."

"No, *exactly* how long, I mean. Because Aunt Sallie dropped some offhand comments about you two working cases during the Cold War, and she died old as shit and you look like you're *maybe* sixty."

Aunt Sallie was Scott Wilson's predecessor as chief operations officer. Auntie—as she was often called—had been with Church for decades, and only recently passed away following a terrible stroke suffered just as the DMS was shut down and RTI started.

"Are you getting to a point of some kind, Colonel?"

"I'm asking you to tell me the truth," I said. "I think I deserve that much."

"In what way has our shared experiences in this war led you to the belief that I owe you—or anyone, for that matter—access to my life story?"

"Hey, how about the fact that I have been putting my life on the line for your goddamn war?" I snapped. "How about the fact that I just came from where my entire family *died* in your war? How about Grace Courtland, John Smith, Khalid Shaheed, Gus Dietrich, Brick Anderson, and all of the other people who died for your war?"

When Church next spoke his voice was colder than I'd ever heard it. He did not shout. He was just ice.

"My war? Interesting that you frequently phrase it that way. The truth is that this is your war as well, Colonel. This has been your war since those teenagers attacked you and Helen. Don't pretend otherwise. Tell me . . . have you told the people closest to you *everything* about what happened? Even Dr. Sanchez or Junie Flynn? No need to answer because we both know that answer. There are all kinds of secrets and some are secrets of the heart and soul. Things we don't share because it would pollute the hearts of the people about whom we care. You have your secrets, Outlaw, and I have mine."

I began to say something to that, to reply with a sharp rebuke, but then I realized I was talking to dead air.

Beside me, Ghost whimpered very faintly.

# INTERLUDE 4

## THE GRAND EXPERIMENT
## LAROQUE ESTATE
## VILLAGE OF MONTAILLOU, FRANCE
## NEW YEAR'S EVE, 1236 CE

Sir Benoit LaRoque walked through snow and winter shadows in the cemetery where so many generations of his family were buried. Some of those graves and crypts held nothing but memories, with the bodies lost to the Crusades and the brutal sands of the Holy Land.

The priest who walked beside him lagged a respectful half-pace behind. He was a small man with a shaved head, no beard, and eyes that seemed to take on different hues depending on the old man's mood. Benoit did not like him. Not at all. And he feared the priest, too. There was a painting from the year 1009 that showed an ancestor, Sir Hugh LaRoque, standing with the family priest—an Italian who had come to France on the order of Pope Sergius IV. That priest and the man who walked with Sir Benoit looked like twins. Or more than that. Benoit had spent hours in front of the painting and knew every inch of the wizened priest's face—every scar, every line—and could not reconcile how a man living in modern France could look so like someone from two hundred and twenty-seven years ago.

When he'd asked Father Nicodemus about the resemblance, the little priest's only reply was a small, oily smile and an offhand remark about family resemblance.

Sir Benoit did not believe that.

Yet he was bound to the priest now. The lessons on how to read the Book of Shadows in the coded language had begun, and now Benoit was due to take his vow as Scriptor with the new year. It was agreed that the *Scriptor's Diary* be withheld until Sir Benoit had mastered the secret language and read every word of the Book of Shadows. Only then would the young Scriptor be ready for the full weight of the truth.

They entered the castle, handing off their wool cloaks to servants before entering the library, where a roaring fire and glasses of mulled wine waited. Once they were seated by the blaze, with the Book of Shadows open between them, Father Nicodemus reached out and placed his small, cold, damp hand atop the young nobleman's.

"Now that we are alone, my lord," said the priest, "I will ask you three questions. What happens next—and happens tomorrow and for years to come—will depend on how you answer. Do you understand?"

Sir Benoit, not yet eighteen but educated and intelligent, did not reply quickly. Instead he withdrew his hand and used it to raise his wineglass. He sipped the warm, spiced liquid and allowed it to linger in his mouth to release its subtleties. Then he stared at the fire. Pine logs were mixed with oak and beech, and the fragrance brought him back to when his father taught him to play *jeux de tables*. They had gamed away many a winter's eve when his father was at home and not in the Holy Lands. Now the game board that had been so skillfully inlaid onto the tabletop was obscured by the weight and reality of Le Livre des Ombres—the Book of Shadows. Though to Benoit, it should have been branded as the Book of Horrors or, at the very least, the Book of Sins.

He took another sip and nodded. "Ask your questions, Father."

It galled him to call Nicodemus *father*, with his own father barely cold in his grave. Manners, however, and the customs of civility must be obeyed, he told himself.

Father Nicodemus nodded and smiled. One of the many, many kinds of smiles that always haunted his gaunt features. "My first question is this," he said. "Do you understand the nature of the Holy Agreement?"

"Understand it?" Sir Benoit nearly followed that with a statement of his true opinion, and it was an effort to bite back those words. Instead he repeated, "Understand it? Yes, Father. I understand full well."

"Very good," said Nicodemus, pleased. "My second question is this: Do you accept that the burden of this knowledge falls to the lord of La Maison LaRoque?"

A log shifted, spilling glowing embers onto the hearth.

"I accept that as a truth and an obligation," Benoit said, then washed his mouth clean with wine.

Father Nicodemus leaned slightly forward, and when Benoit glanced at him, he saw firelight reflected in eyes that seemed black within black.

"And my third question—the most important of all," said the priest in a voice that was oddly low and guttural. Almost a growl. "Do you accept your role of Scriptor and all that goes with it?"

The flames danced along the new configuration of logs. Benoit closed his eyes and tried not to weep.

"Yes," he said in a voice filled with shame and doubt, with fear and loss. "Yes, I accept the role of Scriptor of the Red Order of the Knights Hospitaller."

The old priest leaned back in his chair and sighed deeply, almost as if with erotic pleasure.

"Then we have much to do, my son. The future whispers to us, and we must answer, for we are doing God's holy work."

Sir Benoit watched the fire, certain in his heart that it was not God who sanctioned such horrors. But he was trapped by his role and his heritage and the inflexible requirements of his faith.

"Yes," he said softly. "As God wills it."

## CHAPTER 12
### LEDGER FAMILY FARM
### ROBINWOOD, MARYLAND

After that call with Church I felt frustrated and angry and more than a little confused.

"Well," I said to Ghost, "that was weird."

He wagged his big bushy tail.

Once I was absolutely positive no one was tracking me, I drove out into the country, leaving Baltimore behind as the urban and suburban sprawl gave way to long, twisty roads lined with trees. There were winter-bare trees looking like some of Wyeth's less verdant paintings, but there were also farms and ranches. Cows clustered together for warmth and watched the big man and his dog drive by. Horses with blankets strapped around them ran alongside slatted fence rails, racing me for the joy of it.

Some stretches were green with pine trees, but out here there was still snow on the ground and it suggested an echo of Christmas in the country. As a boy, when my parents would drive Sean and me out here, the excitement was everywhere, from a flaming red cardinal on a snowy pine bough to green wreaths on red farmhouse doors, and chimney smoke promising warmth and hot cider by the fire.

But then a few years ago a little killer named Rafael Santoro had paid that awful visit to my uncle's farm and blew all of those lovely memories into fragments.

I saw the entrance to that farm up ahead and I slowed to look at what time and effort had accomplished. One of Church's countless "friends" who owned one of the largest construction companies in the South had worked miracles. As a Christmas present last year, Church teamed up with Rudy and Junie to have them build a new house. Not a replica—thank God—but a new design. Big, sprawling, but with a Victorian vibe that was quite lovely. Lots of corbeils and dormer windows, gingerbread and gables. Six bedrooms, six full baths, and something like eight thousand square feet. That didn't include a horse barn, a roomy equipment shed, various small buildings I had no idea what they'd ever be used for, a hangar for a small plane, and the beginnings of sophisticated landscaping that promised a gorgeous blooming schedule.

Junie told me that Church paid for it, and he declined to tell her what the price tag was, but my guess was two or three million dollars' worth of material and labor. So, yeah, as much as the Big Man pisses me off at times, he does stuff like this.

As I reached the top of the hill, I could see how far the work had progressed, even in only three months. The house looked nearly complete, and the crews had poured the concrete foundations for the outbuildings. It was beautiful and painful to look at because of who was not, and could not, be there. I could almost see the ghosts of my family standing on the big wraparound porch, their eyes turned expectantly toward the road, Dad and Sean both wearing this year's ugliest Christmas sweaters.

Damn.

But it was also beautiful because this was in no way a cheap and sentimental attempt to imitate the past. My uncle's house had been big and rambling, but never elegant. Never high-end. The new house could have graced the cover of *Town & Country*.

Even so, this was the Ledger farm and it was where the Ledger family line ended. I have no living male relatives, and I don't plan on ever having kids. Can't, really. During the Code Zero case, Junie was shot and the bullet did irreparable harm to her uterus. Sure, we've talked about adoption, but really . . . who in their right mind would ever want to bring new life into a world as cold and cruel as this? Certainly no one who does what I do for a living.

Ghost leaned over and laid his head on my thigh, and when I glanced down, he looked at me with the uncomplicated love that all dogs possess. It's their greatest superpower. He could feel my pain. I think he understood it, because he had played here with my nephew and niece. And he came close to dying here at least twice. Maybe three times. Christ, I've actually lost count of how often I'd nearly gotten him killed here on my home soil.

I scratched the thick fur between his ears and told him he was a good boy. His eyes were sad but his tail thumped against the passenger door.

I fished a dog biscuit out of my shirt pocket and gave it to him. He took it, laid it on his seat, and ate it with those same small, delicate bites. It was so at odds with his titanium fangs and battle scars.

"You're as weird as I am, you big fuzz-bucket."

His tail thumped even faster.

I took my foot off the brake and let the car coast down the hill toward the driveway entrance. Then followed the pale gravel drive up to the turnaround. The front door opened as I turned off the engine, and a figure stepped out onto the porch. It wasn't Junie, who was currently in Philadelphia as a speaker at a conference of tech companies collaborating on soil reclamation projects. She texted me a photo of her with the actor Ian Somerhalder, who had produced *Kiss the Ground,* a celebrated documentary on the subject.

No, this person was medium height, with a comfortable belly mostly disguised by a red-and-black flannel shirt left untucked. He had black hair shot through with premature gray, and a thick mustache. Dark eyes and a smile that was as honest and true as Ghost's expression.

He held a coffee cup and saluted me with it before taking a long sip.

Rudy Sanchez.

My former shrink. My colleague in Church's war. And the best friend I have ever had.

So, maybe this place could be a kind of home after all.

# CHAPTER 13

## PHOENIX HOUSE
## OMFORI ISLAND, GREECE

Mr. Church rode up in the elevator to the top floor of the ancient castle that sat atop the shell of an ancient and long-dead volcano. The castle had been bought from a holding company in Romania, carefully disassembled, and shipped to the island to be Church's home. It was huge, with towers and courtyards, and many rooms. The lower floors were given over to suites of rooms for the executive staff and special guests, offices, and storage for the bulk of Church's private collection of art and oddities.

He stepped out into a long hall and was greeted by Luke Merishi, a Moran—a Maasai warrior from Kenya—and a former member of the Lion Guardians. He wore a standard gray patrol uniform but with a red-and-black-checked Maasai sash along with ornate multicolored arm bracelets, necklace, and earrings. He had a pistol in a belt holster and a slung rifle, but also carried a twenty-inch rungu, the deadly throwing club made of polished ebony wood.

"Good evening, sir," said the guard.

"Good evening, Luke."

The young man fell into step beside Church as they walked along the winding corridor. Luke's grandfather had been a close friend of Mr. Church a very long time ago, and together they had stopped a huge poaching ring.

"How is the training coming along?" asked Church.

"Very well. I spent most of today learning how to de-arm bombs. Tomorrow we will be on the live fire range."

Church nodded. Luke was studying to be an RTI field agent, though Church was conflicted about that. He liked the young man, and had great respect for his intellect, physical skills, and state of mind. The instructors gave him exceptionally high marks; however, Church was not at all sure putting him in the field was the best way to honor his grandfather's sacrifice. The older man—also named Luke—had died on a mission with Church that had nothing to do with lions or poachers. Old Luke, as he was called, had run missions against teams capturing Maasai children for forced sex work. Church had promised the dying hero that he would look after young Luke. So far he'd made good on that promise by funding the young man's education, providing money and care for his village, and offering him a job at Phoenix House. There was no doubt Luke could hold his own in any kind of combat, but at the same time there was a gentleness in him that Church did not want to see destroyed by involvement with the war.

For a while he considered taking Luke on as his personal bodyguard and valet—stepping into the shoes once filled by Brick Anderson and, before that, Gus Dietrich. But both of those good men had died violent deaths *because* of that service. Church did not want to have to bury Luke or explain to Old Luke's ghost that he had failed in his promise of care.

Luke did not ask about any future team assignments or promotions, though. He wouldn't. He was too well mannered and dignified. So like his grandfather.

When they approached the door to Church's apartment, the RFID chip embedded in the fatty tissue of his upper arm triggered the security system, and a panel of faux stone folded outward to reveal an off-market biometric scanner. Church removed his right glove and placed the pad of his ring finger on the screen and quietly spoke today's code phrase. The locks clicked and he pulled open the heavy door, which was a slab of steel alloy sheathed in antique hardwood.

"Good night, Luke," he said. "Get some sleep. I won't be needing anything else tonight."

The door swung shut silently behind him.

*"Usiku mwema, Simba,"* said Luke as he closed the door.

*Good night, lion.*

The apartment lights came on and Church paused for a moment, as he so often did, allowing the day to fall away and the quiet of his private rooms do what magic it could to calm him.

He had a large suite with a number of bedrooms, a full kitchen, an elegant dining room, bathrooms, a huge library, a meditation chamber, a gym, and several rooms set aside for his collection of artifacts. There was art on every wall, and some of it quite old.

He smelled some interesting aromas and wandered into the dining room to see several covered dishes arranged in front of an elegant table setting. Mrs. Karasu, the elderly Japanese woman who took care of his apartment and meals, had outdone herself.

Lately Mrs. Karasu had been experimenting with Romanian dishes, and that night prepared sarmale, a popular dish consisting of pickled cabbage rolls filled with a mixture of minced meat and herbs, served with polenta, sour cream, and pickled green chili pepper. The aromas brought back very old memories for him, leaving him wistful but smiling as he sat down to eat. There was a single candle standing tall in a silver holder fashioned to look like tentacles wrapped around the base of a lighthouse. The flame swayed gently back and forth.

"Calpurnia," he said, activating the artificial intelligence interface, "play Op. 57 V. E-flat major, adagio."

"Playing," said the soft, lush voice of Calpurnia, the AI component of MindReader.

He ate alone, listening to music from days gone by. Different parts of the composition suggested old memories, and as he dined, Church felt the presence of ghosts of friends and enemies, lovers and allies who had been consumed by war and time.

One face appeared over and over again in that chain of memories.

"Nicodemus," murmured Church. "Will you ever leave me in peace?"

The music flowed all around him, and he thought he heard a single word whispered into the spaces between notes.

*"Never,"* it said.

Church stared into the candle flame and whatever truths he saw there he kept to himself.

## INTERLUDE 5

### THE GRAND EXPERIMENT
### LAROQUE ESTATE
### VILLAGE OF MONTAILLOU, FRANCE
### 1240 CE

Sir Benoit LaRoque, master of the estate and Scriptor of the Red Order, was one day past his twenty-second birthday and already he felt old. When the footman knocked discreetly on his chamber door to announce the arrival of Father Nicodemus, Benoit cursed him back to seven generations of his misbegotten line and punctuated it with a pewter goblet he snatched up from his bedside table and hurled the length of the room.

He swung his legs out of bed and sat there, face in his hands, wondering how the world he once loved could have become so cold and bitter a place. He could not remember the last time laughter echoed through the halls of La Maison LaRoque. Certainly not in the four years since his father's death.

"Damn my soul," he told the shadows in his room. Then, as if lifting a massive burden, he heaved himself out of bed and padded across the cold stone floor to where his slippers crouched beneath a wooden chair. His dressing gown, though heavy, did little to conserve his body heat, and he pulled it tightly around his slender body as he went down to meet his personal devil.

"My lord," said the little priest, "I am so sorry to wake you at this hour."

"Could this not wait until morning, damn it?" growled Sir Benoit. "You know there's always a room and bed for you."

Father Nicodemus took off his rain-soaked black traveling cloak and hung it on a peg in the foyer. "I have brought someone for you to meet, my lord," he said. "He is a person of great importance who does not prefer to travel by day's harsh light. I'm sure you will understand."

Benoit looked around but saw no one else. "Where is this person?"

"Outside. Shall I invite him in on your behalf?" There was a strange gleam in the priest's eyes as he said this.

*No,* thought Benoit. *No, no . . . let me bar the door against this visitor.* He did not know who was out there, but he was certain he knew what waited for the invitation to enter. "As God wills it," he muttered at length. "Bring him in."

Father Nicodemus bowed and opened the door to reveal a tall figure dressed in a smoke-gray cloak with the hood pulled forward so that his features were entirely shrouded in darkness.

*How appropriate,* mused Benoit, wondering if evil things really did try to hide from the world, or if there was an element of theatrics about this. Probably both, he decided.

The man paused ever so slightly as he raised his foot to cross the threshold. Then he completed the step and Benoit saw a shiver ripple through him with enough force to make the cloak swirl. Benoit led his guests into the library, where a servant was just finishing the work of reviving a fading blaze.

The cloaked man did not remove his outer garment until the servant had bowed himself out of the room, and then he simply let the sodden thing drop onto the floor. Even then he seemed wreathed in shadows until he walked closer to the fire. Benoit busied himself pouring wine into three goblets, all the time covertly studying this person.

The man was slender and tall and moved with the eerie elegance of a dancer in one of those obscure performances of the poet Chrétien de Troyes's Arthurian romances. His feet made no sound, not even a wet slap as he walked toward an offered chair. He had hair so blond it looked like ice, and a beard that hung to below his heart. His clothes were simple and of a style popular in the last century. He had worm-white hands with long fingers and eyes that were as red as a dungeon rat's.

Benoit handed a glass to Father Nicodemus, who gave a small bow and sat in his usual chair. The visitor, however, shook his head and sat next to the priest. The young lord found it odd that the priest had not yet introduced his companion, and he sipped his wine while he waited.

"My lord," said Nicodemus, "this man has agreed to accompany me here from Kievan Rus', one of the Slavic states. His family is well known and so out of respect for them he prefers to use a traveling name."

"Which is . . . ?"

"Borisov," said the stranger.

"Is that your surname or . . . ?"

"Borisov," repeated the man.

"Very well," said Benoit. "You may call me 'my lord.'"

The pale man considered this, then nodded once.

Father Nicodemus said, "I expect that you can guess to which branch of the human family Borisov belongs."

Sir Benoit pursed his lips for a moment. "Why bring another of *them* here?"

He looked for a reaction from Borisov, but the man's face might have been stone for all the emotion it showed.

"Oh, my friend Borisov is a person of remarkable qualities," said the priest. "Look at him, my lord, and tell me if you can guess his age."

It was a weird question, but Benoit shrugged. "Forty, perhaps. Give or take five years."

Borisov made an expression that might have been a smile or a sneer. Father Nicodemus chuckled.

"Do you find me so amusing, Father?" demanded Benoit hotly.

"No, my lord," said the priest. "It is merely that my friend here is a bit older than he looks."

"So am I. What of it?"

Father Nicodemus turned to Borisov. "Please tell the Scriptor the year in which you were born."

The stranger shrugged, and in a heavily accented voice said, "I was born in our year of the lord 1093."

Benoit burst out laughing. "Is this some kind of joke? I am surprised at you, Father, for waking me in the middle of the night to play a prank upon me. Ten ninety-three? You think I am such a boy, such a credulous fool as to believe this fellow is one hundred and forty-seven years old?"

The old priest contrived to look wounded. "My lord! I would never play a joke on you. Not on you. You are the Scriptor of the Red Order and I am but a humble priest. No, no, no, my lord. I brought Borisov here because he truly *is* that old. His father was older still, and died on his two hundred and first birthday, and only then because ignorant villagers poisoned him with garlic oil."

Benoit got slowly to his feet, uncertain of what he was going to say or do. He wanted to call his men at arms to thrash this Slavic liar to within an inch of his life and cast him out into the rain. He wanted to write a stern letter to the Vatican and have this madman defrocked. He even thought about his father's sword—his own now—hanging above the glowing fireplace.

What he said was merely one word. "Why?"

In answer, Borisov's face split into a wide grin. A very wide grin. It stretched his cheeks and showed all of his yellow teeth. There seemed to be far too many of those teeth in the stranger's mouth. And all of them were as sharp as daggers.

Father Nicodemus leaned back in his chair and looked at Sir Benoit over the rim of his wineglass. "I do not know your mind, my lord, but as for me . . . I would very much like to know how the men in his family have managed to live to such a great age. And whether that gift is something *we* can share."

# CHAPTER 14

## LEDGER FAMILY FARM
## ROBINWOOD, MARYLAND

Rudy and I sat in front of the fire, drinking beer and watching pine logs sizzle and burn. It snowed again and now everything outside the big French doors was an unbroken vista of brilliant white and eighty thousand shades of pale blue and gray. The first stars were igniting and it gave the landscape a quality that was hard to define. Not the cheery Christmas vibe, and not the solitude of deep winter. This was more like the world pausing to take a breath.

I'd told Rudy about the day's events and we chewed on it like a couple of terriers all through the meal he'd prepared. Tossed, baked, and extra rare, and plenty of Taildragger 5G, a superb wheat beer by Saddle Mountain Brewing Company. Rudy had some Afro-Brazilian jazz playing, the volume turned low. Ghost lay sprawled on the hearth, slowly baking his doggie parts.

We'd gone back and forth about the Sabbatarians, the Red Knights, the Red Order, the Assassins Code affair in Iran, and wrestled with those inferences we could draw. It was mostly speculation, though, and a good deal of it may be past tense. As far as Bug and his computer team could tell, the Red Order didn't survive what we did in Iran. After all, we outed the entire group and shared all of the information we'd gathered with the appropriate law enforcement agencies. The witch hunt that ensued was thorough. In countries where there is no active death penalty, a few surviving members of that group were doing *very* hard time. In Iran and a few other countries, any Red Order members who were apprehended were entertained in prison until their usefulness was done and then they were stood against a wall. Five of them were actually beheaded in Syria. I want to say that I mourned, but why would I lie?

"Hey, O learned Dr. Sanchez," I said, "you ever heard of something called the *stregoni benefici*?"

He worked out the translation. "Beneficial sorcerer?"

I explained what Church said about the translation being closer to *beneficial vampire* or *Vampirii Lui Dumnezeu.* Rudy stared into space for a few moments, then shook his head. "Thought I remembered something from one of Circe's books, but I can't quite grab it."

Circe was Rudy's wife who was back in Corfu with their kids, and in a different time zone.

"Ask her when you talk to her next," I suggested.

"Have you looked it up on the Net?"

"I tried. Almost every reference was for a character in those *Twilight* novels. But, like I said, Church said it was a rumor in medieval Europe."

"So," he reminded me, "was the belief in a heliocentric solar system, and that dragons lurked out beyond the edge of the known world."

"Fair point."

We returned to speculations about the Red Order, but soon exhausted the topic because they had gone quiet and were presumed dead or disbanded.

"You said Nicodemus is sick," Rudy mused. "I will admit to having no discernible feelings of sympathy for him."

"How's that square with the ol' Hippocratic Oath?"

"The oath is more of a guideline than a rule. Nor, I should add, is that oath in any legal way enforceable."

"Duly noted." I raised my bottle. "To Nicodemus . . . may he cough up his lungs and die cold and alone beneath an underpass."

Rudy did not join my toast, however. I drank heartily.

Then, as so often happens when we two are alone, the conversation drifted to the enigma that was Church.

"You know, Rude," I said after taking a long pull on my bottle, "ever since I came to work for the Big Man, I knew there was something weird about him."

Rudy gave me a look. "Weird? Church? I'm shocked you would say so. Shocked, I say." He has a rich baritone voice and his Mexico City accent sounds exactly like Raul Julia from the old Addams Family movies.

"Yeah, ha-ha," I said dryly. "But I'm making a point here. The longer I know him, the more convinced I am that he's hiding more than just the truth of his actual identity. I'm not scared of very much, but he scares me. He scares me a whole damn lot."

"More than the Red Knights?"

"A lot more."

"More than Nicodemus?"

"Yep."

Rudy considered that. "What about him *scares* you? Specifically, Cowboy." Rudy is the only person who still calls me by my boyhood nickname.

"I guess because I need to believe in him," I said.

"And you don't?"

"That's just it, I'm not sure."

"What's that mean, though? Do you suspect his motives? If so, why and in what way?"

I sipped my beer and thought about how best to answer him. "He asks a lot of me. Of all of us. He knows everything about me. Hell, he read my psych evals and told me flat out that he had back when he first interviewed me for the old DMS. As I recall, you were ready to call your congressman about it."

"I actually did," Rudy admitted.

"Really? You never told me that."

He shrugged. "It came to nothing. I made the complaint and then suddenly everything escalated. You were all but shanghaied into the DMS and were immediately sent out into the field. Two or three combat incidents on your first day with him."

"That was wild. That whole *seif al din* case. The they're-not-zombies-but-they're-really-zombies thing. That first fight at the meatpacking plant in Claymont, Delaware. Then Room 12 and the crab plant . . . Jesus, there wasn't time to think."

"I joined, too, Joe," said Rudy.

"I know. My point is that all that craziness kicked what little understanding I had in the shape of the world squarely in the nutsack. Since then it's been . . . what? Clones, genetically enhanced super-soldiers, secret societies, aliens, nonsupernatural vampires with nuclear bombs, a machine that makes earthquakes, a rage virus . . ." I trailed off, shaking my head. "I know this is all science and not magic, blah-blah-blah, but the cumulative effect on me is every bit as strong as if this stuff *was* magic. I've lost real trust in the fabric of reality. All for Church and his war."

Rudy nodded. "We were both caught up in the tidal surge that is Mr. Church's war."

"The war is the war," I said, reciting Church's favorite catchphrase. For him, that answers most questions and explains all motivations. "*Which* war, though, Rude?"

"*The* war . . . ?" he suggested. "You've never needed a definition before."

"Maybe I do. Maybe I was too quick to trust. Back then, the bad guys were capital B, capital G. Very obviously the enemy, and very obviously needing their asses kicked. The math was simple."

"And it's less simple now?"

"That's just it," I admitted. "I don't know. The sides in opposition aren't always political, because sometimes the enemy of my enemy is my friend, and sometimes the enemy of my enemy is *also* my enemy. And sometimes my enemy *is* my friend. It's complicated. The Sabbatarians are technically good guys, but I've had to kill a shit ton of them. It's stuff like that that makes me doubt my grasp on the rules that govern reality."

"Consider how complicated it is for me," said Rudy. "I married his daughter. His only known living relative."

"Yeah . . . about that—"

"No," said Rudy, cutting me off. "Circe doesn't know his life story, either. She isn't even certain she knows his real name, and very likely does not."

"Really?"

"Truly."

"Well . . . that can't be a fun way to live."

He snorted. "And people wonder why Circe and her father are estranged."

"Must be fun when he comes over for the kids' birthdays or the holidays."

Rudy shook his head. "Every visit is a masterclass in acting. Circe acts loving to him because we don't want our children to grow up hating their grandfather. Church acts like we're a normal family. I act like I'm not appalled."

"Jeez, man."

A log shifted in the fire, filling the firebox with swirling sparks. We sat and watched them swirl.

## CHAPTER 15

### LEDGER FAMILY FARM
### ROBINWOOD, MARYLAND

"Well, Joe," said Rudy, "let's face it—as any objective student of history will tell you, there is no easy answer. There's not even a chance of one. Not every enemy is as clear-cut a monster as, say Harcourt Bolton, Hugo Vox, or Sebastian Gault. The math always gets complicated when the enemy is prosecuting his worldview and ideology, and believes his cause is just. Fighting such a person causes emotional conflict for any empathetic person in the war. And you, my friend, are empathetic to a very high degree."

I snorted. "Junie insists that's a superpower. But . . ."

"Oh, she is correct. It is. And it is the foundation of why you fight," Rudy said, gesturing to me with his beer bottle. "You know what it feels like to be overwhelmed by hatred and violence. You and Helen experienced a kind of war and a very real defeat. It's why you joined the jujitsu dojo. It's why you joined the army and then the Baltimore police department. It's why you allowed Church to bring you into the Department of Military Sciences, and why you followed him when he shuttered that group and founded Rogue Team International."

I finished my beer, got up and fetched two new ones from the fridge. There was already a battalion of dead soldiers lined up on the table between our chairs. I put his near his elbow, uncapped mine, and took a moderate pull.

"I don't fight for flags or nations or causes, Rude," I said. "I sure as hell don't fight for political parties, and I couldn't give a rat's ass who's in the White House or sitting on a throne somewhere or yelling in parliament. For me the math is a lot simpler than that. It's right and wrong."

"Nicodemus might argue that it's order and chaos."

"Fuck that freak." I took a swig. "As for the empathy thing, there are a lot of people—including military scholars—who would beg to differ with your view of it as any kind of freaking superpower. Not that I don't feel empathy, but that empathy is dangerous. It goes against that bit of advice they give everyone in basic training and at the police academy—to not get emotionally involved."

"I'm very familiar with that viewpoint," said Rudy. "And I know that empathy is very much a double-edged sword. But you accept the cuts that blade makes because the pain is what drives you."

"Jesus," I complained.

"Tell me I'm wrong."

"If you're suggesting I'm addicted to pain, then—"

"Oh hush," he snapped. "You know that's not what I'm saying. I'm saying that you are aware of your damage going in and accept that kind of emotional damage as the cost of doing business. And before you accuse me of minimizing, let me add this. That empathy also allows you to understand what drives the kinds of people we fight. They are not abstractions to you. They are not THEM and therefore a nameless, faceless, irredeemable enemy. No. You see them as people. Not saying you like them, but your viewpoint is closer to what I do in many practical ways. By understanding what drives them, you can better position yourself to respond to their attacks with precise counterattacks. It's clinical, surgical, and therefore effective. This is you being a philosophic warrior rather than someone merely following orders." He smiled. "It's why you were never much of a joiner and why you would be immune to ever being seduced into a cult."

I thought about that as we watched the fire burn. "And yet," I said, "I sometimes feel like I'm *in* a cult."

Rudy, wise and sharp as ever, nodded. "The cult of Church," he suggested.

"For want of a better word, sure," I agreed. "And our prayer is 'the war is the war.' The litany of Church's followers."

Rudy got up and walked around the room for a bit, straightening things that didn't need to be straightened, looking out the window at the darkening fields. Then he came back, sat down, and opened his next beer.

"No," he said.

"No what?"

"It's not a cult. Neither of us are followers. On some level, we *do* trust Mr. Church. On some level we know that, despite his obfuscation and evasions about his past, he is fighting the good fight. We see the goodness in him that is guarded behind iron walls."

"Yeah, but what started him down this path? How did he accept this war as his to fight? Christ, Rudy, who *is* he?"

Rudy leaned back in his chair, the bottle resting on his belly. "I really don't know."

I looked at him. "Are you just saying that because of doctor-patient confidentiality? I mean, you have to know more than anyone else. Maybe even more than your wife. I mean, hell, Circe's his daughter but she doesn't seem to know any more about him than I do."

"While I will not break the seal of my oath to my patients," said Rudy, "I can tell you with one hundred percent honesty and candor that I do not know who Church really is. I don't know that anyone has that knowledge."

"Lilith . . . ?" I suggested. She was Church's lover and they apparently had a lot of history. But Rudy shook his head.

"She knows more than I do, to be sure, but I don't think she has all the answers, either."

"What about Nicodemus?" I asked. "He keeps hinting that he knows Church better than anyone."

"And he is a notorious liar, given to clever and manipulative exaggerations," countered Rudy. "Like when he kept calling Church 'kinsman.'"

"And Church said that was horseshit."

"Yes," said Rudy.

"Do you believe that?"

Rudy shook his head. "I . . . really don't know, Cowboy."

We drank in silence, watching as the fire burned the logs down to glowing coals. Outside the evening wind began to moan and sleet started hammering against the window glass.

# CHAPTER 16
## PHOENIX HOUSE
## OMFORI ISLAND, GREECE

Mr. Church was about to step into the shower when the intercom buzzed.

He gave the wall-mounted speaker a baleful glare, then leaned over and punched the button.

"Go," he said.

"Sorry to interrupt you after-hours," said the crisp voice of Scott Wilson. He did not sound at all sorry. "But a matter has come up that needs our attention."

Church did not ask if it could wait because not even his chief of operations would have called him for anything of lesser importance. Church rubbed his eyes, then pinched the bridge of his nose for a moment.

"Tell me," he said.

# INTERLUDE 6
## THE GRAND EXPERIMENT
## LAROQUE ESTATE
## VILLAGE OF MONTAILLOU, FRANCE
## 1242 CE

Sir Benoit entered his study and paused, surprised at the changes.

It was his first trip home after being abroad for nearly a year. First, he had thrown in with Theobald I of Navarre, but as that began to falter, he joined with Richard of Cornwall, and again saw that the energy of the Crusade was failing. Then he followed Conrad IV of Germany in a crusade against the Mongols, but that fell apart after only a few weeks because the threat itself was withdrawn.

It felt to him as if history was leaving him behind, and during the long journey he wrestled with his feelings about that. On the one hand, the constant Crusades were a heavy financial drain on the member states. As prices rose along with the body count, interest waned. He wondered if that was a sign that the Holy Agreement itself was naïve in its forecast.

On the other hand, as he caught up with accounts and met other travelers, he gradually realized that it wasn't the war that was failing in its intent to fill churches, but a lack of enthusiasm for the specific causes. Farmers in rural France, Russia, and elsewhere had no real understanding of the subtleties of the many so-called holy causes. The Holy Land might as well be on the moon for all it touched the lives of those folk. The lords who owned the estates on which these farmers lived lost so many sons that family lines were dangerously close to collapsing.

All of this worked within Sir Benoit's nimble brain, and as the miles fell away on his final trip back home, he found that a new perspective was taking hold within him.

What if the Red Order had it right all along?

That was the key question with which he wrestled. It was his own mistake, he realized, to conflate the goals of the Crusades with those established by his own forebear, Sir Guy LaRoque. The battle did not need to rage on the Holy Land per se. What mattered was that the *threat* of invasion by the Saracens or the Mamluks be strong enough that people throughout Christendom felt sufficiently threatened that they clung more tightly to the skirts of the Church. That, he now saw, could be accomplished without the absurd and often pointless expenses of a Crusade. Besides, only the Templars were profiting from those so-called holy missions, and as a Hospitaller, Sir Benoit had little love or trust for those arrogant asses with their white mantles and red *cross pattée.* They were getting fat off of the Crusades while honest soldiers of Christ were dying penniless, their lives spent like bent coins.

No, as Sir Benoit reckoned it on that last journey home, Sir Guy had been right, but the Holy Agreement itself required a course correction to keep it from running aground on the rocks of indifference and bankruptcy.

Now he was home, and the intervening months had seen much happen at La Maison LaRoque. It seemed as if every torch, hearth, and candle in the blaze burned with the light of industry and excitement. The first impression as he entered his library, though, was the smell. The air was redolent with a thousand scents of wood and minerals being burned or boiled, distilled or dissolved, sublimated or fermented. It was a heady scent—with perhaps a bias to both sulfur and floral essences—and was not unpleasant. It was strong, though, and he had to pause for a moment to take it in and make some sense of it.

The big room had been changed. Instead of chairs for reading or conversation, there were a dozen worktables, each draped with cloths embroidered with arcane symbols and outré designs. On most of the tables were small metal or stone athanors filled with oil, and on these rested instruments of every kind—beakers and retorts, alembics and crucibles, sand baths and aludels. Small silver chests stood open to reveal stones and crystals of incredible variety. There were baskets of herbs—dried and fresh; bundles of flowers, buckets of sand that ranged from gray-white to volcanic black.

Men and women moved throughout the room, each dressed in robes of uniquely patterned brocade. A few wore strange hats, floppy or conical. All the men were extravagantly bearded, and the women wore garments similar to wimples yet marked with symbols that predated the birth of Christ.

"There you are, my lord," said a voice, and Sir Benoit turned to see a smiling Father Nicodemus threading his way through the crowd. He took the young lord's hands and gave them a warm squeeze of welcome. "I am delighted to see you, for there is much to show you."

Benoit gently took his hands back and gestured to the activity. "When you wrote to say that you were going to invite some alchemists here, I had no idea it would be like this."

"Oh, my lord," said the priest, "there are more in the basement, in the east tower, and in one of the stables."

"To what end? Before I left, you promised me that there was a way for us to receive the gift of immortality from the Upierczy. Have you made any progress at all?"

The little priest beamed at him. "We have made great progress."

"Is it ready, then?"

"What? Oh, dear me no," laughed the priest. "But we have made an excellent and promising start. We have learned so much. Oh yes, my lord, so very much."

They stood together, watching the alchemists at their labors. Each was focused on their tasks, their whole beings seemingly wrapped in a cloak of obsession.

Father Nicodemus edged a bit closer and lowered his voice to a confidential whisper. "We have brought many of the Upierczy here, and they are quartered in the subcellars. They prefer dark places and do not consider their residence here as a punishment. In fact, they are eager to help."

Sir Benoit thought he caught a false note in that last statement, but did not say so.

"What we will need fairly soon," continued Father Nicodemus, "are volunteers on whom to test the elixir our alchemists have promised to deliver."

"Is this concoction safe? Are we even ready for such a drastic step?"

The smile on the priest's mouth was a cruel one. "How will we know until we try?"

"Should we not experiment first on less important people? The prisons are filled to bursting."

"And if the potion is successful, we will be giving the scum of Christendom immortality and possibly other qualities. Does that seem like a good idea, my lord?"

It was rare for Sir Benoit to feel a coldness that matched, or even eclipsed, that of the strange priest. And yet, he said, "We can keep them in chains, and if they become . . . something dangerous to us . . . I am reliably informed that fire cleanses. Mistakes can be thus erased."

The cruel smile turned to one of delighted admiration, and Father Nicodemus bowed. "As my lord wishes."

## CHAPTER 17

### LEDGER FAMILY FARM
### ROBINWOOD, MARYLAND

When my cell rang, I looked at the screen display and showed it to Rudy. "Speak of the devil," I said.

"Maybe don't answer it, Joe," he said. "You were promised a full week of downtime."

It rang again.

"Might have something to do with what happened today. After all, I was in a pretty nasty gunfight . . ."

*Ring.*

Rudy shook his head. "And RTI has a lot of *other* people, equally skilled, who are *on* the clock."

We both waited through the next ring.

"Let it go to voicemail, Cowboy." There was almost a pleading note in Rudy's voice.

I smiled at him. My friend. My brother.

Then I answered the call. Even before the caller spoke, I heard the soft *whup-whup-whup* of a helicopter landing in the front yard.

# MAGNA PESTILENCIA

# PART 2

"My first wish is to see this plague of mankind, war, banished from the earth."

—GEORGE WASHINGTON

"Near the gates and within two cities there will be scourges the like of which was never seen: famine within plague, people put out by steel, crying to the great immortal God for relief."

—NOSTRADAMUS

# CHAPTER 18

## CORVIN CASTLE
## HUNEDOARA COUNTY
## TRANSYLVANIA REGION OF ROMANIA

We came in in that silent time of dark stillness of three in the morning.

There was almost no sound except for the arthritic groan of old trees being bullied by an east wind, and the desultory drip of water from melting snow. Three inches had fallen the afternoon before, but the temperature had begun to climb before sunset and by dawn all of that snow would be gone. Even so, we were careful not to leave visible prints. There were a lot of rocks and bits of broken masonry to use as stepping stones.

We'd gotten most of the way in by air, gliding down on TradeWinds MotorKites, a kind of self-powered parasail rig that looked like we were each dangling from the clutches of giant bats. Very appropriate to the locale.

Transylvania.

I've been to Romania several times, and even to this county before, but there is something about this "land beyond the forest" that always triggers the imagination. We've all seen too many vampire movies, and although Corvin Castle was never the home of Vlad Tepes, it was still an ancient castle near the gloomy Carpathian Mountains. It came with implied dread baked in by centuries of creepy literature and a regional connection to one of the greatest mass murderers in history.

The place looked like something out of a Dracula movie. It was actually a replica of the original Corvin Castle, rebuilt after devastating fires. They aged it well enough to look like it had been around for centuries. It's in that zone between ostentatious elegance and creepy-as-hell.

It was a vast Goth-Renaissance pile that was close to six hundred years old, and they had been hard years. Part of the place had burned down and although there had been a partial restoration, there were still broken walls and fallen stone littered throughout the surrounding landscape. It was often used—under various names—as the setting for horror movies, and anyone could see why. My rational mind wrestled with my imagination, insisting that the darkened windows were not eyes slyly watching us, nor were the huge front doors a hungry mouth.

I had only half of Havoc Team with me for this gig. Top Sims and Bunny Rabbit, the two warriors who'd joined Mr. Church's war at the same time I did. Bunny was recovering from injuries sustained in Pine Deep, but he had that healing engine youth provides. He was only a few years younger than me, but seemed much younger. Full of vigor and never bogged down by the slings and arrows of our shared outrageous fortune.

The rest of the team—our sniper, Belle, and the crazy Cajun tech expert, Remy—were on vacation and too far away to reach us in time. Though they were traveling back to Greece and would likely meet us at the airport on our way back. If all went well and we *got* back.

We dropped down at the far end of a rampart bridge that spanned a deep ravine, landing out of sight of those windows. We punched the release buttons on the kites, catching the harnesses to keep them from banging on the ground. The release button also caused the big wings to fold back and into the backpack housing. We set them aside, entering a three-digit retrieval code. If we did not return within two hours to deactivate the controls, thermite charges would be triggered that would reduce them to slag. They could also be remote destroyed if there was a chance someone was fiddling with them. This allowed us to use the tech without risking it falling into the wrong hands.

Ghost had hung from my chest during the flight, and the kites managed my two hundred ten pounds and his one-oh-five.

Then we flipped down our night vision and went hunting.

There were no visible sentries, but even so we deployed a handful of nightjar drones. They looked exactly like the common birds of the region as long as you didn't get closer than six feet. The drones flew high and circled the whole castle, sending high-def data streams to the ultrathin tactical computers strapped to our forearms. With the Scout Glasses we wore, that feed was transferred to the inner screen of one oversized lens, shaded so as not to interfere with the night vision. Very high-tech, though it made us look like pop-eyed ghouls. Even Ghost had a set of goggles and had been trained how to use them.

We moved like ghosts through a landscape that *felt* old. Some places are like that, storing specific energy like batteries. I used to live in Baltimore and its energy is like that of a delinquent teenager. When I lived in San Diego, it was like being back in my college frat days. But here . . . it felt ancient and unwelcoming. It felt the way certain cemeteries do, where you are pretty sure the dead are not all resting quietly.

When we reached the foot of the castle, we paused. The quality of light was changing and Top tapped me and indicated the sky with an uptick of his chin. A waning crescent moon was slowly slicing through the cloud cover.

We took the Scout Glasses off and waited until our eyes adjusted to the pale, blue-white light.

"Almost looks pretty," said Bunny quietly.

"No it don't," countered Top.

I thought they were both right.

"Ghost," I said, bending to speak into his ear. "Go look. Come back quiet."

We had spent thousands of hours training together. We had our own private set of commands, and he was one very smart animal. He has a weird habit of opening and closing his mouth once with a wet *glop* sound, which I've always interpreted as his way of saying "Aye-aye." Or, more appropriate to the dog of a former Army Ranger, "Hooah."

His bushy tail gave a single flick and then he was gone, vanishing into the gloom.

I tapped my tactical computer and we three bent low to study the feeds from the nightjar drones and Ghost's bodycam.

"No sentries," said Top.

"Then let's go," I said.

Our entry point was a wooden oak door banded by thick strips of steel, aged to look like ancient iron. The lock was new, though, and Bunny knelt to run an anteater over it, checking for any kind of alarm system.

"It's wired nine ways from Sunday, boss," he reported.

"Run a bypass," I told him.

Bunny removed a device from a pocket. It was made of flat gray metal and was the size of a pack of Juicy Fruit. He removed a strip of plastic to expose a strong adhesive, then gingerly placed it on the wood next to the lock. This allowed MindReader, our super-spooky computer system, to remote access the chip governing the alarm. MindReader is built around a super-intrusion software package that can invade virtually any computer or piece of electronics. It does so by overwriting the target software and making it believe that MindReader is a part of that system. Then it takes charge and allows us an incredible measure of control. Once its job is completed, it rewrites the conquered software to remove all traces of the intrusion. Nifty, dangerous, and spooky.

The MindReader device Bunny planted would fall off after fifteen minutes, as the adhesive oxidized and became neutral. Once it fell off, tiny thermite inside would melt it so that even the hardware leaves no useful evidence.

Mr. Church buys us all the best toys.

The door clicked open.

Top and I stood in combat crouches, our HK416s ready in case things got dramatic. Bunny finger counted down from three to zero and then opened the door.

No sirens blared and nothing went bang. I sent a comms signal to Ghost and he came back quick and quiet. Yes, my dog has an earbud.

Together, the four of us entered the castle and the door swung silently shut behind us.

# CHAPTER 19

### CORVIN CASTLE
### HUNEDOARA COUNTY
### TRANSYLVANIA REGION OF ROMANIA

We entered a small combination utility and mudroom. Raincoats on pegs, boots standing in rows, a barrel filled with rakes, hoes, snow shovels, and spades, and two long wooden benches. Ghost moved ahead of us and sniffed the floor. He did not sit, which would have been his way of warning us of anything that smelled like a bomb. Nor did he lie down, the signal that there was someone close by.

I took point, moving forward with my rifle butt snugged into my shoulder. The inner door stood ajar and I checked it to make sure there were no trips or traps. Nothing. That could either mean a level of comfort in their security setup, or maybe the intel was wrong and this was nothing but an antique tourist trap. It wasn't all that much of a comfort, though.

There were dim yellow service lights leading away down a long hall, and we followed it, with Top and Bunny taking turns to try the handles of different closed doors along the way. Four opened into storerooms, and one into a bathroom. No guards, no surprises.

At the end of the corridor, we paused. It was a T-juncture, with longer hallways going left and right. Top edged up and showed me the floorplan on his tac-com. Left was supposed to go to a generator room that powered the whole place, and right led to a flight of stairs going up.

Our intel was passed down the line by a field operator from Barrier, the UK's above-top-secret special projects group. They were a couple of rungs up a shady ladder from MI6 and not generally known to the public. Church had helped set it up shortly after 9/11, and the agent was Oskar Freund, son of one of Church's former spooks and a good friend of mine. If he said there was something here, then there probably was. He wasn't the kind of cat to make mistakes.

The question was, though, where was he?

"Supposed to be right here," said Top.

"Yeah, damn it," I replied.

He looked down both halls. "Class trip or two-by-two?"

"Let's stay together and go left first. He said that there was an entrance to a lab near the boiler, and that'll be off the generator room."

"Copy that, Outlaw," he said, using my combat call sign. His was Pappy and Bunny was Donnie Darko.

We moved down that way, each of us wondering where the hell the guards were. The anteaters scanned the walls and floor, but if there were sensors here, they were inactive.

Bunny moved up close. “Is it me or is this too easy? I mean, in a creepy kind of way.”

“It ain't you, Farm Boy,” said Top. Despite Bunny being a beach boy from Orange County, Top insisted he looked like he walked off a farm in Iowa. Bunny tended to call Top “Old Man,” which was fair enough. Top was in his forties, with a salt-and-pepper goatee and a shaved head. Lots of lines on his face, but a lot of them, I knew, were scars. He'd been through some shit, even before he joined up with Church. I was well aware that my face was starting to show signs of wear. Miles, not years. Bunny, though, still looked like he did the day I met him. Bastard.

We kept going, but instead of hurrying because it all looked safe, we slowed down. I don't trust a gift horse worth a damn, and yes, I will look at its teeth.

At the end of the corridor, we paused and I used a dentist's mirror to peek around the corner. That hallway ran forty feet and stopped at a plain wall with an ordinary-looking door of the same faux antique steel-banded wood. But Ghost immediately lay down, telling me there were guards. Not on this side of the door, but he must have smelled them beyond it.

“Fake door,” said Top, not making it a question.

“Fake door,” I agreed.

I pulled out another drone—a rat one this time—and sent it scuttling down the hall. It reached the door, stood on hind legs, and scanned with a variety of sensors located behind its eyes and in its belly. The signal coming back to our tac-coms was both encouraging and disturbing.

Top said, “Good news, we found the lab. Bad news, there's a shit ton of people in there. I'm counting thirty heat signatures.”

“Shit on toast,” sighed Bunny.

We stayed on our side of the corridor bend.

“What's the play?” Top asked. “Call in the cavalry or storm the Bastille?”

“Oskar said there were test subjects in there,” I reminded them. “That could account for the high count.”

“Yeah,” said Bunny, “and Oskar could be one of them. If they're doing some mad scientist shit in there, we might not have time to wait for backup."

That was true enough. Added to that mix was some concern that the Romanian Secret Police might have some leaks. Particularly in the Department for Foreign Intelligence. Some text messages sent their way wound up in the wrong hands. As a result, our mission here was off-book and we were in country without official sanction. Any help we could call in would have to fly in by stealth chopper, and those were all on the back lawn of a private estate in Serbia. That was six hundred kilometers away. We couldn't even risk high-altitude drones.

"We're on our own," I said. "Either we go in or we go home."

I knew what they would say, but out of respect I let them say it.

"Oskar's been there for us," said Top.

"He's family," said Bunny.

"But let me ask, Outlaw," said Top. "Rules of engagement?"

That was the tricky question. We came armed for war, but lethal force wasn't our only option. We all had Snellig 22A-Max gas dart guns strapped to our thighs. They were loaded with 50-round magazines filled with Sandman, a cocktail of hinky chemicals that has the veterinary drug ketamine as its main component, but it was heavily seasoned with BZ / 3-Quinuclidinyl benzilate—to cause intense and immediate confusion—and DMHP / Dimethylheptylpyran, a derivative of THC—for muscle failure. Sandman is a one-hit, instant-drop option. Doesn't kill, but whoever gets shot with it spends the next six to eight hours having the worst kind of freaky-shit trip. Wild hallucinations, loss of bladder and sphincter control, and—weirdly—occasional violent orgasms. You do not enjoy it, and you wake up questioning every life decision that led up to being in the path of that shot.

I slung my rifle and drew my dart gun. The others did the same. Bunny did so with great obvious reluctance. He was carrying a Franchi SPAS-12 combat shotgun with an after-market drum magazine. It was heavy, clunky, and a lot of SpecOps guys hate them, but Bunny's tinkered with his and plays it like a musical instrument. But it wasn't the right tool for this job, so he slung it.

The rat drone told us that there were cameras on the upper and lower corners of that wall, which meant we couldn't approach unseen unless we knocked them out.

Top took a pair of small but plump single-use drones of a kind we call a nightbird. They look like overfed thrushes, and their sole function was to deliver a small-field electromagnetic pulse blast. The pulse knocks out anything with electronics, so we faded well back from the turn.

"Do it," I said, and he tossed the nightbirds into the air. Their wings deployed and they hurtled off around the corner. Bunny took a breeching charge from his pocket and held it ready.

There was a soft *pop-pop* and the threat sensors fed by the rat drone instantly went dark. We were up and running at once, with Top and me covering Bunny as he ran forward, pressing the adhesive on the charge to the wood beside the lock, and then we faded back again.

We put our Scout Glasses on, with the visual setting dialed to thermals. Bunny thumbed the detonator and there was a heavy *whump*. Then we ran into the swirling smoke and dust. The heat signatures flared on our screens, and we could see soldiers falling from the blast, and others turning toward the destroyed door, arms lifting weapons.

All three of us opened up at once.

It did not matter if a heat signature was a hostile or friendly. We weren't there to kill. If we tagged Oskar by mistake, then we'd carry his unlucky ass out of there. He was a practical guy and would rather have drug-induced nightmares than be tortured by the bad guys.

Several of the guards went down in our first assault, but then gunfire erupted from beyond the cloud of smoke. We got low and fast, racing to find cover. As we cleared the fumes, I got a look at the room and instantly understood why Oskar called this in.

It was a lab, no doubt about it.

A lot of the thermal signatures were men dressed in either brown security uniforms decorated with whipcord edging and lots of gun belts, or men and women in white lab coats. And the whole place was packed with every kind of exotic machine known to modern science, and many I'd never seen before.

It was a big room, maybe a hundred feet per side, with lots of tables and computers, vats of bubbling chemicals, steel dissecting tables, metal cables and bundles of wires trailing everywhere like octopus limbs. In the rear, behind the chemical tanks, there were a dozen glass-fronted holding cells, each with two or three people in it.

It was like stepping inside the twenty-first-century version of Frankenstein's lab.

It was a horror story.

And we were badly—laughably—outnumbered.

# CHAPTER 20

### CORVIN CASTLE
### HUNEDOARA COUNTY
### TRANSYLVANIA REGION OF ROMANIA

The guards opened up on us. AK-47s are an inexpensive gun but that's not why they're so popular. They are also durable, efficient, and reliable. The big banana magazines carried thirty rounds. The air was alive with the roar of gunfire and aswarm with lead.

We returned fire as we dove, hoping to drop some or make them grab their own cover. I felt a hard punch between my shoulder blades as one round hit me. The vests we wore were tough enough to stop the bullets and had the extra benefit of that graphene tubing for sloughing off foot-pounds of impact. Even so, the shot sent me into a sprawl that likely saved my life as another shooter filled the air at what had been my head height.

I skidded, slewed, and came up kneeling behind a heavy toolbox on wheels, and immediately returned fire. Everybody in that chamber seemed to have a gun. Even some of the lab coat crowd had produced handguns. Fun bunch of folks. Must be great to party with.

I caught the shooter who'd hit me with a dart that went into his mouth as he opened it to shout something. He pitched back twitching, then rolled over and threw up before collapsing bonelessly into what looked like a steaming pool of borscht.

Another shooter took his place and he did his best to try and turn the toolbox into splinters and junk. Pieces of tools whapped against me. Off to my right, Bunny was trying to squeeze his massive bulk behind the last in a row of super-computers. A man in a lab coat knelt fifteen feet away behind an overturned table, screaming at everyone within earshot to *not* shoot those mainframes. No one was paying any attention. Made me wonder what was so special in those databanks that he was willing to risk his own life in a situation where hiding or flight seemed like the better options.

I put another guard down and then a lab coat, but more guards seemed to be materializing out of the goddamned air. Top and Bunny were earning their paychecks, but the situation was threatening to go south.

Somewhere out of sight I heard a man screaming in that unique way that let me know Ghost was keeping busy. He's lost some teeth on previous missions and they've been replaced with titanium fangs. Ghost *loves* those choppers, and when he is on the hunt there is no "dog" left—he becomes something closer to a primal wolf. Fast as hell and efficient in his viciousness. He is trained to take enemy combatants out of the fight. Sometimes that means killing them, but in situations like these he goes for severe injury instead. I knew that when this was over, we'd find guys with savage wounds and missing hands.

The people in the glass cells had dropped down, arms wrapped around their heads as if that could save them from bullets. Most of them were screaming, but the glass was too thick and the gunfire too deafening for their cries to be heard. I did see some of that shatter-resistant glass take heavy rounds and spiderweb cracks appeared. That scared me every bit as much as the gunfire because they were clearly test subjects and I had no way of knowing if they were already infected. Me and my guys were wearing body armor, but it wasn't hazmat-level.

The lab coat guy who kept shouting actually stood up, arms spread wide and hands open to show a lack of weapons. He turned in a circle, yelling in Chechen. *"Kompjyüterş yac! Kompjyüterşna the gerz ma toxa!"*

*"Not the computers,"* he pleaded. *"Do not shoot the computers."*

Not sure who shot him or why. Wasn't me or Havoc Team. But suddenly he began to judder and dance as multiple rounds tore into him. The white coat blossomed with awful red flowers and his shout turned into a gurgling, high-pitched scream. One round blew his kneecap to red junk and he fell, but even while he lay on the floor, bleeding and dying, he begged for the computers to be spared.

"Pappy," I called via the comms, "light them up."

A moment later I heard, "Frag out!" And then a flash-bang arced over the overturned surgical table behind which he hid. I ducked down and pressed my palms over my ears and hoped Ghost buried his head under something as he was trained to do.

The flash-bangs we have can be set according to three levels of effect. One is the standard, same as the ones used by the military. Two is a higher setting that is used by SpecOps when doing hostage retrieval in a situation where exact enemy numbers are unknown but predicted to be high. And then there was the level Top used, which he calls God's Talking, which amplifies the flash and bang to the point where eardrums may never recover and retinas burn out. Nonlethal, but if you're caught unprotected in the blast radius you kind of wish that it was.

A moment later he threw a second, going for a downfield pass to the far side of the room. Even with my gloved hands over my ears it was like getting kicked by a moose. I reeled, hissing in pain, and then rose up to view the effect.

Nearly three-quarters of the guards and all of the lab coats were down, writhing, screaming, clawing at their ears and eyes. The people in the glass cells were rolling around, hands over their eyes. They were probably not deafened, but any of them that had been watching the fight were going to have eye problems for the rest of their lives. If they had any future, that is.

The other guards began backing away, some of them shaking their heads stupidly, blinking to try and clear their eyes. We rose up and rushed them, firing the Sandman darts at them first, and then at every other guard, no matter how badly injured. It took maybe twenty seconds and then the room dropped into a weird silence. Gun smoke drifted around us like ghosts, and it called to mind a similar image from the cemetery in Maryland.

I got to my feet, swapping in a fresh magazine.

"Clear," I yelled.

"Clear," came the calls from Top and Bunny. They stood, too. If I looked as bad as them then I must look like shit. They were bleeding from metal and glass cuts, and both had that post-firefight glaze in their eyes. Not quite a thousand-yard stare, but in that zip code.

Ghost came staggering out from cover, shaking his head, too. But he looked at me and I could see that he had found useful cover. His white muzzle was now dripping scarlet and his side heaved from the fear, exertion, and excitement of the battle.

The blind, deaf lab coats crawled helplessly or lay shivering in terror. We walked among them, and as Top covered them with his Snellig, Bunny and I secured them all with flex cuffs.

I went over and knelt by the scientist who had been begging us not to damage the computers. He was bad, circling the drain. I tore a coat from one of his sleeping colleagues and used my knife to cut it into strips, applying them to the worst wounds, but it was only a holding action.

He was about forty, with a professorial face and a thin beard covering a weak chin. His eyes were jumpy with shock. His lips formed words and I had to bend to hear them.

"Am I dead?" he asked.

"Not yet," I said.

He seemed to think about that. Then his eyes sharpened for a moment. "Are you . . . a . . . red . . . ?"

"Red? Red *what*?"

He mumbled something I couldn't follow.

"Can you hear me?" I repeated it in English, Chechen, and Romanian, but his reply was a weak head shake. So I angled myself so he could at least try to read my lips.

His nod was small, but it was there. He fought to speak. It was painful to watch him force words out.

"Saturday?" he asked.

"What? No, it's Tuesday."

The man shook his head. "N-no. Puh-puh . . ." He faltered, stopped, then tried again. "The people. Saturday?" And again there was that rising inflection, making it a question. His eyes were going in and out of focus as he struggled for control.

"I don't know what that means," I said. "What is in that computer? Why is it so important?"

"C-control," he stammered in bad English.

"Control?" I repeated, and he nodded. "Control for what?"

"The re-re-release . . ." The sibilant S sound came out like the hiss of a deflating balloon.

"Release of what?" Then I pointed to the glass cells. "Are the people in there already infected?"

"The Saturday . . ." Those two words came out clear, but then he mumbled other words that were garbled nonsense.

"You need to tell me about the release," I coaxed. Gentle, but firm.

For a moment his eyes were filled with conflicted emotions—horror, guilt, fear—and that gave me the answer to my question. I glanced over at the people and saw some of them trying to stand. Most could barely sit, and now that I had a chance to really look, it was clear that their faces were pale, gray, or sallow, and glistening with sweat. A few wept. Some merely stared at the cracked glass walls in front of them with no expression at all on their faces. Shock? Sickness? Both?

I looked down at the dying scientist and saw his face grow oddly calm. I think that was the moment when shock began insulating him from the agony he had to be feeling. It was the moment when he not only knew he was dying but had accepted that inevitability.

"Play—play . . ." he began but failed and shook his head in frustration.

"Sound it out for me. Do your best."

He was fading, the light starting to go out of his eyes. He took a ragged breath and tried it once more.

"Play . . . plag . . . uh . . ."

That last syllable came out as a long, protracted exhale. His last. His eyes stopped looking at me and instead went wide in a terminal surprise as death took him down into its dark kingdom. Leaving me kneeling there, pressing a bandage to a chest wound that no longer bled.

My head rang. Not from the flash-bang, but from the last word. It had cracked apart as he died, but he got enough of it out.

Not play.

He was trying to tell me that the computers held the key to controlling the release of plague. I whipped around and looked at the people in the cells again, and now I understood what I was seeing. Test subjects. All of them sick.

All of them dying of plague.

God damn.

## INTERLUDE 7

**THE GRAND EXPERIMENT**
**LAROQUE ESTATE**
**VILLAGE OF MONTAILLOU, FRANCE**
**1243 CE**

The Christmas bells rang throughout the land, heralding the celebration of the holy birth. It was an hour shy of midnight on that sacred eve, but La Maison LaRoque was alive with activity. The alchemists worked tirelessly, rarely taking time to sleep or eat. Sir Benoit thought the whole castle stank of unwashed flesh that reeked as intensely as the chemicals. And it sounded like the Tower of Babel, with the alchemists nattering on in a score of languages.

Benoit retreated from the din to a tower where he had set up a new study, albeit much smaller than the one his father had loved. There, with only faint incense and the richness of burning pine logs, he made his daily devotions, read the correspondence from across the known world, and studied the Book of Shadows, adding entries in the coded language that he could now read and write without the code key.

When a discreet tap on his door roused him from a reverie, he called, "Enter."

The door opened and Father Nicodemus leaned around, his seamed face split with a look of unfiltered joy.

"My lord," he said, "may I entreat you to accompany me down to the dungeons?"

"Why?" sighed Sir Benoit. "I do not need to see another deformed prisoner beheaded. I am weary beyond words with having my soul damned to everlasting torment by our *volunteers*. I've had my fill of such disasters."

"Well, my lord, perhaps the spirit of this holy season has cast its blessings on us all."

Benoit frowned. "What do you mean . . . ?"

"Come, Sir Benoit," said the priest. "Come and see what we have wrought."

## CHAPTER 21

### CORVIN CASTLE
### HUNEDOARA COUNTY
### TRANSYLVANIA REGION OF ROMANIA

Top and Bunny hurried over to a door that led deeper into the castle. They had to pass the glass cells to do it, and I watched the silent interplay between them and the prisoners. A couple of the healthier people began banging on the windows, shrieking in total silence for help. Top's face was a stone, and I knew which gear his pragmatism was in. He moved past them, not directly engaging because there was critical work to be done in the short term.

However, Bunny stopped by one cell where a woman in her mid-thirties sat against the wall with the head of a young teenage boy in her lap. Both of them were drenched with sweat. The teenager's eyes were closed, and from where I stood there was no way to know if he was alive or not. The woman did not scream, but she looked up at Bunny with large, wet, blue eyes. There was no pleading there, but instead a kind of acceptance. Maybe she understood the full extent of her situation. Maybe she had spent the last coins of hope already and was just waiting for the night train to come and take her down.

Bunny placed one big hand flat on the glass and he stood there for maybe three full seconds. She gave him a small, sad smile and a smaller nod. When Bunny turned away, I saw his face change from the expression of encouragement he'd tried to show her, to a crumpled grief, and then to a red and murderous rage. Top saw him and gave him a single, silent shake of his head. That said as much as a speech, especially with the telepathy they had—as so many soldiers have who have walked together through the Valley of Shadows too many times to count. Bunny nodded, but I could see how much it cost him.

They went out.

I called into the TOC and ran through it. As I did so, I turned slowly to allow my bodycam to send clear images back home. I lingered on the cells for a bit before forcing myself to turn away and give them a good look at the row of computers.

"Any idea what he meant about Saturday?" Scott asked.

"Sabbatarians," I said. "Kind of has to be."

"Did he have a tattoo . . . ?"

"Not visibly, but I didn't have time to do a strip search."

"Not sure we can trust much of anything he said," observed Scott.

"Maybe. I hope like hell he was being delirious and not really talking about some new version of the plague."

"I daresay," agreed Scott. "We are coordinating with contacts in the Romanian government to bring in a medical team. They should be at your location in under an hour."

"Tell them to take the fast lane."

"Red tape dictates that, and we're not on home turf," he said. "We are not sanctioned for actions on Romanian soil. We are working through back channels. I need you to gather as much intel as possible, including whatever you can download from those computers, and any samples you can safely transport and be out of there in twenty minutes. That is a hard out. You cannot be there when local authority arrives."

"What about those people?"

"They will be given all possible medical care."

"Don't jerk me off, damn it," I snarled. "What about those people?"

He paused and there was a click on the line, letting me know he was closing everyone else out of the call. When he spoke again, his tone was different. Colder, with no attempt at coddling me.

"Listen to me, Outlaw," he said. "We don't know what kind of plague we're talking about here. Our intel was that a group of Chechen radicals were using that facility to build a small bioweapons lab. We're only now knowing that at least one of their projects is plague. That's bacterial, and a lot of groups have pioneered new ways to modify and weaponize different strains of *Yersinia pestis.* Over the last fifteen years we and our allies have encountered more than two dozen deliberately mutated strains. There have been rumors that someone has been developing a strain that is immune to antibiotics. Until we know which kind—or *kinds*—of plague have been used against those prisoners, we cannot make any predictions for their care."

"I don't want to hear that," I said.

"And I don't want to bloody well say it," he fired back. "But the world doesn't bend to our desire. We have to adapt to its realities."

I closed my eyes, not wanting to see anything in that room. Not wanting to look at the innocent people in those cells for fear they would be able to read what I felt.

"The clock is ticking, Outlaw," said Scott, his voice a shade more human. "I don't know if we can help them, but if we get enough information, then maybe we can get in front of this and stop it before we have a new Black Death."

I so wanted to hit him. Or . . . anyone.

Instead I said, "Copy that."

And went to work.

I took a handful of MindReader uplinks, which were each about the size of a flash drive, and plugged them into the computers. I placed a signal booster unit on the middle unit and uplinked to a satellite. The data began flowing at incredible speed, with MindReader devouring it.

We all had BAMS units clipped to our belts and I used mine to sample the air. These are small but powerful bio-aerosol mass spectrometers that draw in ambient air and hit it with continuous wave lasers to fluoresce individual particles. Critical molecules like dangerous viruses, fungi, bacillus spores, and certain vegetative cells are identified and assigned color codes. There's a small, color-coded display that ranges from a comforting green to a terrifying red.

The light was green and I let out a breath I didn't even realize I was holding.

With great care I went to a series of small glass-fronted storage units mounted on the wall and, after checking each with the BAMS unit, I used gloves and tongs to remove several dozen vials marked with letter-number codes. A clipboard hanging on a nail held the key to the code, and the words I read on it scared the shit out of me. I must have checked the BAMS fifty times before the cases were filled, and I set them by the door.

One of the prisoners had begun banging his fist weakly against the glass of his cell, but—coward that I am—I did not look at him. This was hard enough as it was.

Just as I was finishing that task, Top's voice spoke over my comms.

"Outlaw," he said. "Building's clear. We found a few more people and darted them all. We taking prisoners?"

"No," I said, and very quickly told him what I found.

"Well, shit," he said. Then added, "I'll see your plague and raise you something that . . . well . . . hell, boss, I think you better come take a look."

"Clock's ticking."

"Then find me fast," he said, and told me where to look.

## INTERLUDE 8

### THE GRAND EXPERIMENT
### LAROQUE ESTATE
### VILLAGE OF MONTAILLOU, FRANCE
### 1244 CE

Sir Benoit LaRoque sat at one end of a huge oak table. His favorite hound, Claude—last of a pack of siblings Benoit had hand-raised—lay wheezing and twitching on the floor next to him. The big hound's limbs were twisted by arthritis but Benoit did not have the heart to put the animal down. It was the very last link to the optimistic, empathetic youth he had once been. To close that door instilled within the young nobleman a superstitious dread, as if to do so would be to close himself off forever from the values he *thought* his father had cherished. Now he understood the nature of his father and the holy yet dreadful work undertaken in Christ's name for the preservation of the Church. Claude was proof that Benoit had not been born corrupt but had only accepted the twists and stains on his soul because to do God's work often meant sinning against mankind. A paradox and a bitter truth.

Father Nicodemus sat to his left, and five austere-looking men clustered at the far end. These strangers were much like the other alchemists who had come and gone through the halls of La Maison LaRoque, but also unlike them in very specific ways. They were deeply learned in classical studies, with degrees from honored universities; moreover they each had the blessings of the new Pope Innocent IV.

Benoit listened as introductions were made and credentials read out, trying to refine his personal judgment. The little old priest named the group Quinque Patres—the Five Fathers—and they were Hungarians from a monastery in the Carpathian Mountains of the Transylvanian region. It was clear that none of them were hand-wavers or charlatans who wore wizard's hats and spoke in languages that were likely made up. These were true scholars and philosophers of nature, and they were among the most revered alchemists in Christendom.

"The Quinque Patres have brought with them ancient books filled with lore," said Nicodemus as he concluded his introductions. "Some of which date back to the glory days of Egypt, for the study of alchemy is an old one. There are even books written by Saracen mathematicians and thinkers, too. And, while this may be troubling from a political perspective, it is a means to an end. Knowledge, my lord, is neither good nor evil; its merits or deficits are calculated by the way in which that knowledge is used."

"Yes," said Benoit, "I am aware."

When the priest was finished and the standard formalities and compliments given, Sir Benoit waved all of that aside.

"Forgive me for being abrupt," he said wearily, "but can we get to the heart of this matter? Yes? Excellent. Here is what I need to know if I am to give over to you the administration of this grand experiment."

The five men inclined their heads with great dignity.

"The challenge we have faced is that we want the best qualities from the Upierczy—impervious health, a robust nature, and longer life—without sharing these qualities with anyone not covered by the blessings of the Red Order. Nor do we want any of the Upierczy's less savory qualities to pollute the pure blood of our Christian knights. What we seek are knights of great strength and health who can continue to do God's work without their full potential to be squandered by the cruelties of time. And with no unholy taint from the monsters we have been forced to use in this shadow war."

"Of course, my—" began Father Nicodemus, but Benoit silenced him with a raised hand.

"I wish to hear from the Five Fathers," said the young knight. He looked at the strangers. "Do you speak French?"

One of them, a very tall man with pale gray eyes, inclined his head. "I speak your language very well, my lord. And also Latin, Greek, Arabic, and Hebrew."

"Very well," said Benoit. "Now . . . tell me how we can remake the Red Order so that it will last until the Day of Judgment."

# CHAPTER 22

## CORVIN CASTLE
## HUNEDOARA COUNTY
## TRANSYLVANIA REGION OF ROMANIA

I ran from the lab and climbed eight sets of stone stairs. Bunny was waiting for me at the top and he wore an enigmatic expression that I could not begin to decrypt.

"What is it?" I demanded.

"Oh, you got to see this firsthand, boss." He led me into a large library that had uncountable bookshelves floor to ceiling. Between each bookshelf, though, was a large painting. Very large and very old. Top stood in front of one of them, arms folded, head cocked to one side. When he saw me approach, he said nothing but merely nodded at the portrait in front of him.

I stopped beside him and stared.

The painting was of an eighteenth-century gentleman wearing a burgundy brocade coat decorated with a large many-pointed silver star, an ornate cravat, a powdered wig, an embroidered vest, and with the hilt of a dueling sword rising from the lower right corner. The face was a young one and somewhat delicate in appearance. However, it was obvious that someone at the castle had been messing with it to reveal a second image beneath. I knew that was not at all uncommon with old paintings—somebody falls out of favor and gets painted over, or a poor artist buys old and unimportant paintings since stretched canvas is costly. They gesso over whatever's there and paint something new. On a nearby worktable were a variety of tools used to uncover older works—a palette knife, rags, sponges, and cotton swabs.

None of that was what Top and Bunny wanted me to see.

More than half of the face of the original portrait was visible now, and this showed a man of about sixty but powerful and fit. His eyes were dark and penetrating and his mouth unsmiling and uncompromising. The original painter had gone for ultrarealism and it was like looking at a living person, even down to a few small scars on his face.

I stared at it. I literally gaped open-mouthed.

Then I said, "What in the wide blue fuck?"

Bunny, who had come to join us, said, "Yeah. That's pretty much what I said."

Top's comment was a long-drawn-out, "Shi-i-i-i-i-it."

The older painting was done in a different style, one I'd seen in enough museums to guess it was much older than the foppish dandy whose likeliness was painted over it. Enough of the top layer had been removed to show an older costume as well. This was far less ornate, with no medals or crests or frippery. It was the far less ostentatious garment of what appeared to be a Templar Knight.

We stood looking at this man, ignoring the nobleman whose image had been used to obscure the original. Obviously both men were centuries in their graves.

And yet . . .

At that moment I wasn't all that sure of that, or of any goddamn thing at all.

We all knew that face. The older one. We knew those eyes, that stern face, those small scars.

We looked up into the eyes of a man who looked exactly like Mr. Church.

I tapped my earbud to get the Big Man on the line.

"Go for Merlin," he said, using his current combat call sign. Like his "name," Church frequently changed his call sign.

"There's something I think you should see. Maybe without a crowded room."

"Very well," he said, "I'm switching to a secure channel. It's just the two of us."

"Check this out," I said and stepped back to allow my bodycam to get a nice, clear view. "I think I fought a painting of one of your ancestors, boss."

There was a significant pause, then in a cool, quiet voice, he said, "I would very much appreciate it if you wrapped that painting and brought it back to Phoenix House, Outlaw. And, as a favor to me, don't show it to anyone."

"Why not?"

"Because I asked," said Church, and the line went dead.

I stood there for a very long time looking at the painting. There was no logical, rational, or sane reason why his request should bother me. But it did.

Yes sir, it bothered the living hell out of me.

THE DARK INSIDE

# PART 3

"No man chooses evil because it is evil;
he only mistakes it for happiness, the good he seeks."

—MARY WOLLSTONECRAFT

"How the early priests came into possession of these secrets does not appear,
and if there were ever any records of this kind
the Church would hardly allow them to become public."

—HARRY HOUDINI

# INTERLUDE 9

## THE GRAND EXPERIMENT
## LAROQUE ESTATE
## VILLAGE OF MONTAILLOU, FRANCE
## 1244 CE

Sir Benoit walked side by side with Father Nicodemus through the cemetery where generations of LaRoques had been interred. It was midyear's day, and the sun was a white ball of fire in a flawless blue sky. Thousands of birds sang in the trees, and the air thrummed with bees flitting from one to another of the countless flowers.

"Six months," said the knight. "Six months and how many have we buried now? Two hundred prisoners? Twenty volunteers from the foot soldiers of the Red Order? All of them buried here or burned to ash. And what have we accomplished?"

"Much, my lord," said the priest.

"Much? On Christmas Eve you swore to me that the elixir was perfected, and yet that man died screaming six days later. He did not even make it to the first of January."

"And we have disciplined the alchemist who made that claim and swore to its efficacy with a hand to God. He was given the next version of our elixir."

"Yes," drawled Sir Benoit. "I recall him screaming for his mother and he bled from his eyes and rectum and cock. A smashing success."

"Alas, there have been disappointments and setbacks," said the priest ruefully. "Much has occurred since then, however. Since the arrival of the Quinque Patres, we have made great strides."

Since the arrival of the Five Fathers, most of the lesser alchemists were dismissed after swearing on their immortal souls to keep the secret of what they worked on while at La Maison LaRoque. Those whose word was in question simply vanished from all knowing, and even Sir Benoit did not ask as to their disposition. As Scriptor, he had long since prioritized the needs of the Holy Agreement over that of common decency or even mercy.

He asked, "And what have the Five Fathers done to justify the enormous expenses in bringing them here and equipping their experiments?"

"Let me show you, my lord," said the priest.

They stopped at a crypt in which four of Sir Benoit's favorite hunting dogs were entombed, each having lived a full life. Claude, the last of the pack, was expected to pass soon and join his littermates in eternity. Sir Benoit loved those dogs more than he loved anything else. The five of them had been with him for nearly fourteen years, gifts to him from his father. The thought of the last of that litter passing away was a cold stone weighing down his aching heart.

"I am in no mood for more promises, Father," warned Benoit as he touched a marble stone inscribed with Claude's littermates. There was room for one more name, and the thought of ordering that small task to be done tore at him. "If there is nothing of substance to tell me, then leave me here with my dogs."

A pair of swifts darted and raced through the air above and both men paused to watch.

While still looking up, Father Nicodemus said, "They have perfected the elixir, my lord."

"Please, Father," snorted Sir Benoit. "How many times have I heard that? Do you not tire of disappointing me?"

"I swore to withhold such pronouncements after the debacle on Christmas Eve, my lord."

"And yet here we are . . ."

"Oh, yes . . . here we are," said Father Nicodemus. "And it is not idly that we have come here to this sad place."

"Why? I need no reminders about the impermanence of life, Father. Death comes for us all, and soon Claude will sleep with his brothers and sisters." He turned to glare at the priest, who still watched the birds. "You try my patience, old man."

Father Nicodemus lowered his eyes and turned to face the Scriptor. "They say that seeing is believing."

"What, then, am I to see?"

The priest stuck two fingers into the corners of his mouth and, crude as any yeoman's unschooled child, blew a piercing note. When nothing happened, Sir Benoit felt his anger rising, but before he could speak his fury, the bushes parted and a great, dark creature bounded out and leapt at him. Not to knock him down, but to lick his face.

The creature moved with all of the bottomless energy of a puppy even though it was a very old hound.

*"Claude . . . ?"* gasped the Scriptor as the dog pranced and jumped and twitched and wagged in happy abandon. Sir Benoit turned to Father Nicodemus. "But this cannot be. Claude cannot even run, let alone walk or . . . or . . . no, this is a trick."

"It is no trick, my lord."

"But . . . how?"

"The Quinque Patres knew of your love for this hound, and knew that death was calling in a louder voice than that of his beloved master. So they asked if I would grant permission to try their version of the elixir on Claude. And . . . well . . . seeing *is* believing."

The hound was a brute—nearly as much wolf as hound—and on his hind legs stood as tall as Sir Benoit. His face was still streaked with gray and white around the muzzle and eyes, and there were still the old scars from countless hunts and several battles. And yet . . . the animal's body was swollen with new muscle, with sinews rippling beneath his coat. His eyes were clear but the irises had taken on an oddly crimson cast.

There was no doubt, though, that this *was* Claude. Not only brought back from the edge of death, but made strong again. He was once again in the full flush of his canine power. And the joy of his renewed life was there in every leap and bark and wag of bushy tail.

Sir Benoit sank to his knees and hugged the dog to him, holding it with effort as the powerful animal squirmed to try and lick every inch of him. Tears streamed down the young man's face, and if the priest heard his sobs, he was tactful enough not to comment.

After a very long time, Sir Benoit spoke without looking up.

"Is the elixir ready for testing on prisoners?"

"That has already been done, my lord. Sixteen men have been given the draught prepared by the Five Fathers."

"And . . . ?"

"In the weeks since they were dosed, each of them has healed from every disease and injury. We have even experimented with new injuries, and these have healed within hours. Days for the most severe injuries." He paused. "We cannot bring the dead back from life, nor can a one-legged man regrow a missing limb, but otherwise . . ." His voice trailed off.

"Where are those prisoners?"

"In the cells of the east dungeon," said Father Nicodemus. "Well away from all eyes except mine and the Five Fathers." He took a delicate step closer. "No one else lives who knows that this has happened."

Sir Benoit had his face buried in the furry ruff on the back of Claude's bull neck, his arms wrapped around the dog's barrel chest.

"Tell them this," he said without looking up. "We will begin testing the elixir on those whose lives are sworn to God, the Church, and the Red Order. Do you hear me? Only us."

"Of course, my lord," said the priest. "Would you like to pick the first candidate for this blessing? I can make several recommendations."

"I have already made my choice."

"Ah! And who shall it be?"

Sir Benoit turned his head and looked up. He held the dog tight to his chest. "Me," he said.

## CHAPTER 23

### THE TOC
### PHOENIX HOUSE
### OMFORI ISLAND, GREECE

Scott Wilson stood watching the huge array of images on the screens at the front of the tactical operations center. The live feed from Havoc Team was being replayed on some of them, while others were related to different cases. The team on that shift were busy, each of them focused on their work with the relaxed concentration of expert technicians and analysts.

It was a good group, and in many ways Scott felt sorry he would be leaving that family.

Well, possibly leaving. Perhaps probably.

Few of them knew that he was about to catch a chopper to the mainland and a quick flight to Heathrow, and from there to the headquarters of Barrier. It was his second visit in a fortnight, and if all went right, he would remain in England after this trip and take charge of that group. It was something he'd worked toward for years, and now there was a chance. A very good chance, according to Mr. Church.

He wondered, idly, how many of these family members would miss him. Certainly not that musclehead Joe Ledger. Maybe Major Mun would miss him. They'd become close. A few others, surely. Doc Holliday, Ron Coleman, Yoda and Nikki from Bug's team. Bug was uncertain because he seemed to like everyone, which meant that it was all façade, with his true feelings always a question.

Would Church miss him? Or had the Big Man's endorsement for the Barrier job been more out of bias than respect?

He wasn't sure.

For his part, he could bear to part with most of the staff at Phoenix House. And those with whom he shared an actual friendship were never more than a call away. Also, Barrier often did jobs in conjunction with RTI, so there was that.

Barrier would be a fresh start, a new life. And people closer to his own viewpoint. Greece was lovely but it was not England.

He glanced over at his personal workstation, where a small metal statue of Dover Castle sat. When he'd gone to London for the initial interview, that statue was a gift from James Rockwell. An original piece sculpted from beams salvaged when they tore down the old Barrier headquarters. It was made to look like that storied stronghold that guarded the gateway to the realm for nine centuries. That castle, in silhouette, was the symbol for the Barrier organization. Rockwell's message was very clear—this is where Scott Wilson belonged.

"Going home," he murmured.

A tech looked up enquiringly, but Scott merely smiled and shook his head and went deeper into his own thoughts.

## CHAPTER 24
### DRIVING IN ROMANIA

We drove to Bucharest in a Dacia Logan that looked exactly like all of the tens of thousands of that make and model in Romania. Which was, of course, the point.

Our driver was a local asset who didn't say a word the whole way. That was fine, because the three of us had a lot to think about. We'd changed at an Arklight safe house in Sarmizegetusa, dumping our combat gear and changing into street clothes. The driver was waiting for us outside, silently chain-smoking Dunhills. By the time we were showered, changed, and climbing into the car, he had lined up nine butts in a row on the ground, having arranged them neatly with the toe of his shoe.

As we drove to the private airfield in Bucharest, Ghost sat in the back, sandwiched between Top and Bunny, covertly getting doggie treats from both. I was in the shotgun seat. None of us felt particularly chatty with a stranger—even one under our umbrella of trust—in the mix.

When I called in to the TOC at Phoenix House, I was told that Mr. Church was in a series of virtual meetings with power players at the UN and NATO, likely discussing the threat assessments related to what we found in that lab. When I asked to be transferred to Scott Wilson, a tech told me that he left for London at around the same time Havoc left Corvin Castle.

"Who's on deck?" I demanded, feeling oddly miffed. And I am not prone to miffiness. Okay, that's not a word, though it should be.

The person to whom they transferred me—Dr. Ronald Coleman, the senior molecular biologist on Doc Holliday's team—was not in the usual command structure, but given the nature of the threat, was next in this particular pecking order.

"Outlaw," he said, "we're still working on that data, if that's what you're calling about. We won't have much to share for hours. Maybe a couple of days."

"I just needed a sounding board," I admitted. "The things the scientist had said—or tried to say—are gnawing at me."

"Try me," said Coleman. "I've been read in on the Assassins Code mission and am familiar with most of the pertinent details."

"Cool. So . . . the scientist I interviewed. He asked about Saturday. Then he asked if I was red. On the surface that sounded like word salad from a failing mind, and yet . . . There was something there. Or I thought there was. But it was one of those things that no amount of mental hand-grabbing seems able to catch. Red. Saturday."

"Individually, of course," said Coleman, "red and Saturday are maybe obvious. Saturday is likely a reference to the Sabbatarians, right?"

"Probably," I said.

"What makes you uncertain?"

"Today's Tuesday. Saturday itself is coming up. I don't want to make an ass out of you and me by assuming that the reference to Saturday *has* to mean the Sabbatarians."

"Pretty obvious though, isn't it? I mean, you just got into a scuffle with a bunch of those guys less than forty-eight hours ago."

"Scuffle," I echoed. "That's an interesting word choice. But, sure . . . there's that, but don't forget that this started off with Nicodemus fronting me at the cemetery. He never tells the truth—or at least the *straight* truth—when a lie is more entertaining. I could build a case of probability that he sent the Sabbatarians after me to establish the concept of 'Saturday' being about them as a distraction for something a lot more dangerous happening on an *actual* Saturday. You see where I'm going with this?"

"I do," he said glumly. "Wouldn't that require that he had some foreknowledge that Havoc would be undertaking the mission you just finished?"

"There's that," I said. "But over the years he's found different ways to gain info about our actions. Don't forget that he worked with Hugo Vox for years and then with Artemisia Bliss just recently in Pine Deep. So, he may have direct knowledge of some of our actions."

"Only some, though, don't you think?" Coleman asked. "He can't have complete access or we'd never beat him ever."

"Fair enough, but if we step back from absolute knowledge, it still leaves a lot of pretty damned uncomfortable wiggle room. How much deep data does a son of a bitch like him need to start trouble and in doing so confuse the frothy carbonated piss out of us?"

"You speak like a poet, Joe."

"Two things about that—fuck and you."

He laughed.

I said, "Nicodemus has been at least pretty tricky in the past, so let's not put anything in the 'no, it's preposterous' category quite yet."

"Note to self," said Coleman.

"To that point, do you know of anything of significant importance happening on Saturday that involves us or any of our allies?"

"Wow . . . I don't know. Scott would be the person to ask, but he's in London."

I muttered a few foul remarks, then said, "Do this, okay? Turf this over to Bug and Nikki. If there's any kind of actionable pattern here, Nikki and her team should find it. Tell her what I said. Then, when Church is free, tell him to call me."

"*Tell* him or ask?" Coleman asked.

"Fuck it. Tell him. And tell him I told you to tell him."

"Sure. It's your ass."

"You're a nice man most of the time, Ron. Today isn't one of those days."

"Been a long couple of days here, too," he said. "Speaking of which, I'd better get back to work or Doc will have *my* ass."

"Okay, Cuddle-bear," I said, using one of the many nicknames Doc Holliday uses for him. Coleman repeated some of the obscene things I'd just muttered, though he directed them all my way.

I turned to Top and Bunny, who'd listened in on the call.

"So it ain't just me that's confused about which end is up," mused Top. "Good to know."

Bunny wore a thoughtful expression. "That whole 'red' thing the lab guy said . . . ?" he said. "Could he have been asking if you were a Red Knight or one of those Red Order assholes?"

"Maybe," I said. "Maybe even probably, though you'd think those cats would know the Red Order is gone."

"Unless they're not gone," said Top. "They been around since the Crusades, and we know that there are some long stretches of time where they went quiet. So, maybe the Sabbatarians know something we don't."

"And that other name," said Bunny. "Rigatoni Benihana?"

*"Stregoni benefici,"* I corrected, and explained what I'd been told about the supposedly reformed vampire hit men for the church. "Possibly also known as the *Vampirii Lui Dumnezeu*. They probably don't exist, though. The Big Man didn't seem to think so."

"And yet that Sabbatarian jackass thought you were maybe one of those? I can see it—the black tuxedo, the opera cloak, and the long fangs." Bunny shook his head. "Those fucktards are so stupid they don't know they're stupid."

"On the other hand," said Top, "this is plague, so maybe he was trying to warn us. I heard you talking to Coleman, so I know you think the Saturday reference is linked to those Sabbatarian lunkheads, but Saturday could also be a launch date for some kind of bioweapons hit."

"Yeah, okay," said Bunny. "Which would make that 'red' comment some kind of shorthand for bleeding out."

I shook my head. "Plague isn't hemorrhagic, far as I know."

"Two words," said Top. "Designer bioweapon. Who knows what bells and whistles they built into this thing."

"Hell if I know," I admitted. "Might be something as simple as a red car with important bioweapon shit in the trunk driving somewhere on Saturday. Let's face it, guys, kind of hard to build something on two words, especially when Nicodemus is in the math."

"And that lab guy was dying and all," Bunny added. "Shape he was in, maybe he didn't even know what he was saying."

Top sighed. "There's that."

We lapsed into silence for the rest of the trip.

Red. Saturday. There was *definitely* something there. My spider-sense was jangling, but the more I tried to grab hold of whatever this was, the more slippery it became until it was entirely gone, leaving me doubting my own thoughts.

The car drove on.

# INTERLUDE 10

**THE GRAND EXPERIMENT**
**LAROQUE ESTATE**
**VILLAGE OF MONTAILLOU, FRANCE**
**1244 CE**

Father Nicodemus looked up from the prayer book that was open on his lap. Father Lászó, the senior among the Quinque Patres, stood waiting, his face a mask of anxiety.

"What is the news?" asked the old priest.

Father Lászó's face was grave. "The news is unfortunate."

"Tell me."

"Perhaps it is best if you come."

Nicodemus set his prayer book aside and followed the Hungarian alchemist in silent procession down several flights of stone steps, through the library and down more steps to the second level of dungeons in the east wing. The other cells were still occupied, but the men there were chained as well as behind bars, and their eyes watched with the patience of the doomed as the two men walked past.

A door stood closed and guarded at the end of the hall. The sentries snapped to attention, fists closed tightly around the shafts of their halberds. Father Lászó paused just out of earshot and turned to his companion.

"I know the Scriptor is young, but does he have an heir . . . ?"

"No. He never married."

"He has a brother, though, does he not?"

"Yes. Henri, who is but a lad. He lives in Toulouse with his aunt. Why?"

"Arrangements may have to be made," he warned. "This may be hard for you to see."

"I have seen many hard things in my years," said Nicodemus. "I will see this."

The alchemist acknowledged with a bow and they passed by the guards and entered the room. It was dim in there, lit by a single candle on a sconce set high on one wall. The other sconces were on the floor, broken and twisted, their fittings torn from the stone. A man—a physician—lay in one corner and Father Nicodemus saw that two of the candles had been thrust into the doctor's eye sockets. The corpse lay in a pool of blood and Nicodemus could see why—the doctor's throat was torn out and only ragged crimson tatters remained.

In the other corner huddled Sir Benoit. He was naked, filthy, smeared with blood and feces, his hair hanging in dirty streamers. Heavy chains were shackled around him and their lengths anchored to rings newly set into the wall. He crouched there, panting like a rabid dog and glaring up with eyes that burned nearly as red as the blood that glistened on his lips and teeth.

Father Nicodemus made the sign of the cross.

"I . . . do not understand," he gasped. "He was himself not seven hours ago. He was responding to the elixir. His mind was clear and his heart true. What has *happened*?"

Father Lászó shook his head slowly.

"The elixir worked on the dogs. There is nothing abhorrent to nature in the way Claude behaves. It worked on the prisoners."

Nicodemus wheeled on him, his face livid, teeth bared in barely contained fury. "So why is the Scriptor of the Red Order covered in shit and another man's blood, damn your eyes?"

"I . . . I do not know, Father. I—"

Nicodemus struck him across the face. The blow was hideously fast and unexpectedly powerful, and it sent the Hungarian priest spinning into a wall. He struck his face, breaking his nose and splitting his lower lip. He reeled back, knees buckling. Nicodemus grabbed him by the scruff of the neck and slammed the alchemist's face into the unyielding stone. Again and again, painting the wall with blood and spit and tears.

Then he stopped short of outright murder and released Lászó, allowing the whimpering, bleeding man to collapse, where he lay weeping and trembling, half of his face ruined and shapeless.

Father Nicodemus staggered backward, gaping at Benoit.

"No, no, no, no . . ." he breathed. "No, this cannot be. I will not *allow* it."

The Scriptor lunged at him, straining against the chains with such passionate intensity that brick dust fluffed out from where the bolts had been driven deep.

It took a great deal of control for Nicodemus to master himself. He stood there, sweating, panting, tears bright in his eyes. When he looked at his hands, they were trembling and spattered with blood.

He took a tottering step toward the crazed young lord, stopping just outside of the range of snapping teeth.

"My heart breaks for you, my son," he said gently. "You could have heralded in a new age of the world. Immortal warriors of God sweeping across the Holy Land and driving the infidels into the sea. I know how much you sacrificed by accepting your role as Scriptor. I know that it was a hard road for you, and you spent the last of your youth too soon. All of this is my fault, and I pray that the Lord takes your soul into his hands and gives you peace."

As he said this, he quietly plunged a small dagger into the Scriptor's heart. The blade was so thin and narrow that with all of the other marks of violence on Sir Benoit's skin, that last wound would never be noticed.

The young man stiffened and for a single moment his eyes cleared of madness and he stared at Father Nicodemus.

"Please . . . " he whispered, and that was all he said.

His eyelids fluttered and closed and there was nothing but stillness, sorrow, and loss in that terrible place.

# CHAPTER 25

## THE ROYAL HORSEGUARDS HOTEL AND ONE WHITEHALL PLACE, LONDON
## 2 WHITEHALL COURT
## LONDON, ENGLAND

He flew to England and booked a double room with a lovely view of the Thames River, the London Eye, and the South Bank.

In the afternoon he took tea in the lounge, though his coughing disturbed the other guests. Management said nothing, but Nicodemus did not want to draw too much attention to himself and thereafter had his meals sent up.

The meal that day was wonderful, starting with carrot and coriander soup, which had an herb drizzle and sunflower seeds. He followed this with lamb shoulder roulade made with quinoa, asparagus, baby onion, mint yoghurt dressing, pomegranate & rosemary reduction, and a generous side of green beans with confit shallots.

He spent time considering which wine to choose. Lamb was always so wine-friendly that many would wonder if there was any wine that did not go well with it. Most critics would die on the hill that insisted that the Cabernet Sauvignon–based wines were the best choice, but Nicodemus seldom ran with the crowd. So, he bucked tradition and ordered a Catena Zapata Malbec Argentino, 2021.

He ordered enough for two. His stomach tended to rebel at inconvenient times, and he threw up the first meal, wine and all. He spent a few minutes washing Dramamine down with triple-bagged ginger tea, then dug in again. This time the food stayed down, and that was well enough for him.

When he was finished dining, he spent some time watching the television news and some time coughing up blood. After one particularly dreadful bout, he found himself sitting on the bathroom floor, between the toilet and shower. His stomach attempted an insurrection, but this time the ginger won and things eventually settled.

Before getting up off the floor, he pulled a cell phone out of his pocket—a burner that was completely untraceable—and made a few phone calls.

One call was to a local contact. Not a friend exactly—Nicodemus had long ago resigned himself to the fact that he was not the chummy type—but a person he liked and with whom he was doing some business.

"Line?" was how his friend answered the call.

"Clear."

"Where are you?"

"Everywhere and nowhere," laughed Nicodemus.

"Oh, very clever. I am rather busy, as you know . . . what's the reason for this call?"

"I wanted to know if there is anything else I can do for you before I leave."

"Leave?" grunted the man at the other end of the call. "Leave where?"

"Just . . . leave," Nicodemus said. "By the time things kick into high gear, I'll be far away and out of touch."

"Oh really? I had no idea you were planning a trip. Especially now."

"It may surprise you to learn, my friend, that some things are beyond my control. So, yes, I'll be leaving. This is likely the last conversation we'll have."

That resulted in a pregnant pause. "I . . . thought we would have more to do together. That's been the tradition, after all. There's always been a Scriptor and a Father Nicodemus."

"Well, you're not exactly the typical Scriptor, my friend. Nor am I quite the same Nicodemus who helped form the Red Order."

"No, of course you're not the same, but you're in that role . . ."

"Things change," said Nicodemus. "Life happens. Besides . . . you have all that you need to make your own presence known."

"What can I say or do to encourage you to stay?"

"Nothing at all. But again, tell me if there is anything I can do for you? This is the last opportunity you'll have."

The Scriptor paused. "Well . . . there are one or two small things," he said.

## INTERLUDE 11

### THE GRAND EXPERIMENT
### LAROQUE ESTATE
### VILLAGE OF MONTAILLOU, FRANCE
### 1244 CE

It came with the fall of night.

It came inside a torrent of rain so intense that it felt like a punishment from God. Thunder exploded above and all around La Maison LaRoque, the force of each blast landing like the blow of an angry giant on the walls. Ancient trees outside bent beneath the assault, and one oak tree that had endured for eight hundred years died with a groan of sorrow and defeat, its trunk splitting open to disgorge terrified squirrels and fifty thousand termites.

It came through the woods, following a small path marked out by decorative stones, each one of which had a psalm painted in black on their face. The thing passed each of these, ignoring them so completely their prayers might have been scrawled gibberish.

It came to the turnaround in front of the castle and paused for but a moment, glaring up at the battlements and turrets and embrasures. It opened its mouth to say something, but only a wordless cry of despair troubled the air. Several windows were bright with firelight and the promise of warmth within.

It came to steal that warmth.

It came to steal all heat. The heat of the hearth and the heat of beating hearts. It came to the call of meat and blood.

It came to the very door and began pounding on it. Each blow was soft, limp, the motions nearly without purpose. And yet each strike sent echoes whispering along the halls and up the stairs and into locked chambers. Soon more lights were lit and voices could be heard even through the tumult in the skies above.

When the door was opened to inquire of some lost traveler, it came inside.

And then the screams began.

## CHAPTER 26

### IN FLIGHT OVER BULGARIAN AIRSPACE

Once we reached Bucharest and boarded *Shirley,* my private jet, we loosened up. But only partway. The whole affair had been weird from the jump, and I was still a bit freaked from my encounter with Nicodemus and my subsequent call with Church. I didn't particularly dig the way Church shut down that conversation. Seeing a painting of someone who looked like him didn't help.

We settled into the comfy leather seats and began drinking our way through a rare fifty-year-old bottle of Caol Ila. It's a sherry-matured single malt released as part of Gordon & MacPhail's Private Collection. Distilled in 1968 and only released from its single cask in 2018. A gift from Benson Childes, former director of Barrier—the British equivalent and forerunner of the Department of Military

Sciences. He sent it to me on the anniversary of Major Grace Courtland's death, saying that it should be drunk in her honor.

Which we did, clinking glasses and saying her name loud enough to reach Valhalla where, no doubt, she was kicking ass and taking names.

The ceremony of toasting matters to guys like us. Soldiers are a ceremonious bunch, and this was a moment of purity in an otherwise off-kilter day. The bottle was unlikely to survive the eleven-hundred-mile flight.

Each of us had an after-action report to write, and generally those are done without interaction with one another. Not this time. All three of us wanted to tear apart everything that had happened, from the gunfight to the weaponized *Yersinia pestis* to the poor bastards in the glass cells.

Bunny put it well when he observed, "I know RTI is like DMS in that we're reactive rather than proactive, and we have to figure shit out on the fly. But this one has a different feel. Like we're not trying to catch up, but like we gave whatever this is a glancing blow, feel me?"

"Copy the hell out of that, Farm Boy," growled Top. "I hope those data files make sense to somebody, 'cause I'm in the dark."

I looked at my watch. "And the brain trust back home has had some time with it. Let's call the Big Man again."

I tried, but he was still unavailable. The duty officer, a former field guy named Brightwell, answered this time and he told us that Church was on a series of calls and wouldn't be free for anything except missiles inbound for the rest of the day.

"Nudge him," I suggested, and he laughed, then switched the call to Bug and kept it on speaker.

"Hey, Joe, whaddya know?" Bug said with a happier tone than the day deserved.

"Hey, Bug. Are you caught up on what's going on?"

"As much as anyone, I guess. I've got a couple of teams working on the data, and we're coordinating with Doc and her mad scientists. Guess you heard Scott's in London and Church has pretty much gone to his room and nailed the door shut."

"What's up with them?"

"Well, Scott's at Barrier HQ because they're going to offer him the top job there. James Rockwell, the cat who took over from Childes, is stepping down. So, we may lose Scott."

"I will try not to break down and cry."

"Be nice," chided Bug. "You don't see him every day like I do. He's not so bad. Sure, he's a stiff and probably has his underwear starched, but he's family."

"Sure, Bug, I'll give him a nice sloppy kiss as a going-away present."

He made a sound like he'd snorted Red Bull through his nose. Which was a likely guess.

"What's with the Big Man today?" I asked.

"No idea. He went all quiet after you guys wrapped things in Romania and I haven't seen him since."

"Does it have anything to do with the painting we found?"

"No reason it should."

"Ask to see it when we get back. I'm telling you, it looks exactly like him."

"I can ask, but he'll probably say no and make some noise about it being a waste of time and resources. Which, given the state of that computer data, he's not wrong. Besides, it wouldn't be the first time someone thought they found a picture of Church on the Net. He has that kind of face, and there are a bunch of old paintings and statues and shit that look like him."

"Are they his relatives?" I asked. "I mean, the one we found is weirdly similar. I'd go with identical, but that's stupid, since this thing is at least a couple of hundred years old, and maybe a lot older. Have you found any of his confirmed ancestors?"

"Nope," said Bug. "I mean, sure, I found a boatload of paintings, woodcuts, line drawings, and all that of people who look a lot like him, but he always says they're no relation."

"What made you look in the first place?"

"Idle curiosity, too much time on my hands, a tendency toward believing conspiracy theories, and the world's fastest computer," he said.

"You ever tell Church about them?"

"All the time."

"He ever go sulk in his room?"

"I didn't say he was sulking, Joe. Let's be real. This is Church."

"What *was* his reaction?"

Bug thought about that for a moment. "Mixed. When it was an actual photo of him, like with one of the past presidents or something, he had me scrub it from the Net. I wrote a bunch of seek-and-destroy software for stuff like that. And for pictures I couldn't delete, I used AI to alter them."

"How?"

"Oh, that's easy. Facial recognition has gotten so sophisticated and specific that it sometimes gets in its own way."

"Meaning what?"

"Okay, with disguises," said Bug, "you can change things like thickness of lips using collagen injections, hairline with wigs, nostril shape with wire inserts, cheeks with padding. But some things stay the same. Facial recognition analyzes and maps face geometry and facial expressions. It also identifies facial landmarks that are key to distinguishing a specific face from other objects and from faces that lack key points, like the distance between the eyes, distance from the forehead to the chin, distance between the nose and mouth, depth of the eye sockets, shape of the cheekbones, and contour of the lips, ears, and chin. Some of that can be modified, but unless you do surgery to have bones shaved, there are going to be some stable elements that can't ever be changed. The system then converts this stable data into a string of numbers or points called a faceprint. Just like fingerprints, each person has a unique faceprint, similar to a fingerprint. The information used by facial recognition can also be used in reverse to digitally reconstruct a person's face."

"So, Church had you erase or change any photographic images of him stored on the Net?"

"Yep. And before you go looking for something weird about that, he's had me do this for Aunt Sallie, Scott Wilson, and a bunch of DMS and RTI people. Hell, I wiped all traces of my face off the Net and cut the number of photos of you and everyone else doing fieldwork down by seventy percent. And MindReader is poised to blank you out completely if you ever need to vanish."

"That makes sense," I agreed. "It's creepy and weird, but we're in the creepy and weird business."

Bug laughed. "Yeah we are."

"But that doesn't explain him reacting to the painting we found."

"Joe, you're making a big assumption here. He's been spooked ever since Nicodemus and the Sabbatarians took a run at you at the cemetery. And the stuff with weaponized plague dumped on him right after. I think the painting is a lot less of a thing with him than you're making it."

I gave that some serious thought and realized he was probably right. "Yet he wanted that painting brought back to Phoenix House."

"Sure, and it'll probably wind up in the break room or in his library. More of a novelty than anything of importance."

"Maybe," I said. "Shifting gears. What can you tell us about the plague?"

"Let me talk to Doc and I'll get right back to you."

He ended the call and I sat back, aware that Top and Bunny were studying me. They said nothing, though, and I wondered if they were thinking that my interest in that stupid painting was proof that I was losing what few marbles I had left.

I did not feel sufficiently well armed to engage in any convincing refutation.

## INTERLUDE 12

### THE GRAND EXPERIMENT
### LAROQUE ESTATE
### VILLAGE OF MONTAILLOU, FRANCE
### 1244 CE

"Kill it!" screamed the last four of the Five Fathers.

Lászó was unable to lend his voice to the pleas as he lay on the point of death down in the dungeon where his failure had been played out. No one was allowed to go to him to offer succor, and there were only red-eyed rats waiting like courtiers.

The screams of the other four were half-erased by earsplitting bursts of thunder. The storm was directly over the castle now and it seemed as if even that place, which had withstood sieges and war, must yield.

"Kill it, for the love of all that is holy!"

The thing hissed and turned toward the youngest of the four. It peeled back its lips and snarled like a feral dog. Like a beast.

Soldiers shoved their way into the room, pushing the priests back and standing firm between them and the monster. Only the night sentries were fully dressed and armed, while the others wore whatever they could pull on, and held daggers and pikes.

"What is this madness?" cried a voice and everyone—even the monster—turned as Father Nicodemus strode into the room, wearing a dressing gown and a nightcap that trailed down his back. He held a torch in one hand and a crucifix in the other.

When he saw what it was—what kind of thing had invaded the castle—he froze and his eyes went wide with shock and horror.

"What madness is this . . . ?" he breathed.

The thing crouched there, its body dripping mud from the grave from which it had torn itself. Rainwater and blood trickled down its limbs and dripped from the burial garments. On the floor was the unlucky guard who had opened the door. His face was nearly gone, ripped to shreds by hungry teeth, and yet he still lived—eyes staring in horror, knowing that he was toppling into death's valley—chest rising and falling with rapid, terrified breaths that were becoming shallower with each fading heartbeat.

"No," cried the priest faintly. "No, say it is not so."

The monster took a heavy step toward him.

Father Nicodemus held up the cross. "Back, I command thee in the name of the Father, the Son, and the Holy Ghost."

The creature looked at him.

Not at the cross. Not at the other hand that was raised for a gesture of blessing or condemnation. He looked only at the little priest's face. At his eyes.

No one else in that hall could see Father Nicodemus's eyes. Had they, to a man they would have screamed and run, or made the sign of the cross and hurled prayers of protection at him. For those eyes darkened until there was no white left to see; and the color changed from iris brown and pupil black to a swirl of all the uglier shades of yellow and green. These colors swirled like inks or paint that had neither the grace nor will to blend together. The first sunset of chaotic creation might have moved with those colors; or the last sunset of the world as it burned down.

The creature recoiled, hissing, pawing, and slapping at the air between him and Father Nicodemus.

"It is the cross," cried one of the Five Fathers. "See it! He fears the crucifix. It is shamed at the sight of the Redeemer who died for all our sins."

Others brandished their own crosses, but the monster was transfixed by the one held by the small priest.

"Stay back," he warned, meaning it for the others but they took it as a command to the undead thing that stood dripping in the hall. When Nicodemus realized this, he saw it as an opportunity. "Who here has a spear and is not afraid to use it to do God's will?" he demanded in a bold voice, filling it with all of the righteous anger he could summon.

A soldier stepped forward. A big and doughty man, scarred from many battles, and he held a pike that he'd used on the bloody fields near the walls of Jerusalem.

Nicodemus saw him and said, "You are Gabriel, sergeant of arms. Do you fear God?"

"I do, Father, and I serve the House LaRoque and the Holy Church."

"Your name means *God is my strength,*" said the priest, loud enough for all to hear. "Will you use that strength to save us all? Will you use your God-given strength to strike down this demon who pretends to be your lord?"

Gabriel licked his lips. His eyes jumped with fear at the thing who stood there held by the gaze of the old priest. "By my honor, my faith, and my love for Sir Benoit LaRoque, I so swear."

"Then strike, Gabriel. Strike him to the heart and send the demon back to hell so that your lord may rest in the healing arms of Christ."

It hurt the big soldier to do it, but his aim was true and his hands powerful. He stepped forward and thrust the spear at the creature with such passion that the steel tip passed entirely through the torso of what had been Sir Benoit. It tore out from between the walking corpse's shoulder blades, having pierced white flesh and slack muscle, barely grazing the heart but slicing neatly between two vertebrae. The beast collapsed at once, the spine collapsing and the shock extinguishing the spark of unnatural vitality that powered it.

Silence fell and all of them stood like statues, staring at the impossibility of all that happened. From their master's death three days before, to the coming of this *thing* . . . their world was shattered and each of them knew the pieces could never be reassembled to make any shape familiar to them.

Nicodemus lowered his head and murmured a prayer for the soul of the dead. He did not raise his eyes until he was sure they were normal.

His mind was working, though.

*They believed it was the cross that frightened Sir Benoit,* he thought. *That could be very useful.*

"The blade passed through him," said the priest, "but he did not fall until the wooden shaft of the pike had transfixed his heart. Gabriel . . . of what wood is your weapon fashioned?"

The soldier blinked a few times before he had collected enough of his wits to answer. "I . . . it is . . . " he began, then cleared his throat and tried again. "Rosewood, Father."

"And that is holy wood," pronounced Father Nicodemus, jumping at the opportunity to expand on this new set of useful lies. "A shaft of rosewood banished the demon and restored the grace of God's own eternal sleep to our lord. Let us pray."

And they prayed.

All the while, Nicodemus had to fight to keep the smile off his face. He managed it, but it was so very difficult a feat.

*Beautiful,* he told himself.

# CHAPTER 27

## PHOENIX HOUSE
## OMFORI ISLAND, GREECE

She answered on the fifth ring.

"Saint Germain," said Lilith. "This is unexpected."

"It's becoming that kind of week," said Church.

He was in the library in his apartment. A bottle of Château Pétrus Pomerol, an entertaining French red blend, was open on his desk, though his glass stood untouched. The air was sweetened by Corelli's exquisite and soothing Concerto Grosso No. 10 in C Major, Op. 6. The orchestra was working their way through the adagio. That was one of a number of pieces that he usually found calming, but he felt no inner peace at the moment.

"Is everything well with you?" she asked.

"To be determined."

"Tell me, then."

Church picked up the wine, studied the flickering firelight through the dark red liquid, took a small sip, and set the glass down. His plump gray Scottish Fold, Bastian, jumped up into his lap. He idly stroked the cat's thick fur and it began to purr quietly, displaying a contentment that Church did not share.

"Joe Ledger and his team were in Romania," he said. "In Corvin Castle. And they found a certain painting . . ."

Lilith paused very briefly. "Which one?"

And he told her all of it.

# CHAPTER 28

## IN FLIGHT OVER BULGARIAN AIRSPACE

Bug called back in ten minutes, but it was Doc Holliday who opened the conversation and did it in her unique style.

"Joe-freaking-Ledger," she said, her voice dripping with ebullience. "My favorite brain-damaged psychopath. How the heck are ya?"

And that's Doc Holliday right there.

Understand, she is arguably one of the smartest people currently alive, and that isn't an exaggeration. She's earned more PhDs than I've had hot dinners, and Scott confided to me once that her IQ was *estimated* at 270-something. Right up there with YoungHoon Kim of South Korea, who has the highest-ever documented IQ at 276. Johann Wolfgang von Goethe is believed to have been in the low 200s, along with Da Vinci and the nineteenth-century Scottish mathematical physicist James Clerk Maxwell. To give you some perspective, Albert Einstein's IQ was 160.

Mine is likely single digits. God only knows what Church's is, and he is the only person who gets both deferential and polite comments from Doc.

Dr. Joan Holliday is a legit descendant of the famous gambler, dentist, and gunslinger from the O.K. Corral. Except the sound of her voice always conjures up an image of someone closer to Dolly Parton on steroids. She's as tall as me, with improbable curves, outlandish cowgirl clothes, and a wicked grin that lets you know she was fully aware of how her appearance affected anyone with a pulse. Bawdy, often crude, hilarious, cartoonish, and a multidisciplinary super-genius.

"Hey, Doc," I said. "Hope you guys have some updates for us. I'm here with Top and Bunny."

"Oh my," said Doc. "I can smell the testosterone from here. You have Big Brown Daddy and that yummy slice of Southern California white bread there. With you and me, that's a reverse harem novel waiting to happen."

"Christ," muttered Top under his breath. Beside him, Bunny mouthed the words *Big Brown Daddy.* Top saw it and mimed cutting Bunny's balls off. Ghost heard her voice and wagged his tail.

"If the Prince of all Dogs is there, too," said Doc, "give him some belly rubs from me. Make sure you find his happy place."

"Meanwhile, here in the real world," I cut in, saying it like the discreet news announcer at a golf tournament, "there is the lingering threat of a global pandemic of weaponized plague."

"Yeah, yeah," said Doc. "Ask your questions and we will reveal all."

"That's just it," I said. "We don't know what you know, so you guys start."

"Lovebug . . . ?" said Doc.

After clearing his throat, Bug said, "We were able to coordinate with local authorities about the lab. Cover story is that one of the guards working there was with a radical group with ties to Hamas. The hit has been blamed on the terrorists, and the domestic threat level has been elevated. Nothing that we need worry about, though."

"And the people there?" asked Top.

"Authorities medevaced eighteen people to a secure medical facility in Constanta."

"Eighteen?" gasped Bunny. "Wait a minute, there were twenty-five of them."

"Sad to say that seven have died," Bug said. "And another six are on life support."

"From *plague*?" I demanded. "Since when does it work that fast?"

"You boys stuck your peckers in the wrong hole with this one," Doc said. She always sounds happiest when things are at their darkest.

"Care to break it down for us?" I asked.

"Well, honeybuns, that's one of those good news–bad news things, with the bad news winning the blue ribbon by a lot."

"Swell. Hit me anyway."

"Okay," she said, "first the bad news. The information you uploaded is, at best, fragmented. There was a little bastard of a software tapeworm in there that was activated as soon as the upload began. It corrupted about ninety percent of all the data we thought we were recovering. Poor little Bug was in his office crying into his Red Bull."

"She's not entirely wrong," said Bug.

I closed my eyes. "Shit."

"Shit on toast, in fact, Outlaw. There was also some software in there that sent a flash notice that the system had been hacked."

"I thought MindReader prevented that kind of thing," said Top.

"So did Bug, hence the torrent of tears," Doc said. "And to add sprinkles on that dish of dog poop, now that Bug is noodling around inside the data, he says he recognizes the fingerprints of who it belonged—and that's past tense—to."

"Who?"

"Hugo Vox," said Bug.

"You're shitting me."

"I shit thee not," chirped Doc. "And I can just bet you don't want your blood pressure taken right now, do you, boys?"

Top made a low, feral growl. Ghost made the same noise. I felt like doing it, too.

"Yeah, yeah, okay, that sucks," I said. "But Vox is dead because the Big Man put a couple of rounds through his brainpan."

"Never said it *was* him, sweet-cheeks. What Bug's saying is that someone got their grubby mitts on Vox's tech. I wasn't around for that hootenanny, but from what everyone tells me, Vox not only pretended to be the goodest of the good guys and then turned out to be the actual *head* of the Seven Kings, but he knew enough about MindReader to have tech built—cell phones and suchlike—specifically designed to thwart our toys."

"I remember," I said, putting some edge on it.

Bug said, "Unfortunately, there's a long list of people who might have either had access to Vox's tech and took it to some off-book genius to reverse engineer, or they found the schematics of the stuff in some way. In either case, it ups the game for us. Like by a lot."

"It does," I agreed. "It means they know about MindReader."

"And about us," said Bunny. "Which, y'know, blows and all."

"The upshot," said Doc, "is that it leaves us with only scattered bits of data. Enough to know that, yes, they were working on some new strain—almost certainly deliberately weaponized—of *Yersinia pestis,* good ol' pneumonic plague, but not enough to know its scope or purpose."

"Or, how it ties in with Nicodemus and the Sabbatarians," I muttered.

"Or that, yes."

I asked, "And the good news?"

"From what little we could gather from the data fragments, there's a reasonably decent chance that we're catching this early."

I gave that a beat. "Why is it that I find 'reasonably decent chance' to not be all that comforting?"

"It's what we have, sugar," she said.

"Shit."

I looked over at Bunny, who was slowly banging his head against the wall. Top just blew out his cheeks and said nothing. Ghost underscored it all with a loud and generous fart.

"Okay," I said, vigorously waving the stink back in Ghost's direction. "How can we pin this down so we are more than 'reasonably' certain?"

"We're working on that," said Bug. "I got everyone on this. We'll figure it out."

"Uh-huh."

"Pinky swear to try," said Doc.

"I'm going to hold you to that," I said, and immediately regretted it. Too much of an opening. But Doc just laughed and dropped off the call.

"Look," said Bug, "despite the virus damage, we did retrieve a fair amount of data, and Ron Coleman is heading up a team to analyze it and extrapolate from what's implied."

"I'll feel more comforted when we have someone me and my guys can take a direct run at."

"With you on that," Bug said, then he dropped out, too.

I took the bottle of scotch and refilled all three of our glasses. We drank. After a long moment of silent reflection, Bunny asked, "I'd be okay if the pilot cut the engine and we all crashed into a mountain. Be an easier and more fun way to wrap the day. Just saying."

"No argument," I said.

"Hooah," grumbled Top.

## INTERLUDE 13

### THE GRAND EXPERIMENT
### LAROQUE ESTATE
### VILLAGE OF MONTAILLOU, FRANCE
### 1245 CE

"Tell me of this so-called elixir of life," said Sir Louis, the eighth Scriptor of the Red Order.

"My lord," said Father Nicodemus, "surely this can wait until you have had sufficient time for mourning and prayer."

The young nobleman smiled thinly. "My father will be dead for a very long time. It will not matter to him if we let him rest while we attend to important matters here in the world of the living. Or . . . does my boldness shock you?"

The burial of Sir Henri LaRoque had taken place that very morning and now it was only an hour past noon. The newly minted lord of the manor was a cold, ambitious, and devious man, newly returned from doing some work as a counselor between various groups of Crusaders, the pope, and the Mongol leader, Abaqa Khan. Though young, Sir Louis had earned a reputation for diplomacy, bravery, and innovative thinking. His letters back to Europe helped guide policy and interactions with the Khan during a time of civil war, thereby digging like a tick into the skin of the Mongol political structure. Very useful against the Mohammedans.

He returned only when his father, Sir Henri—never a very strong man and an even weaker Scriptor—was taken ill. Scrofula—the king's evil, as it was often called—was burning its way through many of the great houses and it had killed Sir Louis's father, mother, two aunts, and four siblings. All that was left of the LaRoque family line was himself, though Father Nicodemus was reliably insured that Lady Marie, Louis's wife, was pregnant.

"As you will, my lord," said Nicodemus, privately pleased at his new master's brutal efficiency and apparent lack of sentimentality. That was good, because it was a solid enough rock on which to continue building the Red Order, which had faltered following the death of Sir Benoit, and with the Crusades continuing to inspire little public or papal support.

"The elixir," prompted the Scriptor. "I've read the accounts and met the most recent group of graybeards calling themselves the Five Fathers. I've read the accounts of the Tariqa and how effective their Hashashin have been, and how they are *not* growing weaker. And, while the reports detail the mischief our pet monsters have gotten up to, what I don't see is any reports about the elixir of immortality being anything but a vain dream. If I misstate these facts, Father, then, pray . . . set me straight."

They sat at a small table placed before a window in a high tower. Outside, reapers were walking in staggered lines while swinging their scythes to cut the late-spring grass. It was the kind of early afternoon in rural France that made a belief in a kind and loving God an easy story to sell, and that was always pleasant to Nicodemus.

"Well, my lord, there is some very encouraging news," he said. "A great and learned man, versed in the many natural philosophies, is on his way here."

"Who is it this time? Another magician? Another alchemist who will beg for only the rarest elements and potions from across the world so he can waste even more time and money?"

"Hardly that, my lord," said Nicodemus. "No, this man stands above the rest. He is a Dominican friar and well respected throughout Christendom. His name is Albertus Magnus."

Sir Louis grunted. "Isn't—or wasn't—he the Bishop of Regensburg? They used to call him Doctor Universalis, or so I heard. I thought he was dead. He must be better than eighty, if he still lives."

"No, my lord, though he is old, his strength endures. He was born at the end of the last century, if I'm not mistaken. He has written many learned books, and these are used to teach the best and brightest, and to read out his full list of credentials would take a week."

"He sounds expensive."

Nicodemus spread his hands. "He is worth any investment, my lord. Though, in truth, his interest in alchemy and other fields matters far more to him than gold. The Quinque Patres have already told me that they would donate the entirety of their salaries to fund whatever Albertus Magnus requires."

"Say you so?" mused Sir Louis, surprised. "That is great praise indeed. Hold them to it, though."

"Of course."

"When will he arrive?"

"By sunset, my lord."

"Does he bring another entourage like the others?"

"He does not," said Nicodemus. "He travels only with an attendant, two apprentices, and four guards. I have taken the liberty of detailing eight men of arms to accompany him."

Sir Louis waved that away and stood. "I am not the patient man my grandfather was, nor as weak and confused as my father. I will see the Red Order rise to greater power than ever before, and anyone who impedes that progress will make a bitter enemy of me. Hear me now, Father. We know each other well enough to know that I am aware of the shadows that move beyond the light cast by Christ's cross. I know who and what you are, just as you, I believe, understand me. When this Albertus Magnus arrives, I want *you* to explain the shape of things to him and to judge if he can be trusted."

"Trusted in what way, lord?"

"In two ways," said Sir Louis, nodding appreciation of the question.

"He must provide results within one year or he will be cast out, penniless and reviled. And, more importantly, whatever secrets we share with him about the Red Order and the Grand Experiment he must then promise to keep, even unto his death. I will outlive that old man, and if he betrays our trust, Father, then I will see to the extermination of his entire bloodline. My wrath will erase his family from history. I say this bluntly to you because you alone will understand. Or am I wrong about that?"

Nicodemus rose, too, and gave the young nobleman a deep bow. Meaning it, too, which was not common for him. But he liked this new Scriptor. He admired him, for in him he saw the shadow of the first Scriptor, Sir Guy.

"I am your servant, my lord."

As Nicodemus straightened, Sir Louis studied him, searching his eyes. "No," he said. "You are not that. You are a monster, Nicodemus. Of what kind I do not know, but you are not a man. Not truly. Nor are you the grandson or great-grandson of the priest who helped form the Red Order. No . . . you are something else. Perhaps it is something that has no name. Not a demon nor a ghost. But, hear me, priest . . . I am a monster, too. In my way, and without apologies or regrets. *We* are allies, and as an ally you have my trust. Together we will shape the world to come. Together we will be monsters fighting monsters, for this war—the seed that bore the fruit of the Holy Agreement—will never end."

"The war," said Nicodemus, "is the war."

"Yes," said Sir Louis. "The war is the war."

Then he did something that no one else had done to Nicodemus in uncountable years. He drew the old man to him and embraced him. The little priest was so surprised that he had no words. A true first for him.

But he returned that embrace.

And he meant it.

# CHAPTER 29

## BARRIER HEADQUARTERS
## HADRIAN TOWER
## ROPEMAKER STREET
## LONDON, ENGLAND

Scott Wilson stepped from his taxi and looked up at the elegant, glass-fronted building. It was an impressive thirty-eight stories high and Barrier—Britain's rapid-response counter- and antiterrorism organization—had the top four floors. More than 12,500 square meters of office space. More than three times larger than it had been when he worked there on his way up the military intelligence ladder.

Barrier was originally designed to be the faster, lighter, more mobile younger brother to MI6, but over the years it had grown in unexpected directions. The overall brief was to be able to put fully qualified teams in the field with virtually no prep time—a feat that even the nimble Secret Intelligence Service could not do. The effect was more or less that the standard international espionage group handled long-range, deep-cover, and similar projects—things that required a more complex infrastructure but came burdened with the reality of the committee structure and lots of red tape. Barrier had been codesigned by Mr. Church to be ready to go out the door at once.

It was the model that Church had tried to sell to the United States first, but which was rejected because of its price tag. 9/11 changed the math on that, and so Church built the Department of Military Sciences using the model he'd developed for Barrier.

Now the DMS was gone, shuttered due to political interference and backbiting. There in the UK, Scott was pleased to see that Barrier continued to thrive and lost only half a step getting to base.

"Let's see if we can shave some seconds off that time," he told himself as he brushed his Eton College Threefold tie by Benson & Clegg nice and flat, and tugged the hem of his Prince of Wales Shelton suitcoat down. It was a quiet gray suit, but anyone who knew menswear would see its quality. Not the most expensive, which would have been vulgar, but finely made by a company known for crafting clothes for executives in government. His wristwatch, an Audemars Piguet

Royal Oak 67651 Quartz Stainless Steel model, was a bit more ostentatious, but that had been a gift from Mr. Church, and he wore that for luck.

He went inside, passing through the lobby security without a blip, and was ushered into a small foyer that provided access to the elevators set aside for Barrier's exclusive use. The car doors opened into a reception office that had more elaborate security, including retina scan, fingerprint scanner, voice scan, and a three-tiered code sequence. With that completed, he was shown into a waiting room and someone brought him a nice cup of tea.

It was a moderately long wait, though, and twice he went into the toilet to spruce up. There were rows of enclosed stalls, urinals with privacy panels, and sinks that were higher-end than was typical in government bathrooms. Hidden speakers played soothing classical music, and the bathroom air was subtly perfumed by aerosol dispensers mounted high on the walls. He sniffed the hand soap, and nodded approval. Very nice without being overly scented. Marble floors with interesting veining, and fixtures of flat black in the current Spanish style.

The elegance of the bathroom made him feel at home, because Church always went the extra mile to provide tasteful appointments to everything from the coffee in the lounge to the high-end finishes in the bathrooms. It demonstrated a respect for the entire staff and created an atmosphere of sophistication that coaxed everyone up to their most professional standard. Part of what Dr. Sanchez called Church's habit of *benign* manipulation, and Wilson was pleased to see it reflected here in the new Barrier offices.

He dried his hands and returned to the waiting room, where a fresh cup of tea was waiting for him, along with a plate of biscuits.

The schedule was complex and would take two or three days. The first day was all about interviews with screeners of various kinds. Some were from MI5 and the questions focused on personal background, his politics, his official military career, and his association with key players in British government. That consumed most of the first day without Scott meeting with the real power players.

Between meetings he was expected to wait, and Scott knew that how he waited was almost certainly being observed and evaluated.

The unseen watchers would look for nervous tics, unusual body language, whom Scott chose to speak with, and so on. Small details that, when combined, gave whoever was assessing the data a chance to make decisions on the mental and emotional condition, which was at least—if not more so—as important as his answers when grilled.

He even wondered if there were CCTV cameras discreetly hidden in the executive washroom, which he was allowed to use. Unlikely in the stalls or above the urinals, but possibly near the sinks. Scott was used to being observed like this, and even once looked into a good spot for a hidden camera and smiled his most charming smile.

During his fifth interview that day, he realized that he was perspiring and paused to determine if the room heaters were deliberately turned high to literally make him sweat. That was an old trick. Just as it was not uncommon to have tables set a few inches too high and chairs with one leg a bit shorter than the others so that the interview subject was never completely comfortable.

Scott dabbed at his sweaty brow only once, but without remarking on the heat. He projected calm self-assurance, knowing that the people he was scheduled to meet the next day would have received a complete brief on every detail of what happened on day one.

At no point was Scott Wilson genuinely nervous.

Although he should have been.

## INTERLUDE 14

### THE GRAND EXPERIMENT
### LAROQUE ESTATE
### VILLAGE OF MONTAILLOU, FRANCE
### 1286 CE

"Will it *ever* work?" asked Sir Louis. The sacred *Scriptor's Diary* lay open in his lap and a quill in his liver-spotted hand. The new entries needed to be written while he still had his health.

The Scriptor was feeling his years. Though not actually an old man, the weight of everything that happened since he took charge of the Ordo Ruber seemed to be welded to him like a suit of armor. Or a device of torture. Sometimes it was difficult to tell the difference between the burden of responsibility and that of punishment.

Father Nicodemus stood with one hand on the mantel as he stared without blinking into the fire. The hickory logs were dense and slow to burn, and filled that cold room with needed heat. Outside it was snowing and there was already a foot of it covering the landscape, cloaking it all in the pretense of innocence and purity.

"The elixir?" murmured the priest.

"Yes."

"Perhaps."

Sir Louis blotted the ink on the page and closed the book. Then he got up heavily and lumbered over to the window where he stood staring out at the blizzard, turned away. "*Perhaps* is hardly a comfort."

"It wasn't mean to be, my lord."

"How *strong* a possibility is there? We have spent so many years and a mountain of gold and all we have produced are madmen and monsters." He went over to the sideboard and poured himself a glass of deep red wine. "God above, I think even the Upierczy are laughing at us behind our backs."

Nicodemus turned his head to glance at the Scriptor. "And what of it? Do you care that they mock?"

"Mockery I can endure. But what poisons me is that they are probably right. Whatever deviltry is behind their longer lives and their other powers, perhaps we need to accept that it is born with them and dies with them. We can no more steal their immortality than we can turn lead into gold."

"Oh, that is unfair," said Nicodemus as he pushed off the mantel and sat in the opposite chair. "Turning lead into gold is at the heart of alchemy."

"It is the bait on the hook, my friend," said the Scriptor, "but have you ever known it to be accomplished? No, do not bother to answer. I know they have not. We both know it. Frankly, I am not certain of what good any of this has done for the Order."

He sipped his wine and cursed softly under his breath. A log shifted in the fireplace, spitting red sparks onto the hearth.

"Something must be done," said the priest. "We both know that the Upierczy are long-lived but they are not truly immortal. We have seen Upierczy, even some of the most powerful among them, die of old age, even if after greatly more than a century. The Mohammedans' power grows constantly while we lose ground. Our knights cannot compete with their league of assassins. We cannot let the balance slide toward them unchecked."

Sir Louis suddenly sat up straight, eyes wide, lips parted.

"What is it?" asked Nicodemus in sudden alarm. "Are you unwell?"

The old Scriptor held up a hand. "Wait . . . wait . . . give me a moment . . ."

They sat in silence for nearly two full minutes before a change came over Sir Louis. Where there was doubt, now there was a look of hopeful amazement.

"Father," said the Scriptor, "that is it. That is our answer."

The priest frowned. "What do you mean, my lord?"

"You said it yourself. Our knights cannot compete with the enemy."

"Yes, and . . . ?"

"Our *knights*, Father. That's the key. *Our* knights."

"I beg forgiveness, my lord, but I do not follow."

Sir Louis rose from his chair and began pacing the room. "We have been fools, Nicodemus. Blind fools. Greedy blind fools at that." He stopped and turned. "How many of our own have died in this vain pursuit of immortality? How many knights, how many of my own ancestors have been lost to this senseless quest? This alchemy? It's a fool's dream. It is presumptuous because immortality is granted by God or it is not. Who are we to attempt to steal secrets from the divine? Don't you see, we've been punished for that arrogance."

"I—"

"No, hear me out," said Sir Louis, his voice rising with his excitement. "What if the Upierczy were our warriors?"

The priest looked blank. "I fail to follow, my lord. We have used them to undertake our holy crimes for centuries."

"Yes, yes, but that's not what I mean. Have you ever seen them in action? They kill, to be sure, but there is no joy in it for them."

"They drink the blood of our enemies."

"They drink blood because they must," said Sir Louis. "They kill because they must. We force them to do it. And how do we reward them? We lock them away in our dungeons or make them live in caves. They are dependent upon us because we understand what they are. They know *we* know how to find them. The church hunted their kind to the edge of extinction since the time of the gospels. We treat them like monsters, like devil spawn and abominations."

"Which they *are*."

"Oh, let us both face the truth, Nicodemus," snapped the Scriptor. "We are all monsters. The difference is that we of the Red Order and our brothers in the Hospitallers are celebrated for what we do. We are honored, feasted, blessed by the Holy Father and priests like you. Laurels are set upon our brows and mantles of fine silk set with jewels draped on us. When one of us dies, there is mourning and his name entered into the Book of Shadows as a saint in our cause. But . . . what of the Upierczy?"

The priest was listening now, leaning forward, the fires of understanding beginning to flicker in his eyes.

"We treat the Upierczy worse than dogs. We revile them even as we demand so much of them. And what is the outcome? They hate us and they curse us in the dark. God knows that if there were enough of them, and all harboring such resentment, they would rise up and wash the whole of the world in blood."

"Then tell me of the alternative," said Nicodemus very softly.

"We change it," said Sir Louis. "Instead of abusing them, we honor them. Instead of keeping them in chains we let them have such homes as would make them comfortable. Instead of threatening them with eternal damnation for natures which are not theirs to change, we give them a reason to feel pride. Instead of keeping them in slavery, we give them purpose and hope. Do you hear me, Father? We elevate them so that they are our allies and never again slaves who cower in the dark and curse our names."

"My lord, this sounds as if you are describing an order of chivalry."

"And what if I am?" demanded the Scriptor. "Do you find fault with what I propose? The Hashashin who fight for the Mohammedans are given palaces and riches and are rewarded with concubines. The Upierczy know this. The air reeks of their jealousy. Why not come to them and say that we are so proud of what they have accomplished that we want to celebrate them, to reward them with honors and distinction."

Nicodemus looked aghast. "The people will never accept this."

"Why should they ever know? The soldiers in the armies of Muhammad do not know much beyond rumor of the Hashashin. No, it is only the key players in this game who should be made aware. His Holiness, key priests that you feel can be trusted, and the Knights of the Red Order. More importantly, the Upierczy themselves will know that they are our allies in our Holy Agreement."

Nicodemus took his winecup and sipped, eyes hooded as he looked inward.

"Subordinate to us, yes?" he ventured.

"Naturally."

The priest nodded. "Yes . . . Yes, my lord, I see it. A subordinate order of chivalry, answerable to the Scriptor of the Red Order, but honored by all who serve God through our Agreement."

"Yes," said Sir Louis.

"Les Chevaliers Rouges," said the priest.

"Oh, yes," agreed the Scriptor.

# CHAPTER 30

## THESSALONIKI AIRPORT MAKEDONIA
## THESSALONIKI, GREECE

The two missing members of Havoc Team met us at the airport. They sat slumped in plastic chairs at baggage claim, each wearing scowls of disapproval. I was about to say something conciliatory when Bunny grinned and asked, "So . . . how was the vacation?"

Belle, a thin, dark-skinned woman from Mauritania, rarely smiled. She rarely even spoke. But she aimed a finger pistol at Bunny and used her thumb to drop the hammer.

Remy, the young Cajun who handled all the tech stuff for Havoc, gave each of us a crisp salute with an extended forefinger.

"Least nobody was shooting at you two juvenile delinquents," observed Top. "While you were in preschool, we were out saving the whole damn world."

"There is a saying from the writings of the poet Rumi," said Belle. "It goes something like this. And bear in mind, I'm quoting from memory. He wrote—*fuck you, old man.* Or words to that effect."

Remy pointed to her. "Ditto."

"When we get back to the house," said Top, "I'm going to hide in my room 'cause you two are mad at me."

We took the bags around to another part of the airport and then out to an elegantly appointed Bell 525 Relentless helicopter that was waiting for us. Ghost trotted along beside me, tail wagging as if it was his own private ride and we were his entourage.

It wasn't a long flight, but we settled into the leather seats and pretended we were all millionaires. During the trip, we brought Belle and Remy up to speed on everything that had happened, starting with Nicodemus at the cemetery.

"I'm not sure I'm following y'all on this," said Remy. "What's the Red Order and are we really talking *vampires*? And Saturday people? My aunt Viola was born on Saturday and she hasn't taken to running around with hammers and stakes."

"There's a case file on it," I said, "but the bones of it are this: It all started during the Crusades. Sir Guy LaRoque, emissary for Philip II of France, was a senior member of the Knights Hospitaller, which is a noble order dedicated to good works."

"Like the Templars?" asked Remy.

"Yes. Created with good intentions, more or less, but like any organization where there is money and power to be had, it developed some internal cancers. Anyway, this Guy LaRoque was both an advisor to the French king and also a kind of ambassador. Sometimes openly, to discuss treaties and things like breaks in combat to deal with wounded. Normal stuff on the surface, but behind the scenes he met often with Ibrahim al Asiri, who was basically his opposite number for Sultan Saladin. They privately agreed that in times of war, especially Holy War, church attendance spikes, and in peace it falls off. It was so noticeable a thing that they felt compelled to take advantage of it."

"How?" asked Belle.

"They agreed between them that it serves God and their respective religions if holy wars, both large and small, were to continue. They created what they called the Holy Agreement. It spelled out just how they would keep the fires of religious and ethnic hatred burning, but to mutual benefit."

"Jesus Christ," gasped Remy.

"It gets worse," said Bunny.

I nodded. "Sir Guy created a secret splinter group of the Hospitallers called the Ordo Ruber—the Red Order. Red for the Blood of Christ, red for the blood of the infidels spilled in God's name. Red for the sacrifices that needed to be made. And the advisor to this new suborder was a man known as Father Nicodemus."

Remy touched the gris-gris—a small cloth pouch of lucky charms the young Cajun wore beneath his shirt. "Nicodemus . . . as in that *peeshwank* we've been trading punches with?"

"Same name," Bunny said. "Obviously not the same guy."

Top said, "It gets better. There's been a Father Nicodemus working with the Red Order ever since. I sleep better at night when I convince myself it was a whole bunch of guys, probably all part of the same family, who took the name and the job."

Belle's eyes narrowed. "But . . . ?"

"But I don't *always* believe that."

"You are saying this is the same man we've encountered during the Kuga thing? And just recently in Pine Deep? The man who called himself Mr. Sunday?"

"Same name, at least," said Bunny. When Belle and Remy looked at him with raised eyebrows, he added, "I don't believe in ghosts, demons, or any kind of immortal chaos whatevers."

"Chaos spirit," I said. "That's just a theory, and I don't buy it, either."

Remy was now clutching his gris-gris through the material of his shirt. Despite education and travel around the world, he was still a Cajun from the farmlands around New Orleans. His personal belief system was nominally Catholic, but like a lot of folks down in the Big Easy, there was a strong flavor of *vodou* sewn into his beliefs.

Top looked down into the depths of his glass of bourbon and said nothing.

"Getting back to it," I said. "The Red Order was on the side of Christendom. Their counterparts in Islam took the name Tariqa, which means 'the Way.' Each side had its leader whose identity was often kept secret, even from the general membership. The Red Order is governed by a Scriptor, and the Tariqa by a Murshid. As far as we know, the Tariqa is gone, torn down after our mission in Iran a few years ago when its presence and history was disclosed to the world."

"Courtesy of Bug and MindReader," said Bunny. "Heads literally rolled."

"As is appropriate," said Belle quietly. Despite breaking from many elements of the patriarchy, she was still a devout Muslim.

I saw that my glass was empty and before I could reach for the bottle, Remy snatched it and poured a generous knock for me and a larger one for himself.

I nodded my thanks, took a sip, and continued. "At first the two parties in this Agreement decided to commit murders of their *own* people, people belonging to the Crusades, or pilgrims visiting the Holy Land. The logic there being that these deaths would be selected for great effect but without doing substantial harm to either side. Symbolic deaths. Martyrs whose deaths would inspire hate and bloodlust."

"And send everybody back to God," said Top. "Only that didn't work out so well for them."

"The effect worked," I said, "but there was too much of a toll on the members of the Red Order who had to commit those crimes. And so, the Agreement was amended so that each side was allowed a set number of murders and slaughters and burning of holy places."

"Fuck me up, down, and sideways," breathed Remy.

"The Tariqa decided they needed some specialists for the wet work," I said. "Highly skilled assassins who had no emotional connection with anyone they were asked to kill. There was already a group of highly skilled killers operating in the Middle East, an order of Nizari Ismailis founded in 1080 during the First Crusade. The Hashashin. It's where the word assassin comes from, by the way. These killers were amazing. Kind of like Middle Eastern ninjas. Top of the game. And they began doing selected hits on the Crusaders and pilgrims. The kicker was that the Red Order had nothing on a par with them. They had some kick-ass knights, but they weren't the same kind of killer."

"So, did they form their own SpecOps team?" asked Belle.

I shook my head. "Not in the same way, and this is where Father Nicodemus comes back into the story. He knew of some people—humans, more or less—who were *believed* to be supernatural creatures. They were stronger and faster, and they had an incredible natural wound repair system and their lifespan was sometimes twice or even three times that of regular people. They were known by a lot of different names around the world, but wherever one of these genetic freaks lived, the stories of supernatural monsters grew up."

Belle was nodding, clearly seeing where I was going. Remy was a half step behind her, but he caught on, too.

"Vampires, right?" he asked. "That's what you're getting at, isn't it?"

"Yes and no," I said. "These creatures were called Upierczy. But before you ask, no, they are not supernatural. They don't turn into mist, they don't sleep in coffins, they can't command storms, and they don't transform into bats or wolves. They are essentially human, but each Upierczy has a similar genetic defect that causes physical and behavioral changes that are the origins of the vampire myth. I told you about their strengths, but they have weaknesses, too. They are severely allergic to garlic and they can be killed by a bullet or knife just like anyone else. But it has to be a hit to a vital organ, because they really do heal fast."

Remy's eyes were as big as saucers.

"The Upierczy were found by priests and brought to the Red Order. There were never many of them, though. Not at first, anyway. The Red Order tried to breed them to build numbers, but the creatures are close to being genetic mules. There are no females of that subspecies, and the males are often sterile, or if they did impregnate a woman, most of the babies were born with horrible birth defects, or were stillborn. Father Nicodemus and the Scriptor were really determined to solve the problem, though, and they sent agents out to abduct women and keep them in breeding pits in underground tunnels where the Upierczy lived."

Neither Remy nor Belle said a word. I'm not sure they could have.

"This went on for centuries," I said, feeling sick by even telling this story. "Female offspring were either killed or were raised to be breeders. Their word, not mine. Every now and then a healthy male

Upierczy would be born. When that happened, the birth mother would be forced to bear as many children as possible. Some bore a child every year for over twenty years."

Belle's mouth formed a single word. *No.* But there was no sound. My heart went out to her. Although she hadn't been forced to bear children, she'd undergone so many horrors. She was sent to a camp in her home country that performed sexual mutilations that includes clitoridectomies to remove any trace of possible pleasure from sex. Her skin was a roadmap of scars, each of which compounded the horrors of what she'd endured. When Violin and an Arklight team raided the camp, Belle picked up a gun and used it on the men who had committed those atrocities. She hasn't really put the gun down since, and Violin tutored her into becoming one of the most dangerous snipers in the world.

I took a strong sip and continued. "With these breeders, the Red Order have been able to greatly expand the numbers of Upierczy. Though, even then there are fewer of them who are one hundred percent combat ready for tier one ops, and some who have enough minor genetic damage to be useful only as foot soldiers. Now, there are some things that have changed this dynamic. First, the Holy Agreement is gone. You may remember hearing about a top Iranian politician named Jalal Rasouli? He was in line to be the next president, and off the public radar he was the current Murshid. He broke the agreement, and the last known Scriptor was killed during our op. That's one part. The other thing is that among the children born from this program of rapes were some girls who possessed some of the abilities of the Upierczy. They are faster and stronger, harder to kill, and they live an unusually long time. They are called dhampyrs. Some of these women were forced to become breeders themselves, and their forced births often resulted in some of the strongest and most genetically stable males."

"Dhampyrs?" echoed Remy. "I've seen them in anime and shit."

"They're all through fiction," said Top. "Blade, from the Marvel comics and movies, is one. But he's male. In real life, there aren't male dhampyrs."

"Far as we know," I said. Actually, Mike Sweeney in Pine Deep, who worked with us to tear down a murderous militia group, was almost certainly one. I knew that from odd remarks the town's chief of police, Malcolm Crow, has made over the years. But now wasn't the time for a conversational side trip.

"Tell him the good part, boss," said Bunny.

"There's a good part?" Remy asked.

Belle gave me a look of understanding. She knew what was coming next. There was a predatory gleam in her eyes.

"You'll actually like this, kid," I told Remy. "A few decades back, one of these dhampyrs, who was a breeder for many years, somehow orchestrated a rebellion. She led her sisters in an escape that resulted in a bloodbath. A lot of Upierczy were killed, and one of their breeding centers was burned down. These women got free, taking as many of their children as they could. Once free, they formed an organization called the Mothers of the Fallen. Their organization, though not publicly known, has become one of the powerful and effective forces in play against all forms of human trafficking. They have a militant arm, and both of you have met some players on that team."

Belle nodded. Remy took his time with his guess. "Wait, are you talking about Violin and Tommy? You're talking about Arklight."

"Yes I am."

"Wait, wait . . . Violin's mother is Lilith, right? She's Arklight. Is she one of the women who broke out?"

I smiled. "Oh, Lilith's more than that. She's the woman who organized the whole uprising."

"But you said that the woman who did that was a dhampyr. Does that mean . . . ?"

I said nothing.

"And . . . Violin? Is she . . . ?"

When nobody answered, Remy tried to drink from his empty glass. He stopped and stared down into it as if it was going to make sense of the world.

"I . . . I mean . . . but . . ."

"Yeah," said Top.

And that's where we left it. As we flew through the clear blue skies above Greece, I saw Remy sitting, half-turned away from the rest of us, staring out the window, his fingers still touching his amulet of protection.

This world is so much larger and stranger than people think. It's bigger and badder and darker than even your dedicated cynic believes. I felt bad that we had just increased Remy's awareness of that darkness. He was a good kid, and this was going to mark him as surely as a knife or bullet, and—like Top, Bunny, Belle, and me—he would wear that scar for the rest of his life. Even after it faded from open wound to a thin, pale line on the skin of his soul, he would always, on some level, be aware of it and all that it implied.

Ghost came over and laid his head on my thigh. Wanting to be petted, but always wanting to be there for me. I pulled his ponderous weight up onto my lap and as the miles burned away, we comforted each other. Two members of our small pack. Flying from horror into uncertainty, both of us knowing that red days and darker shadows waited for us.

As they always did.

## INTERLUDE 15

### THE GRAND EXPERIMENT
### LAROQUE ESTATE
### VILLAGE OF MONTAILLOU, FRANCE
### 1287 CE

"Kneel," commanded the Scriptor of the Red Order.

The thing stood there. Tall, pale as midnight snow, impossibly strange. It looked down at the clothes it wore—fine linens and brocade, silk and soft wool. Boots of fine leather and a broad belt from which hung a dagger. Never before had he, or any of his kind, been allowed to bring sharpened steel to a meeting with the Ordo Ruber.

Slowly—very slowly—the monster knelt, though it stared with open defiance at the gathered knights, the priests, and the Scriptor.

"Name yourself," said the nobleman.

The Upierczy felt a rush of humiliation at the question, but wrestled with it, unsure if this was some kind of trick.

There were so many of the knights in the hall, and all of them had their swords drawn. They each stood with their sword in front of them, the blades nearly touching the stone floor, one hand clasped tightly around the handle, and the other laid atop that hand. The crosspiece of their swords represented the crossbar that Jesus had been forced to carry to Golgotha, and the length of naked steel the upright. Fifty knights of the Red Order, each openly a Knight Hospitaller, standing with their symbolic crosses. Their foreheads glistened with wetness from the junior priests tracing the sign of the cross on them with holy water. Every face was grave and all eyes watchful.

The kneeling Upierczy spoke slowly, fighting with the extravagance of sharpened teeth and the muffling limitations of lips.

"I am called fiend," he said. "I am called unholy and forgotten of God."

"I did not ask what others who are not Upierczy named you," said the Scriptor. "I asked what you call yourself."

The question nearly took the creature's breath away. Not once in all of his sixty-seven years of life had anyone of hot blood—the sunlight people as his kind called them—even asked if he *had* a name, let alone asked to hear it.

"I . . ." began the kneeling monster. He paused and tried again. "I am Dömötör. I . . . have no surname."

"Does your father live?"

"He does not, my lord," said Dömötör, hating that his fangs mangled his speech.

"What was *his* name?"

"His father called him István, lord."

"Tell me, Dömötör son of István, do you worship God the Eternal?"

"Yes, lord."

"Do you accept Jesus as your Savior?"

"We pray to him who died and was reborn immortal," said Dömötör.

"And do you pledge your life and your honor to the Red Order?"

Dömötör felt confused, and the fear of being tricked became more intense. When he hesitated, the old priest spoke.

"Speak, my son," said Nicodemus. "God is watching."

The Upierczy felt tears burning in his eyes. "Father," he said, "how can I make a pledge such as this? We have been told for centuries that we are beasts and not men. We are slaves and therefore have no honor with which to pledge."

He hated the note of pleading in his own voice, but this was the truth and he was bound to speak it.

The Scriptor took a small step forward. Two knights began to move forward to offer protection but he gently waved them back, bidding them stand in silence. Then the nobleman reached down and pressed his warm palms against the cold flesh of Dömötör's cheeks.

"That time has passed," he said softly. "I cannot step into yesterday to change any of what has been done to you. However, I tell you now—and all within the sound of my voice—that the oppression of the Upierczy ends here and it ends now. I will brook no mistreatment of those who have served us so well and for so long."

The Scriptor looked around, though his palms still pressed against Dömötör's face.

"Is there any man here—knight or priest—who will oppose my will?"

There was no answer.

"Is there anyone here who will rebuke me or tell me that I do not act in God's name and for His glory?"

Silence.

Dömötör wanted to look into the eyes of the knights, but dared not look away.

"God in His majesty and wisdom has brought the family of Upierczy to us, to serve us and to stand *with* us in this holy war. Who will gainsay me?"

No word was spoken.

Then the Scriptor did something that astonished Dömötör. Still clasping him, he bent and kissed the vampire's forehead. Dömötör's heart hammered in his chest.

Then Sir Louis released Dömötör and held out a hand to his own son, Phillip, who would one day be Scriptor after him. The young man had stood silent, a great and storied sword held reverently across his arms. Now he bowed, turned the sword, and placed the handle in his father's grasp.

Sir Louis weighed the sword for a moment, and then touched the flat of the glittering blade to Dömötör's left shoulder, then his right, and finally touched the top of the Upierczy's head.

"Here, in the presence of God, His priests, and the Knights of the Red Order, I dub thee *Sir* Dömötör Istvánson, a soldier of Christ and first among Les Chevaliers Rouges. Now and forever, the Upierczy are an order of chivalry to whom all trust and respect are due. Now, Sir Dömötör, rise and stand in the sight of those who honor you and call you brother."

The Upierczy was so stunned and shaken that for many seconds he was unable to do anything. But as the expectant silence in that room grew heavier, he heaved himself up and stood there, blinking back his tears as the gathered knights filled the chamber with the thunder of their cheers.

Beside the Scriptor, the strange eyes of the priest, Father Nicodemus, swirled with light and with colors.

# CHAPTER 31

## ROGUE TEAM INTERNATIONAL HEADQUARTERS
## PHOENIX HOUSE
## OMFORI ISLAND, GREECE

We returned to the island. To the place that has been home for us since Church shuttered the old Department of Military Sciences.

That closure had been a hard decision for him and for all of us. The DMS was created to be the rapid response group doing the jobs that other Department of Homeland Security agencies couldn't do. And by that I don't mean the other alphabet groups suck. Not the case at all. But government bureaucracy shits out red tape, committees take too long to decide which shoe to tie first, and the great big machinery that is the United States gets tangled in its own wiring. Most of the time, there's allowance for that. But when there's no time left at all and response teams need to be wheels up right damn now, an agency like the DMS mattered. The challenge for us was that changes in who's running what within the government often put Church's do-it-right-now approach at odds with evolving political exigencies. Bottom line, we didn't have time to stroke egos and that made us unlikable.

So, Church created Rogue Team International. We answer to no one, though we frequently take special projects from the United Nations and, yes, Uncle Sam. Though we do it with the understanding that we do it our way, and at our speed. Anyone who doesn't like that can go and hire the second-stringers.

Church surprised us all by buying that island in Greece and then having an old Transylvanian castle disassembled and reassembled piece-by-careful-piece on the island, basing it on and around the remnants of an ancient volcano. There was still enough thermal activity deep down to provide geothermal heat and power for us. And the location was nicely placed to allow our teams to reach most places in Europe very quickly; and the isolation of the island increased overall security.

Of course, we busted Church pretty hard for both having an actual spooky castle and then erecting it over a hollowed-out volcano. I mean, that's right out of *Austin Powers* and *Dr. No.* He had everything he needed to be an evil mastermind. Even has a cat who likes sitting on his lap and being stroked during mission briefings. Luckily, he's one of the good guys.

Rudy and I have spent hours debating whether Church did a lot of it for the theatrics, or for the effect. Everyone at RTI has a theory about our new home. Mind you, we've never landed on anything we believe wholeheartedly, and Church refuses to be drawn into our discussions. He did make a rare mistake once, though, and put up a suggestion box for the official name of our headquarters. But after offerings like Dracula's Castle, Dr. Evil's Lair, Castle Von Doom, and the Dungeon of Despaur, he removed the box and sent a group email saying that it was to be called Phoenix House. And that was that.

Bug insists this is a missed opportunity. Bunny and Coleman agree.

As for our new role as international troubleshooters, if anyone had doubt about us finding work, it turned out we were busy from day one. The three field teams we started with—Havoc, Bedlam, and Chaos—have grown. Now there's the Wild Hunt, Asgard, Olympus, and Avalon Teams in training, with another six in early planning. And we have satellite field offices in London, Paris, Bangkok, Sydney, and Canada. All one big, stressed, overworked, unhappy, deeply weird family of science nerds and shooters.

A tech came over, hand clamped to his head to keep his Padres baseball cap from flying off. He ran hunched over through the rotor wash, saw the hold was empty, looked around and spotted me. He grinned sheepishly and trotted over to where I stood with Top and Bunny by a wall of packing crates. It was Dan Heaton, the third or fourth or fifth in command under Scott Wilson. One of those people who seemed ill-suited to a job with a bunch of science geeks and pistoleros. Dan used to be a high school gym teacher in Carlsbad, California. One of the many people who work for Church but who I've never really gotten to know. My fault, I suppose. He shook our hands and then leaned forward to shout through the diminishing roar of the chopper's engines.

"Joe, Scott wanted to be here to meet you personally," he said, "but he flew to England."

"Why? Is there trouble?"

"There's always trouble," said Dan with a laugh, but then shook his head. "No, you know James Rockwell, head of Barrier, right?"

"Know of," I said. "Never met him. I heard he's stepping down, though, right? Wife's sick?"

"Yeah. Ever meet her?"

"No. Why would I have?"

"She was in the trade," said Dan. "Beautiful woman, too. Former MI6 spook. Great laugh." Dan shook his head. "A month ago, when she was making breakfast, she asked Rockwell if he wanted another cup of celery. When he asked what she meant, she snatched up the coffeepot and shook it at him and yelled 'celery.' Then she dropped the pot and passed out. Docs took some pictures and she has all kinds of tumors in her head, poor lady. They opened her up and took some out and left. They did radiation and chemo and all, but the doctors said it was maybe a year too late. So Rockwell is going to be there for her all the way to the end."

Top nodded somberly. "All kinds of heroes in this world. All kinds of wars to fight."

We stood in the silence of that for a moment.

Dan said, "Scott was short-listed for Rockwell's job before Mr. Church hired him away for RTI, but the prime minister wants him back to fill in, and maybe to take over."

"Good guy for the job," said Bunny.

"Who'll be filling in for Scott here?"

I expected Dan to have used this conversation to announce his own promotion, but that wasn't it. He chewed his lip for a second before answering.

"Major Courtland," he said.

And that hit me like a punch.

Top bristled. "That some kind of fucking joke, Dan?"

The tech looked genuinely surprised. Then his eyes lit up with understanding. "Oh, jeez, I must be a total dumbass. I forgot. I . . . I never knew the *other* Major Courtland."

"You ain't making a lot of sense, dude," said Bunny. "Grace Courtland died a few years back. What do you mean by 'other' . . . ?"

"Major *Claire* Courtland."

"What are you talking about?" I demanded. "Grace didn't have a sister."

"No, no . . . Claire's her cousin. Was in Iraq and Afghanistan, racked up some kills, too. Working with MI6 over there, though officially attached to the Royal Army Medical Corps, though that was just a cover. She was way off the radar doing special projects. Like a zillion call signs and code names. Only surfaced under her own name in UK intelligence circles a couple of years back and has been climbing through the ranks like a rocket. A quiet rocket. She's worked so many off-the-books missions with Barrier that Rockwell recommended her for this gig. Pissed off some old boys who were lining up for the big chair."

"Well . . . damn," I said. Hearing that name—Major Courtland—really shook my cookie-bag. Top caught my eye and studied me for a moment, then nodded and turned away.

"If she's anything like Grace," said Bunny, "then she'll be hell on wheels."

"From what I heard," said Dan, "she looks like she was Grace Courtland's twin rather than her cousin."

I tried not to wince. Having a Grace look-alike could be very weird and likely disturbing for those of us who knew her.

"When's she get here?" Bunny asked.

"Dunno," said Dan. "Pretty much anytime now, I guess."

"Well, well," murmured Top. "This should be interesting as all hell."

"Going to be weird as fuck," I countered.

Dan nodded. "Yeah, well . . . I wanted to tell you about Scott, Joe. I know you two are tight."

He jogged off.

"Tight?" said Bunny. "You and Mr. Stick-up-his-ass?"

"Must be interesting to be that clueless," Top observed.

Bunny said, "Major Courtland? Now, ain't that a swift kick in the nutsack."

I declined to comment. Even though I was deeply in love with Junie Flynn, there is always a small, locked room in the soul of everyone who has ever loved and lost a person. I have all of my memories, hopes, and crushed dreams of Grace locked away, and I make no apologies for opening that closet every now and then and just *being* with the memories we shared, and with the regrets for everything that was stolen from both of us by an assassin's bullet. Junie even knew about that small corner of my heart that will always be connected to Grace. Just as there are similar places for Helen and for Violin. Junie has her own memories and we are adult enough to not only accept this truth but understand it. There is no value in lying to oneself or one's lover that there was no one else of importance before them. That's shallow teenage bullshit.

Even so, how would I react when confronted with the reality of a *new* Major Courtland? It would be a bit of a mercy if she did not look like her cousin. Again, I caught Top watching me, and again we shared a small nod of mutual understanding.

We stayed there near the chopper, watching as techs handled the unloading of the painting, and that drew our attention more acutely. We'd crated it, so there was nothing to see but wood and nails. Way less complicated that way.

As the workmen passed us with it on a hand truck, Bunny murmured, "Normally this'd be just a—y'know—weird coincidence like you see on Instagram. I saw a meme once with a couple of statues that looked like Sam Elliott and Woody Harrelson."

"Saw those, too," said Top.

"But it's the facial scars that are twisting my nuts with pliers. I mean, we've all *seen* those scars up close. Am I wrong or am I crazy or what?"

Ghost made a low sound. Not a growl or anything like that. Closer to a sigh, but his meaning was indistinct.

I said, "Yeah."

Top had a toothpick in his mouth and took it out, looked at it as if it could provide answers, sighed, and put it back between his teeth. "I love this job," he said in a way that conveyed an entirely different meaning.

## INTERLUDE 16

### THE WARRIOR AND THE WAR
### CASTLE OF MIRAVET
### ON THE EBRO RIVER, SPAIN
### 1289 CE

They called him Le Chevalier Bâtard—the Bastard Knight—but he took no umbrage. He even referred to himself that way, using what was normally an insult as his armor. In his youth, a few arrogant fools had risen to that challenge, but they were bones in the ground. The Bastard Knight had no true name, and that was fine with him. On formal ceremonies he allowed himself to be called Sir John Temple, which was not his name.

The Bastard had not taken his father's name out of a balance of respect for the family and a strong dislike of the old man who now lay dying in his estate. There, the old man was surrounded by pimply inbred heirs whose only merit was a marriage certificate.

However, the Templar brotherhood had welcomed the bastard in, and Jacques de Molay, Grand Master of the Order himself, orchestrated a knighthood for him, but that honor seemed to mean little in these troubled times. That lack of family and the air of anonymity was something he used, and over time Sir John Temple became the silent, secret left hand of the Grand Master. De Molay even sometimes referred to him as Le Fantôme. The Ghost. And that worked, too.

Anyone who spoke the sobriquet of "Bastard" in goodhearted jest was a friend. Those who called him that as an insult were thwarted if hoping to publicly embarrass him, for he either ignored it or laughed in their faces.

It was a very difficult thing to get him to draw steel over words. He was far too controlled for that, and his coolness of reaction and studied approach to all matters of conflict made him indispensable. He had been invited into the Poor Fellow Soldiers of Christ and of the Temple of Solomon, and took the solemn oath to be a Templar.

He often stood at the right hand of Jacques de Molay, and was comfortable providing special and discreet services. Sometimes his missions were as simple as delivering a letter or cutting a throat; other times he was called to practice the subtle arts of espionage. De Molay had charged him with investigating a series of brutal murders of their fellow Templar Knights.

Now he crouched on the floor of a bedroom that was awash in blood.

What was left of Sir Rudolfo of Monzón lay scattered across the floor. It took the Bastard Knight time to make sense of what lay there, deciding which pieces made up the fallen knight and which belonged to his wife and two children. The butchery had gone far beyond swordplay and into madness.

"What are you seeing?" asked his son, who also went by the false name of John Temple, though without the prefix of knighthood. To his father's inner circle he was Young John, or simply the Bastard Son. "Is this the Hashashin?"

"No," said the Bastard, shaking his head slowly. He looked around, lips pursed in thought. "No, this is something else."

"What then?" asked Young John. "Did a bear break in here? Or perhaps a tiger let loose from someone's private menagerie?"

"Neither."

"No? But surely, Father, this was the work of a beast. Look at the wounds. They were never made by sword, spear, or even axe. Poor Rudolfo and his family were torn to pieces. This is devil's work."

"Not devils either." The Bastard stood. "I've seen this before."

The lad frowned. "In God's name, Father, *where*?"

"Damascus, Jerusalem, Acre . . ."

"So you *are* saying that the Mohammedans did this."

"No, my boy, I firmly believe that they did not," growled the big man. "This is the work of monsters, but not beasts of forest or field."

The lad suddenly understood, and he spoke a word that many of even the boldest knights would not speak. "Upierczy."

The Bastard Knight nodded, pleased that his son was so quick-witted. "And to commit such an act against a Templar Knight as revered as Sir Rudolfo of Monzón tells me that our true enemy—the Red Order—has turned our past skirmishes into a war."

"War, Father . . . ?"

"Oh yes, lad, and all of the signs I have been seeing these last months tell me that it will be a great war. Perhaps it will be fought on battlefields, but I do not think so. Formal, *declared* wars have some measure of honor in them. This . . . ? There is no honor here. There is hate. And there is subtle cunning. Aye, even in butchery such as this, for Rudolfo was a key liaison between our brothers in the Templars and His Holiness the pope. His loss will weaken an already fragile alliance with Rome."

He walked to the window and looked out at the night. His son came and stood beside him.

"War is upon us, my son," he said. "This is not a war between states or crowns or even which version of God is worshipped, though I dare say some will claim otherwise because that is the shield behind which they hide. No, this is a war of a kind that has raged since Cain slew Abel. A war between those who hunger for power and those who, in faith, believe power will protect them. Kings and thrones will fall and turn to dust and this war will rage on. My own father, fool that he is, said as much to me, and now I tell you this hard and difficult truth: This war will never end."

"But . . . if the war cannot be won, then—"

"No," said Sir John Temple, "that is not what I said. I said it will never end, for there is no path to a decisive and lasting victory. Greed and hatred are the greatest sins."

"The priests say otherwise," said Young John.

"Priests are often corrupt, lad, for beneath their vestments they are ordinary men. Their vows do not cancel out their hungers. Kings are no different. Hear me well when I tell you to trust not those who would put themselves above other men." He sighed and shook his head. "This is not a war that can be won by armies. A single man with a true heart may do more than ten thousand armored knights. And the battles of this war will be fought by good men—aye, and good women, for they are always underestimated."

"Why are there not histories and tales and songs of such warriors?" asked Young John.

His father gave a cold and bitter laugh. "Because praise is glory, and a warrior with a true heart does not require these things. A warrior is different from a soldier, my son. A warrior understands that honor is not built on a pile of enemy bones, nor in any title given, nor even in the traditions of a family name. Honor—real honor—is to stand between those who cannot defend themselves and those who prey upon such innocent weakness, and to make that stand with no thought of reward or even thanks. Honor requires neither. Honor requires commitment to stand when others flee the field, and who—knowing that the fight may then be of one opposing many—will be steadfast."

"Like you, Father."

Sir John looked at his son with a mixture of sadness and love. "The war is not about glory or even an ultimate victory. The war itself is the war. The war is the reason we stand and the reason we fight. For if not us, then who?"

The young man, who was as tall and broad-shouldered as his father, stepped closer and laid a big hand on the hilt of his sword.

"Father," he said calmly but firmly, "tell me how I may help."

## CHAPTER 32

### BARRIER HEADQUARTERS
### HADRIAN TOWER
### ROPEMAKER STREET
### LONDON, ENGLAND

Scott Wilson came back from the men's bathroom after a short break, sat on his side of the conference table, picked up his glass of scotch, and looked briefly down into its amber depths. It was Bell's. Never his favorite. When he drank scotch, which was far less often than gin or wine, he preferred a single malt, and in his view even a mediocre single malt beat *any* blend. Worse still, it had been served over ice. Nevertheless he took a small sip and gave a bland smile to the others.

The three people seated across from him all seemed to like the Bell's. He chalked it up to a deficiency in their education. None of them had gone to Eton, and though it was small of him to hold it against them, he nevertheless did.

There was a fit-looking middle-aged blond man, Clive Cooper, who was the number 3 person at MI5; a short woman with fierce green eyes, Catriona MacPherson, who was in the corresponding position in MI6; and a tall, powerful-looking man with a head as bald as a billiard ball. This was Barrier director James Rockwell, and Scott surmised there would be a *Sir* in front of the James, likely as a retirement present from a grateful government.

Scott shook hands and told Cooper and MacPherson that he knew of them by reputation and was impressed. They gave him the kind of smiles people give someone at the beginning of an interview—the kind that gives nothing away, neither doubt nor encouragement. Rockwell's greeting was much warmer, and Scott decided he liked Rockwell well enough, though he suspected Rockwell was the one who chose the whisky. No one was perfect.

One thing that amused Scott was the small statue of Dover Castle placed on a circle of purple velvet in the center of the table. It was identical to the one Rockwell had gifted him. Scott wondered if its presence here on the interview table was a message. If so, he took it as an encouraging one.

"This last part shouldn't take too long," Rockwell said. "Just a few I's to dot and T's to cross."

"It's all fine," Scott said affably. "I'm in no hurry."

Rockwell's eyes searched his face and Scott saw a flicker of concern there. "I did want to ask, though . . . are you feeling quite well?"

"What? Oh, yes. I'm fine."

"You're quite pale," said MacPherson. "I hope we haven't been giving you too hard a time with all the hoops we're asking you to jump through."

"No, I'm good," said Scott.

Cooper chuckled. "Maybe you've caught a cold. London in March is a bit of a drastic change from Greece."

"Truly, I'm fine," insisted Scott.

"Then," Rockwell cut in, "let's get back to it, shall we? Yes? Excellent. Before the break, Scott, you were going over the liaison work you've been doing while acting as COO of Rogue Team International. Our mutual friend has given a green light for you to be as frank with us as we are with you."

Their mutual friend was Mr. Church, and Scott thought it odd how often the players in MI5, MI6, and Barrier tended to use euphemisms instead of saying Church's name. Were they afraid that speaking the name would conjure the man out of thin air? He saw no real value in using descriptors unless they were all that habitually spooked by the big American.

If, he thought privately, Church was actually American. Despite his New England Kennedy accent, Church could shift to quite a few other languages, all without accent. His colloquial French was as Parisian as someone raised there; and the same was true with Church's Russian, Chinese, and so on. That talent for languages was remarkable, and even more comprehensive than Joe Ledger's polyglot skills.

Aloud, he said, "Picking up where I left off, RTI always has agents on deck, even when the three main teams are deployed."

"And you're training new teams?" asked MacPherson.

"We are. At its peak, the DMS had thirty-five field teams operating on US soil, and of those thirty-five, nine were occasionally deployed for matters overseas. We have been building a similar structure."

"Isn't that awkward, given that RTI has no true governmental connection?" asked Cooper. "You're based in Greece but are not under their jurisdiction."

It was a leading question, but one Scott had been expecting. "The RTI charter gives more weight to the United Nations than any independent nation state. Even with that, Mr. Church retains the right to pick and choose which cases we will take."

"How involved have you been with making those calls?" asked Rockwell.

"I am always consulted."

"Consulted, yes," Rockwell continued, "but how much say have you been granted?"

"Quite a lot. More often than not, I have selected cases to bring to Church. We then debate the merits on a case-by-case basis, and typically proceed only when we are in agreement."

"So, it's similar to the arrangement our mutual friend had with Aunt Sallie?" suggested MacPherson.

"Quite," agreed Scott.

"And what was her real name?" Cooper asked, making it an offhand comment.

Scott smiled and sipped his scotch. He set the glass down before answering. "Sarah Elizabeth Harper."

Cooper nodded. Clearly he knew the answer, and the question was intended to determine how deeply into Church's trust Scott was. Scott knew that there were less than a dozen people worldwide who knew Auntie's real name. Joe Ledger, he mused, was not one of them.

"And what is your employer's real name?" asked MacPherson.

Scott felt the weight of the combined gazes of all three.

"I do not know," he said, telling the absolute truth.

Cooper and MacPherson looked disappointed; Rockwell nodded with what looked like approval.

The questions went on and on for nearly three hours. When things drew to a close, Rockwell stood up and offered his hand to Scott, who rose to take it.

"We will discuss things internally," Rockwell said. "I will, of course, need to speak to the PM and there may be one more follow-up tomorrow, if our friend can spare you for one more day."

Scott smiled warmly. "I think he . . ."

His words faded out as the room began to spin. It was very sudden and very intense, and he felt the floor tilt under him. For a wild moment he thought there was an earthquake, and his analytical mind snatched at the trivia that London hadn't experienced a serious earthquake since 1580. But even as this flashed through his mind, he was acutely aware that he was the only one affected. He saw alarm blossom on the faces of the other three. Rockwell and MacPherson both reached for him as if to keep him from falling.

*How odd*, he thought as he fell.

# CHAPTER 33

## PHOENIX HOUSE
## OMFORI ISLAND, GREECE

My cell rang and I stepped away from the guys to take the call.

I was expecting it to be Junie, but the number came up as *Unknown Caller*. Considering how many burner phones people in my trade use, it could be business related, so I answered with a careful, "Yeah?"

What I heard first was the tail end of what sounded like a pretty nasty coughing fit.

"If this is you, Nicodemus," I said, "I hope you die."

The cough turned into a creaking laugh. "You are such a lovely person," he said. "If I had a daughter I didn't like, I'd let her marry you and nag you to death."

I immediately hit the button for a trace. Burners foil nearly all call-tracing technologies, but Bug's been futzing around with some new things so it was worth a shot.

"You have a reason to call or just want to play more dumbass games?"

"Oh, how I'll miss this when I'm gone."

"Gone . . . ? Please tell me that you have cancer and that it hurts really, really bad."

He laughed at that, coughed some more, and finally said, "I hear you found something of great interest in Transylvania."

"I'm hanging up now," I said.

"No, you're not. You can't risk being impolite when there's even the slightest chance I'll say something useful."

"Do you actually practice being a cartoon villain, Nick ol' buddy? Or are you that clueless about how you come off?"

"Nick? That's adorable."

"Well, it was a toss-up between that and Shitty McDog-ass. Nick's just easier to say."

Ghost looked up at me and wagged his tail.

"I'll have that put on my tombstone," said Nicodemus. "But listen, Ledger, for my time is genuinely short. Despite what you think of me—and I don't blame you for every nasty thought you've had about me because that's part of the game—I wanted to let you know that

I have enjoyed all of this. You, the DMS, RTI, the Seven Kings, Zephyr Bain, Artemisia Bliss, all the fun and games. I've had a marvelous time."

"Fuck you very much."

He ignored that. "You'll hear from me a few more times. Like this. Keep your cell handy."

"Why should I bother?"

"Because my going-away party includes some parting gifts."

That was the phrase I used when joking about him to Church. Probably a complete coincidence. But it gave me a jolt.

I asked, "Which means what?"

"Which means that with each call, I'll allow you to ask one question and get a useful answer."

I stiffened. "More games?"

"Always more games," he said. "I am the veritable prince of games."

"Whatever that means. What *kind* of questions?"

"I'll let you decide."

I cut a look at my team, but they were twenty feet away and deep in a private conversation.

"Why would you answer any of my questions?"

"Why wouldn't I?"

"Maybe you'd be afraid I'd pick something up and use it to track you down. If you're sick, I could get some jollies watching you waste away in a cell. Somewhere nice and dark and dank. I hear Gitmo has an opening, and they're a swell bunch over there. Very accommodating."

"Yes," he said, "I've been there, and on both sides of the bars."

"What's that mean?"

"Is that your question?"

"No," I said quickly.

"Good, because the answer to that would not save a single life. So, ask carefully."

There were so many questions I could have asked and so much he could tell me, but I was on the spot. What I eventually asked surprised me, because it wasn't what I thought I was going to say.

I asked, "Who is Mr. Church?"

There was a sound that might have been a gasp or maybe a laugh. In either case, it was followed by a pause so long I had to check to make sure the call was still active.

When Nicodemus spoke, his answer came totally out of left field.

"He is the Last Templar Knight."

Then the line went dead.

I stood there, the silent phone still to my ear, and stared at absolutely nothing.

*The Last Templar Knight.*

What did that mean? Was it another of his jokes? Or was it a clue? I thought about the painting we'd brought back with us. That man—the original person who stood for the portrait, not the foppish clown who was painted over him—was dressed like a knight, though without insignia. There was nothing to indicate any connection to the Templars.

Which told me what?

I looked around, but no matter where I looked, there were no answers to be found.

## INTERLUDE 17

### THE GRAND EXPERIMENT
### PALAIS DE LA CITÉ
### ÎLE DE LA CITÉ, FRANCE
### 1292 CE

King Philip IV sat across from an old, wizened priest and they spoke of dreadful things. There was no one else within earshot for these were not true matters of the royal court.

"The Holy Land is lost," said the king.

"Yes," agreed Father Nicodemus. "We saw it coming. The Mamluks have prevailed, and we have gone running like frightened children."

A rebuke rose to the king's lips, but he did not give it voice for he feared this little priest. People who were true to him and whom he kept close for counsel warned him that Nicodemus not only had the ear of the pope, but was deeply involved in the machinations of the Red

Order. It was not openly known that Philip's own father and grandfather were members of that order, as was Philip III's father, whose canonization was being discussed.

Instead, the king said, "The people have lost faith in us, Father. They blame us for losing Jerusalem and all the rest. The tremors of their displeasure can be felt even here in this place." He gestured to indicate the palace and all it symbolized.

The priest had strange eyes that, in the uncertain light of a few candles, made it sometimes seem as if their color changed and swirled in ways that made the king feel deeply uneasy. He had to restrain his hand from crossing himself.

As if knowing this, the priest looked amused. He said, "We are adults, sire. We both know that discontent can hammer cracks into the foundation of your kingdom, the holy church, and all of Christendom. And that cannot be allowed."

"You speak as if we can put it to rights with the wave of a hand."

"No, sire, but it can be addressed with the stroke of a quill."

Philip frowned at him. "Meaning what?"

"Meaning, sire, that there are opportunities to assign blame for what has happened and thereby redirect the animus of the people." He paused. "And in doing so restore some balance in other areas."

"You speak in riddles."

"Then let me be very clear, my king," said the priest. "The centuries of the Crusades have seen our fortunes rise and fall. And by that, I mean not only our attempt to reclaim the Holy Land. Those Crusades were enormously expensive, and the cost has ruined more great houses than can be easily counted." His dark eyes sparkled and swirled. "It is my understanding that you owe the Templars a considerable amount, and that the amount is likely to rise."

Philip ground his teeth and nodded, but did not dare to speak.

"Soon your debt to the Templars will be such that repayment may not be remitted in gold but in consideration in more political matters. Already they have their hands in the coffers of half the royal houses in Europe."

"They have never asked for anything except repayment with interest."

"So far," said Nicodemus, "but surely you are wise enough, sire, to know that gold is not the true coin they seek. The Templars have long ago made a farce of their vows of poverty. And their new Grand Master, Jacques de Molay, is already held to be—shall we say—aggressive in matters of collecting outstanding debts. As we are currently without a pope in Rome thanks to backbiting among the cardinals, there is no real check on what the Templars do, and their excesses will run rampant."

"What of it? The popes have never been able to check the Templars."

"That may change," said the priest. "Depending on whom the cardinals elect. However, they are so divided it will be many months if not years before we are blessed with a new Holy Father. We know that de Molay and his lot will take full advantage of that delay to both invite lords and kings to dig themselves more deeply into debt, while also squeezing every scrap of gold from their betters."

"I know, damn it," snapped the king. "The Templars are the bankers for nearly all financial operations of any consequence here in France. I can barely send a patrol of scouts across a busy Paris street without borrowing more from them. But, again, Father, your words stab me with truths of which I am deeply aware. And with no pope to whom I can appeal for help, I am adrift in debt and my boat is springing leaks."

Nicodemus picked up the wineglass that stood untouched on the table between him and the king. He sniffed the rich wine, but did not drink. "Did you know, sire, that it is rumored that the Templar Knights are not true sons of Christ? Those whispers say that in their secret ceremonies, they will spit upon the cross. That they will squat to shit on icons of the saints. And that they worship Baphomet and praise his name while buggering young boys."

King Philip gaped at him in horror. "Surely not," he cried. "I dislike them, yet I cannot believe such accusations. Who is it that whispers of such crimes?"

The priest smiled. "No one," he said. "Yet."

# CHAPTER 34
## PHOENIX HOUSE
## OMFORI ISLAND, GREECE

I told Top and Bunny about the call.

"First," said Bunny, "what that hell?"

"No idea," I said.

"Second, what the *actual* hell?"

"Sounds like he's starting a new game and just called to yank your chain," suggested Top.

"Maybe."

"And . . . Last Templar Knight?" Bunny grinned. "I know Church is supposed to be a bit older than he looks, but the Templars went out of business a couple hundred years ago, right?"

"More like seven hundred and change," said Top.

"So . . . again I say, what the hell is he talking about?"

"Maybe Templar or Knight were names the Big Man used once upon a time, and Nicodemus is fucking with us. 'Cause we all know how he likes to be weird and mysterious and shit."

"Emphasis on the shit," I said.

We looked at each other.

"I got nowhere to go with it," I admitted. "Maybe Bug will know. He's been with Church longer than anyone else. Or he can do a keyword search."

"Worth a shot," said Top. He glanced at me. "You going to call the Big Man himself and ask?"

"Maybe," I said, and then amended. "Probably, but I think I'll ask Bug first."

The conversation seemed to run dry after that. Top and Bunny headed inside to take showers and get some chow. I loitered outside by the helo, squatting on my heels and scratching Ghost's thick pelt. A shadow fell across us and we looked up to see Church himself standing there. Even Ghost hadn't heard him approach. Spooky bastard. I straightened and we shook hands.

"The Corvin Castle mission was handled well, Colonel," he said. "You have my thanks."

"Another day on the job," I said.

Church nodded. "Doc Holliday and Dr. Coleman are in possession of the samples, and Bug's team is working on the computer files. Both departments are going to need time because there is a lot to do. A lot to understand."

"Yeah there is," I said. "But there's something else. Three guesses who I just got a call from?"

He didn't guess and waited for me to tell him. So I went over the whole conversation. As he listened, his expression went from stone-faced nothing to stone-faced nothing. Absolutely no visible reaction.

"This mean anything to you?"

Then he smiled. "I was never a Templar Knight, if that's what you're asking."

"Well, duh. But is there some kind of meaning in what he said?"

"Nothing comes immediately to mind," said Church. "As for questions for future calls, should he live up to his promise, I'll take that under advisement. We can put together a good list of key questions that are unambiguous. I'll make sure you get them within the hour."

He glanced out to sea, where gulls were diving and swooping into a school of bait fish.

"On more pressing matters," he continued, "I've scheduled a meeting for 0800 hours tomorrow. By then we should have a rough sense of the scope of this. Since there's nothing much to do at the moment, Dr. Sanchez has returned from Maryland—you could take one of the helos and visit."

"Trying to get rid of me?"

"I'm trying to give you some time to process what's happened," he said frankly. "We've known each other long enough for me to be aware that you are more prone to cognitive leaps when you have some hours to let things marinate."

I gave that some thought and nodded. Church rarely shares the whole truth about things, and sometimes he outright lies if that suits his needs in any given moment. This felt like one of those times. But his suggestion was a good one. Not only to allow time for me to process but for me to go over it with Rudy, who was smarter and more insightful than me on any day that ends in a Y. More importantly, Rudy knows me and understands how I think and as a sounding board, he's the best in the biz.

"Maybe," I said. "But I'm not sure how much processing I can actually do. I mean, what *is* this? We have Nicodemus jerking my chain in Maryland, then siccing a bunch of halfwit Sabbatarians on us. Then the Corvin Castle thing and maybe a kind of weaponized plague. Are we talking about two cases? Three? Or one?"

"What would your guess be?"

"One."

"You seemed to have that answer chambered for firing," Church observed.

"It's all gut," I admitted. "Yet I can't shake that guess." I paused and looked out to sea for a moment. "Truth is, boss, I don't know how they're connected beyond some of Nicodemus's cryptic comments—him talking about blood and plagues and what-not. And the Sabbatarian asking me why I drank the devil's blood. What's that even mean?" I shook my head. "I feel like I walked onstage during a performance and no one bothered to hand me a copy of the script."

The Big Man actually smiled at that. "And how is that different from our last ten cases? Our last *fifty*? We are a reactive organization. Our whole process has involved catching bits and pieces of things as they fly by and then the scramble to make sense of it in time to respond."

"You should put that on a recruiting pamphlet."

"Perhaps I should."

"It does suck, though, you have to admit that."

Church brushed an invisible piece of nothing from his tie. "I think we would all sleep better if the bad guys included us in their planning briefings."

"Yeah, yeah, yeah," I groused. "I just feel that big clock ticking and every fiber of my being is aching to be on the move, doing something, stopping this . . . whatever it is."

"Very much so," he agreed.

We stood and watched as the helicopter blades began turning. The bird lifted off, angled into the afternoon sky, and flew away. When the rotor drone faded, the day seemed unnaturally silent. Even the ocean waves were hushed.

"There's two more things," I said.

Church waited.

"That message Nicodemus wanted me to pass along. *Tell your lord and master this. Tell him that he* owes *me and the debt has come due. Tell him that and, as I said, watch his eyes.*"

"If there is any sense to make of it," said Church, "we will figure it out. As vague as Nicodemus enjoys being, when he wants to be understood, he usually is."

"Like his remark about watching your eyes. Will that make sense at some point?"

"I can't see how."

Church gave the smallest of shrugs, dismissing it.

"The other thing, boss," I said, "is that painting. Now, before you tell me it's none of my business—"

"Which it isn't."

"Maybe. But that painting isn't just a passing resemblance. Top, Bunny, and I all saw it up close. We saw those little scars, the ones you've had since I've known you. That's not something I can just let go."

"That," said Church, "is between you and your own personal mechanism for frustration management." He bent and gave Ghost's head a brief scratch, nodded to me, and walked back to the house.

"Well . . . fuck," I said.

Ghost looked at me and wagged his tail. Dumb dog.

## CHAPTER 35

### IN FLIGHT OVER THE IONIAN SEA

The day started to get so long that it annoyed the crap out of me. After mooning around Phoenix House for a couple of hours, basically making a nuisance of myself and clearly interfering with important people doing important work, I took my currently unimportant ass out of there.

Church had suggested I go see Rudy, so I decided to do exactly that. I got a buddy of mine to fly me from Omfori Island to Rudy's place on Corfu. It was only a couple hundred klicks away. The AS365 Dauphin got me there in a little better than an hour.

I was halfway to Corfu to see Rudy when I got a call from Bug.

"Hey, just the computer-obsessed maniac I was thinking about calling," I said.

"If you're going to ask about that corrupted computer data, don't," said Bug with more irritation in his voice than is usual for him. "We're working on it."

"Nope. This is something else." I told him about my most recent conversation with Nicodemus. "What, if anything, do you make of that?"

"Wow . . . that's kind of creepy that he's calling you now."

"Gives me the warm fuzzies."

"Must be nice to be popular."

"Not as much as you'd think. So . . . what was it you called about?"

"Huh? Oh, right. The painting."

"Church showed it to you?"

"As if. No, he had it taken upstairs and locked away. But Bunny took a cell picture of it and gave it to me on the down-low."

"Sweet," I said, wishing I'd thought of it.

"I ran image searches on both faces. The older one, the one that looks like the boss . . . that got nothing. No hits at all."

"Not even similar faces?"

"Similar, sure. We always get those," he said. "But none of them are the *same* face."

"But . . . ?"

"But nothing. Not really."

"C'mon, Bug, I know that tone."

He laughed. "Okay, remember I was telling you about how I did that comprehensive search for any image of Church online?"

"Sure."

"Well, the face in the older painting—the knight, I guess we can call it—didn't bring up that painting or that face, but it did get a bunch of hits for the artist. I'm about 99.9 percent certain it's an unknown painting by a famous Flemish painter named Jan van Eyck. Born in Maaseik, Belgium, in 1390, died in Bruges in 1441. He was known for his nearly photoreal paintings. Very famous cat then and now. Only about twenty of his paintings are still around. A bunch were lost to different wars or are in private collections."

"Was he known for painting Knights Templar?"

"Not at all. He was a teenager when the Templars were wiped out by the Church, so he wouldn't have been painting them anyway."

"Any thoughts on how he came to do this painting? Or who the subject might be? I mean, this *has* to be one of Church's ancestors. Or maybe Nicodemus hired someone to fake it."

"No idea. But that brings me to the other painting. The one of the guy wearing clothes from the late eighteenth century who kind of looks like George Washington."

"What about it?"

"That face, even messed up the way it is now, got a hit right away. And get this, it's one of several paintings of a guy who went by a whole bunch of different false names."

"Uh-oh . . ."

"Yeah. Gets crazier. Among the fake names are Marquess of Montferrat, Count Bellamarre, Knight Schoening, Count Weldon, Count Soltikoff, Manuel Doria, Graf Tzarogy, and a few others."

"Okay, what's weird about that? Apart from that guy doing what Church does and using a lot of fake names. I do it, too. We all have call signs and false identities."

"No, no, listen, Joe. Those other names aren't the reason I got freaked."

"Okay, hit me."

"The name he's most well known by is the Count of Saint Germain."

I don't think I even breathed for the next thirty air miles.

"That's what Lilith always calls Church," said Bug. "And, Joe . . . according to the history sites I went to, this Saint Germain guy always claimed that he was five hundred years old."

I said, "What in the wide blue fuck is going on? I mean, this clearly can't be what it looks like. And, more than ever I think Nicodemus is playing some kind of game. Though what *kind* of game is totally beyond me. You have any theories that'll make my nuts climb down out of my chest cavity?"

"No theories, but there's one more bomb I gotta drop, and you are really going to hate it."

"I already hate it and I haven't heard it yet. Not sure I want to."

"Trust me," said Bug. "You don't."

"Tell me anyway," I said, and braced for it.

"One of the stories this guy told people was that he was the son of Francis II Rákóczi, a Hungarian nobleman who—"

"—ruled as the Prince of Transylvania," I completed. "Jesus H. Cartwheeling Christ."

And that was the castle Church paid to have moved from Romania to Omfori Island.

"What are we into here, Joe?" asked Bug, and for once he sounded truly frightened.

"I . . . don't know," I confessed.

Which was a big goddamn understatement.

## INTERLUDE 18

### THE WARRIOR AND THE WAR
### KOLOSSI CASTLE, LIMASSOL, CYPRESS
### 1299 CE

They sat before a fire that had burned bright enough to light the entire room but was now dwindling to scattered flames, glowing embers, and black ash. The two men seated before the fire watched the blaze die.

"I'll try not to read a portent into that," grunted Jacques de Molay, the Grand Master of the Templars.

"It does appear to be a sign," said his companion, Sir John Temple. "I might have said 'a jest' but there's little humor to it."

They watched a log crumble into coals and sparks.

"We will not last," said de Molay. "You do understand that, yes?"

"Oh, hell, Jacques, I can read the writing on the wall as clearly as the next man," growled Sir John. "Especially when it's writ large as it is now. We have more enemies than friends."

"The loss of Acre is a wound from which we may never recover," mused de Molay.

"Sadly, I agree," said the Bastard Son. "We are not popular in Rome or much of anywhere else. Not these days."

"And yet the war goes on, my brother."

"The war is the war," agreed Sir John.

They smiled at one another as if this was a jest, yet each of them carried the weight of memories and fears. Their scars troubled them less than the scope of the war that seemed to tower around them.

"Perhaps we should have taken the offer to become a single order with the Hospitallers," said de Molay wearily. "The pope and the king both want that. And, in truth, it would simplify things and possibly give us the chance to rebuild and become relevant again."

The Bastard turned to study his friend's face. "You think that can ever happen?"

"The union of the orders . . . ?"

"No. Becoming relevant again." The Bastard shook his head. "Alas, I do not. Although we have had no formal declaration from the king, and only vague letters of displeasure from the Holy Father, the days when the Templar name *meant* something have passed. They see us as a threat, and resent their debts which we hold. Frankly, I'm surprised there has been no formal move against us."

De Molay said nothing. But after a moment's thought, he nodded.

The Bastard rubbed his tired eyes. "The Hospitallers have their Red Order and they have their Red Knights. Those . . . *monsters* . . . are privately viewed as the most potent weapon against the Mohammedans. *We* are considered, at best, to be pompous fools parading around in our red-crossed cloaks and robes, but in terms of the war . . . ? We are old news. We are yesterday and the Red Order may well be tomorrow."

"But they are not fighting *the* war, damn it," growled de Molay. "They have their absurd Holy Agreement, which the Church will not even publicly admit to, yet privately they invest the Scriptors with more power and more support."

"Which only proves my point, Jacques. The Knights Templar—despite all that we have accomplished, all the lives we've saved, all of the dirty little battles we've fought on the side of righteousness—are fading like a dream."

The Grand Master nodded, and if tears glittered in his eyes, neither of them commented on it. "A dream . . ." he whispered faintly.

"But the *war* goes on," insisted the Bastard.

"Does it really, John? We cannot even convince the king or the pope or any of the major houses that the Mohammedans are not—and never have been—our true enemy. The Crusades and the battles to retake the Holy Land were never the purpose."

Sir John waved a hand. "Yes, yes, I know, damn it. Our mission to protect pilgrims was never about tearing down another religion, however much it may differ from what we believe to be the one true faith. Proselytizing with sword and flame is not who we are. It never was. How many times have we *both* said it, that the war we fight has been raging since Cain killed Abel. Hell, Jacques, it's not even a proper *holy* war. It's more fundamental than that. It's good confronting evil."

"Yes, yes," said de Molay, "I've heard that speech a hundred times. I was in the room, if you recall, when you told your son the *full* truths about the war. I was surprised you could lure him away from his books, chemicals, star charts, and compounds long enough to pay heed. He's more scholar than soldier."

"As I have told you many times, Jacques, the boy is *not* a soldier. He had taken no vows, made no pledges except to me, as I have to him. He does not crave a knighthood, and frankly I doubt he would accept one. His studies in history and mathematics and alchemy are turning him into a wise man who understands the ways of this world. He sees things much as I do, and you know that I have never been in lockstep with my fellow Templars. They are true knights and I am what I am."

"Yes," said de Molay. "You explained the difference to the boy. What was the example you used? Something about holding a candle against the darkness."

"At the risk of being pedantic, my friend, that was not how I phrased it."

"Give me your words then, Le Fantôme."

"I told him that there are far more good people in this world," said the Bastard. "I told him that they are the ones we fight *for*. The good people of this world are not defined by the house of their birth, nor is their goodness guaranteed by the flag or throne to which they bow, or the place where they kneel to pray. Goodness is innate. Perhaps it can be learned—and there are many paths to redemption, not all of which follow holy doctrine. I have met people in far lands who have never heard of Jesus Christ and yet live lives that benefit those around them. People who believe that empathy is a power and kindness a kind of grace. It is *they* who hold the candles, Jacques. The people like you and me, some but not all of our brothers in the Order, know this. But there are also people of other allegiances, other faiths, other flags and lands who are the ones who stand inside the darkness, watching to see who is drawn to that light. We are the ones who stand apart and watch as the innocent are called to the protection and healing warmth of that light."

De Molay shook his head and offered a sad little smile.

"These are the people who matter," Sir John said after a moment's pause. "But they are so often unable to defend their beliefs, no matter how pure. For, when they raise candles against the darkness, that glow draws the eye and the ire of the very predators they fear. Their lights of hope are a beacon to the kind of people who sneer at compassion and benevolence. People who play at being honorable knights and servants of God, but who serve only their own hungers. Those people *revel* in that fact that the light shows them where to strike. But we who stand in the darkness use that same light to take aim at the predators. We fight in darkness with darkness."

"You make us sound like monsters, my friend," laughed de Molay, but his laughter was uneasy.

Sir John the Bastard leaned back in his chair and stared long and deep into the hellfire red of the glowing coals.

"After all that I have done in this war," he said slowly, "what else can I be but a monster?"

"And your son?"

"He is the bastard son of a bastard killer. He was born a monster and he has accepted the burden of life in the shadows."

Jacques de Molay looked at his friend. "That is perhaps the saddest thing I have ever heard."

The Bastard said nothing and they lapsed into silence.

## CHAPTER 36

### IN FLIGHT OVER THE IONIAN SEA

After that call with Bug I don't think I was even aware of the rest of the flight.

The Count of Saint Germain. The castle of Francis II Rákóczi, who ruled Transylvania.

Holy shit.

As my chopper flew on, I did my own Net search and found a lot of different paintings of Saint Germain, and they were definitely of the guy whose face was painted overtop the one that looked like Church's. I zoomed in on them, looking for commonalities between the count and Church, but there was absolutely nothing similar about them other than that they were white males.

So, why then was the face of the Count of Saint Germain painted over that of a knight painted centuries before by van Eyck? Why did Lilith always call Church Saint Germain?

I got so frustrated that I called Violin, Lilith's daughter and my ex-lover. She answered the way she always does: "Hello, Joseph."

"Hello, Violin. How are you feeling?"

Like me and a bunch of others, she had been badly injured during the last case. Unlike the rest of us, she healed with eerie speed. Even so, I could hear a whisper of pain in her tone.

"I am well," she said in the way she does when she doesn't want to talk about it. Then she said, "You sound stressed. What's wrong?"

I told her, and since she is well inside our RTI circle of trust, I gave her every single detail, going back to Nicodemus at the cemetery and all the way up to my conversation with Bug and subsequent Net searches. She listened without comment.

When I was done, she said, "What is it you are afraid of?"

"That's an odd question."

"It's not," she assured me.

"I'm not sure I'm afraid of anything. But I'm pretty damn sure I'm on a new level of uneasiness. This is all pretty damned weird, don't you think?"

"Given my life story, Joseph, not really."

"Then what's your opinion or reaction?"

"I think you need to be careful about falling into traps of doubt created by Nicodemus. Even if he is, as you say, ill, he is the most dangerous person I've ever known. More dangerous than you think he is."

"Okay, but what about this Saint Germain thing?"

"What about it?"

"Why does your mother always call Church by that name?"

"I . . . I actually don't know. She's always used that nickname for him."

"Haven't you ever asked her?"

Violin laughed. "Of course I have, and I got exactly the kind of answer you would expect."

"Which is no answer at all," I said.

"Yes."

"Will you do me a favor and ask again? But . . . don't tell her about my conversation with Bug. I don't want to get him in any trouble."

"Joseph . . . have you lost your faith in Mr. Church?"

I thought at first that it was an odd question, but then it sank in more.

"I'm not sure I'm ready to answer that question yet."

"When you come to a decision," she said, "let me know."

"Will you ask your mother?"

"I can promise to try."

And she ended the call without so much as a goodbye.

## INTERLUDE 19

### THE WARRIOR AND THE WAR
### THE BRANCH AND FIG TRAVELER'S INN
### PROVINS, FRANCE
### 1301 CE

The inn was large and old and smelled of a century of apple pies, fig jam, and roast fowl.

The young man traveled as John Temple the Younger, a name that meant nothing to most yet much to some. He had grown tall and strong, more so even than his father. The tavern wenches all gave him slant-eyed glances, but his reply was barely more than a small smile whose meaning he left for them to interpret as they chose.

For four days he stayed at the inn, keeping mostly to his rooms, walking in the forests of Lorraine, or sitting at a corner table with a stack of books and scrolls. He said little to anyone, though he was never rude or crass. Merely solitary.

One evening a couple of soldiers tried to bait him by laughing at his bookishness, but Young John let them laugh. He was wise enough to know that there were always people who found humor in mockery, but it cost him nothing to let them have their fun. The wiser travelers saw the breadth of his shoulders, the depth of his chest, and the cold intelligence in his eyes, and they kept to themselves.

It was on the fifth day, late in the afternoon, when two graybeards—weary and dusty from the road—came in and asked where John Temple could be found. The innkeeper nodded to the corner and promised to send wine and plates of hot food, but he did not usher them to that table. He had been a soldier himself once upon a time, and a very good one, and experience schooled him well in recognizing a true warrior when he saw one. And he had the tact of a good landlord when it came to respecting privacy.

The graybeards went over, bowing as they approached and introducing themselves as Joshua of Antioch, a revered scholar, and Magister Alighieri of the University of Naples Federico.

"Sit, gentlemen, please," said the young man, rising and returning the bow.

When they were settled with food and drink on the table, Joshua leaned forward a bit and spoke in a confidential tone. "Your father is a good man," he said, "and did a great act of kindness for the head of our order. Please convey our best respects to him and tell him that he is always included in our prayers."

Young John smiled. "My father is not a religious man. However, I think he will feel honored to be so fondly remembered."

The graybeards bowed again.

Alighieri looked right and left before he spoke. "Are you here, then, on his behalf?"

"In a way," said Young John. "My father is aware that I have come to meet two scholars, but he does not know why. However, I believe that you do."

Alighieri and Joshua shared a brief look.

"You are here to ask about the Grand Experiment."

"I am."

Joshua asked, "May we ask why?"

"Does it matter?"

"Yes," said Alighieri. "It does."

The young man sipped his wine. "If by that you wonder if I want it for myself, then no. Of course not."

Joshua smiled thinly. "Many have said that about immortality, sir, but I doubt any meant it with a whole heart."

"To be fair, sirs, my interest is more *along* those lines," said the young man. "I am very interested in those who *do* want it, and why."

"Why?" asked Alighieri. "Surely eternal life is the answer to all such questions."

"Is it, though? I, for one, would never want to live beyond my time. Immortality seems like a torment, a punishment. To live through countless years and see everyone I love wither and die? Thank you, but no."

"You could share it with whomever you choose."

"And yet, have you each partaken of it? No, I think not. Would you then condemn someone you love—wife, child, sibling—to a life without end? With no eternal rest waiting at the end of labors?" John Temple shook his head. "What grace is there in that? What purpose? Fear of the grave? Defiance of the natural order? Or an arrogance that views aging and death as unfair?"

Alighieri and Joshua shared another brief look.

The magister said, "So, again we ask . . . why do you want to find the elixir of life?"

"Because those with whom I am in conflict have desired to possess it."

The old men remained silent, their faces expectant.

Young John leaned back and studied them for a long, uncomfortable time before he spoke. "You've come all this way to meet me, and yet you are coy with your answers. What price, then, is required for you to tell me what I want to know?"

Magister Alighieri looked offended and was about to vent his outrage, but Joshua touched his arm. "Peace, brother," he said. Then he gave John Temple a searching, reappraising look. "Your question is either a trap or a test."

The young man shrugged. "Answer as you see fit."

"If you think we are here seeking gold, then you are mistaken, and we have all come a very long way for no good purpose."

"Give me a better answer, then, sir."

"We want the elixir destroyed," said Joshua.

"By God, so we do," growled Alighieri.

John sat there, idly tracing a circle using a drop of spilled wine on the wooden tabletop. "That is an interesting answer from two of the most respected alchemists alive."

"Alchemy is a search for truth and answers," insisted Joshua. "The transmutation of one substance into another is part of nature. The church itself supports that."

"And not because the church has a notorious hunger for gold?" asked the young man. "After all, statues of the saints do not gild themselves."

The two elders glared for a moment, but John Temple outlasted them, and as the open truth slowly pushed through their automatic defense of the Church, their eyes fell away.

"That," muttered Alighieri, "is a matter for another time."

"Agreed," conceded the young man. "And, speaking to your point about alchemy . . . I, myself, have made a study of that art. I do not pretend to a level of knowledge even remotely approaching yours, but I am aware of its potential and of its value. I do not mock the practice, but given the many disturbing rumors that have circulated around the search for what the ancients called the *philosopher's stone* . . ." He half-smiled. "A misleading name, since it is not a stone at all."

"Do you know what it is?"

"I prefer the word 'tincture,' since it is clear that the philosopher's stone refers—rather vaguely—to a collection of compounds that, when combined in the right way and in the correct amounts, can enable transmutation. Most of our colleagues in alchemy have sought it to support their labors to turn lead into gold. Though there are about three thousand years of searching by many very learned scholars for the way to use those same compounds to transmute mortal flesh into something that will be free of disease, heal from even the most mortal wounds, restore a feeble mind to clarity, and prolong life. That particular application is sometimes referred to as the *elixir vitae*, and that is, as I understand it, what the Red Order attempted to achieve."

"Without success," said Joshua.

"With questionable success," countered the young man. "But not with certain failure."

"The elixir they created drove whoever took it to madness."

"Most, yes," said John. "Not all. Or, as I understand it, while most of those who took this draught went mad, some of the people who were forced to take it as part of the grand experiment survived with their wits intact. My sources tell me that the Red Order ceased their investigations into the elixir when one of their Scriptors went insane and became vicious and uncontrollably violent. They felt that the risk was too great. Yet . . . since their Grand Experiment was set aside in favor of other strategies, the secrets—the records of the work accomplished to reach their version of the elixir—yet exist. Many have tried to find it."

"As you are yourself," said Joshua.

"As I am, yes," agreed John. "Though for different reasons. As I said, I have no personal interest in living forever."

Alighieri sniffed and nodded. "Extending human life so that it exceeds even the lives of the prophets in the Bible is unholy. Enoch, Methuselah, Abraham, Noah, Jared, and Adam all lived extended lives by the grace of God."

"Yes, as did many patriarchs before the flood," agreed Joshua. "But that is by God's grace and His will."

"And . . . ?" prompted the young man.

"Alchemy is a holy and noble pursuit," insisted Alighieri. "What the Ordo Ruber tried to do was the devil's work. And their *source* of the key essence of the elixir comes from the blood of demons."

"Demons, you say," echoed John Temple. "What can you tell me of them?"

"They are the bastard offspring of Satan," said Joshua, and both men crossed themselves.

John Temple looked amused. "If this is all sorcery and deviltry, then how came each of you—respected scholars whose patrons are devout—to participate in the Grand Experiment?"

Alighieri sniffed. "We were young."

"We were brought into it with lies," said Joshua. "We were told that the Experiment was sanctioned by His Holiness."

The young man nodded. "That is true, though. It is a matter of Church record."

"Because the pope himself was lied to," snapped Alighieri.

Young John let that go as not worth debating. "It is my understanding that the Red Order has abandoned the search for immortality. What then happened to the records of all this? False copies abound. I asked you here to tell me who has them now."

"Perhaps they have been destroyed."

"We both know that is not true. Scholars abhor destroying knowledge, especially that which was hard won. Those records exist, let us not debate that. Tell me who has possession of the elixir and the scholarship attached to it."

Joshua left it to his companion to answer.

"Horace Maxillan took possession of them," muttered Alighieri.

Young John nodded slowly. "Ah," he said. "Yes . . . I've heard the name. He was associated with Albertus Magnus, who, I believe, was consulted on this Grand Experiment but decided it was not for him. Wise choice. I had not heard that Maxillan received the materials. Of all the alchemists, why him?"

"They were offered to Magnus, of course, he being the most revered of our calling," said Joshua. "However, he refused the offer, decrying the whole process as deviltry. Maxillan was an apprentice and is, I believe, a cousin of some sort."

Alighieri said, "A reliable source said that Magnus gave them to Maxillan to hide away in a family crypt or some such. But Maxillan kept them and continued working to refine the elixir."

"That is my understanding as well," John said. "What I want to know is *where* Maxillan has been conducting this work. I believe you gentlemen know."

"Alas, young sir," said Joshua, "we do not."

"We have also looked for him," said Alighieri. "As God is our witness, this is the truth."

"Very well," said the son of the Bastard Knight. "If you find him, will you send word to me?"

"Only if you swear before God not to use the elixir for your own purposes."

"I so swear," said John, though he did not mention God. Even so, the two alchemists looked relieved and nodded. Then the young man added, "And let us all swear, the three of us here right now, that we will aid one another in the search for this elixir and the writings given by Magnus to Maxillan."

He allowed them time to think about it, and they each agreed. They spent the better part of the next three hours working out a method of coding their messages to one another.

When that was finished, John Temple leaned his forearms on the table and studied them with dark, intense eyes. "Thank you, gentlemen. We are brothers now. However . . . before we part ways, tell me all about these *demons*."

# CHAPTER 37

## SANCHEZ-O'TREE RESIDENCE
## CORFU, GREECE

Rudy stood waiting on the fringe of a big lawn, flanked by two of Ghost's offspring—El Santo and Blue Demon. They were nearly even genetic splits of my dog and the monstrous Irish wolfhound, Banshee, that had been gifted to Circe by Violin. Actually, the breeding made them look more like the wolves that wolfhounds used to hunt. Maybe one-fifty each, with extraordinary amber eyes, a thin veneer of puppyhood over predatory potential. As soon as they spotted Ghost, and he them, all three of them lost their damn minds. Tails wagging, happy barks, the bunch of them prancing around like idiots. Hard to believe sometimes that Ghost is a combat veteran and the two younger dogs are combat trained.

I got tackled and comprehensively licked and was then pillaged for the dried goat treats I had hidden in my pockets. When they each had a mouthful, they ran off to shady spots to devour their spoils. Rudy helped me to my feet.

"*¿Qué onda?*" he asked.

"Long-ass couple days," I said. "At least the hellhounds are happy to see me."

"You're an easy mark for those four-legged *bandidos*."

"All good. That's the kind of sneak attack I actually enjoy."

Then I glanced past him to where his wife, Circe, stood on the porch, arms folded tightly across her chest, lovely face cloudy with mixed emotions. Rudy caught my eye and patted me on the shoulder.

"We're *all* happy to see you, Cowboy."

I didn't reply to that as we began walking toward the house.

Years back, during the big *Sea of Hope* case, Circe had joined the DMS in their fight against the Seven Kings. Her full name is a mouthful—Circe Diana Ekklesia Magdalena O'Tree-Sanchez. And she is a staggeringly brilliant woman with a wallful of diplomas and licenses. Maybe not on the same preternatural level of genius as Doc Holliday, but smarter than your average carbon-based life form.

She is also one of the most beautiful women I've ever even heard of. She is average height but beyond that all other uses of the word "average" go right out the window. She has a heart-shaped face framed by intensely black hair that falls in wild curls to her shoulders. Full lips, high cheekbones, and a set of heart-stopping curves. If you ever saw *The Mummy* with Brendan Fraser, his love interest, the librarian played by Rachel Weisz, could have been Circe's sister. Same kind of beauty, with the same self-awareness. The brown of her eyes was so dark that the irises looked black, but those eyes sparkled with wit, insight, intelligence, and disapproval. The latter is usually aimed in my direction.

She and Rudy worked on the *Sea of Hope* thing together, and later on the Assassins Code case in Iran. They made a superb team and—with some help by Bug—decoded ancient texts that were crucial to our battle with the Red Order and the Red Knights. No one was surprised that they fell in love—though I suspect Rudy might have been shocked, since, despite his own good looks, he knew that in that regard he was punching way above his weight.

But here's the thing . . . working with the DMS has put Rudy in harm's way several times, and it got really dicey a few of those times. He lost an eye—since replaced with some fancy-ass gadget that looked real and even had a light sensor that kept pupillary expansion and contraction synced with his real eye. He's also had a knee replacement and other bits of damage. Somehow, Circe blames me for all that, despite the fact that he joined the DMS of his own free will and could retire anytime he wants. Also, I think Circe believes I'm deeper inside her father's circle of trust than I actually am. Rudy, who is therapist to the whole RTI staff, likely knows more about Church than anyone else.

Weird.

I've tried to bridge the gap between my best friend's wife and me, but that's a two-person job and it's been obvious I'm the only one pulling on an oar. I know that's a mixed metaphor, but I'm tired and sore and grumpy.

Before I was even close enough to say hello to Circe, two small missiles blew past her and slammed into me with the same degree of force and enthusiasm as the dogs.

One was a boy about five who had Rudy's tan face and smile but Circe's bone structure. He has as complicated a name as his mom—Albert Joseph Rodolfo O'Tree-Sanchez—but insists that everyone call him Big Al.

The other was a girl, Charlotte Olivia, who was barely able to walk, yet somehow she could run like a greyhound. Odd. She wasn't much for talking yet, but Big Al had given her a combat call sign, too. Or, at least, he kept trying to hang one on her. Circe and Rudy vetoed the last several choices, which included Poopy-Head, Turd-Munch, Stupid-Face, and—weirdly—Gertrude. None of us can figure out where that one came from.

I allowed myself to be tackled yet again, and there was some tickling, belly raspberries, and more pocket pillaging before Big Al pronounced that I was allowed to stay. Charlotte gave me a big smerpy kiss that missed my cheek and landed on one eyebrow and the bridge of my nose. Not a sharpshooter but makes up for it with enthusiasm.

When I looked past the kids to Circe, I saw that her expression had changed. Or maybe I'd read it wrong. The smile she wore was genuine and it was welcoming.

Also odd, but nice.

I got up, dusted myself off, peeled away the two clingy children—each of whom, I swear to Almighty Zeus, had ten hands and fifty fingers on each—then came up onto the porch, offering my hand to Circe. She surprised me by batting it lightly aside and giving me a hug. It was maybe the third time she'd hugged me since we met, and as we embraced, I caught Rudy's eyes and raised my eyebrows. He grinned and mouthed *Go with it.*

Which I did.

An older woman came out of the house and took charge of the little brigands. She was a hatchet-faced former Arklight field agent who had run some of the most brutal field ops in her day but she was now a combination nanny and bodyguard. I don't personally know anyone tough enough, brave enough, or stupid enough to make a run at those kids while Auntie Polina is in the vicinity. Even at seventy she scared the bejeezus out of me. Once, after first meeting her, Top Sims quietly remarked, "I ain't even Catholic but I found myself crossing myself. Twice. And afterward I kinda felt the need to go to church to make sure I'm still good with Baby Jesus."

Polina gave me a quiet up-and-down three-second appraisal, then punctuated it with a wordless nod. Then she, the kids, and Ghost's illegitimate offspring all vanished indoors while Rudy waved me toward a row of wooden rocking chairs. I sank gratefully into one, and for a while I sat there with Rudy and Circe and watched the clouds sail far out to sea.

Polina reappeared briefly with three cold bottles of beer. An Alpha for Circe. It was a beer with a lighter, subtler taste exclusively from Greek barley. Rudy got a locally brewed Corfu beer. And mine was a Vergina beer, a well-balanced pale lager from the Macedonian Thrace Brewery. The tops were off and the glass sweating. We clinked and took our first sips. The beer was cold, but not so cold that the temperature canceled out the taste. Superb for a lovely late afternoon on a Greek island.

We drank in silence for a while. A pair of hooded crows landed on the grass and began pecking where the kids tackled me, looking for tasty leavings.

"Rudy told me about what happened back in Maryland," said Circe after a while. Then she shivered. "Nicodemus." Circe spat the name.

"It was gobs of fun," I said. "He was as charming and helpful as ever. Pillar of our shared, global community."

"He had Sabbatarians with him?" she asked, eyes wide.

"Had, yes."

She thought about that, then nodded. "And then Dad sent you to Romania. Bet that was fun."

"So much fun. We laughed and laughed."

"I bet. Weaponized *Yersinia pestis*?" Circe shook her head. "People are mad. The lot of them. You know that, right? I mean the clinical diagnosis for the majority of the people we meet is bugfuck nuts."

I snorted. "If you're looking for an argument on that point, sister, you came to the wrong shop."

The "Dad" comment still throws me, even after all this time. Circe is, as far as any of us know, the only living blood relative of Mr. Church. His daughter. There's no part of me that can make that sit quietly in my head.

We watched the crows. There were five of them now. One, a scruffy old bird, stood apart and stared at us. Or, maybe, at me.

"This is going to sound weird . . ." I began, and Rudy laughed.

"Weird? Coming from you, Cowboy? The hell you say."

I ignored that and gestured to the bird. "Over the last couple of years, I swear that I've been seeing crows—big, old ones like that one over there—watching me. Crazy as it sounds, I sometimes think it's that exact one."

"Perhaps you should see a therapist," Rudy suggested.

We all laughed at that. But even while she was laughing, Circe gave me a strange look, though she did not make a comment. Overhead, the sky seemed filled with birds, many way up high coasting in the gentle thermal winds.

## INTERLUDE 20

### THE WARRIOR AND THE WAR
### TEMPLE HOUSE
### WINCHESTER, HAMPSHIRE, ENGLAND
### 1301 CE

A rider brought a coded message to a modest manor house in the forests of Hampshire, on the outskirts of Winchester. There was no formal designation as Temple House, nor did anyone in that neighborhood so call it, but within the family of the Templars, and to the smaller cabal Young John formed with the two old alchemists, that was its name.

Sir John was away, traveling in France with de Molay to meet with other members of the Brotherhood and, except for a handful of trusted servants, Young John was alone. He took the message, paid the rider, and then went up to his study, which occupied the whole of the top floor.

The study had a library filled with hundreds of volumes of books, some so ancient they were nothing but bound collections of scrolls. There were even clay tablets among the rest, and careful drawings of hieroglyphs from Egypt and Persia. Large wooden tables and comfortable chairs littered this room, and a fire was always kept burning. A dozen cats prowled around, growing fat on foolish mice and slow rats; and two Alaunt hounds had the run of the entire house.

Beyond the library was a large space crammed with more tables, more bookshelves, but also bins of chemicals, raw materials, compounds, and outré devices for astronomy, dissection, and the analysis of the unknown. Chemical experiments were always in some phase of development, and there were alembics for distillation, retorts and vials, bubbling sand baths and show globes filled with strange concoctions, mortars and pestles, crucibles and athanors.

John took the sealed message to his study, broke the seal, and spent a quarter hour decoding the message, which was written in a blend of ancient Greek, Latin, and Aramaic, with some alchemical symbols used in place of key words.

It read:

*To Our Brother in the War,*

*We have been following leads as to the whereabouts of Maxillan, but so far none of these have proven themselves reliable. We will, of course, continue with this mission.*

*However, we have made what we feel is a discovery of some importance. The rumors of Church support of the Red Order is now confirmed. There is a priest assigned to them who has the ear of the pope. His name is Nicodemus, though little else about him is known.*

*He has been the chief advisor to the Red Order since its inception from within the more extreme members of the Knights Hospitaller. We have come to believe that he was responsible for locating the creatures whose blood is the key ingredient in the elixir.*

*We have this from a priest—Father Andrew of Paris—who had worked with the Red Order but has since recanted and confessed his sins to a parish priest who is more aligned with our views than that of the Order. Father Andrew said that there has been a Father Nicodemus at the heart of the Red Order since it was created, and others of that same name involved with the LaRoques, the family from whom all of the Scriptors have been selected.*

*Father Andrew believed that all of the men known as Father Nicodemus are the same man, and that he is not a man at all but some manner of immortal trickster, much like Loki from Norse beliefs. I have my doubts as to whether that is true, but cannot disprove it, either.*

*Beware of Nicodemus, my young friend. He is powerful, devious, and subtle, and he has the ear of many powerful families as well as the confidence of the last few popes.*

*We are living in dangerous times. There are even rumors that this Father Nicodemus is so closely aligned with the Knights Hospitallers and is therefore set against the Templar Brotherhood. I fear that their rising power may pose a real and certain danger to the Templars. Please warn your father, and ask him to warn the Grand Master. And remind them that the Red Order has its own knights, and by that I mean the demons we hunt. Do not dare to underestimate their powers. Seek for means of protection beyond the sword and the shield.*

*May the Grace of God protect you and all of us who fight this war.*

*—Joshua of Antioch*

# CHAPTER 38

## SANCHEZ-O'TREE RESIDENCE
## CORFU, GREECE

"There's something I wanted to talk with you about," I said.

"To Rudy?" asked Circe. "I can go inside and—"

"No. Please stay. Actually, you're the one I really wanted to talk to, Circe, but . . ."

"But," she echoed, then smiled and shook her head. "Look, let's settle something before we go any further. Rudy and I have had a lot of talks lately. About you. About how we get along."

"Maybe *I* should go inside."

Circe reached over and placed one small, tan hand on my forearm. "No."

There was more that she wanted to say, but her struggle with it was obvious. Rudy came to her rescue. "The bottom line is that you are family with us, Cowboy," he said. "Those are Circe's words, not mine."

"I . . . don't know what to say. Thanks?"

"I'm just going to say this and leave it," Circe said. "You're not the reason Rudy has made some of the decisions he's made. You never wanted him to get hurt. You two love each other. You're brothers. Maybe I was a little jealous of all the years you had with him that I haven't. No, don't try and unpack that. Just leave it. But accept my apology for the time that's been wasted since. You *are* family, and you always will be."

I picked up her hand and kissed her knuckles. "That means more to me than I can say, you have no idea." My voice was thick and I drowned it with beer.

Circe's eyes looked wet and she busied herself with fetching fresh drinks for us.

We sat and sipped and watched the crows for a few minutes. Then I came back to what I'd begun to say. "Like I said, there's something I wanted to talk to *both* of you about."

I told them about the painting. I gave them all of it, down to the small scars on the face of the man in that painting. While I spoke, I watched their faces. Rudy looked surprised and confused, but not as much as I expected. However, Circe began nodding before I was done.

I stared at her. "What? You know about the painting?"

"That specific painting? No. How could I?"

"What then . . . ?"

"You remember that during the Assassins Code case, Rudy, Bug, and I managed to translate the Book of Shadows—what most people call the Voynich Manuscript?"

"I remember. That decryption was pretty much key to us getting ahead of the bad guys. Between the Book of Shadows and the other one—" I snapped my fingers a couple of times to coax the memory back. "The Saladin Codex. Yeah, between those two books there was pretty much a complete account—a confession, really—of all of the murderous acts perpetrated by the Red Order and their vampire goons. And about the Holy Agreement between the first Scriptor of the Red Order and the first Murshid of the Tariqa. All those crimes and deaths as a long game to keep polishing pews with the asses of the faithful."

Circe leaned slightly forward. "Did you ever actually *read* our translation?"

"All of it? No. Church shared the information with Interpol, the UN, and about a zillion other groups, and the Red Order assholes are either all in prison or dead. And we spanked the Red Knights pretty hard, too. Arklight's been hunting down the stragglers ever since." I paused, seeing the lights in her dark eyes. "Why?"

"It's worth reading," said Circe. "There's a lot more in there than the confessions of the holy crimes."

"Such as . . . ?"

"Such as the fact that the Knights Hospitaller—the service group from which the Red Order split off—had a long rivalry with the Knights Templar. The pope at the time tried to arbitrate a truce by asking that the two orders join into one. That never happened, mainly because the Templars—despite the propaganda spread by the Church—were never a bunch of Satan-worshipping pedophiles and criminals."

"It's interesting," Rudy interjected, "that there are always groups grasping for power who hurl unprovable accusations of child molestation and devil worship at their political enemies, knowing that the accusations can never be disproven because you can't prove a negative."

"And people wonder why I think all career politicians should be eaten by rats," I said.

Circe said, "My point is that the Templars, despite some individual flaws, were a more ethical group than the Hospitallers, particularly the splinter groups. Or at least a thousand times better than the Red Order."

"Tell him about the other book," suggested Rudy.

Circe nodded. "The Book of Shadows and the Saladin Codex are more or less the same story told from two different perspectives—the Christian Scriptors and the Muslim Tariqa—but Rudy's correct in that a third book is mentioned in both of those works. It's called the *Scriptor's Diary,* and is believed to contain secrets known only to the LaRoque family, as they have been the only Scriptors throughout history, with Charles LaRoque being the last. And he was killed by a Hellfire missile in Iran."

"Where is this *Scriptor's Diary*?" I asked.

"That's still a mystery, Joe," said Circe. "But it's useful to know about it so you can keep your eye out for it."

"Jeez, I didn't know this was going to come with homework." I sipped my beer. "What about the other thing, the *stregoni benefici* bit the Sabbatarian mentioned. Ever heard of that?"

"Of course," she said. "It's part of Church records, specifically in the histories of the Inquisition. But, like a lot of the so-called official reports by Inquisitor priests and monks, there's not much to it. My guess is that the whole idea of a reformed vampire was concocted to tie in with the post-resurrection redemption concept, establishing that even something as sinful and evil as a vampire could be accepted and redeemed by Christ. A nice marketing plan to sell redemption through efforts of faith, but it petered out pretty quickly and after the fourteenth century there's no mention of them at all."

"Are they mentioned in the Book of Shadows?"

"In passing only," she said. "As part of a list of supernatural beings supposedly conquered by the righteous. That's all. However, in more modern folklore from the last few centuries there's mention of them either under another name or in reference to a splinter group of Red Knights. The *Vampirii Lui Dumnezeu.*"

I picked my way through the translation. "Vampires of God . . . ?"

"Yes," said Rudy, smiling. "Think Angel and Spike from the TV show *Buffy the Vampire Slayer.* Or Nick Knight from that other nineties show, *Forever Knight.* Vampires who fight evil."

"Pop culture points for the Mexican headshrinker," I said, then shifted gears. "Why do you think Nicodemus would refer to your father as the Last Templar?"

"Not sure," she said. "The Templars were exterminated in 1314, so . . . Nicodemus is likely making a reference to Dad's career focus. Fighting the good fight and all."

"The war is the war," I quoted and she sighed.

"Okay, so, Book of Shadows," I said. "And . . . ?"

"And in the Book of Shadows there are many accounts of policies and practices of the Templars that the Red Order opposed. There was their own version of a shadow war, though one without any of the whitewashing provided by the Holy Agreement. This was a good guys versus bad guys thing, and it explains why the Hospitallers supported Pope Clement V when he destroyed the Templars. Denounced them, filed accusations of blasphemy and heresy, had their lands and holdings seized and had the leaders of the group, including the last Grand Master, Jacques de Molay, tortured and executed."

"I saw a movie about that," I said, but she ignored me.

"The Book of Shadows recounts dozens of violent conflicts between the Hospitallers and the Templars. And conflict between the Templars and the Red Knights."

"Must have been a lot of dead Templars after clashing with those fangy bastards."

"Not as many as you'd think."

"Oh . . . ?"

"Buckle up, Joe," she said with a wicked little smile.

## INTERLUDE 21

### THE WARRIOR AND THE WAR
### KOLOSSI CASTLE, LIMASSOL, CYPRESS
### 1302 CE

They came in the night.

They were of the night.

Four dark forms that moved without sound through the October shadows. They wore hooded cloaks over black clothing. No armor, no shields. Nor any insignia or ensign. The only color about them was the paleness of each face and the bloodred hue of their glaring eyes.

The two sentries posted by the coach road never saw them. They were aware only of the night coming alive around them and then they were gone, their throats torn away and their lives consumed.

The killers did not try to pick the locks on the main doors, nor did they pause at the walls, but simply scaled them with the ease of bats, crawling toward the moonlight with worm-white fingers tipped with stygian nails finding the smallest cracks and crevices to pull them upward. From the top of each wall, they simply jumped outward and down, landing and rolling and coming up onto their toes like acrobats. They hunted the grounds to find every patrolling soldier and each spiked-collared dog, ending them with icy efficiency. The sentries' hounds were dark-haired, and that was their doom. Had any of the dogs been white, the shadows would have fled.

Then the four killers scaled the walls of the blocky castle. The upper windows were covered by shutters and drapes, but neither was a true barrier to the things that came by night. The room they entered was one often used by Jacques de Molay when he was in Cypress, and as soon as the creatures were in the room they drew slender knives whose blades were painted a flat and unreflective black. However, here they stopped, for the wood in the fireplace was fresh, as if only set alight minutes ago. And the air was heavy with a cloying incense—frankincense and pine and cloves—that was oddly powerful for a bedroom at night.

"Do it quickly and let us be gone," hissed one of them. It was a man's voice, but guttural and strange, the speech muffled. "He sleeps. Let us feed quickly and end this. We can set the drapes alight as we go."

They crept toward the huge bed, in which a figure slept beneath a heap of furs. The four black blades rose and fell as one, tearing into the body over and over again. There was barely a sound. No cry of alarm or pain; no pleas to God for mercy or salvation.

"Hold, hold," cried the leader of the four, waving the others back. He tore at the furs, flinging them aside to reveal slashed and torn clothes filled with straw and rags. "What trickery is this?"

And a voice asked, "You come as thieves in the night and complain of deception?"

They whirled as a figure stepped out from behind a heavy oak table on which bowls of incense fumed. He was not dressed in the red-crossed doublet of the Templars, but instead wore wool trousers and a loose forest-green shirt. Like the intruders, he wore no armor and like them he held a naked blade. Two, in fact—a simple and unadorned broad-bladed sword in his right and a sturdy battlefield dagger in his left. There was nothing impressive about either weapon except in the way they were held—with the casual competence of the expert. Anyone who knew battle could see at a glance that this was no common soldier but a warrior who was fully confident in both his weapons and his skills.

Yet, as he stepped into the faint glow of the fire, it was evident that the man was no veteran of a dozen campaigns. He was a lad of perhaps eighteen summers. Tall, broad-shouldered, deep of chest, and very fit. He looked strong, but moved with a feline grace that was every bit as silent as the four killers he faced.

"Who is this?" sneered the leader of the assassins.

"Does it matter?" asked John Temple the Younger. "We are not met here to make friends."

The leader stepped forward, nearly within range of that sword. "Listen to me, boy," he said boldly. "Tell us in which chamber your master sleeps and we will grant you a quick and painless death."

"Say you so? My reward for betraying the head of my order is to die a traitor?" The young man laughed. "Les Chevaliers Rouges. Such a grandiose title for a pack of dogs. I hope your Red Order masters do not rely on you for arbitration. You lack finesse."

"And you lack wits," hissed the leader. "You had a chance to call for help, but now that time has passed and—"

There was a flash of silver fire and the leader's head seemed to leap upward, his eyes registering shock and even awareness at his own sudden death. Dark red blood shot to the ceiling as the corpse dropped first to its knees and then toppled sideways. The rainfall of his own blood pattered down around him, spattering the other three.

"A coward's blow!" cried one of the others.

"Say four assassins who creep like vermin through a nighttime window." Young John raised his weapons and set himself for combat. The three remaining assassins rushed him.

They were fast.

Hellish fast.

And they swung their swords with a level of strength out of all sanity. The young man did not even try to meet such blows with direct opposition, but instead parried them and even tapped the swinging blades to add more power to each attack. The result was that the first two blades swung at him struck sparks from the stone floor. The third was a lateral cut that should have cleaved the young man's head from his shoulders, but despite his bulk, the youth ducked the blow and struck out as he did so. He stabbed upward with the point of his dagger, piercing the biceps of the third killer; then jerked it free and smashed the steel disk of a pommel down with crushing force onto the man's instep. Bones collapsed beneath the blow, yet before the killer could even scream, the young man rammed up again, this time with his sword, the eighteen inches of polished steel punching through the soft palate and up through the roof of the mouth and deep into the evil brain.

Instead of trying to tear the sword free, he kicked the dead assassin in the stomach, propelling him backward against another of his kind. The sword, alas, was caught in bone and held by suction and the handle was torn from his hand.

That did not stop the defender, nor even slow him. Young John merely let go of the handle, pivoted, dove forward and slashed another killer across the face with his dagger. The villain tried to block it with his sword arm, but the angle was wrong and the tip of the dagger sliced him from cheek to cheek, cutting completely through the bridge of his nose. The killer howled in pain, and then the young man backhanded him and cut his throat all the way to the spinal column.

That left only one of the killers. Without the slightest hesitation, the young man ducked beneath a vicious thrust that nearly took him in the throat. He punched the flat of the enemy's sword upward—a move that even a knight wearing a steel gauntlet might not have attempted. The punch was true and raised the weapon above him, yet the killer's sword blade turned and cut deep across the fronts of the young man's four fingers. The scent of blood filled the air, battling with the incense.

The young man danced backward to avoid a whirling slash to his midsection. Even sucking in his gut was not enough and the tip of the remaining creature's sword drew a line of white-hot fire across his stomach. Yet this did not give the youth pause as he spun, catching the nearest bowl of incense, and hurled it at the killer's face.

The attacker laughed as he batted the bowl away, smashing it and sending the fuming contents everywhere. Some of the dust got into his face and he spat it out, still grinning.

"I will gut you for . . ." began the killer, but his words immediately disintegrated into a fit of terrible coughing. He staggered, folding forward at the waist, one hand going to his throat. "I—I—God—"

That was all he could manage to force out through a throat that was closing as surely as if a giant had him in a crushing grip. The killer staggered backward, stumbling, tripping, his sword falling from his hand. His knees buckled and he dropped onto them as he clawed at his throat.

John Temple the Younger stood his ground as he watched. He lowered his dagger and studied the face of the Red Knight as it choked to death. The incense—so strong and overpowering—hid the stink of the powdered garlic, and now the effect was there to be read. To be learned.

The Upierczy's face was bloated and dark and there was a mixture of astonishment, confusion, and desperation in his bulging eyes. There was even a note of pleading there.

In the eyes of the young man there was no reciprocal mercy. Nor was there hate or triumph. He watched this death with a scholar's eyes, noting everything, missing nothing.

The creature lay dead at his feet—as dead as the other three.

Yet John Temple stood still as a statue. Watching, seeing, understanding, and learning.

# CHAPTER 39

## UNDISCLOSED LOCATION
## ILFORD, ENGLAND

They were in a large cellar beneath a building tucked back in an industrial park. Rows of folding chairs were set facing a simple podium with a microphone. Behind the podium was a live feed of two locations in London—an office building and a hospital.

The man who stood behind the podium wore a business suit and looked affable and pleasant. He was neither.

"Most of the teams are in place already, and that all went like clockwork," he said. "Little round of applause for Tish Phelps and Geraint Lefèbvre who oversaw everything at the hospital."

The room erupted into thunder as a hundred pairs of hands hammered together in shared excitement. Many of them had been part of this since the very beginning, while others were new recruits from various private military groups around the world. Not all of them were white, but all of them were some kind of Christian. The only Muslims represented in that room were pictures tacked to the wall, and of these more than half had red X's drawn across their faces, marking successful eliminations.

The man at the podium patted the air to silence the ovation.

"I could not be prouder of all of you," he said, and his joy was evident on his beaming face. "This has been a labor of love as much as a mission of faith, and by this time tomorrow the face of the world will have changed. In a week the world will be shouting for war. And in a year, Islam will be a footnote in history."

The applause that followed this statement needed no prompting, and it went on and on and on.

# INTERLUDE 22

## THE WARRIOR AND THE WAR
## KOLOSSI CASTLE, LIMASSOL, CYPRESS
## 1302 CE

Young John stood there for nearly two minutes, and then the door banged open. Castle guards came in first, their faces red with fury and grief and bloodlust. When they saw the four bodies on the floor, they looked first in amazement and then studied the young man who had clearly been the author of the mayhem. Some looked away, jealous that they had not been the ones to avenge their comrades and protect the Grand Master; while others kept glancing around, certain that one youth without armor could not have done this kind of butchery. It would be remarkable against ordinary killers, but against the unnatural Red Knights? It left them stunned. That was simply not possible. Not three years ago two Red Knights had killed eleven Templars in a battle in Palestine.

"Stand aside," growled a voice and the soldiers turned to see the Bastard Knight and Lord de Molay himself. They parted like the Red Sea, allowing these two entrance to the bloody room.

De Molay had a sword in his hand and he went from corpse to corpse, prodding each knight with the tip of his blade. The Bastard moved with him, crouching to push back the lips of the dead men to reveal wicked and unnatural fangs. Every soldier in the room, and the Grand Master, all crossed themselves. After a moment, so did the Bastard.

The young man did not. He merely waited.

The Bastard strode over to him and plucked at the wounded hand, raising it to study the cut across the fingers. "This is nothing," he said gruffly. "It will heal. Now let me see your stomach."

"It is of no consequence, Father," protested the youth.

"Show me, damn it."

The young man sheathed his dagger and pulled his shirt up. The cut was deep and it bled freely.

"You'll need that sewn, boy," pronounced the Bastard. "And you'll need a healer. Some herbs or a poultice."

“See to it,” said Jacques de Molay as he came to join them. “But first, lad . . .”

He thrust his own sword into its scabbard, then knelt and picked up the unadorned sword and handed it to the Bastard’s son. When it had also been sheathed, the master of the Templars took the young man by both shoulders.

“You guessed this would happen,” he said. “You can see into their minds.”

“No, my lord, I cannot,” said the younger Temple. “I recently learned of these creatures—two alchemists with whom I met called them demons—but from their description I knew these were not true monsters. Or, at least, not supernatural.”

“What else would you call such *things*?”

“They are men,” said Young John. “Strange, warped, perhaps diseased, but they are clearly mortal. I spilled Holy Water on the windowsills, and it did nothing to stop them or even give them pause. If they were of Satan, then the Holy Water or the crosses mounted on the walls of every room in this house would have driven them hence, but that did not happen. No, my lord, these are men.”

“They are unlike any *men* I have ever seen.”

“Nor have I seen any like them, but I have traveled far, my lord. I have seen people in the deepest jungles of Africa who—even as adults—are less than half my height. And I have seen giants of better than seven feet tall. We have seen children born with humped backs and clubbed feet. In our own order there is a priest who is an albino with red eyes. None of them look like men as we tend to think, and yet all of them are. The world is vast and what being a *man* can take many forms.”

The Grand Master turned to Sir John. “Watch this one, John. Give him a chance and he will prove that angels are merely visitors from across the sea and not heaven’s sentinels.”

“My son tends to go his own way in thought as well as action.”

“My father taught me to know more than what I learned from my tutors,” said Young John.

Sir John raised his hands as if in surrender. “Guilty as charged.”

De Molay roared with laughter and clapped the lad on the shoulder.

“So,” continued the young man, his face serious, “the Red Order knows we oppose them. And I fear that my own investigations into their Grand Experiment may have alarmed them. An attack of some kind was inevitable, so I let it be known through discreet agents where I might be found. For eleven days we have set this trap to no effect. Now, several of our fellow Templars lie dead outside and these fiends have violated your very house. I have failed to anticipate all of the details, and am thus culpable for all that has happened."

"You saved my life, boy," said de Molay tersely. "I will be the judge of success or failure. And you slew four demons—or whatever they are—in doing so."

"They are not demons, my lord."

"Clearly the garlic worked . . ."

"Garlic is an herb, my lord," said the youth. "Our own gamekeeper here cannot abide onions or leeks. He nearly died three Christmas Eves ago when he ate the wrong dish. No, my lord, I think garlic is like that. Not a charm, but something they cannot physically endure."

De Molay shook his head in mild exasperation. This young man always had a practical explanation for everything. He was the least superstitious person the Grand Master had ever met and—he suspected—the young man was not as devout in spiritual areas as was common. On that subject, he remained silent, as he did with the Bastard's own agnosticism. A sin and a blasphemy, but de Molay knew the true hearts of father and son, and that was what mattered.

He gave the youth's muscular shoulders a squeeze, then released him.

"You have done God's work here tonight," he said, pitching it loud enough so all the soldiers—and the crowd now gathering in the hall—could hear. But far more quietly and privately he added, "And I wish you were my own blood kin. You and your father."

The youth smiled—a rare thing for him.

"Thank you, my lord."

De Molay studied him. "You are an unusual lad," he said. "No, I am unfair. You are a remarkable *man*. You are a warrior and, I think, you understand things about the world that most do not. Perhaps more than I do."

The youth shook his head. "If I may be so bold, my lord, let us understand each other. We understand that this war is *the* war. It is not God versus the devil. It is not the followers of Muhammad versus Christendom. It is not *us* versus *them.* It never has been, though we've let crosses and flags and thrones convince the common man otherwise. No, my lord, this is war between those *people,* singly or in groups, who want to use their hate to set alight the fields and farms, hearts and souls, of this world. And why? Not for faith or patriotism. No, my lord. They wage this war for power. Even the quest for money and riches is merely a pathway to power for them. It is about power and the desire to use it to control, to suppress, to own, to *have.*"

De Molay laughed and slapped his thigh, but then gestured for the lad to continue.

Young John bowed. His eyes were alight with passion. "My lord, we fight those people who respect no laws, yet they hide behind them. We fight those who do not truly believe in any celestial power, and yet who cloak themselves in holy raiment and polish their swords with pages torn from scripture. We fight those who know how this world is made and use that knowledge to hide behind laws and treaties and vows so that they can prey on whomever they choose because they believe that power gives them the right to do whatever they want to do. We fight those who know how to manipulate faith and trick the faithful and guide the hands of kings and priests. That is who we fight, and it is a war that has lasted as long as there have been men on God's green earth. It is a fight that will last until the sun burns cold and dark in the sky. It cannot be won, but it *must* be fought, for it is the only war that matters. This war is *the* war."

The older men stood staring at the young man. "You are your father's son," de Molay said. "And I am honored to call you both friends and kin of the heart."

Sir John's smile was, as it so often was these last few years, filled with sadness and love.

"The war is the war," he said as he laid a hand on his son's shoulder.

Then the last Grand Master of the Templars nodded gravely and said, "The war is the war."

# CHAPTER 40

## SANCHEZ-O'TREE RESIDENCE
## CORFU, GREECE

Circe said, "There were quite a few anecdotes in the book about attacks by Red Knights *on* Templars, and just as many detailing attacks made *by* the Templars on the Upierczy. Successful attacks, with a significant body count."

Rudy nodded. "It reads like a thriller novel in parts," he said. "I'll get you a copy of our translation."

"And while I find that pretty interesting," I said, "haven't we wandered pretty far away from the topic? We were talking about the freaking painting we found in Transylvania."

"We still are," said Circe. I began to ask, but she held up a hand. "In those accounts in the Book of Shadows, there are a whole bunch of anecdotes that refer to someone called '*Bastard Son*,' also known as The Nameless Man, The Ageless Man, The Warrior, *and* The Ghost."

"Whoa, whoa," I said. "Nicodemus said something about that. He called Church the bastard son of a Bastard Knight."

"He is likely trying to confuse you by weaving in facts as well as speculation and rumors," said Rudy. "He *does* that. Mind games would delight a person of his kind."

"All well and good, but what does that say about Church? That he's descended from a knight?"

"Possible," said Circe. "Even likely. The Bastard Knight and son are both mentioned in the Book of Shadows. No actual name ever given, though. My mother thought Dad was a direct descendant of someone involved with the Templars. Not with the main group, but a kind of splinter cell that fought against the Red Order."

"A secret society within the Templars?" I suggested. "Somewhere Dan Brown just got a woody."

"Idiot," said Circe, though she was smiling. "There are nine separate firsthand accounts by Red Order members who survived—or, more likely fled—when this person attacked. Here's one description that really caught my attention. Let me see if I can recite it as close to the book as possible." She closed her eyes. "*'He was a tall man. Deep of chest and broad of shoulder, who had the eyes of the devil. When he moved, it was with unnatural speed and power, even of grace. And even as he slaughtered our brothers and our knights, there was no sign of passion on his face. Not of anger or joy, not of holy or unholy delight in the carnage he wrought.'*" She opened her eyes and looked at me. "Ring any kind of bells?"

"Should it?"

"Don't be dense, Joe," she snapped. "Who does it *sound* like?"

Rudy said, "Tall, deep of chest and broad of shoulders. A deadly fighter who shows no emotion."

"Okay, look, I can see where you're going with this, but it's too much. We found a painting that looks like your dad with a newer painting of the Count of Saint Germain layered over it. Lilith always calls your dad 'Saint Germain.' You have to admit there's some weirdness going on." I held up a hand to stop them from interrupting. "Now, understand me here—I never said it *was* him. Either of those painted faces. Or even thought it *could* be him. I'm just confused by the resemblance in the older painting. Top thinks maybe it's one of your dad's ancestors."

"You mentioned unique scars," Rudy reminded me.

"Let's not forget that Nicodemus is likely turning dials behind the scenes," I said. "He taunted me with references to the plague. He's making crank calls that are clearly intended to turn dials on me so that I get all paranoid about who and what Church is. We know Nicodemus is working with the Sabbatarians right now and worked with the Red Order during the Iran case. Taking an old painting and hiring some art expert to touch it up to screw with my head isn't all that much of a stretch. But then you two come at me with a reference to someone called the Bastard Son or the Ghost or whatever. I mean, I know *I'm* crazy, but aren't you guys supposed to be the voices of reason?"

"Cowboy," said Rudy, "maybe you missed the part where Circe said there were a number of firsthand accounts. The descriptions are very similar in substance."

"Okay, so this Bastard Son got around. Wouldn't be the first time a powerful ancestor is represented genetically and through actions by descendants," I said. "Sure as hell not unusual for facial and other physical characteristics to be passed down. Hell, my nephew, Lefty—had he lived—would have been the spitting image of my grandfather, even down to the way he threw a knuckleball or slider. So, if this Bastard

Son was with the Templars and was that good of a fighter, then they likely used him in exactly the way that Church uses guys like me, Top, Bunny . . . we've kicked ass on all seven continents. And maybe that's why your dad fights this fight, this *war* . . . because it's part of a centuries-old family tradition. And I think we can agree that's a hell of a lot more likely than what you seem to be edging toward."

Circe shook her head. "I'd buy that if they were talking about one warrior in one window of time. But Joe . . . the descriptions of him in the Book of Shadows were written by eleven different Scriptors over a period of seven hundred years. The description of his methods, his physicality . . . they all match."

I stared at her for several long seconds, waiting for the curl of lip to tell me this was the joke it had to be. When Circe's face expression remained serious and fixed, I laughed.

"Oh, come *on* . . ."

"There are other things, too," Circe said. "Things my mom said. Things I overheard. Things Hugo told me."

"This is bullshit. It's . . ." And my words trailed off as something Nicodemus said to me at the cemetery came back with disturbing clarity. "Oh, shit . . ."

Circe said, "I read your after-action report about the incident with Nicodemus, Joe. I can make a really good guess what you just remembered."

I licked my lips, which had gone totally dry.

Nicodemus had said, *First off, I want to give you a message and ask that you deliver it to your master. To the* creature *you call Mr. Church. Stupid name. All full of a feeble attempt at irony. Mr. Church, Dr. Pope, the Sexton, the Deacon, John Temple, Andrew Cross . . . how many others? All in an attempt to put another coat of whitewash on who he really is. On* what *he really is. The bastard son of a Bastard Knight. But* I *know his truth. Yessiree Bob. I know who and—more to the point—*what *he is when no one else is around.*

"No," I said. "The reference to the bastard son of a bastard son pretty much *says* that he's a descendant of that Templar."

"Does it really?" she asked.

"And have you considered therapy?" I pointed to Rudy. "I can recommend a decent shrink."

"You're deflecting, Joe," she said.

When I looked at Rudy, I saw there was no help there. "This is totally nuts . . . you both know that, right?"

And they did not say a goddamned word.

On the grass, the old black crow opened its mouth to caw but made no sound at all.

## INTERLUDE 23

### THE WARRIOR AND THE WAR
### THE OAK AND RAM
### LONDON, ENGLAND
### SEPTEMBER 22, 1307 CE

The messenger found Young John after weeks of searching. The rider was dusty and travel-worn, and John took him to a corner of the tavern at the inn and had food and drink brought.

Once decoded, the message ran thus:

> *To My Brother in the War,*
>
> *I trust and pray this finds you safe, for there are many alarming rumors about King Philip of France conspiring with the pope to bring down the Knights Templar. I fear this is true, and urge you to give up this quest and retire somewhere. I pray that your father heeds this warning as well, for he is a good man. The support you have both shown us will never be forgotten.*
>
> *I have two bits of news, and alas the first is sad. Our brother, Alighieri, has been murdered. He was found in an alley, his throat torn out and the marks of the demons of the Red Order upon him. I have taken the precaution of going into hiding and will leave soon for a monastery in Ireland.*
>
> *The other news is promising. I have confirmed that Maxillan is in France, and am following his trail. Once I have confirmed his location I will send you a message. Until then, please be safe.*
>
> *May the Lord bless and keep you.*
>
> *—Joshua*

Young John read the message twice, then folded it and placed it in a hidden pocket inside his sleeve. When the messenger was finished with his meal, John handed him enough coins to pay for the meal and ensure his safe passage back to France.

When the man was gone, Young John rose and walked to the big fireplace in the inn, where he stopped and looked thoughtfully into the flames. He took the decoded message out once more and read it.

"Now," he said to himself, "is that not interesting."

Then he tossed the original and his translation into the flames and watched until both were utterly burned to ash.

# CHAPTER 41

## THE PINE BARRENS
## NEW JERSEY

He left his car in a ditch, engine running, door open.

He didn't care.

The road cut through a section of the Pine Barrens where few people ever bothered to go. Especially in March. By April, the first of the early-bird campers would be coming over from Philadelphia or down from New York to begin airing out their summer cabins and year-round RVs.

Nicodemus wasn't there for that.

Instead, he walked away from the car and into the deep woods. He did not care about ticks or snakes or wasps. Not then, nor at any time. Even those creatures sought elsewhere for cleaner food. He was never to their taste.

He took nothing with him except the clothes on his back and his cell phone. That was it. He'd even emptied his pockets in a small cedar-water stream, dropping coins and wallet and pistol into the brown depths. No one would ever find them because no one came to that part of the woods for a stroll.

He walked and walked until the road had vanished, taking with it the car and nearly all of his connections to the world. Except his phone. He kept that. There were still a few games he wanted to play before bedtime.

# INTERLUDE 24

## THE WARRIOR AND THE WAR

## FRIDAY, OCTOBER 13, 1307 CE

All across Christendom the word went out from Pope Clement V that the Knights Templar were heretics and blasphemers. The order for their arrest bore the papal seal, and soldier knights—many of them Hospitallers and secretly Ordo Ruber—carried out the arrests.

The captured Templars were handed over to Church Inquisitors, who tore confessions out of them with glowing irons, salt-caked whips, flaying knives, and worse horrors.

It was as if all of Christendom threw back its head and screamed in pain.

# CHAPTER 42

## BARRIER HEADQUARTERS
## HADRIAN TOWER
## ROPEMAKER STREET
## LONDON, ENGLAND

Scott Wilson sat in a chair, a blanket wrapped around his shoulders, and tried to convince everyone that he was perfectly fine.

"Just a touch of a bug," he said. "It's nothing. Please don't make a fuss."

Rockwell and MacPherson remained with him, with Cooper having run off to call for medical aid.

"We'll see about that once we have you looked at," said Rockwell. His smile was so tight that it looked carved out of wax. Scott saw that along with the concern for his well-being, there was doubt in Rockwell's eyes.

*Bloody clever way to apply for a job, you pillock,* he told himself.

"Really, I'm fine," he said.

Even as he protested, Scott began to wonder if he was, in fact, sick. Or, more truthfully, how sick he was. His head felt like it was trying to split apart, as if his brain had outgrown his skull and needed to be let out. The sweats he felt earlier were back, and despite feeling soaked he was also starting to get the chills. Rather intense chills.

"Well," said Rockwell in the kind of placatory tone used to encourage sick people and mentally deficient children, "let's just sit here until the EMTs have a chance to give you the once-over."

"They'll be here any moment," said MacPherson, who had a cell phone to her ear.

"This is all a lot of . . ." began Scott, but his words dissolved into a vicious fit of deep-chested coughs. They seemed pulled out of him, and each burst of coughing was so heavy that his throat felt abraded. He tried several times to calm his chest so he could finish what he was saying, but the coughing only got worse.

Much worse.

After one particularly long bout, Scott looked down at the pocket handkerchief he'd pressed to his mouth and was alarmed to see that it was speckled with blood. Very red, and in some quantity.

"I . . . I don't . . ."

Then he felt himself toppling forward, sliding from the chair and once more falling . . .

. . . falling . . .

. . . falling . . .

. . . into darkness.

## INTERLUDE 25

### THE WARRIOR AND THE WAR
### THE OAK AND RAM
### LONDON, ENGLAND
### OCTOBER 14, 1307 CE

Young John busied himself throwing some clothes and books into a bag because a coach waited downstairs to take him to the port. His father was staying at The Silver Shield Inn near Paris.

By now he would have heard of the decree sent from Rome to arrest all Templars. Without doubt his father would risk everything to find and protect Jacques de Molay, and John knew that any such plan would be suicide.

As he ran down the stairs to the front hall, he heard a knock at the door. A servant girl opened it to accept a message from a rider. She turned and saw her master and handed it to him.

John took the cloth envelope into the drawing room and sat in a chair by the dwindling fire. The seal was a familiar one, and he was both pleased and relieved to see that it was the one Joshua of Antioch used for their communications.

He tore it open and read the short note:

> *To My Brother in the War,*
>
> *I write in haste for my time is short. I have spied soldiers following me. I am hiding in a country inn. Even so, I fear that this will be my last letter. I have bribed the gamekeeper of this inn to carry this message away because I needed to get important news to you.*
>
> *I have found Maxillan! He is at Château l'Hernault outside of Paris. He has been there the whole time!*
>
> *May God Protect You.*
>
> *—Joshua*

# CHAPTER 43

## SANCHEZ-O'TREE RESIDENCE
## CORFU, GREECE

"Are you two going to sit there and tell me that you think Church is—what? An immortal warrior? An angel? Some kind of alien? What is it you want me to believe here? And before you answer, let's all remember that you are both scientists. Credentialed, lettered, rational."

Rudy looked embarrassed and uncomfortable. "That's not what we're saying."

We both glanced at Circe, who was staring out the window while her fingers tangled and untangled in her lap.

"The longer it takes for you to answer," I said, "the more I'm going to start looking for some aripiprazole."

We waited her out.

"I . . . I actually don't know what to think," Circe said at last. "This is something I've wrestled with since I was a kid. It's one of the things that drove my mother away."

"She thought he was a seven-hundred-year-old knight, too?"

Circe shook her head. "No. And, for the record, Joe, I don't actually think that."

"Then what?"

"That's just it, I don't know."

"It is entirely possible," said Rudy slowly, "even likely, that your father *is* a descendant of a Templar Knight, or—if Nicodemus is correct—the illegitimate song of a Templar, and that he has used that to play a role."

"What kind of role?" I asked. "You mean he wants people to think he's immortal?"

"Not sure if 'immortal' is the note he's going for, Joe, but unnatural in some way. Let's face it, he plays the part. He is unusually strong and fast, not just for his age but for any age."

"A life spent in martial arts can do that," I reminded him. "My sensei was in his late sixties and could whoop my ass while reading the Sunday paper. An understanding of physics and physiology can give someone the appearance of being stronger, faster, whatever. Hell, the Shaolin monks leaned into that so people would think they could do magic. It's part of their mystique. A lot of what they claim is chi is really a sophisticated and subtle understanding of basic physics. Mass displacement, leverage, and like that."

Both of them considered that and nodded.

"What about his physical appearance?" demanded Circe. "I'm going to be thirty-six in two months and my dad has looked exactly the same since I was a little girl."

"Ask Paul Rudd."

They both looked totally blank.

"God, how am I suddenly the pop culture expert in the mix? Paul Rudd? Guy who plays Ant-Man in the Marvel movies? He's close to sixty and looks the same as he did when he was in his late thirties. Some people have winning tickets in the genetics lottery, so maybe your dad's one of them."

"Maybe," said Circe, though her uncertainty was evident.

“Let’s face it,” I said, “it’s a hell of a lot more likely he has good genes than it is that he’s hundreds of years old.”

“I guess,” she said. “But what about the people who have known him for a long time? Aunt Sallie comes to mind.”

“I know. I even said as much to your dad earlier today.”

“What was his reaction?” asked Rudy.

“Irritation, but he’s often irritated with me. And before either of you make a crack about that, I know I’m a pain in the ass.”

“I would never say such a thing,” Rudy protested, then under his breath added, “Out loud.”

Circe got up and walked over to the window and stood there for a long moment, arms crossed tightly. Then she turned and leaned back against the glass.

“The easy and maybe *sane* answer is what Rudy said. Maybe Dad’s not immortal, and it does sound pretty silly even saying that out loud, but maybe he’s closer to being a magician. Not real magic, but an illusionist. He’s built the character of Mr. Church or the Deacon or whatever so that he can be a fixed point of calm in a crisis while also being the spotless champion of good works. It’s a good recruiting tool, especially for someone who may still *seem* like he hasn’t changed in years but knows privately that he’s lost more than a step getting to first base. So, he plays a role that’s a bit of Lancelot but without the emotional baggage, and a bigger chunk of King Arthur. Might for right and all of that Round Table mentality.”

“I’ve heard of people doing a lot worse with their lives than that.”

Her eyes flashed for a moment. “I never said he was a bad person,” she snapped. “Terrible father and husband, maybe. Questionable friend, despite all of his so-called *friends* in the industry.”

“I think he calls them friends because it provides a measure of comfort,” said Rudy. “We trust him because he is so demonstrably competent, and so we trust his *friends* because of their association with him.”

I nodded. “Sure. If someone like him trusts them then they—and whatever service they provide—are equally trustworthy. Pretty much understood that from the jump.”

“Yet it brings us no closer to the truth.”

"Maybe yes, maybe no," I said. "I think that sowing doubt about Church is high on Nicodemus's to-do list on any given day."

Circe came and sat down. She took a sip of her beer and studied the beads of sweat on the bottle. "What frustrates me most," she said, "is that my mother never knew his truth. *I* certainly don't. Which means my kids—his grandchildren—might never really know him."

We sat in the silence of that for a very long time. Rudy and I exchanged looks, but he'd probably already had that conversation with her fifty times and the fact that it came to this point told me that neither of them had been able to advance it a single step forward.

I stayed for dinner and played with the kids and the dogs, and then lingered while Circe put the kids down for the night. The three of us sat with cups of decaf, listening to the subtle voices of the night.

Before I left I went and stood briefly in the doorway of the big room the kids shared. I could smell the paint down the hall from the second bedroom they were preparing so each of the kids could have their own space. For now, though, they slept in their twin beds as little devices projected colorful images onto the ceiling. Swirling stars and spinning planets for Big Al and idly drifting tropical fish for Charlotte.

The two kids slept so deeply, so completely, that it was as if the world was a completely safe place and that everyone was kind and happy. An illusion? Maybe. It was the truth for both of those beautiful children, though, and that mattered to me.

They were why I fight. I am a monster so that they don't have to fear monsters.

I thought of Junie. We so wanted kids, but she couldn't. There was some talk about a new kind of surgery using a uterus grown in a lab from her own cells. The process was showing hopeful results, but it was more complicated than that. There had been so much damage inside her that any thoughts that science would catch up and make it all right seemed like the height of wishful thinking. Possibly delusional thinking.

The children slept.

I bowed my head and tried not to weep.

Then I went back to Phoenix House. Kind of surprised the chopper was able to lift off with the weight of all my doubts and fears and unanswered questions.

Halfway there, I got another goddamn call.

## INTERLUDE 26

### THE WARRIOR AND THE WAR
### THE SILVER SHIELD INN
### OUTSKIRTS OF PARIS
### OCTOBER 19, 1307 CE

Sir John Temple and his son sat in a quiet corner of the inn. Neither wore their red-crossed garments and were instead dressed as traveling merchants. Since they were polyglots, they conversed in Portuguese, which none of the others in the room were likely to know.

"The Grand Master arrested?" breathed Young John, who had come to the inn after weeks of traveling in England. This was the first time he had seen his father in more than a month, but there was no joy in it.

"Six days ago, aye," said his father. His face was wooden with strain and heartbreak. "Jacques was arrested at a funeral on the thirteenth of October. Many of our brothers were rounded up."

"On whose authority? Was this Philip of France? Was it the Red Order?"

"Worse," said the old knight. "This was done by papal decree."

The young man sighed. "Joshua warned us of this, but I did not think the corruption could rise so high."

"Ha," snorted Sir John. "Corruption knows no limits. You'd do well to remember that. Men are men. Even if they wear holy robes and live in cathedrals, they are men, and men are weak."

"Even so."

"The decree ordered all monarchs in Christendom to arrest every one of our brotherhood and confiscate all lands and holdings," explained Sir John. "There are already rumors of our brothers being beaten, tortured . . . It's happening in France, Iberia, Italy, England, Germany, and Cyprus. God, this is the end of us."

"We knew it was coming," observed his son after pushing down his emotions and giving it a minute's thought. "You said as much to the Grand Master. He even agreed that the writing was on the wall."

Sir John gave his son a bleak look. "And how does being right soften this blow? For I feel as if I have been stabbed through the heart."

"Where has de Molay been taken?"

"I do not know, though I have many eyes looking."

"And you still believe that you must try to free them? Or that such a thing is even possible?"

"By golden temptation or cold steel, I'll see them free," said the elder Temple, his eyes catching fire.

The young man did not argue. They had already half-come to blows over this on the ride to the inn, and his father was unshakable.

"Do not misunderstand my meaning when I ask, Father," said his son, changing tack, "but what of the fortune? I can guess that this will cancel all outstanding debts, and the monarchs of the countries where this is happening are among the biggest debtors. However, there are the banks—"

"Those assets have been seized."

"Surely de Molay took greater precautions?"

Sir John drained the wine from his glass and signaled for more. After the tavern maid brought another bottle, paused to give Young John a flirtatious smile, and left, the old knight said, "There are places where much has been stored."

"Do you know of these places?

"I do, for both Jacques and his right-hand man, Hugues de Pairud, held me in their circle of confidence."

John leaned forward. "How secure are they?"

"Quite secure," replied his father and gave him a conspiratorial wink.

The young man considered. "Is there enough to raise an army to fight back against this?"

Sir John laughed. "Enough? There is enough to buy heaven itself thrice over. Yet, to raise an army would mean going to war against the pope, and he has all of the monarchs under his control. None of them will risk excommunication. Not to save us. Too many of the lords we could otherwise count on owe us money, and I think they will err on the side of a clean slate."

"And our own holdings? The Brotherhood's, I mean."

"Much has already been promised to the Hospitallers."

"By that I take it that the Ordo Ruber will receive those estates," said Young John.

"Yes."

"And you, Father? What will you do? Granted, we have no estate beyond Temple House, and we have ever been careful to keep it apart from the Templar name. However, *your* name is known, as are your allegiances."

"No, I left my real name behind a long time ago, lad," said the knight. "The name John Temple was used mainly within our Brotherhood and not openly known, so I will continue it. If it becomes stained, then I will let it fall away like an autumn leaf." He reached out and laid a hard palm on his son's muscular forearm. "Do that as well. We are bastards, which means we *have* no family to protect us. There is only us. Your mother, bless her saintly soul, is fifteen years in her grave and you have yet to take a wife. When you do, take also a new name. Whenever you move, leave the name behind and take a new one where you arrive. The Church is as patient as it is relentless, and the Red Order even more so. They know we exist, though not the names under which we go. To our enemies I am the Bastard Knight and you are the Bastard Son. The Temple name was chosen out of love and loyalty to the brotherhood, but—like a broken shield—discard it if its protection fails."

"I will, Father."

"Mark me on this, my son. A name is nothing. The worth of a man—of any true heart—is in the actions taken. A name is a tool to be used and discarded when its use has passed. That has kept me safe for these many years. Be wise in this regard, and be ever wary."

"I swear it," said Young John. "However, I must risk a trip to Château l'Hernault, near Paris. Maxillan has been located."

His father looked appalled. "Even now, with all of this, you still hunt for that alchemist and that elixir? Let it be."

"I cannot, Father, and you know why."

"You have said that it is not for your own use, and you know that I would never take so much as a drop, not if it were to give me as little as a single day. Destroy it, lad. That is the only thing to do with such . . . such . . ."

"Blasphemy, Father? Are you getting religious in your old age?" Young John said it with a smile.

Sir John shook his head. "I am in no mood for jests, boy," he snapped. Then, a moment later, relented. "Forgive me. That was harsh and uncalled for. Only, please . . . consider what I've said."

"I always consider what you say," said the son.

They lapsed into a troubled silence then as the day turned to night and the empty bottles piled up. John Temple the Younger did not ask again if his father would try and rescue Jacques de Molay, for it was pointless to ask a question to which he already knew the answer.

# CHAPTER 44

## PHONE CALL

I knew who was calling as soon as my phone rang.

"What do you want?" I asked.

"Why, you sound as mad as a tick on a store mannequin," said Nicodemus. "Hope I didn't interrupt you in the middle of anything important."

"I'm organizing my sock drawer and you almost made me match brown with blue."

He chuckled softly.

"I'll ask once more and then I'm hanging up," I said. "What do you want?"

"Oh, you wouldn't begin to understand."

"I might," I said as I activated another call-trace. "Try me."

"In reply to your earlier question, Colonel Ledger," he said, "yes, I want to see the world burn. Burn, but not burn *down*."

"Why?"

"The fire keeps me warm."

"And that's a noble goal even though that same fire burns so many innocent people to ash?"

"I said you wouldn't understand."

"Maybe if you tried for once, just for the hell of it, to make plain sense . . ."

"It doesn't work like that," said Nicodemus, sounding almost sad. "It's like asking a physicist to clearly and completely explain quantum field theory in five words or less."

I sighed. "That's a bullshit answer. Personally, I think you're just petty, cruel, and a sociopath. Narcissistic, too."

"True enough," he said with a laugh. "But none of those things are relevant to our conversation."

"I'm still listening."

The meter on my cell screen told me the call signal was bouncing all over the globe. MindReader tried to insist that its most likely place of origin was in the exact center of the Etna volcano. Clearly he had a really good call relocation scrambler.

"Maybe," he said, "if you believed in—and more to the point, *understood*—reincarnation and karma you'd view the fate of all those burning people in a different light."

"Meaning what?"

"That's a topic for some other chat, unless you want that to be your question. Or did you forget my generous offer?"

In truth I actually had. Or maybe it's fairer to say that I hadn't really taken his offer seriously.

"Sure," I said. "I have a question. What's the intended use of the weaponized plague they were developing at Corvin Castle?"

He laughed. "Well, if you thought you'd trick me into revealing my elaborate evil master plan, then you're out of luck, my friend. While I know something about the new Black Death . . . or, maybe, Red Death is a better title, it is not *my* plan. I have surmises as to its use, but that would not be a fair answer to your question. Alas, you've asked the wrong person and that wastes your question. Such a pity."

"Maybe I'll be more specific when you call back," I said.

There was no answer. When I looked at the screen, the call had ended.

# INTERLUDE 27

## THE WARRIOR AND THE WAR
## TEMPLE HOUSE
## WINCHESTER, HAMPSHIRE, ENGLAND
## DECEMBER 8, 1313

The rider came by the dark of midnight to deliver a message from Joshua of Antioch. By now Young John could read the messages without the need for decoding. He read:

*To My Brother in the War,*

*I write in haste, for I have confirmed that the soldiers who I thought might be following me definitely are. I fear that the Red Order knows my name and is aware of my connection with the Templars who fight our war. I beseech you to keep me in your prayers.*

*There is now no longer a doubt that Father Nicodemus was behind the fall of the Brotherhood. It was he who sullied the minds of King Philip IV of France and Pope Clement V. His promises of wiping out their debts to the Templars was the lever he used. Once more the love of money proves itself to be the root of evil.*

*The pope will seek the penalty of death for Jacques de Molay. That is certain, though it may take time for him to win support from among the most senior cardinals. I believe this news may already have reached your father, and we both know how adamant he is with his desire to rescue the Grand Master. Please warn him that the Red Order is aware of this and may set a trap. It would be folly to try, and would likely end with your father's capture, torture, and execution. If he will listen, please beg him to stay clear. His heart is true, but such a rescue would meet with failure.*

*I must finish this and give it to the rider. I do not know if I will be able to communicate again. If I am taken, do not attempt to rescue me. If I am killed, waste not your life in revenge. The war, as we both know, is the war and must be fought. Live to fight.*

*But I include with this message a list of friends who are well placed within the Church, each of the kingdoms, and among unions of tradesmen and merchants. These are people I trust. Friends of mine who are therefore friends of our cause. They will help in any way that they may.*

*May God Protect you and May His Grace be your Shield and his Righteousness your Sword.*

*—Joshua*

John Temple sat back, feeling grief and weariness and fear. His heart told him that nothing he could do would restrain his father from the course on which he had set himself. Freeing de Molay obsessed him.

Would showing him the letter matter?

He hoped so, but doubted it.

And he thought of poor Joshua. Taking great risks to send that message even as assassins hounded him. Would he die in an alley as Alighieri had?

Then he looked at the list of Joshua's friends, and his eyebrows rose. There were more than two dozen names on the accompanying parchment, and each person was either highly or usefully placed.

"Friends," he said.

Outside his hounds howled at the deepening night.

## CHAPTER 45

### ST THOMAS' HOSPITAL
### WESTMINSTER BRIDGE ROAD
### LONDON, ENGLAND

Barrier director James Rockwell stood looking out of a window in the director of medicine's private office there at the hospital. Rockwell's hands were clasped so tightly behind his back that his fingers ached. The pain was useful, though, as it allowed him the discipline to keep his thoughts and feelings off his face. The reflection that looked back at him from the glass showed no emotion of any kind, and that was fine.

Inside, his mind was churning.

Cooper and MacPherson had each returned to their offices, Rockwell having said that there was nothing they could do. He'd expected a quicker answer to what was troubling Scott Wilson, but hours crawled past and whenever he checked, he was told the same thing.

"We are still conducting tests and should have something for you very soon."

Very soon came and went. Rockwell reviewed the event at headquarters. Wilson looked ghastly when the EMTs wheeled him off. His vitals were alarming, his skin flushed to an alarming red, and his eyes blank. By the time he was in the ambulance, Wilson was unable to speak. He was unconscious long before the ambulance arrived at St. Thomas.

Since then it was all a waiting game.

Rockwell listened inside his body, fooling himself several times that he was beginning to feel ill, too. Ever since his wife had been diagnosed with cancer, he had become super-vigilant to any kind of troubling symptoms in those around him. A kind of empathetic hypochondria.

There was a discreet tap-tap on the door and he turned to see Dr. Anwar Suliman, the chief medical officer whose office this was, come in. Rockwell saw the hard lines that only a few hours had etched onto the handsome brown face and guessed what the news was going to be.

"Tell me," he said without waiting.

The doctor told him.

Rockwell stared at him in silence for five full seconds.

"Dear God," he breathed.

## CHAPTER 46

### IN FLIGHT OVER THE IONIAN SEA

After the call with Nicodemus, I contacted the TOC and gave a full report. Bug told me that the trace dead-ended, but that was no surprise.

My chopper was still two hours out from Omfori Island, so I called Junie. It was ten to midnight where I was, but Philadelphia is seven hours behind, so it was late afternoon. I thought it would ring through, but she answered, sounding a bit breathless.

"Joe!" she cried, and in that one syllable I heard surprise, delight, and joy. It made my eyes burn with tears. And it immediately called to mind her wild blond hair and vibrant blue eyes, and that smile that could turn on all of my internal lights. "God, how are you? *Where* are you?"

"Had to go to work," I said.

"Hold on," she said, then, "Okay . . . scrambler's on."

Mine was, too, so I told her all of it. Every detail.

Junie is a scientist and closet conspiracy theory nut, but she is a superb listener. When I was finished, she didn't ask my opinions about Nicodemus or what happened at Corvin Castle. Not yet, anyway. First she asked how I was doing.

I told her how confused and distressed I was about everything, and she was glad I spent time with Rudy and with Circe. We talked about that for a while, then eased back into the discussion about Nicodemus.

"I'm having a hard time sussing out his game plan here," I admitted.

"What's the Cop think about all this?"

That was a key phrase. She is well acquainted with the committee I have in my head, and I guess she was hearing too much from the Modern Man and not enough from the insightful investigator who is my most reliable aspect.

"Well," I said, "he's clearly playing a game. It's the rules and goals that elude me."

"That's just it, Joe," she said. "He's not giving you anything concrete. And he's messing with your expectations. The thing at the cemetery . . . sending those Sabbatarians after you was clearly not intended as a hit. As awful as it sounds to say it, if he wanted you dead he could have arranged it more effectively."

"Yup. Hell, since he came up behind me before I noticed, he could have emptied a magazine into my back before I knew anything. He seems to have a way of not triggering Ghost's senses, too. Which is why I think the fur-monster is so afraid of him."

"He's right to be afraid of Nicodemus. Let's be real, babe, that maniac is the most dangerous person any of you have ever faced. And he keeps coming back."

"Yeah. And Church has been fighting against his schemes for a long time."

"About that," said Junie. "I've had some suspicions about Church ever since I met him."

"Feel free to share," I said. "Please."

"We don't know him, do we? I mean, sure, we know that he's a good guy fighting the good fight. He's proven that time and again. He's had so many opportunities to profit in different ways from the kinds of things the DMS and RTI have done, but he doesn't. Even when he took all that money away from the Seven Kings, Hugo Vox, and Vladimir Putin, he funneled it back into his war chest. He gave Toys and me so much seed money that FreeTech is now the most demonstrably effective humanitarian technology company on the planet. I also know that he channels a lot of money into environmental causes, animal rights, and more humanitarian charities than I can count. He could have bought a small—or even medium-sized—country and set himself up as king, but he never has."

"Even though he has a castle sitting atop a hollowed-out volcano?"

She laughed. "Even then."

"He has a cat, too. Sits and strokes it while contemplating his master plans."

"He's not Blofeld or Dr. Evil, Joe."

"I know."

"And, personally . . . I think the volcano base thing was him having a little fun with the people who follow him. Bug was over the moon when he found out about Omfori Island. Still is."

"And the castle?"

"God only knows," she said, "but when have you ever known Church to do something for no reason? Usually when he does something there are fifty overlapping reasons."

"Which he doesn't share."

"Why should he?"

It was a fair question. Everyone was allowed their own privacy, including or especially the privacy of their own thoughts and motivations.

"Which leaves the issue of the painting unresolved."

"You mean the face with the scars," she said. "The older one under the newer face. Yeah, that's a head-scratcher."

"You're the conspiracy theory expert, honey," I said. "You're saying you don't have a theory."

"Oh, I have plenty of theories, and I've been brooding on them for years now."

"Care to share?"

"And be laughed at? No thanks."

She wouldn't be drawn out and we drifted into other topics.

"Major Courtland," Junie said. "And you say she looks and even sounds like Grace?"

"Eerily similar."

A lot of romantic partners might have taken that moment to make a crack that would hint at jealousy or irritation or unease. Junie's not like that. What she said was, "That must be really painful. So many memories, good and bad. I'm sorry."

"Thanks, and . . . yes. It would be useful if we could just file that kind of stuff away where it can't be found."

"That would make you less of who you are, love," she said. "From what you've told me, your feelings for Grace were intense, and the way she was taken from you was so cruel."

"Yes."

"Feel your feelings, Joe," Junie said. "Maybe talk to Rudy about it, too, because if she's taking over for Scott, then you'll have to deal with her on a day-to-day basis. And, I'm always here for you. For anything you need or want to say."

She did not pursue the topic, but what she'd said was enough. It was what I needed to hear from the person I loved.

Out the window, I could see the lights of Phoenix House.

"Have to go, love," I said.

"When this is over, come home to me."

*Come home to me.*

She wasn't home, either, but that was the point. When Junie said those four words it punched a ray of good, clean sunlight through the cloud cover over the wasteland of my heart.

"I will," I promised.

Yeah, I know soldiers aren't supposed to make promises. Bad luck and all that. But the only rules that apply to what I have with Junie matter more than superstition or tradition. We never said *Goodbye.* Instead it was a gentle demand married to a hopeful request, and then my promise as an answer.

If there was anything that kept me sane, it was that.

## INTERLUDE 28

### THE WARRIOR AND THE WAR
### CHÂTEAU L'HERNAULT
### JANUARY 27, 1314

John Temple the Younger stood breathless and bleeding, the sword and dagger in his big hands dripping with blood. His face was bright with the flames that were quickly spreading all around him.

There were already five corpses on the floor. He had come all the way to the château to find one of those men, but he was dead before Young John scaled the wall and entered through a high window. The other four were Knights of the Red Order. Not, as he expected, Red Knights—a distinction he had only recently learned. The monsters were the Red Knights, while the Knights of the Red Order were mortal men. The similarity in name was clearly meant to sow confusion. The Upierczy were the more powerful and far harder to kill, but the fighters he faced in that château—though human—were all superb swordsmen trained in the Crusades and on countless battlefields. Killing them was no mean feat, and John was at the very edge of his strength.

Alas, there were five knights left, and the room in which they stood was burning.

Tables filled with potions and mixtures and distillations fumed and bubbled in their retorts. Many had already reached the bursting point, and the air in that room was a poisonous fog. He felt the toxins burning in his lungs and hoped he had not killed himself in this mission.

One of the knights, a lithe man named Sir Hugo who was known as a master duelist, held his longsword in one gloved hand and had a cloth pressed to his mouth against the fumes. Behind him, sitting on a table which had only now begun to burn, was a stack of books bound with red silk. Atop the books was a small crystal flask filled with strangely colored liquid, with traces of many shades of yellow, green, and brown that swirled together but—like oil and water—did not blend.

Sir Hugo's four men were clustered behind their leader, but at a word from him they began fanning out. Only the intense clutter of the alchemist's workroom kept them from easily circling the young man.

"I know you," said the knight. "You are the bastard son of the Bastard Knight. You're John Temple's whelp. Tell me, boy, who was your mother? I never could tell if she was an English whore or some French slut."

If the insult stung, it did not show on Young John's face. He looked calm, almost placid, despite his wounds and the sweat that coursed down his face.

"They say you aspire to be an alchemist, too," mocked the knight. "You? A pathetic piece of unwanted street trash whose father licks the balls of the Grand Master of the Templars. What a farce."

On cue, his knights laughed heartily but without real humor.

"Tell me, Sir Hugo," asked Young John calmly. "Did it really require nine of you to kill one old man? What slowed you? His age or the fact that he has but one leg?"

The truth was that Horace Maxillan, the old alchemist who lay sprawled between them, had clearly been tortured with enthusiasm and for a long time. His face and much of his torso had been neatly and carefully flayed. His fingernails were all torn out and laid in a neat row on the edge of the stack of books. His nose and ears and eyelids had been cut away and one eye hung out on a bloody cheek.

"Oh," said Sir Hugo, moving his cloth in order to spit on the dead man's face, "we were greatly entertained. He did not want to share his secrets, yet in the end he was more than willing to talk. He begged to tell us everything. I had to cut his throat just to shut him up."

"With eight men needed to hold him down? Such bravery. I'm sure your Scriptor will be so proud," said the young man. "Though how he will ever hear of it I cannot tell. Certainly a headless man cannot tell him of these brave exploits."

Sir Hugo's eyes flickered for a moment with confusion, and in that fraction of a second, John Temple moved. He threw his dagger sideways at a knight trying to get behind him, and the blade sank to the crosspiece in the man's heart. Before the deed was even completed, the young man darted left, pivoted, and delivered a lightning-fast backstroke with his sword. The look of confusion froze on Sir Hugo's face even as his head leapt into the air trailed by blood.

Then John Temple crouched, ducking under a sword slash as he chopped down through a third man's leg just above the knee. Even as the knight opened his mouth to scream, the young man kicked him in the groin, sending him crashing into a fourth knight. They went down in a frenzied ball of screams and blood.

The son of the Bastard Knight whirled to face the fifth man, a burly giant with a broad-bladed cleaver of a sword raised above his head. As the sword fell, John parried it and used his free hand to punch him in the eye, knocking him sideways off balance. Then John chased him with a rising slash that sheared through both wrists. The huge sword fell and the young man silenced the brute's screams with a deft thrust through the heart.

He turned again to see the fourth man disentangle himself from his crippled friend, but the timing was all wrong for the knight. He looked up as the edge of John Temple's sword blurred with silver fire, and then most of him fell one way and the top of his head the other. A last, quick thrust killed the legless man.

Then it was over.

John Temple had only paused to trade barbs with Sir Hugo long enough to catch his breath and regain a useful calm.

But the room was burning furiously now. Bottles exploded, showering him with stinging crystal shards. Many of them cut into his face and scalp, cutting deeply. The chemicals on them soaking into his blood. The air was unbreathable, and Young John staggered, his eyes nearly blind and his head swimming. He lurched toward the table with its stack of books and the flask, but the books were burning. The liquid in the flask itself swirled with those disparate colors which still refused to blend.

There was a moment of nearly fatal hesitation because of the poisons in the air. He reached for the books, but snatched his hands away as his gloves caught fire. He slapped at the flames, and then felt heat as his sleeves and trousers began to burn.

With a snarl of fury, he reached through the flames and snatched the bottle, then spun toward the window and hurled himself out into the night.

He landed badly, feeling bones break and muscles tear, but the lawn was a slope that sent him tumbling down to the muddy bank of a gurgling brook. Young John rolled into the water, having only enough presence of mind to hurl the flask onto the mud. The waters closed over him and he nearly passed out.

And, perhaps, did for a bit. No more than a minute, though. A fit of terrible coughing snapped him awake, and it took every ounce of what little strength he had to flop and splash onto the bank.

The flask was there. Still corked, still intact. How it had not exploded was beyond his dimming mind. That it didn't was as close to divine intervention as he would ever believe. He pulled it to him, gasping, bleeding, feeling all of the many hurts this night had bestowed.

John almost smashed that flask. He knew full well that he should. Yet something stayed his hand. Although he tried to convince himself that he wanted it for research only, that was a lie. His father was off on another wild attempt to rescue Jacques de Molay. Over the last few years he had tried five times to accomplish that impossible goal, and each time the elder Temple had returned home wounded. He was spilling his own blood and wasting what few years he had left in a fruitless quest.

Young John looked at the flask.

"For you, Father," he said, forcing himself to speak the truth.

It took a very long time for him to get to his feet. The pain was dreadful and he knew that he was badly hurt. The thought of climbing into the saddle and riding with so many burns and broken bones sounded like the Judgment of Hell.

Even so, he staggered brokenly through the shadows, away from the burning château.

# CHAPTER 47

## PHOENIX HOUSE
## OMFORI ISLAND, GREECE

"James," said Church as he answered the call. "I hope you're not giving Scott too hard a time over there."

"Listen to me, Deacon," said Rockwell. "Something's happened. Is this line secure?"

"It is. Tell me what's happening."

"I . . . I mean it's . . ." Rockwell started and stopped, and Church could hear him take a steadying breath. That alone was enough to put Church on high alert, because Rockwell was a very controlled man who was not prone to a case of the Victorian vapors.

"What is it?" he asked gently.

"It's Scott Wilson," said Rockwell. "He fell ill during our interview. I had him brought to St. Thomas and I'm here with Dr. Suliman, chief of medicine here. I'm putting this call on speaker. The room is secure. Just the two of us. I'd like the doctor to explain it to you."

"Very well," said Church neutrally. He braced himself for whatever was coming.

The next voice was very mildly accented—an Indian who had lived in England for a long time. Church thought he heard a Jodhpur flavor.

"For security reasons I was told not to ask for your name," said the doctor.

"Please proceed, Doctor. What has happened to Mr. Wilson?"

"The patient was brought in four hours ago. He was unresponsive when he arrived and has not regained consciousness. Prior to his collapse, he complained of a headache and was visibly sweating, flushed, and short of breath. He has a severe cough and X-rays show that he is developing pneumonia. His sputum is bloody and watery. His current temperature is 104.8 and we are going to pack him in ice and alcohol to try and bring that down."

"Is there a preliminary diagnosis?" asked Church. He stood in his office, gripping his cell phone so forcefully the plastic case creaked.

Suliman paused for a beat before answering. "We have done extensive bloodwork and have detected a severe bacterial infection. The blood culture test has, ah . . . yielded disturbing results. Has Mr. Wilson been in the Democratic Republic of Congo, Uganda, Tanzania, Zambia, Brazil, Peru, or the Southwest United States anytime over the last few weeks?"

"He has not."

"Not in Mongolia, Vietnam, Algeria . . . ?"

A chill swept through Church. "Mr. Wilson has not been anywhere outside of Greece in five months, Doctor. Tell me, why those specific countries?"

"They, ah, are where the most recent cases of this infection have been reported over the last few years. None, though, as aggressive as what we are seeing with Mr. Wilson."

"Doctor, please," said Church. "I understand a fair amount about medicine, so put a name to this, if you have one."

From that list of countries, though, Church already thought he knew what name the doctor would say. When he heard it, he hated that he was correct.

"Sir," said the doctor, "we have confirmed that the patient is experiencing a severe infection of *Yersinia pestis*. Do you know what that is?"

"I do," said Church. "Plague."

"Specifically in this case pneumonic plague, yes," said the doctor. "And it is by far the worst case of it I've ever heard of, let alone seen. And that is deeply troubling because Mr. Rockwell has informed me that the patient underwent a complete physical only yesterday. Chest X-ray, complete metabolic panel, bloodwork . . . all of it."

"And . . . ?"

"And there was no trace of *Yersinia pestis* in his sputum or blood twenty-four hours ago. Unless the labs who did his workup yesterday were grossly incompetent, then our Mr. Wilson has been infected by a strain of this bacteria that is far more rapid and aggressive than anything I've ever seen. More aggressive than anything nature could create. Do you . . . ah . . . do you understand what I am saying? Given the nature of where Mr. Rockwell works and what he says Mr. Wilson does for a living, I have to think that this was not a naturally occurring infection."

"No," said Church hollowly. He cleared his throat. "What is your prognosis?"

Dr. Suliman took a moment before answering that. "We need to knock that fever down. That is our most critical immediate goal. We are using streptomycin, but if that doesn't work, we'll try gentamicin, an antibiotic that has been effective as an alternative to that. If neither works, there are others we can try. Levofloxacin, moxifloxacin, ciprofloxacin, tetracycline, and chloramphenicol. Early antibiotic therapy is essential for treating any kind of plague. In addition to antibiotics, he is on oxygen, intravenous fluids, and is being given respiratory support." He paused. "Mr. Rockwell says that you are Mr. Wilson's friend as well as his employer."

"That is true."

"I am also told that you have considerable resources at your disposal. Access to medical records including those belonging to various—shall we say—clandestine military laboratories."

"If you have a question, Doctor, ask it. Let's waste no time with etiquette."

"Then I'll be blunt," said the doctor. "This strain of *Yersinia pestis* does not belong in nature. This has to have come from someone's lab. And if they developed it, then perhaps they have some idea of how to treat it. Isn't that how bioweapons research works? Invent a disease but coinvent a cure so that the weapon is not a danger to the home team? Am I correct?"

"Close enough," said Church. "If that information is available, I will move heaven and Earth to find it and get it to you."

Suliman sighed. "I would not spend too much time with that, sir. I really would not."

## CHAPTER 48

### PHOENIX HOUSE
### OMFORI ISLAND, GREECE

Ghost and I got off the chopper and headed inside, but immediately saw Church hurrying toward the door we'd just come through. The young Maasai warrior, Luke Merishi, was with him. Both of them were pulling suitcases. I moved to intercept them.

"Fleeing the jurisdiction?" I said, but the joke landed flat. Neither of them even slowed for me.

"Now isn't the time, Colonel," snapped Church. "We're wheels up in three minutes."

"Why? What's happening?" I demanded. "Has something come up? Is it Nicodemus or those Sabbatarian asshats?"

"It's Scott," said Church. "He's in London and he is very ill."

I hustled along with them and in a few clipped sentences, Church brought me up to speed. By the time we reached his helicopter, the blades were turning and my head was spinning.

"Plague . . . ?" I gasped. "But he wasn't exposed to the samples we brought back from Romania."

"No," said Church. "He was not."

He paused for a moment and turned to me.

"Scott was in good health yesterday. They did a full physical on him."

"But plague doesn't come on that quickly."

Church just looked at me.

I said, "Shit. How . . . how bad is Scott?"

"Bad," said a voice, and I turned to see the barrel-chested Dr. Ronald Coleman hurrying up, a duffel bag slung across his body and the handle of a wheeled metal equipment case clutched in one hand. Luke stepped up, took the case and the duffel as if they weighed nothing, and handed them up to the chopper's crew chief.

"Is this the same thing they were working on at Corvin Castle?" I asked.

"What else could it be?" asked Coleman. He gave me a crooked, awkward smile and climbed aboard.

Church lingered. "Listen to me, Colonel," he said. "With Scott ill and me heading to London, that leaves you in overall charge. I will be reachable as often as possible, but I need you to get things organized. Meet with Doc Holliday, Bug, and the other division chiefs and come up with an approach protocol for this. There may be crucial and useful information in the records you obtained. We're already frighteningly behind the curve. Catch us up."

Before I could even reply, he turned and climbed onto the helicopter. I walked backward through the rotor wash, hand over my eyes against the setting sun as I watched the bird rise into the air. It turned and shrieked away into the distance.

I stood there, feet braced but feeling as if the ground was crumbling beneath me.

# INTERLUDE 29

## THE WARRIOR AND THE WAR

**TEMPLE HOUSE**

**WINCHESTER, HAMPSHIRE, ENGLAND**

**FEBRUARY 9, 1314**

The Bastard Knight lay on his deathbed.

Jacques de Molay was condemned and would soon burn. Nothing Sir John had tried to do worked. It was a kind of cruel joke of fate that the Grand Master would outlive his old friend who tried so many times to rescue him. Cruelty seemed to rule the world. The Poor Fellow Soldiers of Christ and of the Temple of Solomon were no more. Many had been tortured to death. Others hanged or beheaded. Some were scattered, leaving behind their names, their lands, and their hope.

Sir John Temple lay on a small bed in his old manor house and his son sat with him. Both were in great pain, though Young John's many wounds were healing, albeit slowly. His father's wounds, he knew with the clarity of horror, were mortal.

"Father, please, I beg you," pleaded Young John. He held the flask of elixir close to the older man's lips.

"No, damn it," snapped Sir John. "Pour it out, for the love of all. It is devil's brew."

"You don't even believe in the devil, Father. Nor God. The elixir is life. It can save you. Heal you. Please!"

"My time is done," said the old knight wearily. "All of my friends—my brothers—are gone or soon will be. They wait for me beyond the door of shadows. It is right that I lay down my sword and shield and go with them."

"But we must fight on," protested his son. "Their forced confessions are being copied and nailed to every church door and tavern in Christendom. People will *believe* that the Templars were the monsters described because of the signatures upon them."

"Bah! Confessions are lies told to stop the pain," scoffed Sir John. "Only fools believe such lies. This is a tool of war that has toppled more kingdoms than swords ever will. Torture and coercion are the sharpest knives."

"So use the elixir to heal yourself. It will protect you even if you are taken."

"Enough," growled Sir John, though the effort tore a fit of coughing from him. Those coughs were too deep and too wet and the sound drove knives of fear into his son's heart. When the old knight was recovered enough, he said, "The Hospitallers and the Red Order have won this battle, my son. Let them believe that the secrets of the Templars—our truths and our fortune—die with Jacques de Molay. They will believe it. We have left some caches of gold for them to find, enough to convince them of their victory."

"Why reward murder, Father?"

"Because when the wicked think they have won, they often become complacent. They gloat and they count their gold and think that the world is theirs. Yet *you* will carry our truths onward. Through your life and the lives of your sons and the allies you will make along the way."

"Father, I . . ."

"No, listen. Time is short and I must say these things, and you must hear. Swear it."

"I swear."

Sir John patted his son's arm weakly. "Good lad. The strife between the Templars and our enemies will end, and in time perhaps we will be forgotten. Or history may remember us only as the lies told about us. I do not care. Glory and praise, even fairness in recollection, are meaningless to those of us called to fight this war."

Young John nodded, accepting this precept even though it hurt.

"But the treasure that we have hidden away is known to none but me. All the others who aided me in carrying out de Molay's last orders are dead. I have recorded it all on a piece of parchment and hidden it where I once hid your mother's jewelry. You know whereof I speak. That money is for this war, do you understand?"

"Of course, Father, but I—"

"Hush and listen. Our secret brotherhood of warriors is in ruins, yet it is not gone. That flame *must* endure. And even though I love you, my son, and despite the sins I have committed by drawing you into this war, I charge you with rising and standing firm against our many enemies. I also charge you with the task of finding others who, like us, are willing to take up any sword that fits the hand and use it to keep those safe who deserve mercy and who will find it nowhere else. Be the good man I know you to be. Be strong. Be steadfast. And fight this war for as long as you can."

The young man took his father's hand and held it.

"Please find the grace in your heart to forgive me for what I ask, my son," said Sir John weakly. The light that had always burned so brightly in his eyes was dimming, burned down to embers by the terrible wounds he had taken.

"You may ask anything of me, Father," swore the young man.

Sir John smiled and said, "The road ahead will be a lonely one, my son. As my own road has been lonely."

A little drop of blood appeared in the corner of his father's mouth and rolled down across his chin.

"Such as we," he whispered, "are truly bastards. We have no family name worth bearing. Change your own. Leave the false name of John Temple behind. It was never my name or yours, as we both know. Take whatever name you require, and use the fortune of the Templars to build your own army. It will not be large, because the bigger the army the more it becomes the target of hatred rather than a real threat to those who hate. They think they are safe in the shadows, but I tell you to move *through* those shadows. Hunt them in the dark. Be the serpent who bites, the scorpion who stings. Be silent and secretive and subtle. Be not merciful toward those who have no mercy in their hearts. When you find other warriors, look closely at them and be sure that they are *our* family. *Your* family now. Blood will not bind you, but there are things about each true warrior that will bind them to you, and you to them." He closed his eyes for a moment. "Stand, my boy. Stand and be true."

Another fit of coughing took him then, and all the spittle was a terrible and glistening red.

When he could speak, Sir John squeezed his son's hand, and the young man's heart broke as he felt how little strength was left in that once mighty grip. "My beloved son, can you forgive me for asking so much of you?"

"Father," cried Young John, his voice thick with unuttered sobs, "there is no need for my forgiveness. I have long ago accepted my part in this war. I will do whatever I can to stand and to fight, and for as long as I am able."

Sir John opened his eyes once more and looked up into the face of his son. "I . . . I do not know if there is a God, or if He has even a splinter of mercy for mankind. But there is something greater than us. There is magic and wonder and, most precious and powerful of all, there is hope. I love you, my son, my heart."

"I love you, Father."

The old man smiled. Faint, and small, and fading, yet it was a true smile.

"The war is the war, and it will rage as long as hate endures. It must be fought, no matter the cost, no matter . . ." he said, but the words trailed off as that last fragile spark of fire in his eyes flickered and went out. It darkened his eyes and darkened the world around his son. Still, his father died with that smile on his lips.

The young man kissed his father's slack hand and then pressed it to his own heart.

"The war is the war," he said, the words soft as shadows. "And I will fight it. Hear me, Father . . . I will stand and I will be true."

After a long while he placed his father's hands, one atop the other, over the deep chest and that noble, silent heart. Then the young man took a cloth and sponged away the blood.

When he stood, the wounds inside his body shrieked with agony. The broken ribs had knitted but still felt fragile. He still pissed blood, and sometimes he coughed it up as well. The powders and poultices he used every day helped, but there was such a long and uncertain road toward full vigor. He stood swaying and nausea swirled in his acidy stomach.

*The war is the war.*

It was almost as if his father had spoken those words again.

Young John looked at the small bottle of elixir he held. It was the last of the brew, and the secrets of how it was made were lost, perhaps forever. It had also boiled from the heat of the fire, and there was no way to know what that had done to the chemicals. Perhaps it was now powerful, or it could have become a far deadlier poison. And the toxic fumes he'd breathed in during that fight in the château still made him feel deeply unwell.

And yet . . .

"The war is the war," he said aloud. "I swear to you, my father, that I will do whatever I can to stand and to fight, and for as long as I am able."

He glanced down at the flask.

"For as long as I can . . ."

Then he raised the flask to his mouth and drank it.

## CHAPTER 49

### PHONE CALL

Another call from Nicodemus.

I almost didn't answer it because of what Church just told me. There were about a thousand things I needed to do. And, let's face it, Nicodemus was doing a workmanlike job of pissing me off, and I was halfway to believing that was his entire point with these reach-outs. But . . . if there was even a splinter of a chance that there was something useful in his comments, I had to play along.

"What?" I snapped.

"Hello to you, too, Colonel Ledger."

"Kiss my nutsack. Why are you calling?"

"Just feeling chatty. How are you and Mr. Church getting along lately?"

I wanted to punch something that would scream. Instead I applied what little self-control I possessed and demanded, "What *is* it with you and Church, for fuck's sake?"

"Which church? The institution or the monster?"

"Cute. Since you seem to have arrived on the short bus, I'll be specific. Why do you hate Mr. Church with such persistent intensity?"

"I never said I did."

"Dude, it's implied."

"How so?"

"You're always trying to kill him."

"Am I?"

"Aren't you?"

"My dear boy," said Nicodemus, "tell me, do you play chess?"

"That's off topic."

"Indulge me."

"Yes. I play chess."

"Are you any good at it?"

"I hold my own," I said.

"Is there someone with whom you play who challenges you? Someone who *presses* you?"

"Sure."

"Have you ever tried to kill that person?"

"Of course not."

"Well then," he said, "there you go."

And he hung up.

## CHAPTER 50

### BARRIER HEADQUARTERS
### HADRIAN TOWER
### ROPEMAKER STREET
### LONDON, ENGLAND

Barrier director James Rockwell sat in his office, chair turned to the window, and looked out over the City of London. That afternoon's rain had passed after scrubbing the skies clear and leaving them cloudless and blue. The skyscrapers and landmarks all gleamed as if lacquered, selling the illusion that all was clean, and bright, and correct.

He put his feet up on the sill and rested his teacup on his flat belly while he fielded an endless stream of calls from Number 10 Downing Street, every member of Parliament who wanted to get his or her name into the media, a rapid-response team from UKHSA—the UK Health Security Agency—countless public health offices, key players over at CBRN—the UK's Chemical, Biological, Radiological, and Nuclear group—and even the civilian group, REACT. Everyone wanted in, even though the situation was still in its infancy. Rockwell expected that kind of thing because there were a lot of elections coming up, and every politician and agency had to maintain the right public face because social media could make or break anyone and anything.

He was happy that there was a generous knock of brandy in the cup, and this was his third cup. Rockwell wasn't buzzed, but he could feel the faintest tingle at the corners of his eyes. He glanced over at his copy of the Dover Castle statue, and gave it a little nod.

After the craziness of Scott's collapse, the EMTs, the rush to the hospital, and his call to Mr. Church, and all those calls, the day should have felt spent. His own physical and emotional batteries should be tapped out.

And yet James Rockwell sat in his chair, ankles crossed, whisky warming his stomach. His door was closed and he was alone. Just him and the enormity of all that was happening.

# THE WARRIOR AND THE WAR
# PART 4

**"The greatest way to live with honor in this world is to be what we pretend to be."**

—SOCRATES

**"There is no act of treachery or meanness of which a political party is not capable; for in politics there is no honour."**

—BENJAMIN DISRAELI

# INTERLUDE 30

## THE WARRIOR AND THE WAR
## ILE AUX JAVIAUX
## PARIS, FRANCE
## MARCH 18, 1314 CE

The young warrior found himself amid a crowd of yelling, sneering, cursing, shouting people as the world caught fire.

Jacques de Molay, the 23rd Grand Master of the Knights Templar, a seasoned warrior, and a man of seventy years, was brought out in chains. The great man's body showed the scars of what had been done to him with lash, hot irons, blades, and fists. And yet, despite his age and the horrors committed upon his person, he walked with head upright. Even the chains and the occasional brutal blow did not humble him.

On the platform, the judge of the trial—a man deep in the pocket of Pope Clement V—read out the charges and then quoted liberally from the confession. With each line of that recitation the hounds and ghouls in the crowd hooted and screeched.

". . . did deny our Lord and Savior Jesus Christ . . ."

More jeers.

". . . did abuse the crucifix in a sacrilegious way . . ."

Rotten fruit and offal were hurled, and if some of it hit the guards bringing the condemned to the pyre, they did not rebuke the people.

". . . did commit unclean acts with other knights of their accursed order, and with children . . ."

Some small stones were thrown with expert accuracy, and one of these opened a fresh cut above de Molay's right eye.

". . . and is hereby condemned to burn in the purifying fires of righteousness so that . . ."

There was more, but John Temple the Younger listened with only half a mind. His main focus was on the man himself, trying to catch his eye. But de Molay was fighting to retain his dignity, which had been so cruelly stripped from him by the Inquisition.

The confession was all lies. The bastards in Rome knew it. King Philip knew it. Every whore's son in the Red Order knew it.

Perhaps even this crowd knew it, but they were a savage lot. The kind who thrived on the entertainment of misery, humiliation, and execution. John understood this as an abstraction, but it was so far away from his own heart and mind that it was like looking at a race of beings to which he owned no relationship.

So he stood and endured the spectacle, feeling each hard word, each thrown piece of dung, each peal of laughter chip a splinter off of his soul.

*And these are the people for whom we fight?*

That question filled his mind and he wrestled with it, for it would be so much easier to simply walk away. To abandon all hope of doing measurable good in this ugly world. To leave behind John Temple and become someone else. Perhaps travel to the East and lose himself among people who have never heard of this kind of thing. The pull on him to go and never come back was nearly overwhelming, for he already felt alone and adrift.

His father was dead. He had no other family. The Templars *were* his family, and now the last of them was being herded to the stake.

But then something happened that changed everything about the moment, the day, and his life.

When de Molay was bound to the stake, the priest overseeing the execution asked, quite mockingly, if the condemned had any last words. No one really expected so brutalized a man as de Molay to speak, or if he did, it would be to beg for mercy.

Instead, the last Grand Master of the Knights Templar stood straight and with a powerful voice spoke out with such force that it silenced the entire crowd. He spoke even as his bloodstained clothes began to burn.

With great dignity, he said, "It is just that, in so terrible a day, and in the last moments of my life, I should discover all the iniquity of falsehood, and make the truth triumph. I declare, then, in the face of heaven and earth, and acknowledge, though to my eternal shame, that I have committed the greatest crimes but it has been the acknowledging of those which have been so foully charged on the order. I attest—and truth obliges me to attest—that it is innocent! I made the contrary declaration only to suspend the excessive pains of torture, and to mollify those who made me endure them. I know the punishments which have been inflicted on all the knights who had the courage to revoke a similar confession; but the dreadful spectacle which is presented to me is not able to make me confirm one lie by another. The life offered me on such infamous terms I abandon without regret."

The crowd stood still. A few tried to jeer, but their words died in the air.

Then, de Molay pronounced a great curse upon King Philip of France and His Holiness Clement V. He called upon Christ to prove the innocence of the Templars by bringing judgment from God on their persecutors. "Pope Clement," he cried in a voice like thunder. "King Philip! Before a year, you will appear in the court of God to receive your righteous punishment! *Cursed! Cursed!* All cursed up to the thirteenth generation of your races. This I swear by Almighty God."

And then the flames enveloped him. The crowd only began to jeer once the fire stole the Templar's voice, and those of three others of the Brotherhood who burned with him.

Young John Temple stood there, hearing those words and that curse that echoed in his mind. And in them he found two things he believed lost. He rediscovered a sense of purpose and with it the sure knowledge that he would never abandon this war. He would fight on and on for as long as there was life left in his body.

And such life there was. The elixir was alive within him, burning him. Healing him. *Changing* him.

*"Righteous punishment,"* he said, though the roar of the crowd was such that no one heard him. "The war is the war."

With that, John Temple turned away from the horrors and vanished into the throng.

# CHAPTER 51

## PHOENIX HOUSE
## OMFORI ISLAND, GREECE

When the shit hits the fan, you don't just stand there and gawp. Nor do you let an annoying phone call from a notorious psychopath serve as the rudder for navigating troubled waters. You dial it to eleven and get your ass in gear.

Lots of mixed metaphors in there, but I was feeling stressed.

Church's helo vanished into the dark. I tapped my comms for the command channel, which put me in the ear of everyone in charge of a key division. The medical team, the computer division, logistics, field support, departmental administration, all of it.

"This is Colonel Ledger," I barked. "I want all stations to stop whatever you're doing and listen to me. This is a Class A emergency. All other concerns not related to this are rescinded. Acknowledge."

As I ran down the hall toward the elevator, they confirmed. Doc Holliday, Bug, and the rest. I punched the elevator button and gave them the news about Scott Wilson.

"The Big Man and Ron Coleman are heading to London," I said. "They need answers and we need to level up and make that happen. Bug—a lot of this is on you. I don't care what you have to do to salvage data from Romania, but do it. Take any other resources you need."

"Joe, I—"

"Don't talk—work."

*"Bang,"* he said and was gone.

"Doc, you have those samples from that lab. As soon as Church can arrange it he'll send samples back here from London. He'll set that up and it'll likely take a few hours. You need to be ready for them, and by the time they're in hand I want you to know every motherfucking thing about what Havoc brought back from the castle. Is that clear?"

In almost every other circumstance she'd have made a joke or some wildly inappropriate crack. Not this time. She said, "Count on it."

I gave more orders to different divisions and then tapped into the channel dedicated to field teams and ordered everyone who was in-house to meet me in the staging hall. This was a combination arsenal and training facility on one of the lower levels. By the time the elevator took me down, Top and the rest of Havoc were there waiting. Bedlam and Chaos Teams were away, but their team leaders—Major Mun Ji-Woo and Luis Salazar—were larger than life on big screens.

A third team leader's face filled another screen, and it was someone with whom I've had a kind of hate/somewhat less intense hate relationship for years. He was a thin, handsome young man with large eyes, a sensual mouth, and a nearly constant smirk that suggested he was privately laughing at a joke whose punchline he alone was slick enough to grasp. Alexander Chismer, known to everyone as Toys, and team leader for RTI's take on the Dirty Dozen—a bunch of former criminals of one stripe or another who were given a chance of personal redemption by Mr. Church. The team, known as the Wild Hunt, mostly did small espionage jobs by infiltrating their previous colleagues in the criminal underworld and international terrorist community. Lovely bunch. Useful in about the same way as toilet paper. You don't like to think about it but you don't want to be without it at key times.

I stood on a section of the matted training floor so everyone could see me.

"Give me your location and team status," I said without preamble. "And let me know how soon you could be wheels up if it comes to that."

Major Mun was one of South Korea's finest field agents who now worked for RTI. She had been injured in Germany during the last case, but she looked fit and ready to eat lead ingots and spit bullets. She said, "We're in Bangkok. We've been chasing down some of Kuga's former execs. We're close to putting a few of the top players in the bag."

"This is more important," I told her.

Mun's expression was a mix of skepticism and interest. "What is happening?"

"Team go-status first," I snapped.

"If we have to drop this case, we'll lose these guys. It'll take months to find them again."

"That's not what I asked, Major."

She nodded. "We can be at the airport in under two hours. Flight time is thirteen hours."

"Copy that. Stay on the job, but be ready. I'll have Bird Dog get in touch to finesse logistics. He can get you on a faster noncommercial plane. Count on it."

"Understood."

"Chaos, what's your ready status?"

Luis Salazar was medium height, fit, with a bald head and a dark goatee going prematurely white. His kind eyes and ready smile were a mask that dropped when things went south. Chaos and Havoc have rolled out together, and Salazar could dance the dance as well as anyone I know.

He said, "We're ready to roll now, Joe, but we're in São Paulo. If we head to the airport we can be in Heathrow in fourteen hours. Maybe a smidge less if Bird Dog can back our play."

"He will," I told him. "He'll be in touch before you get to the airport. But wait for the briefing. It'll be quick."

"Hooah," he said. Not everyone in the RTI field teams was a former Ranger like Top and me, but we'd started using "Hooah" as our company standard response for everything from "yes sir" to "fuck you," and now everyone uses it.

I turned to Toys's screen. "Where's the Hunt?"

"At the moment," he said, "I am in Cockermouth."

Even I had to take a beat on that. "Is that some kind of fucking joke?"

"Sadly, no. It is a market town in Cumbria, in the Lakes District."

"You're in England?"

"And unhappy about it, though we are making considerable headway with a dirty little matter Wilson sent us to sort out. Why? What's so important that you want us to—"

"Scott Wilson is in London," I cut in. "He's in intensive care and from the talk around the shop, he's right out there on the edge."

"Christ," gasped Toys. "Was he shot? If so, by who?"

"Being shot would be a best-case scenario," I said. "Scott has been infected with pneumonic plague."

They gaped at me as I told them all of it, starting with Nicodemus and the Sabbatarians. I didn't go into every detail, just the pertinent headlines.

"Is this a bioterrorism attack?" asked Mun. "Is this the Kuga or the Russians or—?"

"We don't know, but I can tell you right now that we have to find out. We have to get in front of this and stop it before this turns into another global pandemic."

Salazar shook his head. "Outlaw," he said, "I'm not sure why this is a panic situation. We've had plague cases in the little town where I grew up in South Dakota, but only in animals. Prairie dogs and rodents. Heard of cases out west, but I thought they just gave you some antibiotics and that was that."

"I don't think Nicodemus is lobbing sick prairie dogs around London," Toys said acidly.

"Even so . . ." said Salazar, though with no real emphasis.

I said, "I want you all on deck and stand ready if I need to put you in play, so—"

"Excuse me, Colonel," said Mun, "but to hell with that. I'm shutting my op down and heading to the airport right now."

"Yeah, me, too," said Salazar.

I glanced at Toys, and he nodded. "Oh, please, Ledger," he said with a wicked grin. "You're about to dive into what could easily be a new Black Death, and that means you're going to want to take scalps." His grin was deeply unpleasant. "And that you do *not* do without me and my lads. I'll see you in London."

He signed off—and then so did the others—and I turned to my guys. "Church told me to stay and run things here," I said.

"Well, pardon me if this is me speaking out of turn," said Top, "but fuck that noise."

"Yeah, boss," said Bunny. "We're ass deep in pencil-necks around here. Let one of them run the shop. I say we go find someone who needs to be hurt really, really bad and then exceed their expectations."

"Hooah," echoed Top. Even Ghost gave a single, definitive bark.

"Hoo-fucking-ah," I agreed, then shot a look at my dog. "And you, Mr. Fur-monster, are staying here. You'd look absurd in a ChemRig and, besides, you wouldn't be able to bite anything. Or anyone."

He looked unhappy.

The rest of us ran to get ready.

# INTERLUDE 31

## THE WARRIOR AND THE WAR
## ROQUEMAURE, GARD, FRANCE
## APRIL 20, 1314

The sky was dark with clouds and the damp wind threatened a great storm.

The Nameless Man stood in the shadows thrown by a monstrous old elm tree, his smoke-colored wool cloak pulled around him. His dark hair snapped in the breeze as he watched a wagon race toward the big house next to the church. Soldiers and knights were everywhere. Priests hurried in and out of the place. And the courtyard was crammed with people.

The air was ripe with tension, and the sound of prayers—whispered and cried aloud in a dozen languages—told the tale of fear, worry, and anticipated grief.

The pope was dying.

Few actually said that, but it was clear to the traveler that everyone thought it. They all feared it.

Except for him.

He watched the latest group of wise healers descend from the wagon and run into the house, pulled and pushed by priests and men-at-arms. One rumor openly whispered was that Pope Clement had swallowed a dish of powdered emeralds on the orders of one of France's wisest doctors.

The Nameless Man smiled at that.

The emeralds would do no good now, just as they would not for anyone no matter what their ailment. It was the rich man's version of a spurious folk remedy, with evidence in favor of its efficacy merely anecdotal, and actual proof nowhere to be found.

Not that it would matter.

The terrible pains the pontiff felt, the agonies that tore the screams from him, could not be cured. They were not cancer, as many insisted. There was no tumor, no disease to be fought.

Poison was a subtler art, and there were so few methods of detecting it. Arsenic was its base, but alchemy offered so many intriguing and useful additives. Some to disguise the poison, and others to greatly amplify the symptoms. No chance of dignity would be on offer, and the dying, though moderately quick, would be awful in every possible way.

The Nameless Man did not smile, nor did he gloat. This was not about personal satisfaction. Nor even precisely revenge.

This was justice.

He turned away and made his way through the growing throng to the small stable by a roadside inn. He ate a hearty meal that night and slept through eight untroubled hours.

The bells woke him, and he lay there, eyes open and staring upward at nothing as the tolling began its slow, mournful proclamation.

# CHAPTER 52

## COMPUTER SCIENCES DIVISION
## PHOENIX HOUSE
## OMFORI ISLAND, GREECE

His name was Jerome Taylor but no one ever called him that.

He had been nicknamed Bug when he was the smallest kid in first grade. The name took on new meaning when he discovered a passion for computers. The machines themselves—hardware, circuit boards, memory chips, all of it; and the software—reading, writing, hacking.

Even his mother had called him Bug. He never thought of the nickname as any kind of slight. He was a bug, and liked being a bug in the works.

When he was in high school, he had hacked into the school's computers to mess with the grades for himself, his friends, and—in a rare spiteful mood—those few kids who bullied him. He had barely graduated when he hacked the CIA with the goal of using their resources to track down Osama bin Laden.

Within twenty-four hours Major Grace Courtland and Sergeant Gus Dietrich showed up at his door. They took him to see Mr. Church, who offered him a deal with pretty simple terms—go to prison or come to work for the Department of Military Sciences. When Bug hesitated, Church gave him ten minutes to play with MindReader, the world's most powerful and sophisticated computer.

In those ten minutes, Bug hacked the White House and left a bunch of *Zits* cartoons in the online folder for the president's daily security briefing. Then he agreed to work for the Big Man.

Since then he actually *did* help locate bin Laden, painting a target on the terrorist chief for SEAL Team 6. He also rewrote and expanded much of MindReader's software, making it even more powerful and far more dangerous. And he constantly upgraded the whole MindReader system, eventually marrying it with the world's first fully functional quantum computer that he helped take away from the mad genius Zephyr Bain.

Now, MindReader Q1 was many times more powerful than the last system and much faster than anything else out there by an order of magnitude. His staff, all of whom he had identified and forwarded for hiring, were a collection of misfits and socially awkward geniuses who shared Bug's view that justice and humanism were more important than laws.

He also knew that Church trusted him completely, and was content in the knowledge that this trust was warranted. Though small, physically weak, and lacking any combat skills, he was one of the most dangerous people in the world. That would have been a burden to some, a temptation to many, but it was a comfort for him. It allowed him to do measurable good and to stay as anonymous as he chose.

In short, he was a very happy man with a career he loved.

Beneath the surface of that happiness, a fire burned. Although it never showed on his face, he had been cultivating a fiery hatred for the kinds of people who held to a warped worldview with such fervor that they were willing to do anything to see it come to pass. The kind of people who would spend millions to develop bleeding-edge technologies and then use them for crimes ranging from racial genocide to trying to bring about the actual apocalypse. The kind of people who would use bomb-carrying drones to target the families of their enemies.

As was done when Sebastian Gault sent such a device to kill Bug's mother.

He sat at his desk in an office crammed with terminals and screens and drives and a fridge stocked with Red Bull, Coke, and bottled espresso. His shelves were crammed with action figures from the Marvel films, with a bias toward the entire cast of the *Black Panther* films. The top-fidelity speakers mounted in the corners of the ceiling played bizarre playlists whose contents ranged from Wu-Tang Clan to Vivaldi to Mbaqanga. When people passed his office, they usually saw him grinning as he typed. Only those who knew him very well saw the heat in his eyes and the occasional tightness of that smile.

Now he worked on the material Joe Ledger, Top, and Bunny had recovered from Corvin Castle in Romania. There were maybe four people in the entire world who could do what he was doing with that fractured data. One of them worked for a Russian bot farm; two of them worked for Bug. And the fourth, the king of that peculiar species—*Homo sapiens computeris,* as Doc Holliday classified it—was Bug himself.

Someone was planning on releasing a weaponized and super-virulent strain of Black Plague. That Big Bad was working with Nicodemus, or maybe *was* Nicodemus. And their first salvo was to infect Scott Wilson. Not Bug's favorite person, but a member of his family. A member of the RTI family. A fellow warrior in Church's war, which was also Bug's war.

"No you don't, you fuck-knuckle," muttered Bug as he worked. "No you damn well don't."

And his fingers flew over the keys so quickly they were only a blur.

## INTERLUDE 32

### THE WARRIOR AND THE WAR

### ROYAL COUNTRY HOUSE OF FONTAINEBLEAU
### ÎLE-DE-FRANCE
### NOVEMBER 29, 1314

The Nameless Man stood amid a cluster of doctors and other learned men in a drawing room set aside for their use. He had arrived with several others, and his forged credentials were accepted more out of desperation than anything else. Doctors were arriving from every corner of France, and he was merely one of many.

All of them had a theory, with apoplexy being the most frequently forwarded and agreed upon. And that was well enough. Some held that the king was still in grief over the death of His Holiness Clement V—though anyone with an acute understanding of politics knew this to be nonsense. Clement was an ally out of financial need only, and never an actual friend. In fact the pope had spent a lot of effort trying to limit Philip's powers.

But, as the Nameless Man knew so well, there was a streak of sentimentality running rampant during death watches such as this. The year was a deadly one for many people in power. Jacques de Molay had burned. The pope died of a ruptured stomach. Many knights fell with the Templars, or died in pointless battles far away.

Now King Philip IV of France stood tottering on the ledge above the abyss.

Near where he stood, two doctors were explaining things to a court scribe who was tasked with recording every detail. The doctors had already covered the incident that brought the monarch low, describing how the king cried out in sudden pain while hunting in the Forest of Halatte a few weeks before, and grew steadily more ill.

"There are four humors that need to be kept in careful balance," said the elder of the two physicians. "Blood, phlegm, yellow bile, and black bile."

"Oh yes," agreed his companion, "and any imbalance in these fluids can cause a condition such as this. Which is why we are trying to rectify those humors."

"Good sirs," said the scribe, "how can this be done?"

"It is being *attempted*," said the elder, careful not to make promises, especially when every word was being written down. "We are trying all of the best methods appropriate for treating apoplexy."

"Indeed," said his companion. "Bloodletting and purges, of course. Special leeches have been applied."

"Cupping, too."

"Oh yes. And a close examination of the patient's urine tells us much."

"Urine?" echoed the scribe.

"Of course. The color, viscosity, and particulates in urine have much to say," said the younger doctor. "There are also many herbs and flowers whose essences . . ."

The Nameless Man moved away.

No one accosted him except for news, and he merely passed along whatever bits of nonsense he heard. Even if he was, for some reason, searched by the guards, they would find an excellent set of forged credentials and little else. The slender tube with its tiny darts had been discarded in the woods after that single use. It was a souvenir of his many wanderings before the fall of the Templars—a gift from a friend in Persia and relatively unknown in Europe. A breath arrow, the friend called it. So simple—a smooth-bore tube three feet in length, and darts carefully fletched and dipped in a blend of natural and alchemical poisons.

He left Fontainebleau and was many miles away before the bells began tolling.

# CHAPTER 53

## FREETECH NORTHEAST REGIONAL OFFICE
## PHILADELPHIA, PENNSYLVANIA

Junie Flynn wrapped the last meeting of the day, shook all of the important hands, thanked her staff, and took the elevator to her private apartment on the fortieth floor.

Once inside she kicked off her shoes, started the water running in the big, jetted tub, told the household AI, Calpurnia, to play Bach's Unaccompanied Cello Suites by Yo-Yo Ma, and built herself a very large and very dirty martini. Halfway through her second sip the phone rang. When she saw the display, Junie smiled.

"Hey, Rudy," she said. "This is a pleasant surprise."

"It's a Happy almost Birthday call."

"You're nineteen days early."

"Never too early to celebrate."

"Well . . . cheers. I'm drinking the world's largest martini."

"Then cheers for sure," he said. The call fidelity was excellent and it sounded like Rudy was standing there with her. She wished he was. Joe was her love, but Rudy was her brother. Closer than anyone to whom she was related by genetics.

Junie leaned against the window frame and looked out at the

Philadelphia skyline. The air was gray with clouds and smutch, but a few slanting beams of sunlight found their way through. Junie took that as a sign.

They talked about Circe, their kids, and Joe. They talked about dogs and life. It was an aimless conversation, and Junie didn't feel that Rudy was just being kind and reaching out because she was lonely. Rudy often called. He was like that.

"How's the big presentation going?" he said, gently shifting gears.

"Just spent five hours listening to my chief scientists read papers that I can almost recite word for word."

"How many times have you done this presentation?"

"This month or this year?"

"That bad, huh?"

Junie laughed, sipped, and said, "It's all good, really. The fact that we're filling every seat with an investor capable of looking past their own profit margins and charitable donation tax breaks to see actual benefits is a good thing. Ditto for politicians who at least *pretend* to care more about helping their constituents than angling for the best optics to secure votes."

"So young to be so cynical."

"Oh, bite me."

There was the high-pitched scream of children in full rampant delight. That made her smile, too. Then her smile became fragile. She wanted children very much, but was unable to have any. And the doctors trying to sell her on a lab-grown uterus using her own DNA and stem cells were swearing that it might work.

Might being a terrible little word.

"I saw Joe a couple of times recently," said Rudy. "In Maryland and then here in Corfu. He misses you terribly. But the job . . ."

"Yes," she said. "The job. Or maybe we should call it what Mr. Church calls it. The war."

"Yes," said Rudy.

They were silent for a while.

Then he said, "He won't always gallop out to fight dragons, you know. He will retire. He'll want to."

"Maybe he will," she said. "But I don't know if he wants to."

"He does, just . . ."

His words trailed off, but Junie picked it up. "Just that he knows right now he can't."

Rudy sighed.

"I hope," said Junie faintly, "that he decides to walk away from the war sometime soon. Walk away rather than be carried off on his shield."

"He will," said Rudy.

Junie sipped her martini and looked out at the jagged teeth of the city skyline.

"I pray that's true," she said.

# CHAPTER 54

### PHOENIX HOUSE
### OMFORI ISLAND, GREECE

We were packed and ready in record time.

We grabbed our gear and headed back up to the helipad when we heard the signature *bing-bong-bing* that signaled the arrival of a helicopter. The elevator doors opened and we stepped out in time to see a sleek black Bell 525 Relentless touch down lightly on pad 2, just in front of ours.

"New toy?" asked Remy, but I shook my head.

Even before the rotor whine began to ease down, the door slid back and a woman leaped lithely down to the deck. She was medium height, slender, with short dark hair, brown eyes with gold flecks, and an athletic figure that looked hard in the right places and soft in the right places. She wore a black nylon windbreaker over black fatigue pants. No sign of rank, either, but her bearing was officer level. She had a Sig Sauer .9 in a shoulder rig and the grips looked worn from hard use.

And the sight of her punched me right in the heart.

"Grace . . ."

I hadn't meant to say it. Sure as hell didn't want to say it. The name just came out. I felt as much as saw Top give me a sharp look.

The woman looked around with those brown eyes, saw me, and I saw one eyebrow go up. I knew this wasn't her, but everything about her was the same, even to that sardonic lift of the eyebrow. This was not Grace.

But God damn.

In the space of about a full second I felt such a tidal surge of complex emotions. The memory of loving Grace was still there, and it flooded through me like salt water, making every memory flash once more with pain. Grief was there, too. A lot of it. She had been my lover, but she had been also one of the finest tier one special operators anywhere. Her loss made the world less safe.

At the same time, Junie was there in my heart and mind. My love for her wasn't in question, even in that searing moment of memory. Junie was my life, my hope and heart. I loved her even more than I'd loved Grace, and she was adult enough to understand what I was feeling. That was a given.

And yet, in that single second of time, I was in the present but also back at the Warehouse, the old DMS headquarters in Baltimore, where I'd first met Grace. And we were in a crab-packing plant facing hordes of infected people who were driven to mindless cannibalistic murder. Then we were in the Liberty Bell Center in Philadelphia, trying to stop the *seif al din* plague. Suddenly we were on Dogfish Cay, hunting Berserkers and the Jakoby family. Which is where she saved the world but died doing it.

Died in my arms. That moment was forever seared in my mind . . .

*. . . "Grace," I said, pitching my voice sharply enough to wake her from the stupor of shock. "Grace, stay with me, babe . . . come on . . . stay with me."*

*She opened her eyes a little and licked her lips. "That's . . . Major . . . Babe . . ." she said with a smirk.*

*"Yes it is, honey, yes it is."*

*The pounding on the door was incessant.*

*"Joe . . . the laptop . . ."*

*It was on the desk and I pulled it close. There were two words in a little gray box.*

*Message sent.*

*"Grace . . . did Cyrus send the code?"*

*"I—don't . . ." Her voice disintegrated into a fit of coughing. Blood flecked her lips.*

*"Grace, honey, stay with me. Help's on the way."*

*I hoped to God that I wasn't lying to her. I could hear helicopters in the air now, which meant that help was arriving from outside the EMP blast zone. Soon hundreds of troops would be landing. But was it all for nothing?*

*"Joe," she whispered, "listen . . ." She reached up with a weak hand and gripped the front of my shirt, tried to pull me close. "Joe—if the . . . code . . . was sent . . . there's . . ."*

*She broke off into another fit of coughing. I used another strip of cloth from my shirt to dab the blood from her lips. I wanted to scream. I wanted to do anything to get out of this room, to get her to a medic.*

*". . . Joe . . . if the code was sent . . . there's still time."*

*"What do you mean, Grace? How can we stop it?"*

*"Cancel . . . code." More coughing, more blood. "Cyrus knows. If not . . . MindReader . . ."*

*The Berserkers were knocking plaster out of the wall. The whole room shook.*

*"Take the flash drive . . . to Bug . . . tell him." Her eyes drifted shut.*

*"Grace, come on . . . don't do this to me. Don't leave me . . ."*

*Her eyelids fluttered open. "I'll . . . never leave you . . ."*

*But she did.*

*Her eyes closed and she settled against me. Her head lolled forward and she died right there with her cheek pressed against mine. I screamed her name. I screamed and screamed until I tore blood from my own throat.*

*But all the screams in the world could not bring her back from the infinite sea of darkness in which she now swam. I could actually feel her leave. It was like a whisper against my lips. Her last breath, exhaled as I held her.*

*I pulled her against my chest and rocked her back and forth as one by one all of the lights that held back my personal darkness flickered and went out . . .*

"Colonel Ledger," she said, smiling as she strode forward, hand thrust toward me.

Funny, one of the reasons Church hired me was because I'm known for a lack of hesitation. But for one moment longer I was unable to do anything but stare.

Then Top made the smallest sound in his throat, barely heard above the decreasing rotor noise, and that snapped me back to the present. I used every ounce of strength I possessed to hoist a smile onto my face as I stepped up to take her hand.

"Major Courtland," I said. "Welcome to the DMS."

She blinked once and that eyebrow arched again. "Don't you mean RTI?"

"Shit. Yes. Sorry."

We shook hands, but she didn't release mine right away. "I know I'm not her," she said, looking at me, then at Top and Bunny. Then let my hand go and shook everyone else's.

"Pleasure," said Top.

"Is it?" she mused. "Look, I know that you three in particular worked with my cousin. I've read the reports and Mr. Church has given me a pretty comprehensive background on things. I'm also aware of how much Grace and I look alike. Not twins, not even sisters, but I see the shadow of her sometimes when I look in my own mirror. It's freaky. We all know it. So, I think we should be up front about it. This is going to be strange for a while."

"As understatements go," said Bunny, "that takes the cake."

"But," said Claire Courtland, "I'm not her."

"No," I said softly.

"I can see from your faces that she never even mentioned me. That's fine. We'd drifted after her son died. I . . . take it you know about that?"

"Yes . . . the baby was born with a hole in his heart," I said. My voice sounded weirdly wooden.

"I never even got to meet the lad," said Claire.

The rotor noise faded out, leaving a fragile silence.

She looked at each of us with those too-familiar stranger's eyes. "As I said, I'm not her. Looks, name, and rank aside, I am my own person. I'm not her, and I have no intention of ever trying to live up to her reputation. There will be only one Grace Courtland, and she is remembered as a hero. A true hero. Bloody hell, she saved the world. I'm never going to do that. But what I can do is help RTI do its job with as much speed and efficiency as possible, that I promise."

I took a breath and let it steady me. "Since we're laying facts on the table, let me say this. Grace was more than a colleague. You probably know that she and I had a thing. A relationship. We *mattered* to one another. Seeing you right now—especially now as things are quickly going to shit—is a kick in the balls that I don't need. No . . . let me finish. That's my stuff to sort out. Grace has been dead a long time and the world has changed. Me tripping over myself just now is the one and only hiccup. You're the new chief of operations. You're *Claire* Courtland and you're Church's second-in-command. Your predecessor is dying in a London hospital and we are heading there to try and make sense of what's happening and do whatever we have to do to stop it. Anything else will be sorted out by us focusing on the job. Sound good?"

"It does," she said.

And it sounded good to me, too, even though some of it was bullshit and a lot of it was going to take a while to process. Right then I did not have the time to go somewhere quiet and call Junie and Rudy. So, I crammed all of this weirdness down into its box and signaled our pilot to spin up the helo that would take us to the mainland.

Major Courtland nodded and stepped aside. "Good hunting, then," she said.

## INTERLUDE 33

**THE GRAND EXPERIMENT**
**LAROQUE ESTATE**
**VILLAGE OF MONTAILLOU, FRANCE**
**DECEMBER 31, 1314**

The Nameless Man stood in the great hall with a sword in one hand and a torch in the other.

The dead lay all around him.

A dozen knights of the Ordo Ruber.

Five of the Les Chevaliers Rouges.

And the Scriptor.

Sir Louis LaRoque had not died well. The dying itself had been punctuated with screams and cries for mercy. The Scriptor was the last to die, and by the time the Nameless Man came for him, Sir Louis huddled in a corner, seated in a pool of his own piss. The air stank of shit and blood and fear.

He had begged and wept, clinging to the boots of the Nameless Man. Kissing them. Promising gold and titles and estates in exchange for life.

Killing him had not given the young warrior any pleasure. It was a task to be undertaken, a thing that needed doing. And so his sword rose and fell. One single stroke, despite the temptation to hack the man to unidentifiable pieces.

Murder was best accomplished with efficiency, though. And the son of the Bastard Knight was a practical man. He felt the urges, the hatred, the bloodlust, but he did not allow them to dictate how he conducted his war.

Now everyone in the place was dead.

"It will do you no good," said a voice, and the Nameless Man whirled, holding the torch to one side and raising his blade.

A man stood in the doorway. Small, slender, wizened, and dressed in the cassock of a priest. There were no guards with him. He stood alone and unprotected, and yet he smiled. It was a ratlike grin of red delight.

The young man nodded soberly. "I know who you are," he said.

"Oh, do you now?" The priest took a few steps forward, though he stopped well beyond striking range.

"I know your name."

The priest's dark eyes sparkled with amusement. "And I know yours."

"I doubt that is true," said the young man.

"You are John Temple the Younger, son of the Bastard Knight," said the priest.

The Nameless Man shook his head and smiled. "No," he said mildly, "that is not my name. It never was. Nor was it ever my father's."

The old priest looked only mildly disappointed. "Then what makes you think that you know *my* name?"

"You are the one called Father Nicodemus," said the young fighter.

"Are you so sure that is my true name?"

"I don't particularly care. Priests take names from the Bible."

"That was also my father's name," said the priest. "And my grandfather's, going back many generations."

"No," said the young man.

"What?"

"I said that I do not believe you are the last in a long line of priests who took the name of Nicodemus." He lowered his sword point a few inches. "I think it has been you all along. You have always been Nicodemus."

The priest ignored that. Instead, he gestured to the many dead, and to some of the furniture which had already felt the kiss of the young man's torch and was beginning to burn. It was oven-hot in the hall, and the air shimmered with that heat.

"Do you really think that this will stop the Red Order?" asked the priest. "Do you think the Red Knights are defeated as well because you butchered one foolish old Scriptor?"

"No, of course not."

"Then what is it you think you've accomplished with all of this? There will be another Scriptor. The pope in Rome has given over much of the Templar gold to the Ordo Ruber, and they are recruiting from among the very best houses. They will come back stronger."

"And they will be met with a stronger response," said the young man. "For that is how war is fought. Few single battles are decisive."

The priest laughed and spat into the closest open flame. The spittle hissed and turned to steam. "You think that you can *win* this war?"

It was meant as mockery, but the young man gave a straight answer. "No. I do not believe that the war I fight can ever be won."

"Then—" began Nicodemus, but the young warrior was not finished.

"It can be lost, though. Through inactivity, through a loss of resolve, through a failing understanding, through timidity and cowardice, through inattention . . . yes, it can be lost. But I do not fight to win a war," said the Nameless Man. "I fight because the war needs to *be* fought. I fight because I can, and that is enough of a calling."

Nicodemus took another step forward and now he was nearly within reach of that bloody length of sharpened steel. In the harsh glow from the young man's torch, the old priest's eyes seemed to somehow undergo a process of change. The dark brown faded to be replaced by lighter and less healthy shades of brown, and then greens and yellows of the sickliest kind. It jolted the young man, who recognized that swirl of diseased colors from the way the elixir looked when he first saw it in Maxillan's room. Yet, it was different, too, for there had been a thread of bloody crimson in the elixir—and that had become more vibrant and dominant as the fires in that other room heated the brew close to the point where it would have burst the glass.

"You make a brave speech," growled the priest. "But I have seen a thousand like you before, and all of them are now dead. You are a brave and skilled man, a *bold* man for having done what you did here this night, but you are only a man. You will burn away the few years allotted to you and I will piss on your ashes, for I *cannot* be outlasted. I was born with this world and will die with it, and not a moment before. You cannot even conceive of what I am, let alone hope to stop me."

"I know what you are," said the young man. "You are chaos. You are this generation's Loki. You delight in war because war is chaos. You delight in conflict because that is chaos. No, old man, I know you but you do not know *me*."

Nicodemus laughed. "And what are you except a foolish young man?"

The Nameless Man said nothing. He merely stood there and let the priest make his own judgment. He saw the exact moment when Nicodemus looked into his eyes and saw their colors begin to swirl and change. The greens and browns, the yellows, and that deep crimson. He saw the smile falter and fade into doubt on the priest's face, and he saw something like fear blossom slowly in the eyes of Nicodemus.

"What *are* you?" gasped the priest.

The man who had been John Temple smiled then. Thin, cold, merciless. "Perhaps we are kin," he said.

The priest stumbled back from him then. "You . . . you took the . . ."

Without pausing to finish his statement, Nicodemus spun and ran howling into the night. And the Nameless Man let him go, knowing that to chase him and kill him would accomplish little. To allow that fear to grow and run rampant, though. Yes, that could be interesting.

By the time the last of the priest's cries had faded, the house was ablaze. The young man dropped the torch, cleaned his blade on the cloak of a dead knight, and walked out into the cold of New Year's Eve. He found his horse, mounted, and rode off.

And on the first day of 1315, the Nameless Man was many miles to the east. He had no real plan for his next step, but there was nowhere better for news than taverns in port towns. He would linger there for a while and see what the news of the world had to tell him.

His father was at rest in Scottish soil. Joshua of Antioch was gone, as was Alighieri, de Molay, and everyone else who knew him on sight. That was well.

That was useful.

He discarded all traces of John Temple the Younger and would not choose a new name until one was needed. For now, he remained friendless and nameless. The war itself would give him a name, he judged. Perhaps many names in many places.

He rode on through the French countryside. In the trees, crows and other dark birds clustered on branches to see him pass. One crow—a very old and ragged one—stood on a rock and as the Nameless Man passed, the bird opened its mouth to utter a caw, but it was without sound. Even so, the rider paused to nod in acknowledgment and understanding.

Then he rode on.

Riding away and yet always riding to war.

# CHAPTER 55

## IN FLIGHT OVER LUXEMBOURG

The Cessna Citation X+ tore through the skies at just under the speed of sound. Inside the cabin, there was no sound at all. The cabin was designed to offer absolute quiet when needed for virtual reality meetings using Doc Holliday's ORB technology, or for relaxation and contemplation.

No one aboard was relaxed, though.

The three passengers—Mr. Church, Dr. Ronald Coleman, and Luke Merishi—were each deeply involved in reading real-time data streams. Church had windows open with Bug, Holliday, and a number of his usefully placed friends in various key industries—British government, the United Nations, the Centers for Disease Control in Atlanta, the World Health Organization, Interpol, and others. His fingers danced over the keys, muting one call and going live on another . . . a flow of conversations that was, in its way, like a dance.

Nearby, Ron Coleman was delving deep into sections of decrypted data sent by Bug's team. He also had an additional window open with a direct link to Dr. Anwar Suliman in London. Every now and then he cut a discreet glance at Church, always amazed at how the man could maintain coherence and contribute meaningfully to over a dozen simultaneous conversations. It was both impressive and a bit creepy.

Across from them, Luke was gathering logistical information on the evolving status of Havoc, Bedlam, Chaos, and Wild Hunt teams. He also cut looks at Church, though his were more of surprise than anything else. He was young and still in training for fieldwork, but since the death of Brick Anderson, Mr. Church's former personal assistant and bodyguard, the big man had begun including Luke in more aspects of RTI. He knew that his next move up the ladder would not put him in Brick's slot—he still lacked too much practical field experience for that—but it was clear Church respected his skills as a fighter. So, he was along to protect the man his grandfather once described as "God's warrior." At the time, Luke thought the nickname was grandiose, and he still did not make any religious connections with his employer, but he understood a great deal about Church's "war."

Even though he had never once fired a shot in anger, Luke had already accepted that war as his own. He just didn't know what role he would eventually play in the conflict. As he worked, he tried not to be seen looking. Somehow, though, he knew that Church was acutely aware of that, and of everything going on around him. It was both an encouraging thought—given that Church led this fight—but also a disturbing one. There was something about Church that was beyond Luke's ability to articulate it.

As he worked, he felt his heart racing.

The miles whipped past as the jet soared toward London.

# INTERLUDE 34

**THE WARRIOR AND THE WAR**
**THE BLACK DEATH**
**NORTHUMBRIA, ENGLAND**
**1351 CE**

*"They stole my baby!"*

The woman collapsed under the weight of horror and grief. Her bony knees smacked into the mud, spattering her threadbare dress with filth, yet she did not care. The rain beat at her, driving her onto hands as well as knees. Each drop was like a thrown stone, and there was too little meat on her body to shield her from the uncountable impacts.

Her hair—what was left of it—hung in dripping rattails. The blue of her eyes was faded to a milky gray-white, and only two rotted teeth remained in her screaming mouth.

She was twenty-three.

She was the oldest of her family, because no one else was left alive. Some were buried in the churchyard, but most had been tumbled into mass graves, doused with oil, and burned before gravediggers pushed the dirt over the ashes.

The only member of her family younger than her was the baby that the monsters had stolen.

Monsters who looked like the baker's son and the daughter of the cooper, and the senior apprentice to the cooper. Those three. All known to the screaming woman. All friends, or at least friendly to her before the darkness came.

Before the Black Death.

"God, help me!" she wailed. "They stole my baby."

Her words were nearly lost beneath the roar of the rain.

Then a shadow fell across her and the woman looked up, reaching with pleading hands before she even knew who it was. She faltered though, because the face of the tall man in front of her was unknown. He was big, well-made, with broad shoulders and limbs heavy with muscle. With *flesh.* Everyone else in town—in all of England—was, like her, a mockery of what they once were. They were scarecrows. Yet here was a man who looked well-fed and strong.

The sight of him was like a punch to her heart. How could anyone look so healthy when the whole world seemed to be dying? How could anyone have that much meat on their bones when famine walked abroad?

She recoiled from him, fearing that this was something unnatural. A ghost, perhaps, or Satan come to mock those he was starving to death.

The man looked down at her. He wore a thick gray riding cloak with the hood pushed back so that the rain fell on his dark hair and pale face. His eyes were a strange mix of brown and green that the woman did not like at all. Had she the strength she would have fled. As it was, all she could do was turn and begin to crawl in the direction the three monsters had taken. Even now the mud and rain were dissolving their footprints.

The man said, "Who has taken your child?"

The woman stopped and looked up, one final flicker of hope still burning. His eyes were strange but his face was calm, with no sign of cruelty or malice. There was great sadness there, though. Much of that.

She lifted a muddy hand and pointed to a stable half a block away. "They . . . they . . . oh God, don't let them . . ."

Those seven words cost her so much to speak that before she could say more, she collapsed and lay still.

The man immediately knelt beside her. He turned her over and gently thumbed mud from her eyes and nose and mouth, and then pulled her close, wrapping his cloak around them both.

"Be at peace, my sister," he said softly.

But he spoke to the wind and the rain. The woman was beyond hearing.

After a moment, he laid her down, removed his cloak, and covered her with it. Then he rose, eyes burning, and looked at the stable.

Then he was running.

He ran swiftly through the rain, twice leaping over other huddled shapes. The town was dying. It seemed as if most of Europe was sick with the Black Death. In most of the towns and cities he had visited, close to half of the people had died.

The thought staggered him.

Millions of people.

And no enemy to fight. The Ordo Ruber and their Red Knights had nothing to do with this, for the recent Scriptor and half of the members of that order were dead, too. No one knew the cause. The priests rattled on about this being another punishment by God, yet there was no logic, for the innocent and faithful died as easily as sinners and atheists. But that was the way of priests—thanking or blaming God for everything.

In the early days, many believed that it was something brought on purpose by enemies . . . but as the plague spread to other nations, that theory faltered and collapsed.

The Nameless Man believed that there must be a cause because he did not—would not—accept that the impossible existed. Everything had to have a cause, no matter how obscure.

Over the last weeks he had begun rebuilding his alchemy studio and was out collecting samples of hair, skin, blood, and more; as well as stories of people who lost family and people who had the disease and recovered. The answer would be in there somewhere. And even though the death toll was slowing, it was uncertain as to whether the worst was past or if there were simply too few to keep it raging.

He ran.

The stable door was ajar and when he was still ten paces away he knew that he was too late. Even a starving child would be screaming for the mother from whom it was taken.

There was no sound at all.

He drew his dagger, pulled the door open, and stepped inside.

Into horror.

The three of them knelt around the small thing on the straw. They wept as they ate. One of them, a woman, paused frequently to punch herself in the face as punishment for what she did.

"No . . ." he breathed.

He entered and pulled the door shut behind him. As he walked toward the three people and their dreadful feast, he wondered if what he was about to do was punishment or mercy.

Either way, he wept as he went about his work.

## CHAPTER 56

### IN FLIGHT OVER THE IONIAN SEA

"Well now," said Top once we were in the air, "wasn't that interesting as all hell?"

"Freaking surreal," said Bunny.

Remy asked, "Does she really look that much like the Major Courtland you guys knew?"

"So close it'd break your heart," Top said. I caught the tiny look he gave me.

"Did Violin ever know her?" asked Belle.

"Before her time," I said.

They lapsed into silence, maybe taking some subtle cue from Top.

We logged some flight time before anyone spoke again.

"Hope Scott's okay," said Remy.

We all nodded. The man was a dick, but he was family.

"We gonna spank someone hard for this, ain't we?"

Top gave him a long, cold look that said everything on that subject that needed to be said.

A few minutes later, I called ahead to make sure *Shirley* was fueled and ready. Bird Dog—Brian Bird, head of RTI logistics—assured me it was.

"And I packed all the fun toys, too," he told me.

Bird Dog was a good guy, and he'd been with us since the DMS days. Not a field operator, though he'd pulled triggers more than once when situations demanded it. He had a large team and anytime me and mine needed or wanted something, he made it happen.

"The other teams are coming in from Thailand and Brazil," I said, "and they'll need—"

"They don't need either jack or shit," he cut in. "I spoke with all team leaders and we got them all covered. Bedlam and Chaos will be met at Heathrow with everything they need and all tied up with fancy ribbon."

"And the Hunt?"

"They haven't even used what I sent them out with, Outlaw," he said. "Even so, your jet, *Shirley,* is ass-heavy with extra gear. You want to start a war, you're covered, and then some. Oh, and I loaded every single ChemRig in the locker. Enough for everyone and some left over in case we have any guest stars in this shindig."

The ChemRigs are a radical new design on the MOPP 4 chemical warfare protective overgarment. For years we've been using special-design Saratoga Hammer Suits, but Doc and Coleman thought they could do better, and damn if they didn't. The ChemRigs are exceptionally durable and flexible, allowing us to move normally, with no material drag on legs or arms, nothing to foil agility. They have ultracompact air filtration systems that could scrub out anything up to and including Marburg virus, and attachable air tanks if even more protection is needed. At full-seal, you could line dance in a biohazard hot room even if all the little monsters were out of their test tubes. They cost something like $1.4 million each, but as far as I was concerned they were cheap at the price.

What made them even better was the Kevlar and spider-silk body armor built into the fabric, with graphene composites to reduce the foot-pounds of impact from most calibers of handgun and long gun. A sniper bullet would get through, but not much else. And the special weave prevents most stab and slash wounds, which Kevlar does not.

"You're the actual Man," I told him.

"This I know," he said and signed off.

# INTERLUDE 35

## THE WARRIOR AND THE WAR
## STRASBOURG, ALSACE, FRANCE
## JULY 1518

They sat together on a slope that looked down on a shallow valley littered with farmsteads in their unique patterns of abstract geometry. Fields of green and fields only half-seen through the dense crowds of white sheep. Smoke rose from a score of chimneys, rising up to a sky as blue as a robin's egg.

Both men were bleeding from too many wounds to count. Slashes and stab wounds, gouges torn by flying arrows and the ragged welts of battle-whips.

Behind where they sat, their horses grazed untethered among the many dead. Their own horses, and those belonging to the group of bandits. The bandits themselves were like irregular islands in the sea of grass. Here and there a spear stood straight as a flagpole, or a sword driven deep but left to mark where its owner fell.

"They've stopped dancing," said the shorter of the two, a redheaded Irishman named Flannery. "Have you noticed?" But before his companion could reply, the Irishman answered himself. "Of course you noticed, ye damn spooky bastard. You notice everything."

The taller man smiled as he reached out and plucked a brown recluse spider from his friend's shoulder, showed it to him, and then blew hard to send the creature spinning away into a stand of creeping thistle.

"Now you're just showing off, Ardeaglais."

"To answer you," said Ardeaglais—though that was not his true name—"yes. They stopped dancing. But we knew they would."

Flannery snorted. "*You* knew they would. All that nonsense about it being mold on bad wheat . . ."

"That's what caused it."

"And the nobles staying healthy because they ate the fresher wheat."

"Yes. It's happened before. Always with a famine or damage to cereal crops like wheat and barley and suchlike."

"That makes little sense to me."

Ardeaglais half-turned and nodded to the dead men behind them.

"It made as little sense to them. They thought it was God punishing the people for failing to properly tithe the church."

"And you don't think so?"

The big man spat onto the grass and left it there as an eloquent reply.

Flannery shook his head. "And that pack of *langers* thought it was all going to be easy pickings."

"They are opportunists and cowards. The famine and the dancing plague left this whole region open to plundering. To steal from those who are too sick and weak to defend themselves."

"Well, mate, the shite-heads are not stealing anything anymore."

Ardeaglais reached to drag over a leather saddlebag he'd tossed onto the grass after the fight. He flipped it open and rummaged inside until he found a thick roll of bandages and a pot of a foul-smelling ointment.

"Take off your shirt," he said. "We have to stop the bleeding. That last pike thrust nearly did you in."

"And it hurts, too. Wait, what's that muck? It smells like my dog's arse."

"It'll keep the wounds from turning foul."

"Gah! What's in it? Satan's piss and what else?"

"Comfrey, some spiderwebs, and a few other things."

"Did you say spider's—wait, oww! *Owwww,* you ham-fisted son of a Scottish she-goat. *Loscadh is dó ort.*"

Flannery continued to complain all the way through the process of cleaning, stitching, and bandaging his wounds. He offered to help Ardeaglais with his own wounds, some of which were every bit as bad as the pike thrust, but the big young man shook his head.

"I'll be fine."

"Well," said Flannery with disapproval, "at least you don't bleed much. Some of those wounds are already closing. Spooky bastard, you are, and no mistake."

They sat and watched the village that they had nearly died protecting.

"They'll never sing a song about us," said Flannery wistfully.

"Why should they?"

"Because we saved them from being butchered and burgled."

Ardeaglais took a stem of grass and placed it between his teeth, chewing the end slowly. "Do you need to be thanked?"

Flannery thought about it, and muttered a few unpleasant things under his breath. But he said nothing and when night fell, they were miles away, riding east to the sea.

# CHAPTER 57

## IN FLIGHT OVER THE IONIAN SEA

After the call with Bird Dog, I tapped into my private channel with Church and he came on pretty quick.

"I hear a rotor," he said instead of hello. "I take it you've chosen to disobey a direct order." There was no question in that, nor any obvious rebuke.

"You didn't hire me to sit around filing reports."

"No," he said, "I did not."

"The other teams are all inbound."

"The war may not unfold in London."

"If it doesn't, we'll go where it is."

"Part of that has been simplified," said Church. "I just got off a conference call with the prime minister, the home secretary, James Rockwell, and the heads of MI5 and MI6."

"Sounds like a party. Was this a general catch-up or . . . ?"

"We talked about you."

I said, "What . . . ?"

"Rockwell is concerned that the plague outbreak was specifically targeted at Barrier. To cripple the organization at a crucial time when they are handling a number of key cases, with their field teams all out of country on critical missions."

"What's his theory? That the plague was launched when Barrier was at its weakest?"

"Yes, because Barrier's teams are more experienced with bioterrorism than anyone else in England."

"Like we were with the DMS back in the States," I suggested.

"Very much the same."

"What's that have to do with me?"

"Rockwell was a protégé of Benson Childes, who always held you in high regard. Rockwell respects you by reputation."

"I feel all warm and fuzzy, but why bring me up in the group chat?"

"First," said Church, "Rockwell and Bedwyr Griffiths, the head of security for Hadrian Tower, are both deeply concerned at how the plague could have been introduced. Neither feels like it could be as simple as a sick person bringing it to work by accident. Not with a weaponized strain. Dr. Coleman agrees, as do the medical experts already at work on this in London."

"What's the alternative? A deliberate attack with a human vector?"

"Everyone agrees that is the case."

"Barrier's new digs are on the top four stories of a new skyscraper, right? And the whole building is filled with various high-security government offices. How much security would such a person have to go through to get onto the floor where Scott caught the bug?"

"Too many to fit into any acceptable theoretical model."

I said, "Ah."

"Yes."

"So there has to be an inside man."

"At least one. Nearly every employee at Barrier was hired from MI5, MI6, the SAS, and a few other critical groups. All of them are trained in spycraft of one kind or another. And all have passed Barrier's intense vetting program. And yet they still brought the bioweapon into the building and targeted the likely incoming new chief of station. Rockwell mapped it out and admitted that he and Griffiths must have either missed something or been betrayed. Possibly both. If either is at fault, it's career ending and may result in charges. Rockwell was already on the way out, so it's not as devastating to him personally. Griffiths is a rising star and this will likely crush his career. The fact that they have openly accepted responsibility and repercussions speaks well of them."

"I know a lot of politicians and bureaucrats who wouldn't have the integrity or backbone to do that."

"And this is where you come into the equation," he said. "Rockwell recommended that an outside team be brought in to handle the investigation. A group that is beyond reproach and led by someone who has demonstrated remarkable problem-solving skills, personal integrity, fierce determination, and who has experience resolving ultracritical missions with either national or global implications. For the record, I am paraphrasing Rockwell."

"And he naturally recommended you," I said. "Makes sense."

"No, Colonel, he recommended you."

I laughed. "*Get* the fuck outta here. I'm a foreigner, I'm a notorious pain in the ass, I don't play well with others, and I can be a dick when dealing with authority figures."

"It is very much *those* qualities Rockwell forwarded as part of his recommendation. He may have phrased it differently, of course."

"And how much laughter ensued?"

"None at all. The PM and the home secretary read his briefing notes about you, though both are aware of your track record and Havoc's from the Rage matter, the London Hospital investigation, and the *Sea of Hope*."

"This is nuts."

"And you are already on your way here," he said. "Now isn't that interesting."

"Havoc's heading there to see if we can help. I'm not trying to crowd out anyone who has actual authority."

"Somebody has to watch the watchers, Colonel. In this case, no one in the UK is as familiar with the structure and functions of Barrier. You're the senior field agent in RTI, and were the senior field agent for the DMS. Both of those organizations are built on the same model as Barrier."

"And you helped design Barrier."

"Yes."

"How are the local teams going to react to this? I foresee a big-ass jurisdictional pissing contest."

"That path is being made straight by the people who were on that call."

I sat there, stunned and confused. "And you think this is a good play on Rockwell's part?"

"It's highly unusual," said Church, "but so is the situation."

There was more, with a discussion of logistics, and then he got a call and had to drop out. I sat there, trying to grasp the full scope of what he said.

# INTERLUDE 36

## THE WARRIOR AND THE WAR
## LONDON, ENGLAND
## 1563 LONDON PLAGUE

They rode into town together.

A tall, somber man with eyes filled with shadows and ghosts; and a shorter man with laugh lines around his mouth, though he was not smiling now.

"Ah, London," said the short man, whose family name—Fletcher—came from generations of arrow makers. "Still a shithole, I see. Ye gods, Iain, the *stench*."

"The city's overcrowded," said his companion, Iain Kirk, late of Edinburgh. "The filth is less obvious where the monied families live, but down here . . . there's nothing but rain to clean the streets."

"Aye," said Fletcher. "Poor folk, poor conditions, and no one gives a dried piece of cattle dung for anyone here. Hell, they hate each other."

Iain shook his head. "It's not hate."

"Then what is it?"

"Hopelessness."

The shorter man cut Iain a look and clearly had a rejoinder nocked and ready, but he let it pass. In the three years during which they traveled together, he had yet to win a single argument. And in the current matter, there was no path forward to anything but agreement and sad acceptance.

They rode through the streets, their horses' hooves and legs becoming increasingly caked with mud and shit. There was no escaping it, and their boots were likewise fouled. Fletcher took a rag from his saddlebag and wrapped it around his mouth and nose. He offered one to Iain, who declined.

"You'd rather smell the shite of a few hundred thousand lost souls?"

"No," said Iain, "it's simply that I've become used to it."

"If I ask if all of this offends you," mused Fletcher, "you'll tell me that the true offense is in the disregard for the poor and destitute, won't you now?"

Iain said nothing, which said it all.

They rode on, pausing only as a cart rumbled past pulled by a dispirited ass. A man with thigh-high boots led the ass, and he wore a scarf wound so comprehensively around his face that only his bleak eyes were visible. The cart itself was half-filled with corpses. Men, women, and children. All of them filthy, all of them gray and ghastly in death.

"What happened here?" asked Fletcher.

The man stopped and looked up at the travelers as if they had descended from the moon itself.

"Happened? *Happened?*" cried the man in a voice ruined by whisky and hard living. "It's the end of the world, that's what's happened."

Fletcher gestured to the bodies. "Was there a fire or something?"

The man looked genuinely surprised. "If you don't know, gentlemen, then you should not be here, and that's the truth of it. It's not a fire, sirs, it's the plague back again after a dozen years. Back and worse than it was when I was younger, that I can tell you. People are dropping in their tracks and it's more than me and my mates can handle. We have diggers making graves day and night, but we're going to have to stop doing 'em individual-like and maybe dig a pit."

"How did it start?" asked Iain.

The man shrugged. "Ask fifty people—if you can find that many still alive—you'll get fifty stories. No one knows, like they never seem to know."

Iain studied him. "But what do *you* think?"

Another shrug. "Came from across the channel."

"From France?"

"Aye."

"What makes you say so?"

"Stands to reason, dunnit? Bunch of lads go off to fight the French and when they come back and go marching from town to town doing their recruiting and suchlike, then the people in that town start getting sick soon's they march off. Weren't no plague 'round 'ere since before we started up with France again."

Iain and Fletcher shared a look but said nothing at the moment.

"How many have died?" asked Fletcher.

"How the 'ell should I know?" The man lifted a section of the scarf and spit into the mud at his feet. "Too many by 'alf. Worse here, but the nobs are falling, too. Maybe not 'er 'ighness, who scarpered off to Windsor Castle, but enough of them that lives up in the big houses stayed too long. It's 'it the army, too. 'it them real bad, or so I 'ear."

Iain looked up and down the street. There were few people visible. Living people, at least. Several corpses lay near houses, ready for collection by the death carts. "How can we be of help?"

The man with the cart looked at him for a moment. If he was surprised at the offer, it did not show. Instead he merely looked weary and sad.

"'elp, sir?" he said. "That's kindly said, but there's nothing to help with. This is the end of the world."

With that he tugged on the lead, and the ass moved on, pulling the grim cart. Fletcher and Iain sat and watched the process as the man went about his horrid work.

"Poor bastard," muttered Fletcher.

"He has a good heart."

"What makes you say so?"

"Look at what he's doing. With all the deaths, there would be plenty of work in the farms outside of London, and yet he stays to bury the dead. That takes a certain kind of person."

"What's that you like saying? That heroes are around every corner."

Iain merely grunted.

Fetcher adjusted his scarf. "He blames the French."

"Yes."

"You think this was *caught* there or *sent* here?"

"You know what I think, Fletcher."

The shorter man nodded. "You think *they're* back again?"

"They never left."

"We killed nigh onto a score of the bastards. Hell, we burned down the Scriptor's mansion just like that other fellow did a couple hundred years ago. What was his name? The one the history books call the Son of the Bastard Knight? John Temple, was it?"

Fletcher's eyes twinkled with strange merriment as he asked, knowing his companion would decline to answer. He never did when Fletcher made comments of that kind.

Instead, Iain said, "They are not centralized in France. They haven't been in years. They have their hiding places throughout Europe, Africa, and Asia, and they spread like lice."

"They spread like the plague itself," suggested Fletcher.

"Like the plague . . . or with it."

Fletcher turned halfway around in his saddle. "You keep saying things like that, brother, but what do you mean? Are you saying they somehow *gave* the plague to English soldiers so they'd carry it back home?"

"Something like that, yes."

Fletcher whistled. "If that's the case—if it's even possible—then why are we here? Shouldn't we be in France, looking for the poxy bastards?"

"You already said it," said Iain. "We don't know for sure if it was sent or brought. We need to do a thorough search here in England before we cross the channel. It may well be that it isn't the Ordo Ruber in France who did this, or one of their chapters. I have been hearing curious things from Wallachia in the Ottoman Empire."

"Oh? Curious in what way?"

"Nothing confirmed, alas, but tales told by travelers of creatures haunting the Carpathians."

"Let me see if I can guess," said Fletcher. "These creatures hunt by night, drink blood, and are hard as blazes to kill."

"The very same."

"Of all the ills in this world, my friend, why are you so obsessed with plague?"

Iain's unusual eyes—brown with strong highlights of green and red—took on a distant aspect, as if he looked through a hole in this world into some other place.

"I have seen death carts too often in London. A century ago there were ten times as many of them. Millions died."

"Meaning you *read* about such things."

"Yes," said Iain vaguely. "That must be what I meant."

Fletcher searched his face for some deeper meaning, but if he had more questions on that subject, he kept them to himself. Instead, in a lighthearted tone, he asked, "And if you find that it is the Les Chevaliers Rouges gathering their power again, what then? Fill the hold of a ship with garlic and go riding off into the mountains?"

For the first time that day, Iain Kirk smiled.

# CHAPTER 58

## IN FLIGHT OVER THE IONIAN SEA

I just finished telling the guys that Havoc Team had a weird new elevated status when my cell rang again.

Church said, "That was Dr. Suliman. In the last hour sixteen members of Barrier have been admitted to the ICU."

"Jesus Christ. Do we know if Scott was exposed there or brought it in with him?"

"Unknown, though my guess is that the exposure was at Barrier."

"Why, because there aren't any cases coming in from anywhere else?"

"Yes. However, that's small comfort because this variant of *Yersinia pestis* is not responding to the standard antibiotics. Dr. Suliman says that he has not yet found a single antibiotic or cocktail of them that has shown any efficacy against this."

"And Scott . . . ?"

"I'm sorry to report that he is in critical condition. They have him on a ventilator."

"Fucking hell," I breathed. Scott.

"I called Director Rockwell and told him," said Church, "and he is locking the entire building down."

"Good call." I paused, then said, "All of this makes me wonder if this was what Nicodemus meant when he made the crack about his 'going-away party.' I mean, he seemed pretty sick when I saw him in Baltimore. Maybe he really is dying and he wants to spill gasoline over everything and toss a match as his way of saying goodbye."

Church thought about that for a moment. "Let's both hope that isn't the case."

"I hope a lot of things. So far those hopes have a piss-poor batting average."

"Nature of the game, I'm afraid," he said, with an edge of sadness that I've heard in his voice a few times over the years.

I thought about everything Rudy, Circe, and I talked about. At that moment, I didn't care one freckled damn if he was an actual immortal warrior or a guy using the role of the eternal champion as some kind of armor for a fight that started before he was born and would outlast all of us. The latter was a lot more likely, and, frankly, made him make more sense. It also dialed up my admiration for him. The war was the war, and the warrior was, by extension, the warrior. And no matter what else he might be, that's who he was. Hard to say if Nicodemus understood that or not. Maybe so. Despite everything he seemed to admire Church. His comment about having a worthy chess opponent might have been his most telling remark.

I forced myself back to the more immediate topic. "Look, boss, we both know I'm as much a cop as a shooter. Maybe more so. Why don't I take Havoc to Barrier and see if I can work it as a crime scene? Might be easier for the locals if we do something quiet like that."

"Yes, do that," he said.

"Even so, it'll mean stepping on toes over there. Nobody's going to want an American stealing their investigation."

"I don't particularly care about anyone's feelings," he said. "Do you?"

"Ha! Have you *met* me? No, I just want to know if your clout will smooth the way for me if I piss anyone off. Last thing we need is someone getting all high-assed and trying to shut us out."

He made a sound that was equal parts laugh and growl. "I can assure you, Colonel, that by the time Havoc lands there will be all of the cooperation you require."

"Copy that."

"However, Colonel, be careful with this. It has an odd feel to it that I can't quite define."

"Getting that same vibe," I told him and tapped out of the call, frowning. Church rarely ever says anything like "be careful," and God knows I've taken my team into some seriously toxic environments. Church actually sounded concerned. Maybe even worried, and that worried the living fuck out of me.

I told my guys the latest. They looked grim and scared and angry, and that was how it should be. I was scared, too. Very scared.

And really, really pissed.

I mean . . . a souped-up, quick-onset, fast-moving version of the disease that many science historians believe did more damage than the bubonic version of the bacteria, meaning that it killed somewhere between 75 and 200 million people in the 1300s. In just two years—between 1664 and '66—more than 70,000 people died in London. From 1895 to 1930 it killed twelve million people, most of them in India. Those numbers are surreal.

Granted, since then antibiotics have slashed the death toll down to a handful here and there, but we were getting pretty convincing proof here that some asshole with a Gee-Whiz Junior Pandemic playset had rewired the little germs to make them even more lethal.

I closed my eyes, hoping for a small patch of unsullied mental ground to stand on and take stock. Plague. In London. Scott Wilson burning up. Scott, who was healthy as a horse two days ago. Sick, maybe dying.

From fucking plague?

I thought about the people we'd rescued from the lab at Corvin Castle. The ones we saved, and the ones who died. It made me wonder how long before Havoc hit that place that they'd been infected. Was that the same strain? Was this an even worse one?

I prayed Doc Holliday had some answers for me.

And I needed Bug and his team to find out where the bad guys were or, at least, where they might be. There was a deep anger setting fires in my heart and black poppies blooming in my head.

The very nature of what I do is reactive. That's a constant topic of conversation and frustration. It's like being a firefighter—we don't roll out unless something's already burning, and by then it's as much damage control as anything. We don't prevent anything. At best, we try and keep something big and bad from becoming any version of "worst-case scenario." So far, we've managed to keep the world from burning to ash.

*So far.*

Those are two very awful words.

So far. Damn.

## INTERLUDE 37

### THE CARPATHIAN MOUNTAINS
### PRINCIPALITY OF TRANSYLVANIA
### WINTER 1570 CE

He staggered down the slope, leaving bloody footprints behind him in the snow.

In one hand he held a longsword whose length was broken, leaving jagged points above midway. The sword was red to the crosspiece, as was the hand holding it. Blood was spattered everywhere, from the man's boots to his scarred and lacerated face. His clothes were torn, and his cloak little more than a collection of rags.

His other hand was clutched into a tight fist, with long strands of black hair seized tight therein. Seven heads hung from the hair, their combined weight causing the man to stagger and sometimes fall.

Each time he rose again, panting, hoarse with cold and effort and pain.

On he marched until he reached the road. The snow was up to his knees and he was soaked to the skin, freezing, half-dead. His horse stood waiting with the patience of its kind. Snugged into heavy blankets, with an open—and now empty—feedbag on the snow and a lead tied to a tree with three fathoms of rope. When it saw him, the animal shied backward from the smell of blood. Then it stopped and waited, watching with curious, cautious eyes as its master lumbered toward it.

The man tripped and fell to his knees. He dropped his grisly burden, letting the heads tumble into the virgin snow. The broken sword fell, too, and for a long time all he did—all he could do—was kneel there, gasping, blinking blood and tears from his eyes. His face flushed red and breath pluming in the frigid air.

The seven heads lay there. A perverse accident made them all face the man as if in judgment. They were so alike—skin the color of mushrooms, eyes red as blood, slack mouths agape to reveal rows of teeth more like those of a shark than anything human.

The tether tied to the horse allowed the animal to reach him, and it stood above him, breathing its warm, damp breath against his face.

He reached up and pulled that huge head close and leaned his forehead against the flat bridge of its nose.

They stayed like that for a long time.

In a nearby tree, an ancient crow watched them, its dragged feathers dusted with snow. Its eyes were black within black and they saw everything.

Absolutely everything.

## CHAPTER 59

### ST THOMAS' HOSPITAL
### WESTMINSTER BRIDGE ROAD
### LONDON, ENGLAND

There were soldiers waiting for them outside of the hospital. Four of them in black body armor, rifles at port arms, and stony faces. Church and Coleman had to show their identification five times between the street and the ICU where Scott Wilson and the Barrier employees were being cared for.

Director Rockwell was not there to greet them, having said that he was undergoing voluntary quarantine at Barrier headquarters. Instead, a tall woman with a Pakistani face and a Yorkshire accent intercepted them. She clearly recognized Church and came right up to him, offering a hard brown hand.

"Colonel Naqvi," she said, giving Church's hand a single pump. "I'm heading up security here at St. Thomas."

Church introduced Coleman.

"We came straight here from the airport," said Church.

"I was advised of that, sir," said Naqvi. "Dr. Suliman is waiting for you. I'll take you to him."

As they hurried along the hall toward a bank of lifts, Church asked about Scott Wilson. Naqvi was a little too long in replying.

"I won't understate things, gentlemen," she said. "But he is not doing very well. He coded forty minutes ago but they were able to revive him. Even so . . ."

She let the rest hang.

Once upstairs, Naqvi guided them to a conference room that was apparently the command center for the unfolding crisis. The doctor was a very thin man with sadness in every line on his face and eyes that already looked haunted. He had a phone in his hand and laid it down on the table as carefully as if it were a live hand grenade.

Then he got up with painful slowness and came over to greet them. He waved his guests to chairs near where he had been seated at the far end of a long table. Naqvi took a seat at the other end and sat as still as a statue except for her eyes—they moved with the flow of conversation and missed nothing.

"Where are we?" asked Church.

"In very serious trouble, I'm afraid," said Suliman.

"I heard about Scott coding and—"

Suliman shook his head to cut him off. "It is with a very heavy heart that I must tell you that Mr. Wilson died a quarter of an hour ago. I am so very sorry. I know he was a friend and colleague."

Coleman sagged back and looked ill. "Oh, God . . ."

Church sat like a statue, staring down at his interlaced fingers.

"It's worse than that," said Suliman. "He was the first to present with symptoms, but two employees from Barrier died before he did. And . . . a third passed just before you arrived."

Coleman suddenly slammed his palms down on the table hard enough to splash tea from Suliman's cup. *"How?"* he demanded. "How is that even possible?"

Suliman gave him a bleak stare. "This is unlike anything I've ever seen. And, understand me, gentlemen, I've worked with infectious diseases for thirty years. I've been read-in on biological warfare threats on several occasions, and I've been an advisor for Barrier, MI5, and MI6. I've seen many dreadful bioweapons. The speed with which this is unfolding has some parallels in threat assessments on file, but we have no idea how it started, or when the actual time of exposure took place."

"Explain, please," said Church.

"While I know Dr. Coleman by reputation, I don't know how much *you* know about this disease, sir," the doctor said to Church. "But I think for your benefit and Colonel Naqvi, let me lay things out so we are all speaking the same language, yes?"

"Please do."

"Pneumonic plague is bacteriological, which means, among other things, it does not require a living host," said Suliman. "Patients develop a high fever, an intense headache, weakness, torpor, and a rapidly developing pneumonia with shortness of breath, chest pain, cough, and sometimes bloody or watery mucus. The disease spreads to the lungs of a patient either as a secondary infection in cases of untreated bubonic or septicemic plague, or when a person inhales infectious droplets coughed out by another person or animal with pneumonic plague. That is the standard model. Pneumonic plague is the most serious form of this disease, and it is the only form of plague that can be spread from person to person. The incubation period of pneumonic plague following inhalation can be as short as one day, though often a bit longer."

"With you so far," said Naqvi. Church merely nodded.

"The timetable of what we are seeing is confusing and deeply disturbing," continued Suliman. "It raises key questions such as did Mr. Wilson have it when he arrived at Barrier? Did he bring it with him? If so, why have there been no cases *outside* of Barrier? None on his flight. We checked, and we have the taxi driver who brought him there from the airport in isolation, and he is completely symptom-free. The Security Service has tracked every single passenger who was on his flight and is rounding them up. None, so far, are sick. Nor is the crew of that plane. There have been no reports of illness from anyone at Heathrow."

Church said nothing but made a small twirling motion with one finger to tell the doctor to continue.

Suliman nodded. "So far, this suggests that his exposure was at Barrier headquarters, but that's where the timetable is the most problematic. For Mr. Wilson to have been exposed there means that he was infected, caught the disease, developed severe symptoms, and collapsed within a matter of hours. Far less than a full day. This is supported by the employees there falling ill around the same time, three of whom were not even in the office a day ago. But *Yersinia pestis* simply does not act that quickly. The pathogenesis here is unnaturally fast. Moreover, there are no vectors we have so far been able to locate. None of the infected have insect bites of any kind that we have so far found."

"Airborne?" suggested Church.

"We are, of course, looking into that, but the pattern of *who* at Barrier became infected doesn't bear this out. People working in offices with several others have fallen sick, but their colleagues have not."

"Have you been able to create a map of movement?" asked Coleman. "Who went where and when?"

Suliman looked pained. "To a degree, but with the symptoms presenting with such aggression it's been difficult to interview the people who could give us the fullest answers. It is also a very busy place, with quite a number of government offices and laboratories. We have a team working on it, however."

"Hit pause right there," said Coleman. "Labs? What kind of labs?"

Suliman nodded approval of the question. "Director Rockwell took me into his confidence and said that there were several kinds of research groups housed in the building. And, yes, one of them has samples of *Yersinia pestis*. However, he has checked the research logs, hot-room access logs, and research diaries and no one has done anything with their samples in recent years."

Naqvi nodded. "What makes it worse is that two-thirds of the in-house security team at the building are either sick or in the bloody morgue."

"I have some people coming in who can help with that," said Church, and he explained about Colonel Ledger and Havoc.

"Surely we have other groups here in London who are best equipped for this kind of thing," said Suliman, looking perplexed.

"We have several," said the colonel. "And two of them are inbound as well. However, from what I was told, Mr. Church's people have more experience beyond simulations and dry runs."

Coleman laughed. "A whole lot more. Besides, Mr. Church helped design Barrier and has been in this game longer than anyone."

Suliman looked skeptical about that claim. He glanced at Naqvi, but the colonel nodded. "I received a call from Number 10 saying that all doors are open to Mr. Church's special investigators. That comes from the top."

The doctor almost smiled. "It seems like the disease isn't the only thing moving with speed and force. I'm impressed, but more than that, I'm grateful. You say this Colonel Ledger has dealt with this kind of thing before?"

Coleman leaned close to Church. "How much do we tell him?"

"Everything. This is hardly the time for secrets."

To the doctor and the colonel, Coleman said, "Buckle up, gents." And he told them about Corvin Castle, with some additional remarks on a number of other high-profile cases Ledger worked. The doctor looked both impressed and aghast.

All Colonel Naqvi said was, "Bloody hell."

## INTERLUDE 38

### THE WARRIOR AND THE WAR
### PUDDING LANE ROOMING HOUSE
### LONDON, ENGLAND
### DECEMBER 15, 1664 CE

A comet hung like Satan's promise in the sky. Everyone who looked up from the streets of London to see it, feared it.

"What do you think it means?" asked the woman.

She was a widow and the mother of four children who were each buried next to their father in pauper's graves with the cheapest of stone markers. Her face and body were marked, too. Whip and fist, knife and ligature, hot iron and burning pipe bowl. Her face, never beautiful, was a roadmap of scars that told her story without words. No one who looked at Red Jane would ever doubt that life was unkind to her, and had been since girlhood, for many of those scars were old.

The man who sat on the edge of her bed holding her hand watched the comet for long moments before he spoke.

"In itself," he said softly, "it means nothing. A comet, nothing more."

Red Jane sat up, pulling the sheet over her breasts. Even they were mangled, a parting gift from a man who once swore to protect her. His lies cost her dearly, and the scars were there to remind her every day that trust was a terrible gamble.

"There's talk," she said.

"About the comet?"

"Yes."

"There's always talk about comets."

Red Jane shook her head. "No, Gabriel, they say that it is a warning from God that something bad will happen."

The man—Gabriel Bethel—smiled faintly. He was a big man, with strange eyes that were older than his face. Like Red Jane, his body was a roadmap of all the pain visited upon him. Most of the scars were old, though, faded to pale lines, though there were some more recent wounds. Even they seemed further along in healing than was normal, and that gave the woman a small thrill of excitement. Fear, to be sure, but something else as well, for she did not actually fear the man. She had seen Gabriel fight and watched him kill, but when he touched her it was with a gentleness unlike anything she had ever known. Despite all of the betrayals that marked her life, she trusted this brooding, quiet warrior.

"Is that what they say?" he murmured.

"It's happened before," Red Jane insisted. "Before battles and plagues and invasions."

"With all that happens for ill in this world, Jane," he said, "there would need to be comets in the sky every night."

"So . . . you don't think something bad will happen?"

He stood up and walked naked to the window, placed the palms of his big hands on the sill, and leaned out to study the comet and its long tail.

"Oh," he said, "don't mistake me . . . something bad will happen."

"But, I—"

"However, I do not think the comet is here to announce it. Evil will come, because that is what evil does, but it comes quietly and without such ostentation."

She got out of bed, letting the blankets fall away, and came over to stand behind him with her arms wrapped around his waist. She laid her cheek against his back.

"Perhaps this once it will pass us by," she said.

"Perhaps," he said, but he took such a long time in saying it she knew that he did not believe it.

She also thought he was wrong about the evil, that maybe it indeed *would* pass. Or that they had already met the most pressing evil—

bloodthirsty monsters who stole children in the night—and slew them all. Gabriel Bethel himself killed eleven of them, and Red Jane killed the other two, using arrows he fashioned for her with spun-glass balls instead of barbs. Those balls were filled with pure garlic oil, and though Red Jane at first laughed at this, the arrows killed those two monsters, and they died hard, too. Spitting and choking and crying out in fear and wonder even as their throats clenched tight and their hearts burst in their chests.

He called them Red Knights, though they looked more like demons to her. When the battle was done, they were able to bring out twenty-six children, some mere babes and the oldest a girl of twelve who had not yet begun to bleed. Seven other children needed to be buried in shrouds so their parents could not see what was done to them.

Those monsters were dead, and the comet burned, and nothing seemed to happen, arguing that Gabriel was wrong, as he so rarely was.

"Tell me, my love," she said as they watched the comet. "What will you do if the Red Knights come to London?"

"If they came in peace," he replied, "I would do nothing."

"You wouldn't just kill them? They are monsters, after all."

He shook his head. "My war is not with any race nor any kind of people. If they do no harm, then they have nothing to fear from me or those who fight this war with me."

"You're a strange man."

"So I've been told," he said, smiling a little.

"If they come to do harm, what will you do? I mean, how far would you go to stop them?"

He did not answer, but watched the comet burning in the night.

# CHAPTER 60

## HEATHROW AIRPORT
## HOUNSLOW, UNITED KINGDOM

When we reached Heathrow, somehow Bird Dog was already there waiting for us.

He is a very tall man, nearly Bunny's height, though of a different body type. Bunny looks like the guy who played Jack Reacher on TV, only bigger. Bird Dog looks like an actual human being. He's as bald as an egg and has a black goatee that was going gray, and insists I was the main cause of most of those gray hairs.

"Car's waiting for us," he said. "Got everything you're ever going to need, and if there's something you want that isn't in there, let me know and I'll get it."

"How about a chartreuse Jet Ski with an ejector seat?" asked Remy.

"I can get it," said Bird Dog. Wasn't at all sure he was kidding. He added, "And Siege sent some playtoys for you. They're in one of the cases."

Siege—shorthand for C. J. Leith—was the RTI armorer, specializing in blades of every kind and use. Knives, axes, swords, throwing blades . . . he was a wizard with steel and a grindstone.

"Just a heads-up," said Bird Dog, aiming the comment more at Remy and Belle than the rest of us. "This is the UK and firearms are pretty much frowned upon except under very limited circumstances. Not saying that you shouldn't return fire if attacked, but maybe rely more on the Snelligs than the stuff that goes bang."

Belle pretended to look helpless. "I seem to have forgotten mine."

But Bird Dog wasn't buying. "Cute, but I packed sidearms for all y'all along with long guns and even the new full automatic rifle. And, yes, Bunny, I have the Snellig Cloudburst, too."

Along with the automatic rifles, the Cloudburst was a pump shotgun version. It hadn't yet been used in combat.

Bunny pointed to himself. "Happy camper, nonlethal edition."

"And," concluded Bird Dog, "more ammunition for each dart gun than you will ever need." To Belle he added, "Sandman darts are a lot lighter than lead rounds, so you can carry more ammo."

"Don't need *more* ammo," she said with a sniff.

Bird Dog rolled his eyes at me but said no more on the subject.

There was a small contingent of airport security and some MI5 cats waiting for us, too. They must have been fully briefed by someone with the right kind of juice because they didn't ask us for IDs. They just made sure we got to our SUV with no hassles. They weren't all that nice about it, either, with a few ordinary travelers getting a tad jostled.

Remy tried to get behind the wheel, but Top told him to mind his manners and go sit in the back. Which was fair, since Remy had never driven in the UK and none of us needed to have him hit a curb and blow a tire.

I lingered for a moment and took Bird Dog aside. "Everyone's coming in. All the teams including the Wild Hunt. You have gear for them all?"

He gave me a pitying look. "You try to tell your grandmother how to suck eggs?"

"My grandmother's dead."

"Goes to show you."

"That makes no sense."

"Get in the fucking car, Joe."

Ten seconds later we blew out of there.

## INTERLUDE 39

### THE WARRIOR AND THE WAR
### PUDDING LANE ROOMING HOUSE
### LONDON, ENGLAND
### SEPTEMBER 2, 1666 CE

That winter, the Thames froze twice and the cold was so intense that it kept people indoors as often as was possible. It wasn't until the spring thaw that the dying began.

And die they did.

Whole families. Whole neighborhoods.

London screamed as it died, and plague stalked the streets on the scuttling feet of rats. Gabriel went away for a while, searching, he said, for the cause of the plague. He did not believe that rats were solely responsible. He vanished for many weeks.

During that time Red Jane became one of the women hired to be searchers of the dead. Plague-searchers hired by parishes in London, to enter homes where people died. Entering there to examine the bodies and determine if these deaths were natural—childbirth, consumption, starvation, self-murder, cancer, or other causes—or if they were victims of the Black Death.

It was brutal work. Sad and dangerous, and it eroded her soul down to a nub of bleak despair.

Gabriel returned to London and began searching for her, and found her in the same bed where they had made love so many times. He stood in the doorway, holding a candle, staring with horror at what she had become.

The stick figure on the bed, withered down to a husk, racked by terrible coughs, and with buboes in her armpits and groin and neck.

"Don't come near me, for the love of Jesus," she cried.

"I must," he said as he crossed the threshold.

"Please, my love, stay away," sobbed Red Jane. "I beg you."

He came anyway, and sat on the bed. The blankets were soiled with blood and sweat and worse, but he did not care. He took her withered hands and held them in his, pressing them to his chest.

"I am so sorry that I stayed away so long," he said as tears rolled down his cheeks. "I tried to get back sooner, but . . ."

He shook his head. The truth was the Red Knights that he chased turned to pursue him, and in such numbers that there was nothing for it but to flee. Through England and into Wales they hunted him. Whenever he found the right ground for it, he would set a trap and carve their numbers down by ones and twos and threes.

By the time he'd whittled them down to a handful, the plague was raging throughout London. Even as he killed them, they mocked him, confessing that luring him away from the city was a plan, keeping him too busy to discover what they were about. Now he knew.

It was all a plan. The plague was not carried by rats, but by fleas that lived on the vermin. Fleas grown for decades by the alchemists of the Red Order. Fleas who carried a disease that had been made much stronger than ever before, and now it was being used to destroy England so that the Scriptor could help France in a plan of total conquest. It is much easier to conquer a land of the dead than a nation thriving with soldiers.

This was done without the sanction or even knowledge of Louis XIV. He would benefit, though, from the outcome only to discover how many of his courtiers were secret members of the Red Order.

England would fall, France would rise, and within a hundred years a French Empire would challenge even the Ottomans. Perhaps they would reclaim the Holy Land.

England was a growing power, and one likely to become a force across the face of the world. They were slow to react at times, but once roused and with their anger focused, they were a considerable threat. Using London as a witch's cauldron to brew a plague powerful enough to sweep across that great island would be a victory from which the nation would never recover. And the Red Order would be thereafter able to go unchecked. It was an ambitious plan, and a sound one. It could work, and likely *would.*

Gabriel explained it all to Red Jane as he sat with her. Her eyes were wide with horror.

"Surely they have already won," she gasped.

"Not yet. The plague is mostly concentrated here in London, which is the seat of power. The Red Order wants it to do all the harm it can do right here."

Red Jane shuddered as waves of pain raced through her. She turned and vomited, and he held the pan for her, then washed her face with a clean rag. Each time she threw up or had a coughing fit she seemed to diminish, to dwindle, as if life itself was made of the fiber of her being and was being leached away.

"But what can you do?" she pleaded. "You're only one man. What can any single person do against such evil? How can you hope to stop such hate?"

"There are things I can try," he said. "Things I must try, for I cannot let this merely happen. Defeat is not inevitable, but to stop this I . . . I must become even more of a monster than I already am."

"What things, my love? What is so awful that you hesitate even now? What in God's name can you do to even try to stop this?"

He kissed her fingers.

"You asked me that before and I didn't answer," he said. "I have given it much thought since."

"Then tell me, my love, if the Red Knights or the Red Order are really behind this plague, to what extreme would you go to oppose them? And . . . do not worry that I will hold it against you if you choose to withdraw from a fight of this kind."

There were tears in his eyes and they fell down his cheeks. "To stop this," he said, "I would burn down heaven itself."

The coughing and shivering returned and would not relent. She wilted against him, trembling at this last assault upon her, this last insult the plague offered. Yet she felt protected in his strong arms.

Gabriel Bethel held her all through the night. Her eyelids drifted shut and the last thing she ever knew was that someone cared enough to keep her safe.

She was gone before the chimes of midnight ceased.

He lingered there to wash her body and her hair, and dress her in a gown of plain white. He combed her hair and spread flowers around her and kissed her face.

The rooming house was next to a bakery, but there was no smell of bread that night, nor had there been all day.

Gabriel went out and came back with bundles of sticks and a small barrel of oil. He arranged the kindling around the bed and doused everything with oil, then went through the empty bakery and every empty house and spilled the oil everywhere.

He took the last candle from Red Jane's room—a stub less than an inch tall with a tiny flame—and placed it in her folded hands. He wept openly as he did this.

Before leaving he stood in the doorway and looked at her. In the repose of death she looked whole and young and, in his eyes, beautiful. The candle fell slowly sideways. When the oil began to burn, it spread quickly.

Very quickly.

He walked up and down the street, pounding on doors to warn the few remaining residents of the fire. The baker, Thomas Farriner, and his family escaped through a second-floor window, with Gabriel there to help. He helped several families flee.

When they were gone, he stood for a while on the street, his face turned to the freshening breeze. The bakery and rooming house and all the rest went up in a sheet of flame. Soon all of Pudding Lane was ablaze.

Then all of London burned. He saw to that.

He would later learn that more than thirteen thousand houses burned, along with nearly ninety churches, the Royal Exchange, the Custom House, St. Paul's Cathedral, Bridewell Palace, and much more. A newspaper in Cairo said that the loss was estimated to be close to ten million pounds.

He did not care.

The fire slowed the plague and soon the specter of the Black Death spread its wings and flew away, leaving England alive to rebuild. History books called it the Great Fire of London, celebrating both its effect and its destructive force.

Gabriel Bethel was never heard of again.

## CHAPTER 61

### ON THE M4 MOTORWAY
### BRENTFORD, ENGLAND

We were halfway to Barrier when Church called via the team channel.

"We're on our way to—" I began, but he cut me off.

"Outlaw, I need you and everyone on Havoc to hear this from me first," he said. "Scott Wilson has died as a result of the infection."

Beside me, Top made a long, low sound like he was deflating. Bunny cursed. Remy and Belle merely exchanged looks.

"I'm really sorry to hear that," I said, and meant it. I was a long way from being captain of Scott's fan club, but he did not deserve this. He was—*had been,* I suppose—a tight-ass, but he was definitely on the side of the angels. And, from what I knew so far of this disease, it was a hard way to go. I added, "And it really pisses me off."

"Join the club," said Church bitterly.

"We'll be there in a bit over forty minutes."

"You'll be there sooner than that," he said. "That sound you hear is a police escort."

"What sound—?" I began, but then I heard it. Two police ARVs—armored response vehicles—seemed to materialize out of nowhere, lights and sirens doing the full-tilt boogie. They settled into formation with us, one out front, one behind, and we broke one hell of a lot of traffic laws.

Oddly—surprisingly—I could feel my heart breaking, too. Scott

Wilson was dead. One of us. One of our family. Murdered. Maybe it was grief I was feeling, or maybe the heart needs to break open wide enough to let all that rage and hate out.

A police helicopter flew overhead, dropping low so that it was barely thirty yards above us.

We raced onward.

## CHAPTER 62

### PHONE CALL

My cell rang again and I thought it was Church calling back, but no. It was dipshit.

"What do you want?" I said, and was answered by a fit of deep, wet coughing. I waited it out, once more trying the call-trace tech even though it hadn't worked either of the previous tries. Hope springs eternal.

"Well, gosh," said Nicodemus. "I think I just hacked up some lung tissue."

"I'll cry about that later."

"Am I interrupting anything important?" he asked.

"I'm washing my dog's ass, so . . . yes."

I put the call on speaker and everyone came to point.

"I just heard that our mutual friend Scott Wilson has now shuffled off this mortal coil and joined the choir invisible."

"Fuck you."

"A cogent argument."

"Did you just call to cough at me or is there a point to this?"

"There's always a point to everything I do," he said. "Except when there isn't."

"Uh-huh. If you listen real carefully you'll hear me hanging up."

"You're not as much fun as I thought you'd be," said Nicodemus. "Yes, I have a reason for calling."

"Tick, tick, tick," I prompted.

"You said you wanted to ask another question. Hopefully something more precise than your last flub."

Top cocked an eyebrow at that, but I shook my head.

"How's this for precision," I said. "Tell me exactly what your current agenda is regarding RTI, me, the Sabbatarians, the Red Order, and the world in general."

"Oooo, that is a good question. Hmmmm, what *is* my plan . . . ?"

"Stop stalling."

"Not actually stalling, Ledger," he said, and then coughed for nearly a full minute. "Lordy, that's set off some fireworks all around me. Hoo-boy. Now, where was I? Ah yes, my plan."

I waited.

"If you are thinking what I have in mind is something you can stop, then you're quite wrong."

"I didn't ask that."

"True, but I needed to say that for context, because my *plan*," he said, leaning on the word, "is both more complex and yet less specific than what I'm usually up to. Nothing as contrived as the militia thing or the weaponized rabies thing. Not as much of a megillah as with the Seven Kings. No, this is more of a make it up as I go sort of thing. I am, after all, sick and that limits my energy and involvement."

"Still telling me nothing."

"There's no way to be as specific as you want, but that's the nature of questions and answers. The answers are what they are because the truth is the truth."

"Tell me the truth, then."

"I want to break the man you know as Church. I don't want to kill him. I don't want him to perish as the world burns, but believe me when I say this is the gospel truth—I am determined to break him as my last act in this age of the world. How's that for both truth and drama?"

He began to laugh, but it became another coughing fit. He hung up.

I sat back and looked at the others.

"That was surreal," said Bunny.

*"Laissez les bons temps rouler,"* muttered Remy. It was a Cajun phrase—*Let the good times roll.*

"What did any of that mean?" asked Belle.

I shook my head. "I have no idea."

Though, in truth, some species of understanding was crawling around in the back of my brain. Out of sight and out of touch, but definitely there.

## INTERLUDE 40

**CHATHAM DOCKYARD**
**RIVER MEDWAY, KENT, ENGLAND**
**NOVEMBER 13, 1666 CE**

He haunted the dockyard by night.

Over the last week there had been quiet murders and Simon Chapel grew concerned that the Red Knights had escaped the London fire and were hunting among the many ships and boats plying the waters around Kent. It was also possible, even likely, that Dutch spies were abroad because England and the Dutch Republic were still engaged in their small but fierce war over trade. But Simon did not think so.

The most recent killing was near a victualing yard used to house stores for naval vessels as well as transport ships that would be escorted across the Atlantic by royal frigates or sloops. During the daytime that area was as busy as an anthill, with people everywhere, carts rumbling over the cobblestones, booms swinging huge nets filled with crates and barrels, and ship's pursers and junior officers yelling at everyone. But by night, it was deserted, cold, and filled with suspicious shadows.

Simon Chapel moved through that quiet darkness as he examined the scene from several vantage points. There were still bloodstains on the ground despite an attempt to wash them away. He came over and knelt by the largest smear, leaning forward to sniff it. Human blood had its distinctive coppery aroma, but the darker blood of the Chevaliers Rouge was stronger, more bitter, and had a hint of sulfur in it.

And that latter stink was what he smelled there.

He sat on his heels and looked slowly around, trying to make sense of it.

A Red Knight had died here. That was obvious, at least to him. The tavern talk said that the victim had been hacked to pieces, and Simon wondered if that had been done to mangle the corpse so thoroughly that its monstrous nature was no longer evident. A fragment of a shattered incisor he found stuck between two paving stones seemed to verify his assumption.

The talk at the tavern also said that the only eyewitness, a peg-legged foretopman who was now a homeless beggar, swore that there had been a single killer. A slim man dressed in black. He and his victim argued in some unknown language and then drew swords. The fight was brief but intense, and the slim stranger won but took severe injuries of his own. The beggar said that after the victim was down, the stranger continued to hack at him while shouting two phrases over and over.

Simon Chapel found the old sailor and plied him with drink, and pressed coins into his hand in order to encourage him to repeat the words as best he could. The man was illiterate, yet his travels on a variety of ships had taken him many places.

"Thought it were some northern speech," he mumbled.

"Where in the north?"

"Russian, mayhap," slurred the drunk. "Or mayhap Poland. I don't rightly know."

"Tell me what you heard. Sound it out," said Simon, and the man had. It took Simon a bit of time to work out which language the sailor heard, and what the likely words actually were.

*Cel care l-a uitat pe Dumnezeu* and *Pacatosul, dusmanul lui Dumnezeu.* Two very interesting comments.

You have forgotten God.

You are the enemy of God.

Simon thought that to be very interesting indeed.

Now he squatted there, wondering what really happened there. It was so unlikely that any single man—any normal man—could have fought and defeated an Upierczy. Granted, he had faced and killed several of them, but Simon knew he was not normal, and never was. Even before the elixir, he was a better and more efficient killer even than his father had been. Or any of the Templars. He knew he was something of a freak, but that freakishness was an excellent and unexpected weapon in this war, amplified now since Maxillan's last concoction.

So, who was it killed the Red Knight?

He thought briefly about something his father and Lord de Molay mentioned so many, many years ago.

*"Vampirii Lui Dumnezeu,"* he murmured to the night.

Were there warrior vampires out there somewhere? Were they, in fact, reformed Upierczy? Or were they something else? His father hadn't known and in the centuries since, Simon never once encountered them. The very concept of them all but vanished from his mind, eroded by the passage of years.

He rose and searched the warehouse and several surrounding buildings. At times he felt that he was being watched, but when he checked there was nothing in the shadows but dust and vermin.

He stayed in the port for a few days, and then bought passage on the *Sutton Flower*, an armed transport taking settlers to the New World.

# CHAPTER 63

## HADRIAN TOWER
## ROPEMAKER STREET
## LONDON, ENGLAND

Getting close to the Barrier HQ building took some time, even with a police escort and the orders already in hand at every checkpoint. Rubbernecker traffic was everywhere, and the cops—bless their hearts—were running themselves ragged trying to keep them out of everyone's way. Crime scene traffic management—talk about unsung heroes. Has to be a job with its own kind of PTSD. Especially the sorry bastards who have to do it in cities like London.

I mean, it's not like London was built according to any kind of sensible grid pattern to make it easy to find stuff. Nope. It was a sprawl of twisty streets, absurdly narrow byways, roundabouts, and make-it-up-as-you-go urban planning that only drunks and madman seemed able to make sense of. It was built for horses, carts, wagons, and coaches. One of the hardest-drinking men I ever met was a Cockney structural engineer whose job it was to keep London city streets from collapsing. After hearing some of his stories I'm glad all people do to me is try to shoot me.

Top, who can drive anything on four wheels pretty much anywhere without losing his cool, got us there and made it look easier than it was. In the backseat, Belle had a two-hand death grip on the leather upholstery and Remy was praying something in Cajun-accented Latin. The AVR vehicles peeled off, and the helicopter, too. Police constables waved us through to a spot close to the building and we piled out.

Bunny looked around. "Hell of a lot of rubberneckers around here. Don't they know what kind of crap's going on? Y'know, the Black fucking Plague and all. Just saying?"

"It's excitement," Belle observed coldly. "People are stupid."

Since we'd already changed into our ChemRigs at the airport the crowd fell into a whispering hush, leaning toward their friends to share theories as to who and what we were. There were no labels, patches, or insignia on our rigs, but we had gun belts strapped around our middles and we all carried heavy equipment bags.

Remy tapped my arm. "Guy just called us ninja spacemen."

Top made a face. "Sounds like one of those eighties New Wave bands trying to sound ironic."

"You know about eighties New Wave?" asked Remy.

"What of it? Can't a guy like me know music?"

"Nah, it's just that you're old."

Top gave him a very bland smile. "Two words," he said pointing a finger like a gun. "Friendly fire."

Remy drew his fingers across his visor, zipping his mouth shut.

Hadrian Tower was a government building, which allowed the local authorities to exert a more definite set of restrictions. Even so, the poor traffic cops were in a losing battle against the curious crowds.

We trooped over to the main door, which was accessed only by a plastic corridor that served as the single-entry point. The rest of the building was in the process of being tented by an impressive array of industrial helicopters and what looked like legions of Spider-Men crawling all over the sloping upper floors. Well, maybe moon men is closer to it as everyone wore a kind of white protective overgarment typically worn at crime scenes over here. Gloves and booties, and helmets with self-contained oxygen tanks. There were these little three-sided shower stalls where techs with high-pressure spray tanks barraged everyone who came out with disinfectant, and even then some of those folks had to sit in exam tents.

"They ain't taking this shit lightly," observed Top, impressed. He likes seeing anything done well, from grilling a good steak to tuning an engine to cleaning up a site after camping. Although he was a combat sergeant, his Type A traits came out when he was a sergeant overseeing training at Fort Bragg.

A tall man with graying blond hair and a whole lotta nose spotted us and hurried over. He wore a hazmat suit but no hood.

"Ken Manning, building manager," he said, not offering a hand, given the circumstances. "You're Colonel Ledger and this is your RTI field team?"

"Call me Outlaw." I introduced the team, giving their combat call signs. "Havoc Team's here on loan. Will there be any problems with that?"

Interjurisdictional issues were tough enough when everyone saluted the same flag, but when it goes international there is nearly always a pissing contest to establish who has the biggest political dick. But Manning surprised me.

"Not a problem, Outlaw," he said. "Word came down from on high that you should be given full cooperation. You'll have full run of the building. Besides, I've personally worked with the Deacon before."

"Ah," I said. Deacon was one of Church's nicknames, though one that's pretty much fallen out of common use. I took a closer look at Manning and saw wrinkles that made me add another ten years to his apparent age. Call it a healthy fifty.

I looked around. "I don't see any CBRN vans."

CBRN was shorthand for chemical, biological, radiological, and nuclear defense.

"Due to the secure nature of the work done in the building," said Manning, "we operate on a special charter, which covers the various departments that do classified work. A DSMA-Notice was issued to the press, of course. Our biggest issue is the crowd outside—everyone has a cell camera and is a YouTube wannabe influencer."

I nodded. DSMA-Notice was shorthand for Defence and Security Media Advisory Notices, what used to be called more simply D-Notice, and stood as an official request to news editors not to publish or broadcast items on specified subjects for reasons of national security.

Manning added, "Moreover, we have our own version of CBRN built into our staffing and protocols."

"That's good to know."

He nodded to my ChemRig. "I don't recognize those hazmats. I thought the Deacon preferred Saratoga Hammer Suits."

"These are next-gen," I said.

"Ah," he said in that very British way that encompasses a lot of meaning and understanding. "Well, we're happy to have you on board with this. Deacon says that you've handled more than your full share of biohazardous situations, particularly those involving deliberate threats."

"Terrorists with funky germs," Bunny said.

"And other toys," added Top.

"Hooah," said Remy. Belle, true to form, said nothing at all.

I nodded to the entrance to the temporary tunnel. "Clock's ticking pretty loud here, Manning."

"Too right it is. You want me to walk you in and show you around? A quick tour of key areas?"

"I'd appreciate it."

He grinned and swept a hand toward the tunnel. *"Lasciate ogne speranza, voi ch'intrate."*

I smiled back and translated for the benefit of my team. "Abandon hope all ye who enter."

Manning nodded approval. "You know your Italian."

"I've read Dante."

Together we stepped into hell.

## INTERLUDE 41

### THE WARRIOR AND THE WAR
### SALEM, MASSACHUSETTS
### AUGUST 1692

"How many of them are there?"

The old woman jumped at the sound of his voice and turned quickly, bringing her knife up with a practiced ease. He did not block or parry the blade, but stepped backward in case she went for a thrust. Recognition came a heartbeat after alarm.

"It's you," she said tightly. "I did not think you'd truly come."

"I gave my word," said the man. He was big and blocky, with strange eyes and a lugubrious expression. His traveling cloak was smoke gray, and the clothes beneath them unadorned black. A pair of flintlock pistols were thrust into his belt, and he had a basket-hilted Scottish sword and matching dagger as well, and throwing knives tucked into the tops of his boots.

The woman smiled at that. Not a nice smile in any way. "Forgive me if I need proof of action before I take any man's word."

"That's fair," he said.

She slipped her knife into the sheath hidden beneath her apron and leaned back to look up at him. Agatha Fowler was eighty years old and looked every minute of it. Her face was creased with age and worry, blue eyes clouded with glaucoma. Even so, her speed with the knife spoke to an inner toughness born of experience and need.

"You've certainly taken your time, Jonah Tabernacle—if that is even your real name."

"Does it matter if it is?" asked Jonah.

"Not very much."

"Like the women you have been gathering, a name is either a burden or something to be discarded."

"And how many names have you left behind you in your travels?"

He gave a small, dry laugh. "Many."

Her eyes searched his. "You don't seem happy about it, even with the freedom it gives you."

Jonah inclined his head toward the nearby barn. "How many of them are joyful at leaving behind their names, their families, their hopes for happy and ordinary lives?"

"All of them," said Agatha.

"All of them," he agreed.

The old woman linked her arm with his and they walked companionably toward the barn. "To answer your question, my friend," she said. "There are one hundred and eight. From Salem and the surrounding towns."

"More than I expected."

She glanced up at him. "Too many?"

But he shook his head. "No. And as the ship doesn't sail until the morning tide two days hence, there is both room and time for more."

"I dare not even try," said Agatha. "Samuel Parris has eyes everywhere."

Jonah nodded. Parris, the pastor of Salem Village, was among the first to make accusations against girls and women in the area. His condemnations were so potent and compelling that it seemed to burst open the floodgates of hate.

"He and the others in town will have something else to draw their attention," he said. "I've planned a bit of a distraction."

"Oh . . . ? What have you and your band of thieves come up with?"

Jonah traveled with a small group made up of like-minded men and women he trusted, even if some of them were technically criminals. The New World was still so unsettled, at least in terms of English law, and that gave him and his followers some useful latitude.

"Nothing too extravagant," Jonah said. "A few small house fires set in the right place and at the right time. Everyone will be looking to the west and we will have a clear path to the docks."

"Do you trust the captain of that ship?"

"Isaiah Croft? Yes. I trust him completely."

"Why?"

"We have traveled a certain distance together," said Jonah. "Enough to have seen him in situations where he could do harm without fear of repercussions, but each time he took the better path."

Agatha reached for the iron handle of the barn door. "Trust is very hard to come by in times like these."

"It is," agreed Jonah.

She paused a moment longer. "And if the men in town try to stop you?"

The smile he gave her was of a kind that might have given the devil himself pause.

"That," he said, "would be an unfortunate choice of action."

The old woman stood on tiptoes to kiss his cheek. "It's nice to know that not all men fear and hate women."

Then she pulled the door open.

# CHAPTER 64

## HADRIAN TOWER
## LONDON, ENGLAND

The place looked empty.

Bunny walked past us with his BAMS unit held high to catch airflow. We all stood and waited, including Manning, who still wore no hood. After a few minutes, Bunny's shoulders relaxed and he turned to show the bright green sensor screen.

"All good, boss."

Manning smiled. "Most floors have their own HVAC system, with exceptions being the three Barrier floors and a couple of other divisions that occupy more than one level. We have BAMS technology built into our air filtration."

"Smart," I said, then looked around. "Where is everyone? And . . . how many people work in this building?"

"On a normal business day like we had yesterday," said Manning, "eleven hundred and forty-six. Staff sign-in numbers confirm that."

"And where are they now?"

"Evacuated," he said. "Once it was determined that the only people getting sick were on the three Barrier floors—levels 83 through 86—it was decided that the rest of the employees should be taken somewhere safer. They're in isolation in an auditorium at RAF Northolt, a base in South Ruislip."

"None of them sick?"

"Not yet," he said, then realized how that sounded and corrected himself. "No."

"That's something."

Manning gave me an appraising look. "It's my understanding that you will be acting as lead investigator for this matter, at least in the short term. How can I best help facilitate that?"

"I want exact numbers of everyone still in the building," I told him. "As well as access to employee information, job descriptions, performance reviews. All of that. Can you do that?"

"One thing I can tell you is that we have a security team here. Alpha Team by name. One of Barrier's Special Projects groups. PMCs, but all thoroughly screened. Forty of them, all in special Hammer Suits."

"Where are they now?"

"On patrols all over the building. Remember, there are eighty-six floors aboveground and four below."

"Can you give me a precise list of who's on Alpha? Names, ranks, images. And also where they are right now and how best to contact them?"

"I can, but the director of security, Mr. Griffiths, can do it a good deal more quickly. I'll take you to see him when we're done here."

"Apart from you, Griffiths, Rockwell, and Alpha Team, who else is locked in with us?"

"There are about thirty people spread out here and there and locked into offices that have been swept for the, um, disease."

"Call it plague," I said. "Keeps it simple."

"Simple perhaps," he said and shivered. "But just that word is rather terrifying to have as a part of any normal conversation."

"Define normal," said Top.

Manning laughed nervously and looked sheepish.

"Okay, I'll need the same info on them as on Alpha. I want to have names, faces, and designations for everyone inside this building. No exceptions. Also, I also want logs, work orders, delivery manifests, the lot for anyone who visited the building over the last three weeks."

"That's a great deal of information." We both knew it was a pain in the ass, and I was a foreigner with a special pass. I knew it was a lot and did not give a rat's wrinkly nutsack if it discommoded him in any way. However, he said, "I'll get everything you need."

"Thanks. Now tell me about access. Who, how, where, why."

"The more sensitive the area," he explained, "the smaller the number of people who have access."

"Different keycards?" asked Bunny.

"Yes. Some are color-coded for different floors and different departments. The maintenance team has salmon-colored badges. The global threat-assessment group has black cards, and so on. Barrier IDs are forest green, and the special security team have lime-green badges. Each badge has a programmable chip which syncs with the security computers to respond to changes in the day-code, emergencies, and that sort of thing."

Remy grinned. "What color badge do we get? I'll take purple, green, or yellow."

Those were the traditional colors of New Orleans, but Manning shook his head. "Plain white. Special all-access passes. The only other person who has that level of access is Mr. Rockwell. Even Catriona MacPherson of MI6 and Clive Cooper of MI5, both of whom were here for Mr. Wilson's interview, had day passes with restrictions."

I nodded. "Does Griffiths oversee all of that?"

"Yes."

"Didn't he used to be director of field support for Barrier?"

"You've done your homework," said Manning, nodding. "Yes, Griffiths stepped away from fieldwork around the time Barrier moved into this building. He served as senior advisor on building security and it's largely because of him this is one of the most secure buildings in Europe."

I looked around. "Big claim for a building with a lot of big glass windows everywhere."

Manning grinned like a poker player about to drop a full house on the table. "That's part of the genius of it all. The glass isn't glass at all."

"Come again?"

"It's a whole new take on what they call amorphous glass or metallic glass. Every window you see is actually a completely opaque panel made of alloy with a disordered atomic-scale structure, tempered to be not only bulletproof but able to withstand a direct hit from anything short of a ballistic missile. Not joking."

"I'm looking right through it," I said. "I can see the damn car we came in. I can see helicopters in the air. How does that make sense?"

"Micro-video sheeting with real-time ultra-high-def display," he said, still grinning. "The outside of every panel is covered with thousands of tiny cameras, and the inside is coated with just as many display screens. The cameras feed the outside images to the screens so the effect is like looking out of a window, but it's not. It's the same technology being experimented with on the next level of stealth aircraft."

"Okay, that's impressive as hell, but what's the point? I mean, I get the increased security for Barrier, but why the whole building? Sounds more expensive than practical."

"Oh, believe me, it cost a bomb. But we need it. There's a lot more to this building than Barrier and a mixed bag of government offices. We have more than twenty cutting-edge labs here, ranging from a few BSL-1's for research groups working on microbes not harmful to healthy people, a few BSL-2 labs working on lower-end biological threats, two BSL-3's and a BSL-4 with the highest level of safety, which is where we would *normally* study something like this plague outbreak. That's where most of the remaining staff are, since their floors are already bio-sealed."

I stood and gaped at him. "Hold on, you have top-level biological research labs in the heart of fucking *London*?"

Manning managed not to look either embarrassed or contrite. "As I said, Colonel, this building is incredibly secure. We have more security features here than they have in your Centers for Disease Control in Atlanta, Georgia. And by quite a larger margin."

"What's stored in the BSL-4 and -5 labs?"

"I . . . well, I don't know the specifics. Well above my pay grade, of course."

"Would Griffiths know?"

"I would doubt it. However, Director Rockwell would know, as Barrier is the centerpiece of Hadrian Tower. All departments report to him."

"And nobody bothered to mention this before now? Nobody even suggested that something you have stored here could be the reason Scott Wilson is cooling meat in a hospital morgue?"

As my tone rose, his smile drained away. Maybe he thought I was going to hit him. Maybe I was thinking really damn hard about doing exactly that.

"I . . . I mean I assumed that your Mr. Church knew all about it. Mr. Wilson certainly did. He even commented on it when he arrived yesterday."

That jerked the rug out from under my outrage. I drew in a deep lungful of air through my nose and exhaled slowly, trying to cool my anger.

"First off, Manning, the whole idea of a having a biohazard lab in the heart of London is stupid."

"Yet the CDC is in Atlanta," he countered with some heat.

"And that's stupid, too," I fired back. "Though that, at least, is not downtown."

"Our security is second to *none,*" he said again. No smiles now.

"You want to know how many 'security second to none' places I've encountered since I came to work for Church? Places that bad guys waltzed into and places *I've* cracked? In this day and age, it's the height of hubris to believe that security is an absolute. Surprised you, as building manager, don't know that."

His face slowly turned the color of a stewed tomato.

"Second thing," I said, swinging back to my topic, "is that this is a poor fucking time to tell *me* about it. There should have been a briefing on all of this while we were en route."

"Wouldn't that be up to your lot?" he asked.

Impasse. I wanted to punch him to make myself feel better, but there was no chance that he was on the policy level. His glare was challenging, but I was in the ring with the wrong boxer.

"Maybe I'd better have a chat with Director Rockwell," I said. "Barrier was built to stop stuff exactly like what's happening here."

"Speak with whomever you deem necessary," Manning said coldly.

"Where is Rockwell?" I asked.

"He'll either be in his office or in the executive gym."

I almost smiled at that. "The gym? Seriously? With all this going on?"

Manning shrugged. "It's a private gym and no one who was sick had access. Besides, Mr. Rockwell is into fitness in a big way. He calls himself a fitness fanatic. And it shows. He's built like one of those movie superheroes. Muscles on muscles. And strong? Like you wouldn't believe. Scary strong. One of those guys who looks strong but is even stronger." He paused, perhaps aware of having a fanboy moment. In a less effusive tone added, "Between you and me, I think the gym is therapy for him with all that's going on. Exercise releases all of those endorphins."

"Good for him," I said dryly. "But I want to see the head of security first."

From Manning's face it was clear he knew he'd lost control of the conversation and wrapped it up with a crisp, "Come along and I'll take you up to see Mr. Griffiths."

## INTERLUDE 42

### THE WARRIOR AND THE WAR

### PARIS, FRANCE

### 1766 CE

"Know him?" laughed Voltaire. "Why, of course I know him. Le Comte de Saint Germain is a wonder-man. He is the man who knows everything and never dies."

"Oh, surely not," said the dinner guest to his left, sure that the host was making another of his elaborate jests.

"Wonder-man. Ha! He's nothing more than an adventurer," growled a colonel of cavalry. "A dandy who puts on airs and makes preposterous claims."

The duchess to Voltaire's right raised one delicate eyebrow. "I've heard that he claims to be more than five hundred years old."

"I heard that he said he was at Golgotha for the Crucifixion," said another guest. Everyone at Voltaire's table seemed deeply engaged by the topic.

"No, no, no," said the host, waving that away. "Those are claims ascribed to him but I can assure you he has never said them. If you ever met him, you'd understand. He is a reticent man who rarely speaks about himself. Even the claim that he is the son of Francis II Rákóczi, the Prince of Transylvania, was made by someone else. Giacomo Casanova, perhaps. He loves to spin a tale when the truth is too boring."

The duchess caught the eye of another highborn lady and they shared a secret smile, both having made acquaintanceship with Casanova.

"Then what does he say about himself?" demanded the colonel. "Surely he had presented credentials to someone."

Voltaire leaned back in his seat and sipped his wine. "We have had many conversations," he admitted. "But he rarely speaks of himself."

"Of what, then?"

"Politics, mostly," said the writer. "His knowledge and understanding of the machinations of every court is prodigious. He is frank about things, and no fan of any monarch who views the world as a chessboard rather than a collection of people."

The colonel sniffed at this. He was the second son of a great family, and he regarded empathy as a sign of weakness. "A piece of courtly fluff," he said.

Voltaire turned to him and offered a wide, devious smile. "Feel free to say so to his face, my friend. That would be quite amusing."

"Why? He's no soldier."

"He is without a doubt the finest swordsman I have ever met."

"Bah, any bloody fool can learn to twirl a ceremonial sword and dazzle the unlearned with flourishes and tricks. He's fought no duels I've ever heard about."

"Oh, he dislikes dueling," said the writer.

"Timid, then?" snapped the colonel, who was a notorious duelist, despite the practice being officially illegal. "I thought as much."

"Not at all," laughed Voltaire. "It is his view that dueling is a game for men who doubt their virility and must prove themselves in public displays of violence."

That hushed the table for a moment, and no one met the colonel's eyes. A few of the women smiled into their fans. Several of the male guests suddenly found their soup quite delicious.

"Let him say as much to me, damn his eyes," growled the colonel, his face reddening.

"If you ever chance to meet Le Comte de Saint Germain," said Voltaire smoothly, "I hope you do tell him that."

"I will."

"And let me know where to send flowers and condolences."

# CHAPTER 65

## HADRIAN TOWER
## LONDON, ENGLAND

A very silent and stiff Manning led us to Griffiths's door. He was about to knock but I shifted to block him. "Thanks, Manning. We've got it from here. Please get that information I asked for."

His affability had melted away and I didn't much care. Sucked for him to be point man on this. My sympathy level was low because if I was in his place I wouldn't have buried the lede in terms of what was stored in the building. I watched him go. Manning didn't exactly flee, but he didn't linger, either. Nor did he look back—just walked off with a ramrod-straight back and a brisk stride.

"Not a happy camper," observed Bunny.

Top stepped close and spoke quietly. "Boy's got a corncob up his ass." To me he said, "You're gonna have Bug hack this place and get the skinny on what's in those labs, right?"

"Oh yes," and I tapped into my comms. Oddly, it took three tries before a connection went through, and when Bug came on he sounded staticky. I quickly told him what I wanted.

"I'll get Yoda on it," Bug said. "I'm still on this Corvin Castle data mess."

"Keep me posted."

I tapped out of comms.

Top said, "There's two ways of looking at this, Outlaw. One is that this building is really top-of-the-line secure *because* of all that goes on, and they went the extra mile to make damn sure. But the other option is that this place is a vault and if it goes into lockdown, then anyone stuck in here is going to share the place with a bunch of nasty-ass germs."

"Uh-huh," I said.

"Can't say I like either option," Bunny observed.

"It's stupid," muttered Belle and flapped a hand at the whole place. "Expensive death trap."

"Personally," said Remy brightly, "I'm okay with us getting the hell out of here and seeing how fast we can get to a nice island, say maybe in the South Pacific."

"Hooah," said Top.

"Hoo-fucking-ah," agreed Bunny. "Tell you one thing . . . I'm not taking this ChemRig off anytime soon."

"Word," said Remy, and they bumped fists.

"Maybe you guys should stroll around and get a read on the place," I suggested. "Eyes and ears. Bodycams on and skepticism dialed to eleven. I don't like anything about this."

"I thought Barrier was our ally?" Remy said.

"Remember the Golden Rule," I said.

"Which is?"

"Trust no one," said Top, Bunny, and Belle all at the same time. They headed off.

I knocked on the door of the security office.

## INTERLUDE 43

### THE WARRIOR AND THE WAR
### PARIS, FRANCE
### 1766 CE

"You should have seen his face when I suggested that he call you out," said Voltaire, who then burst out laughing. "He was apoplectic."

"Perhaps you should not have done that," said Le Comte de Saint Germain.

They were in a Turkish-style bathhouse, both of them pouring sweat as they sat amid clouds of steam. There was incense swirling within the vapor. Voltaire sucked on a hookah that was filled with tobacco lightly soaked in opium.

"I was rather hoping he would challenge you."

"That's unkind," said the count.

"Oh, not unkind to you," insisted the writer. "Colonel Duquesne needs a sound thrashing. Though, as he is nearly as dangerous a swordsman as he claims, he isn't likely to get his comeuppance from anyone else I know."

Saint Germain leaned back and closed his eyes. "So, I'm an assassin now. Charming."

"You've been called worse."

"I have."

"If there is even a soupçon of truth in all the gossip, you are the force behind half of the political decisions in Europe, and the opponent to the other half. All of your plans and schemes. Visiting alchemists and spiritualists. Talking with revolutionaries, cutthroats, pirates, and brigands. God only knows what you're actually up to."

Saint Germain said nothing.

"And," said Voltaire, "I rather think 'assassin' is not far off the mark."

The count began to snore softly, though the writer rather thought it was only a pretense of sleep.

# CHAPTER 66

## BARRIER HEADQUARTERS
## LONDON, ENGLAND

Bedwyr Griffiths looked like he'd spent a lot of his years playing rugby in one of the less polite leagues. He had a gristly left ear, several old facial scars—including a deep one through his right eyebrow—and a nose that had been so comprehensively knocked askew that I wondered if he could even breathe through it. He was about six feet tall and nearly as wide, with bandy bowlegs and impressive shoulders you could land a small plane on and still have runway. I guessed him at around sixty but doing a good job looking fifty. On one sideboard there was a row of trophies from a variety of contact sports including karate, Brazilian jujitsu, boxing and, you guessed it, rugby. He wore a dress shirt tucked into gray wool trousers, a school tie of some sort, and had a small headset with a wire mic wrapped around toward the corner of his mouth.

"The one and only Outlaw," he said with a small, knowing smile. "I've heard stories." Despite the Welsh first name he had a broad Yorkshire accent. Sounded like Sean Bean.

"Oh?" I said.

"You're the kind of bloke who gets talked about," he said. "In certain circles."

"Hopefully very discreet circles."

He laughed. "Only kind I ever travel in, except when I'm taking my granddaughters to ballet."

There were framed pictures on the wall of two adorable preteen twins in ballet costumes. He also had a lot of photos of him with five different prime ministers, one with the queen, one with the king, and many with people I didn't know, each of them in uniforms of various branches of the military. Although it wasn't at all unusual for someone to fill their office with such photos, there was something about it in the office of the director of security that bothered me. Nor could I quite define why.

"Have a seat," he said.

"Can we talk about the elephant in the room first?" I asked. "Like the fact that you're not wearing any kind of protective garments . . . ?"

"Too late for that, I'm afraid," he said. "I was exposed to Scott Wilson and quite a few other staff members who have since gotten sick. Dr. Suliman said that if I hadn't gotten sick yet, I likely have some resistance."

"I hadn't heard about any kind of resistance so far."

"Apparently there is some known immunity among the population of London. Something about our ancestors having survived the historic Black Death and passing on the gene or whatever to descendants. Talk to the medical professionals, they'll explain it better. My family's originally from Wales, but enough of my ancestors lived in London going back to the twelfth century that I suppose I got lucky." He paused and shook his head. "Even though it's nice to be alive, it feels like a lot of more deserving people got the short end of the genetic stick. I'm finding that hard to feel joyful about."

"Guess I'd feel the same," I said.

"Oh, and, just to be sure, they shot me up with every kind of antibiotic they had in the cupboard. I think at this point I'm safe from everything up to and including social diseases."

I gave him a kind of noncommittal grunt and took the seat he waved me to. Have to admit that it was weird sitting there in a Chem-Rig but otherwise having a chat in a well-appointed office with a guy wearing a business suit. Surreal, but not in a good way. It was like looking at ordinary life through a lens smeared with oil—the picture was almost right while being noticeably wrong.

"For all the obvious reasons, I want to keep this brief," I said.

"Here to help," he said. "Tell me what you need and I'll do what I can to make it happen."

"First, as I understand it, you oversaw the security for this building."

"As part of a team, sure."

"How'd that play out?"

Griffiths looked puzzled. "How is that relevant to what's going on?"

"Scott Wilson wasn't sick before he came here," I said. "He caught the plague here and died as a result. Bunch of your employees are dead or dying. How do you not see the relevance?"

"Ah," he said. "I understand. Well, it's pretty simple. I was a field agent for enough years and worked enough of the kinds of cases you know a lot about. Bioweapons, new technologies, all that. When you have to infiltrate bases and labs that have top-notch security, you cultivate a grasp of the technical philosophy of how security works based on need, threat assessment, and design requirements. Not to blow my own horn too much, but I broke into a number of facilities that were considered to be unbreakable. So, when they were designing this place, they brought me aboard as a consultant."

"What was the nature of your consultancy?"

"I worked with the design team to reinforce those areas that often leave an opening for an intrusion team armed with sophisticated technology. They built several computer models and kept challenging me to beat the security. When they got to the point where I couldn't beat it easily, they took the strengths from each model and built on those. Eventually they came up with a design I couldn't even dent, they turned it over to the architects, and two years later we have this place. It's a bloody fortress."

"Manning said the same. You consider this place unbreakable?"

"So far, yes. Based on where we are in our understanding of security science, yes."

"And yet somehow people in this fortress are dying of a weaponized pathogen."

His face darkened a bit and he looked both angry and embarrassed. "Quite," he said, loading a lot of meaning into that one word.

"Care to float a theory as to *how*?"

"There can be only one possible answer," he said.

"I pretty much don't want to hear 'human error' here," I said.

Griffiths shook his head. "Deliberate human *sabotage* by someone who works here," he said. "And believe me when I say that no matter how close you were to Mr. Wilson, you do *not* want to find out who did this more than I do."

"Because your reputation is on the line?" I suggested and watched his face.

“No,” he said with a dangerous edge. “Because some of the people who died today are friends. And my niece is also in hospital on a ventilator. There’s a damn good chance she’s not going to live. So, yes, Colonel Ledger, I have skin in this game that matters more than my job.”

## INTERLUDE 44

### THE WARRIOR AND THE WAR
### VON HAUKE MANOR
### ECKERNFÖRDE, GERMANY
### FEBRUARY 27, 1784

“You are now a dead man,” said Duke von Hauke, handing over a signed certificate of death.

Saint Germain took the paper and held it to the light so he could see both the official signature and the watermark. Then he folded it carefully and handed it back.

“I am dead,” he agreed.

Von Hauke, an old friend, poured them each a glass of excellent French brandy. They toasted his demise, sipped, and watched the snow fall gently over the lawn. The windows were frosted, but there was still enough clear glass to view the storm.

“It’s a strange thing to ask,” said von Hauke. “Stranger still to be a party to it. I understand that you prefer discretion and secrecy, but between us . . . may I ask a question?”

“Between us,” said Saint Germain after a few moments’ consideration. “Ask. And if I can answer, I will.”

“This *role* you have been playing—the mysterious Le Comte de Saint Germain—was it ever real? And if not, how wide of the mark was it?”

“Those are two questions.”

“Indulge me. People have made such extraordinary claims about you that it is impossible to *know* anything. Is there even a grain of truth in the wild stories?”

“Some.”

"Then you *were* at the Crucifixion?"

Saint Germain chuckled. "Of course not."

"Are you an angel?"

"Please . . ."

"Are you Cain, slayer of Abel?"

"Hardly."

"Not a vampire then, either? That's the latest gossip."

They both laughed at that.

"Definitely not a vampire," said the count. "The only blood my appetite craves is a very rare steak."

The duke sipped and studied him. "You are rich as Croesus yet you have no estate. You are a perpetual house guest, and always at the best houses—artists, writers, philosophers, for the most part—and in palaces, too, at times, yet you have no home as far as I know. You could buy half of France and perhaps all of Germany, but you spend your fortune on the network of spies and agents you've created."

"I have a keen interest in politics."

"As I have noted. There's more. You are older than you appear. I've known you for—what is it now? Thirty-five years? And yet you look as young now as when we first met. Or perhaps a year or two older."

Saint Germain said nothing.

"Then there's that painting you commissioned . . . the one Voltaire's friend did of you. That isn't even your face. And I heard he painted it over a portrait that was closer to the mark. Will you at least tell me how old you are?"

The only answer was a small shrug. They sat and watched the snow pile up.

"You're not a soldier and you sneer at duelists," said the duke, "yet how many times have you come here bleeding and half-dead?"

"What is it you want me to say, Heinrich?"

"Not to put too fine a point on it, my friend, but what *are* you?"

"A man," said the count. "Nothing more."

The duke sighed at that answer, knowing it to be false but not at all certain how much was a fiction and how much was evasion. "Do I even know your real name?"

"No one does. Not anymore."

"But why *not*?" pleaded the count. "What are you afraid of?"

"I am afraid of many things, Heinrich, because this world is unsafe and there are people who delight in creating misery and causing strife."

"Yessss," drawled von Hauke. "Like that man you asked about a few years ago. The one with the biblical name. What was it?"

"Nicodemus. Yes, he foments chaos for its own sake. But, there are others who are the shadows behind thrones, the ones who manipulate for gain and care nothing for the pain they cause. I see it brewing in France, and on both sides of the golden line. The bourgeois have taken excess to a grotesque limit, and the people will not stand for it much longer. Yet even among them there are those who do not really care about liberty and equality but light the fires as distraction for what they truly want."

"Which is what?"

"Power."

"Not profit? Not gold?"

Saint Germain shook his head. "Gold allows for the acquisition of power."

The duke considered this. "Do you really think there will be a revolution in France?"

"It is inevitable at this point."

"The people have been grumbling for years."

"Their anger will come to a boil. Just as it did in the American colonies. The age of empires will not last forever. France will burn within a decade, mark me on this."

"Is that what you want?" asked the count. "Is that the prize at the end of all your plans and plots?"

"What? No. It will be a bloodbath, whether the people are victorious or the government puts them down. I take no sides in that, for there are heroes and villains among each camp. But I can read the writing on the wall. I can read the terrain that we, as a culture, must traverse."

"What *is* your goal, then? You spent years in the courts of Europe, making friends at every level and now you are *dead*. Have you accomplished some great achievement? Or have you met with failure and now intend on reinventing yourself."

Saint Germain smiled. "Oh, a bit of both, really. There are wars that did not happen, and some that needed to happen, and have."

"Your doing?"

"With the help of key friends, well placed."

"Ah. I suppose I am one of those."

"You are, Heinrich," said the count. "And a rare one in that you get to ask these kinds of questions. There are very few people I trust as much."

"Yet you do not answer all of my questions."

Outside, a branch of an ancient oak sagged beneath the weight of snow. There was a muffled *crack* as it snapped off and fell.

"I answer what I can, my friend," said the count. "You are a great friend and you are a good man. Better than most, and better even than some to whom you are related by blood or marriage. However, there are some truths that might do you damage to know."

"Shouldn't I be the judge of my own vulnerability?" asked the duke.

Saint Germain shook his head. "I must ask that you trust me when I say that it is better for you not to know some things."

"Like your real name?"

"My real name is of no consequence. You will not have heard of it, nor would anyone alive. My family was not a royal or even noble one. My own father was a bastard, as am I."

"Or your age?"

Count Saint Germain smiled. "Older than I look."

The duke sighed and finished his brandy. He refilled both glasses. "May I ask one last question—and I pray you give me a truthful answer."

"I will if I can."

"Tell me, my friend, are you a good man?"

They sat for a long while as the snow fell.

When the count spoke, there was a deep sadness in his tone.

"I aspire to be, Heinrich."

It was all the answer he gave, but it was enough.

# CHAPTER 67

## BARRIER HEADQUARTERS
## LONDON, ENGLAND

Top Sims and the rest of Havoc walked through the building, doing it at what an observer might have construed as an ambling pace. The reality was that they were trying to feed as much detail as possible via their bodycams.

"Be faster if I just launched some busy-bees?" asked Remy. "Got about a zillion of 'em in my bag."

Busy-bees were one of a wide variety of drones he carried as Havoc's tech guy. They were the size of bees and were basically flying cameras. The audio feed was questionable because of range, but the lenses were excellent; and they sent signals back to Remy's tactical computer, and from there to MindReader.

But Top shook his head. "Outlaw wants us to be coy with the toys we brought. We can deploy the good stuff later after he talks to Griffiths and Director Rockwell. Right now, he wants us to look and pass along our impressions."

"Copy that," said Remy, though he was disappointed. He loved his gadgets.

Belle, the team sniper, silently turned her head this way and that, doing it slowly, taking in a lot more than the average person ever could. Sniper training was as much about patient observation and practical assessment as it was in being able to hit a target at long range.

Bunny fell into step beside Top. He held his BAMS unit in his big hand, the screen continuing to glow an encouraging green.

"Air's clean," he said.

"So? You want to take off your hood, Farm Boy?"

"Not a chance. Though, damn, my nose itches like a son of a bitch."

"Life is hard for some folks."

They walked down a hallway of offices, opening each one and waving the BAMS around.

"Still green," Top said. "I'm good with that."

"Even so," said Bunny, "this place gives me the creeps. Outlaw's not a fan, either, I can tell."

"No shit. Place brags about having the tightest security this side of God's private bathroom and then there's an outbreak of the Black Death? Some version of it that's too nasty for that vindictive bitch, Mother Earth, to cook up? Can't say I'm digging the vibe here, either."

"You feeling anything about that Manning guy?"

Top thought about it and shook his head. "If someone here's involved in this, he wouldn't be near the top of my list."

"But he would still be *on* the list?"

"Everyone's on my list."

"Hooah," said Bunny under his breath.

Then in a sharp whisper, Belle said, "On your six."

Top turned to see two figures dressed in black Saratoga Hammer Suits coming toward them, rifles up, barrels pointing at them.

# CHAPTER 68

## BARRIER HEADQUARTERS
## LONDON, ENGLAND

"Sorry to hear about your niece," I said. "But I need as complete an understanding as possible as to who gets clearance to enter this building. That includes executive staff, general staff, in-house maintenance, housekeeping, visiting maintenance, deliveries, all of it."

"Brief, he says," murmured Griffiths, rolling his eyes heavenward.

"Brief being a relative term," I clarified.

He swung his laptop halfway around so we could both see it. "Then let's be about it."

Unlike Manning, Griffiths was prepared. We went through each tier of the security system, the keycard protocols, the programming of the electronic scanners—retina, breath, voice, finger, and palm geometry—the positioning of all closed-circuit TV cameras, the functioning and shifts in the security office, foot patrols, activity logs from all devices and stations, and a bunch more. There was no hesitation when answering even my most probing questions, and no arguments when I wanted to read classified personnel files.

In short, he gave me everything I asked for, and more besides.

By the time we were done, I was ready to begin a proper investigation. In a weird way, it felt good. This was me doing what I was originally trained for—cop stuff. I was good at it and had one of the highest clear-records with the Baltimore PD. Since coming to work for Church, I've also racked up a lot of closed cases. I knew how to do this, and it defined me a whole lot more than shooting people.

"If there is something to find here in the building," he said, "*find* it. Friends of mine have died today. I don't want my niece to die, too. If the doctors can't find the right antibiotic, more of them are going to die. Anything I can do to help, any resource you need, call me and I will bloody well make it happen."

"Fair enough," I said, rising. "As I understand it, Rockwell is up in his office?"

"He is. Self-imposed isolation. Decided to do it here as a show of solidarity for the staff. You know, sharing the danger his people face. He's like that."

It was said as a compliment for Rockwell, but I thought there was a bit of something else there. Dislike, perhaps. Not sure, and under the circumstances conversational nuance was tough to read.

Griffiths seemed to catch that and quickly said, "He's taking this all quite hard, Colonel. A lot of the people who have died are longtime friends of his. He spent so much time and effort to make Hadrian Tower a fortress and now he feels responsible. It's crushing him. Have to say, I'm feeling a great deal of that as well. This should not be possible with everything we did to prevent it."

"I appreciate your candor and the cooperation, Griffiths. Me and my guys are going to walk the building and see what we can see. If I need something that these keycards won't give me, I'll call."

"Anytime." He handed me a card with his office and personal cell numbers on them, then said, "Merlin told Mr. Rockwell that you used to be a cop, right? Baltimore in Maryland?"

"That's right."

"Word is you were a good one."

I shrugged.

"Well," said Griffiths, "I hope you're a really damn good one, because the guy on my team who headed up our internal security investigations squad died three hours ago, and his two best investigators are in the hospital. Which is why I brought Alpha Team in."

"Don't take this the wrong way, Griffiths, but how good are they?"

"Best of the best," he said with obvious pride. "Look, we may have been blindsided by this, and one of our labs may have been compromised, but from here on we're on high alert and my lads are ready for absolutely anything."

"Good to know."

"What else can I do to help?" he asked.

"All-access badges?"

"Yes, I have them right here," he said, and opened a desk drawer and handed over a set of five white cards with black lanyards. "Had these made as soon as word came down."

I took them and saw that they were all identical, and each card had a tiny gold silhouette of Hadrian Tower. I hooked one over my head and shoved the others into a pocket on my ChemRig.

"I've been seeing cameras everywhere," I said. "I assume there's a security office where all the feeds go to? I want to put one of my people there to review footage going back a week."

"A *week*? Why? Wilson didn't get here until yesterday."

"It's not him I'm looking for."

Griffiths waited, but I didn't explain. Eventually he nodded and told me he'd make the necessary arrangements. We stood and I was about to leave when he stopped and touched the headset he wore. He stepped aside to respond to a call. At the same moment I heard Top's voice—weak and scratchy from a bad connection—in the earbud comms unit I wore.

"Pappy to Outlaw," he said.

"Go for Outlaw."

"Standing here pointing guns back and forth with a couple of guys who say they're with Alpha Team. Like to get some confirmation on that."

As he said that I heard Griffiths say, "No, they're part of Havoc Team."

We exchanged looks.

"Let me handle this," Griffiths said and spoke into his mic. "Longshanks to Alpha Team, stop and listen. This is an executive update."

Then he explained about Havoc Team and our investigation, and was emphatic that we had the lead on deck unless there was a Code Black situation. He waited for confirmation, and when Top told me that guns were being lowered and introductions beginning, I relaxed. A bit.

When Griffiths was off his call, I said, "Code Black?"

"That's the designation for enemy infiltration by person or persons unknown." He smiled. "As I said, Outlaw, we are ready to deal with this no matter what that takes."

I nodded, but said, "I don't want your shooters or anyone else to get in my way. Let's be crystal clear on that."

"We are entirely at your disposal."

# INTERLUDE 45

## THE WARRIOR AND THE WAR
## LES ÉGOUTS DE PARIS
## (THE SEWERS OF PARIS)
## MARCH 1983

The killer descended from the glimmering lights of Paris into a black underworld of rushing water, stagnant pollution, raw sewage, savage rats, and forgotten bones.

He carried no map, but the route was imprinted onto the front of his mind. He went deeper and deeper into the underworld, carrying with him the tools of his trade: a gun, a knife, a silver garrote, and a mind that was far colder than the waters that rushed through the bowels of the Earth.

It had been the work of four weeks to obtain legitimate permits and credentials from the correct departments within the streets management offices, then copy those documents, and return the originals. If anyone ever checked, everything would be in its proper place. The level of proficiency at which the killer worked was both a source of amusement among his peers and the reason this man had never failed in a field mission. The jokes at his expense—"My grandmother's slow, but she's old."—were shared out of his earshot.

The killer did not recognize most of his peers as being on the same team as himself. He had a separate and entirely personal agenda that he chose not to share. They had *this* war, and he had *the* war. The difference was vast, and the perception of it was telling.

The members of his own team knew only what he wanted them to know. Just as his superiors knew only what he wanted them to know, and that included many of the details in his personal file. Nearly all of it was a fabrication that had taken years, much thought, and a great deal of money to construct. Everything there—photos of his childhood, his school records, his medical history, even the samples of blood and hair on file for DNA testing—belonged to other men. Dead men whose lives he had borrowed, combined, and then otherwise erased.

The killer was as certain as he could be that his real name existed in no database in any computer on Earth. Except Pangaea. *His* computer. A computer the killer had obtained in the way he'd obtained many useful tools in his personal arsenal. He'd killed the man who built it and the men who guarded it.

And then he completely rebuilt the computer to suit his own needs.

Now Pangaea was a killer, too. Like him in many ways. It intruded where it did not belong and destroyed things that were too valuable to let stand. For Pangaea, the path of destruction was through the memory banks of other computers. It sought certain information and retrieved it, often deleting the information on the target mainframes, then it deleted all traces of its own presence. The killer spent a great deal of time erasing all records that a computer system called Pangaea ever existed.

One of Pangaea's secret weapons was a new feature that the killer had developed and added to its operational system. A subroutine called "Kreskin" that was designed to search for patterns and collate any relevant information into a set of projections that were as close to human intuition and guesswork as a binary computer mind could achieve. At least with the current technology.

That pattern search had located a target the killer had sought for a very long time. It was why he was down here in the sewer. It was why he was hunting in the darkness like the predator he was.

He moved as quietly as possible, running lightly along the narrow ledges to avoid splashing through the sluggish stream of runoff from last night's rain. The storm drains were vast, stretching for 21,000 kilometers beneath the sprawl of the city above. These tunnels held the drinking and no-drinking water mains, telecommunication cables, pneumatic cables, and traffic light management cables. Following the tunnels took planning, getting lost was simple. Dying down here was common.

He took care. He planned every step.

If his information was correct, then he was near to the target.

The killer slowed to a walk and then stopped at the entrance to a chamber that was part of the channeling system which took water from dozens of culverts and combined them into a larger chute that flowed to the Seine. He crouched in the shadows, silent and unmoving, allowing his senses to fill him with every bit of detail about where he was and what was here. He was not a man to make assumptions, even about an empty tunnel.

There was a rusted service door set into the far wall. A weak bulb in a grilled cage mounted above the door threw dirty yellow light over the churning water. A child's rag doll bobbed in the current and the killer paused for a moment to look at it. The doll was dressed in the checkerboard clothes of a harlequin jester, with bells on its hat and a broad smile of stitched red silk.

It was an expensive doll and it looked well-worn, and not just from the passage through the drain. This was a doll a child had held close for many nights. Something loved, something treasured. And now it was lost here in the darkness, on its way out to oblivion in the ocean. Perhaps if the child knew where it was then she might imagine her tattered friend to be off on some grand adventure. Otherwise . . . it was a friend who was lost and would never be found. That thought came close to breaking the killer's heart.

So many of his friends were lost to him.

So many.

He almost reached for the doll, almost pulled it from the water as the thing bobbed past, but he did not. He remained as still as the shadows and the grime-slick walls and the bones of dead rats. Instead, he watched the harlequin doll drown amid the froth of converging sewer water and rush away into the great nothingness.

After a moment, he turned his attention to that rusted door. According to the records Pangaea had filched for him, that door led to a disused valve station whose purpose had been superseded by a more modern system controlled in an office on street level. The door had been shut and locked and left to rust down there in the dark, becoming yet another of the many forgotten places in these sewers.

At a glance the door appeared to be totally abandoned, with years of rust crusted to the hinges and knob. The low-wattage service light was there to aid with routine inspection of this rechanneling chamber. That was how things looked, according to all official records and even on the service logs of the men who worked these tunnels. They knew the door was there, but they ignored it as they ignored disused tunnels, chambers, holding tanks, ladders, and other detritus of an older age of public sewage. Like the subway systems in New York and London, there were layers of new built on forgotten bones of the old.

However, the killer had a separate source of intelligence which insisted that this door was not at all what it seemed. And that there were more than rust-frozen valves on the other side.

The killer was about to rise from his crouch when he heard something.

Very faint, very soft. A footfall. A scuff. Not an animal sound. Human, though he could not tell more than that.

He did not move, aware that he was so deep inside a bank of shadows that he was invisible. His clothes were as black as his balaclava, and he had black greasepaint around his eyes. Only the whites of his eyes were visible in the light, and no light touched him where he crouched. The gear he carried—grenades, knives, and more—was arranged on his belt with cushions so they didn't clink or rattle.

The sound came from a side tunnel off to his left. From the memory of the tunnel schematics in his mind, the closest street access to that tunnel was at least a mile away. A long way to go in the dark. He raised the black cover of his watch and touched the face, reading the position of the arms. Three minutes past four in the morning. Far too late for the evening maintenance crew, two hours early for the day shift.

He waited.

There wasn't another scuff. Whoever it was knew how to move

quietly. The scuff had probably been a rare accident. An unseen patch of slime.

The killer drew his pistol. A .22 with a sound suppressor. It was poor at long range, but this man never killed from a great distance. He was selective and careful. It was not because killing up close provided him with a physical thrill. That was not a factor in the function of either his heart or mind. It was a matter of not liking to make errors. Distance, especially in the dark, increased the risk of errors.

Errors were the result of sloppiness, nerves, or poor process.

He crouched there, the pistol held in both hands, barrel pointed down, his forearms resting against his bent knees to keep the muscles from fatiguing.

Forty feet down the tunnel the shadows changed. A slender fragment of the darkness detached itself and crept forward with catlike grace. In the bad light it was difficult to tell much about the figure. Small, slight of build, moving with the ease of a dancer or a martial artist. Someone who knew how to move. No visible weapons in the hands; however, the black handles of knives stood up from sheaths on each thigh.

The killer pursed his lips in appreciation.

He watched as the figure approached the downspill of yellow light and paused, becoming as motionless as the killer himself.

Suddenly a sound broke into the moment as the rusted metal door opened. Despite the decrepit appearance of the door it opened with a soft *click* and swung outward on nearly silent hinges. Three men stepped out. Two of them wore boots, jeans, and T-shirts; both wore identical shoulder holsters with .45 pistols snugged into them. The third man wore a hazmat suit with the hood off. The men in jeans drew their pistols and walked to the edges of the runoff trough, looking up and down into the shadows. The killer knew that they saw nothing, that they *could* see nothing; neither had allowed his eyes to adjust to the darkness before trying to look through it. They didn't see the killer and they didn't see the other figure crouched barely six feet from them.

The two thugs nodded to the man in the hazmat suit, who reached in through the doorway and lifted out a Styrofoam cooler of the type used to transport medical or biological materials. A red biohazard symbol was stamped onto the white plastic side. He walked to the edge of the trough and stood for a moment looking down into the eddying water. Then he set the cooler down.

The killer raised his pistol.

His intel had brought him here to this place, this time. His mission projections had him back at street level within eight minutes from first trigger-pull.

Then everything changed.

The figure crouched in the dark moved.

There was a rasping sound, steel clearing leather, but no flash of metal. Like British commando knives, the blade was blackened. The figure rose from its crouch and swarmed among the men. The blade swept right and then left, and suddenly arterial blood geysered up, spraying all the way to the curved ceiling of the brick tunnel. One of the thugs reeled back, fingers scrabbling to stem a flow that could never be stopped. The second man staggered away and turned in an almost graceful pirouette, hands reaching out to break a fall that turned clumsy and artless. They collapsed like discarded puppets onto the stone walkway so quickly that the man in the hazmat suit was unaware of their deaths until bone and slack flesh struck the stones behind him.

He spun and he was on the verge of crying out in shock and alarm, but the shadowy figure moved past him, sweeping an arm across his throat with incredible speed. The man in the hazmat suit dropped to his knees and then fell forward, his slumping corpse humped over the Styrofoam chest.

It was the fastest thing the killer had ever seen. How quick had it all taken? Three seconds? Two? The thugs and the other man lay dead. Blood ran in slow lines down the walls.

The shadowy figure stood facing the open doorway, knife gripped in one hand. The cuts had been so fast, the edge so sharp, that no blood clung to the weapon except a single pendulous drop that hung for a moment from the tip and then fell with the softest *splash.*

The killer watched all of this down the barrel of the .22 he held. He was thirty feet away and if he'd had to paint a fourth corpse onto this tableau he could have done it with impunity. Fast or not, the kill shot was his to take.

But the figure turned—slowly, with grace and without haste—toward him. A gloved hand reached up and hooked fingers under the edge of a mask. Lifted, pulled it away. In the weak lamplight the hair which spilled out from under the mask looked yellow, but the killer knew that it was not. He knew that it was as white as snow. Thick and lustrous, but paler than death. The face it framed was nearly as pale, except for a red mouth and eyes so dark they looked black. It was a beautiful face. Regal and cold and cruel. A face unused to smiles. A face like a death mask of some ancient queen, or a temple carving of a goddess of war.

The killer *knew* that face. She lifted that proud head and looked down her patrician nose at him.

"Saint Germain," she said quietly. There were equal parts contempt and admiration in her voice. "Or do you prefer 'Deacon'? I've heard that people are calling you that now."

He lowered his pistol and pulled off his balaclava. "It doesn't matter."

"Deacon, then," she said. "It's less pretentious."

He smiled. "And we wouldn't want to be pretentious," he said. "Would we, Lilith?"

# CHAPTER 69

## OUTSIDE OF HADRIAN TOWER
## ROPEMAKER STREET
## LONDON, ENGLAND

They lounged against the side of a black two-year-old Land Rover Defender. They were dressed in jeans, jumpers, and scuff trainers, and they ranged between looking vaguely homeless and looking like they had just walked a Paris runway.

The latter image was projected by a fair-haired young man with a somber yet handsome face reminiscent of a young Sting. His was a dangerous beauty projected by a knowing half-smile, piercing green eyes, sharply defined bone structure, and a general attitude that promised everything from a sweaty night on a dance floor to a knifing in a back alley.

The least attractive of the group looked like he just walked out of a supermax prison after serving a full ticket for strangling musk oxen. The others could have been part of a Sex Pistols cover band or a crew ready to do a series of smash-and-grabs on jeweler's row.

"Well, this is all a proper cockup, innit?" murmured the big man.

"Effing plague," said a redhead with a lot of scars on the left side of his face. He tapped the big man. "Gimme a fag, Muppet."

"Smoked the last an hour ago."

"Twat."

Above them, helicopters beat back and forth.

"We cracked on to get here and are we just going to loiter about or are we *in* this game?" asked a very tall man with deep brown skin and a T-shirt that bore the popular Bollywood slogan *Ja Simran Ja, Live Your Life.*

Four of them glanced at the handsome one.

"We bloody well wait until they ring us and tell us what to do," he said.

Muppet, Rugger, Zombie, Rent Boy, and Toys—The Wild Hunt—waited with an outward show of studied insouciance, yet inside all five of them were wired to the eyeballs. Tense, scared, angry, and eager to find whoever was responsible for this disaster and have some fun utterly destroying them.

## CHAPTER 70

### BARRIER HEADQUARTERS
### LONDON, ENGLAND

Top, Bunny, and Belle watched the Alpha Team members move off.

"Am I supposed to feel comforted that they're here?" wondered Bunny.

Belle snorted but made no other comment.

Top stood there, eyes narrowed, watching the Alpha shooters disappear down a corridor.

"Long as they stay out of our way, I'm okay with the extra muscle," he said.

# INTERLUDE 46

## THE WARRIOR AND THE WAR
## LES ÉGOUTS DE PARIS
## (THE SEWERS OF PARIS)
## MARCH 1983

Deacon rose to his feet, his pistol still in his hand but the barrel pointed down. It made the statement he intended.

Lilith flicked her wrist the way a samurai would when shaking blood from a katana, and then slid the black-bladed knife back into its sheath. Without taking her eyes from Deacon, she knotted her fingers in the back of the dead man's hazmat suit and, with no apparent effort, lifted his body off of the Styrofoam cooler and casually swung it up into the rushing water. It was an act that demonstrated a level of physical strength far in excess of what should have been possible for a woman of her size. A very strong man might have had difficulty lifting so limp and heavy a burden and tossing it aside so casually. That, too, made a statement and it was in no way lost on Deacon.

He moved closer and stood a few feet from her and the cooler.

"Are you here for that?" he asked, then ticked his head toward the open door. "Or what's in there?"

Lilith took some time answering. Her expression gave very little away, even to someone as practiced at reading expressions as Deacon. She nudged the cooler with the toe of her boot.

"Do you know what's in here?" she asked.

"I might," Deacon said. "Do you?"

Another pause. "No."

"Ah."

They both looked at the open door.

"That's going to set off an alarm," he said.

"I know."

"If they think they're being raided they'll dump their computers and—"

"It's an old burglar's trick," she said, cutting him off. "Set a smoky fire and watch through a window. Watch to see what people will rush to save. A good man will save his family Bible. A blackmailer will save his cache of evidence. And a scientist—"

"—will save his research," he completed. "Yes, I've read Sherlock Holmes."

Lilith gave him the tiniest sliver of a cold smile. Not at all friendly, but not as hostile as her flat reptilian glare. "Why were you waiting over there? You could have picked the door lock."

"I wasn't trying to get in. I wanted this." He squatted down and removed the cooler's lid. There were three aluminum cylinders packed into carved slots. Each cylinder was pressure-locked with a tight metal cap.

"What is it?" asked Lilith. "A bioweapon? Some kind of germ warfare thing?"

"A performance-enhancing synthetic steroid," said Deacon.

She actually smiled. "'Performance'? What kind of performance?"

"Not the kind you're thinking," he said, returning her smile. "It's the first generation of a formula that combines the select lean mass-building steroids with a synthetic nootropic compound that significantly increases and regulates the hypothalamic histamine levels. In normal pharmacology these drugs are wakefulness-promoting agents often prescribed to prevent shift-work sleepiness. This version is designed to build stamina and wakefulness to a point where the treated person won't tire and won't lose mental sharpness."

"To what end? Super-soldiers?"

"Hardly. Indefatigable factory workers."

Lilith blinked. "Factory . . . ?"

"These drugs are intended for use in Third World countries to increase the efficiency and output of unregulated factory workers. Shift workers who can work twenty-four or even forty-eight hours at maximum efficient output." He sighed. "It's a new tweak on legal slave labor because it's for use in countries where there is no enforceable human rights presence and where governments are easily bought. Earlier versions of these drugs are already being used in Southeast Asia and some places in Africa."

A sneer twisted her mouth. "The new face of slave labor."

"Yes," he agreed.

"Why do *you* care?" She cocked an eyebrow. "Are you here with official sanction?"

Deacon didn't answer. Instead he closed the cooler and replaced the lid. Then he took the container and placed it in the shadowy spot where he'd been crouching. It vanished from sight as if it ceased to exist.

"I didn't see you in the dark over there," said Lilith after a few moments. "Not until you pointed your gun at me."

"Your back was turned when I raised my weapon. You could not have seen the movement. One of these days, I would like to obtain a drop of your blood."

"To do tests?"

"Of course."

"You wouldn't understand the results," she said.

"I might."

She made a mouth of irritation. A very French thing although Deacon knew that she was not French. He did not know everything about Lilith's heritage—and some of what he'd been able to piece together was apocryphal or at the very least doubtful. The most credible version was that her mother had been a Warsaw Jew who had died badly at Sobibor. He had learned that through exhaustive research, but lately he'd come to doubt the story. The reason for his skepticism was a series of references to a woman who fit her description and patterns being tied to the Ordo Ruber—the Red Order.

From what Deacon had been able to piece together about her, Lilith had not been any kind of an ally to the Order, but rather a slave—a *breeder*—in their pits to provide viable male offspring for the Upierczy. These were genetic freaks whose bizarre nature gave them unusual strength, resistance to diseases, and a slower rate of aging. They were also ferocious and predatory, and it was almost certain they were the basis for the belief in vampires. The Upierczy, however, were not supernatural, though they were incredibly dangerous and extremely difficult to kill.

However, those monsters were close to being genetic mules, and when they were able to procreate, the only surviving children were girls. The Red Order's scientists had spent more than a century—and tens of millions of dollars—to locate and abduct women of a certain kind who were able to become more easily pregnant. And who could produce male children.

Deacon had liberated women from two such pits some decades

before, and survivors spoke of a fierce killer named Lilith who had led her own revolt and slaughtered many of the Knights. That woman had taken her only surviving child, a young girl, with her.

Since then, Deacon had become gradually convinced that Lilith and this one were the same. If so, then she was far older than she appeared.

Of course, so was he.

It was clear she knew some of his own history. He admired her for that insight, and for many other reasons.

While Lilith watched, Deacon dragged the two dead thugs one at a time to the edge of the stream and rolled them in. It was clear to them both that it required more effort on his part than she'd used to dispose of the man in the hazmat suit. Neither felt the need to comment on it.

When the last man vanished into the swirling waters, Deacon consulted his watch, glanced upstream and then over at the still-open door, then pushed his sleeve down to cover the watch.

Lilith said, "Those men were out here to hand that cooler off to someone."

"Yes. A four-man team. Two Americans, a Brit, and their local contact."

"When are they due?"

"Five minutes ago," said Deacon.

She opened her mouth to ask for clarification, then thought better of it. She glanced at the rushing water as if expecting to see four bodies float by.

"Ah," she said. "So . . . your part in this is over?"

He shrugged. "I did what I came to do. Now tell me . . . what's your interest here? Arklight has never expressed an interest in this area of *human* rights."

Deacon, for his part, leaned on the word "human." Making the point and leaving much understood but unspoken. It seemed to both amuse and annoy Lilith as various partially formed expressions came and went on her face in rapid succession.

He noted that Lilith did not flinch or rage at his mention of Arklight. Once before she had tried to kill him for speaking that name, for even knowing it. The fact that she had been unsuccessful in killing him formed one of the somewhat shaky pillars of the truce that existed between them. The truce, he knew, was as substantial as vapor and it existed only because they had yet to have directly conflicting agendas. Her tolerance of his use of the name of the highly secret and extremely dangerous group of which Lilith was nominal head and chief operative was as close to an olive branch as he ever expected to receive from her.

Finally she gestured to the open doorway. "The lab in there is partially funded by Ordo Ruber."

Deacon raised his eyebrows. "Is it indeed?"

Lilith said, "There are rumors that the Order has been hiring scientists of all stripes—molecular biologists and others—to try and rebuild the genetic lines of the Red Knights."

"To what end?"

"They want the Knights to become a more powerful and effective organization than ever." Something, some strange fire, ignited in Lilith's eyes. "I can't allow that."

"Then this is a straight hit?"

"No. This isn't their central lab. We don't know where that is. This is more of a processing and distribution center for research materials that will then be sent to researchers who are in the Order's pocket."

Deacon nodded. "And you mean to do what? Get hold of their bulk research materials and notes and use it to find leads to the scientists working for the Order?"

"You were always cleverer than the other little spies, Deacon. Yes, that's exactly it."

"Do you have a team coming to help you?"

"It's only a small lab," she said. "Staff of ten or twelve." A pause. "These are scientists, lab techs, and a few foot soldiers. Three are already down."

"What about the Red Knights?"

Lilith shook her head. "Guard duty isn't what they do. They won't be here."

Deacon looked at the gun he still held. He was about to say something when a buzzer suddenly sounded from inside the open doorway. Loud and insistent.

"Finally," she said, and rested her hands on her knives. They could hear shouts and the sound of running feet. "This part is mine."

Deacon smiled and shook his head. "To be fair," he said mildly, "you helped me when you eliminated the three men who came out here. I feel as if I should return the favor."

But Lilith shook her head. "I don't want your help. Be a nice little spy and go play James Bond somewhere else."

The shouts were getting louder.

Deacon took a breath and let it out slowly. Then he holstered his pistol and turned away. He picked up the cooler and faded into the shadows, watching over his shoulder as Lilith drew her weapons and moved like a blur of shadows and steel in through the open door. The tunnel immediately echoed with the rattle of automatic gunfire and the screams of men in terrible pain.

With the cooler under his arm, Deacon began walking back the way he'd come, a frown etched onto his face. He got almost a hundred yards before another scream split the air. It wasn't the dying scream of a man.

It was the shriek of a woman in agony.

And in terrible fear.

Deacon dropped the cooler, tore the pistol from its holster, whirled and ran back along the edge of the black water as fast as he could.

# CHAPTER 71

## BARRIER HEADQUARTERS
## LONDON, ENGLAND

I went over a few extra details, then thanked Griffiths and left his office. While I waited for the car, I heard a noise. As I turned, there was a quick movement as Griffiths shifted back into his office. It was clear he had leaned out to look. So, I tapped into the command channel.

"Outlaw to TOC," I said quietly.

"Go for Artemis," said Major Claire Courtland. I knew it wasn't Grace, but the voice was so achingly close.

Forcing my head to stay entirely in the game, I said, "I'm on-site at

Barrier. Have someone do a deep background on Bedwyr Griffiths, chief of security."

"I know him," said Claire.

"Give me the headlines," I said, "but I still want that deep dive sent to my tac-com."

"Copy that. Bedwyr has passed every background check there is, including one the DMS did on him a few years ago at the request of the then chief, Benson Childes. He is widely regarded as one of the most astute experts on security systems for critical sites. MI5 and Barrier have both given him top marks for his ability to grasp the subtleties of virtually any hardened facility and puzzle out the weaknesses. His papers on security theory are required reading for anyone above a certain clearance level."

"Personal opinion, Artemis?"

"Very well," she said crisply. "I respect him and trust him but don't like him."

"What creates that schism?"

"Frankly, I've never been able to put my finger on it," she admitted. "He is very good at his job, comes with the highest ratings, and has clearly earned every accolade he has, is known to be a good family man and a patriot."

"But . . . ?"

"But he is unlikable."

"Strictly personal take?" I asked.

"Not at all. I don't know anyone who likes him. Even Benson Childes disliked him."

"Isn't he the one who hired him?"

"Yes, and he made a few private jokes to me on the subject. Said it's useful to have a head of security no one much likes. No personal bias."

"What's Rockwell's take on him?"

"They get along," she said. "I didn't get the impression they socialized off the job."

"Griffiths said his niece is one of the employees who is in ICU with plague. Can you confirm that?"

"Hold on." There was a brief pause, then she said, "Madelaine—known as Maddy—Neale. She's worked there for over a year. Clean record."

"She in his department?"

"No. She lacked any military, police, or clandestine work history. Maddy and her husband, Charlie Neale, ran a cleaning company that had contracts for a lot of government buildings, with the appropriate clearance level for that sort of thing. The business faltered during COVID when so many people were working from home. Fewer paying jobs. They sold the company and she applied for a job at Hadrian Tower when they began hiring eighteen months ago. She had to go through normal channels for approval as her uncle pointedly removed himself from the vetting process so as to avoid any stink of nepotism. Maddy did that without being asked, by the way. MI5 did the background checks and she's clean. Excellent work record managing both in-house and outside company services. Everything from scrubbing toilets to making the mess hall sparkle."

"Is Maddy really on a ventilator?"

Another pause. "Yes. Dr. Suliman has her listed as critical. His personal notes to Merlin indicate that she is losing ground and may not last the night."

"Damn. Getting back to Griffiths himself . . . any skeletons in his closet?"

"If so, no one has found so much as a little toe bone, and believe me, Outlaw, given the critical nature of his position, we have *all* looked. Perhaps the negative personality reaction everyone has is simply bad chemistry. And I mean that quite literally. I've wondered if it was a pheromone thing."

I chewed on that for a moment. "Have Bug put someone on him anyway."

"Copy that." No pause, no argument. "Continue with your investigation, Outlaw. TOC out."

The elevator door opened quietly and I stepped in, but gave Griffiths's office a last look. Had he been spying on me or just watching me leave? Or was it simply that my paranoia was dialed to eleven?

Hard to say.

## INTERLUDE 47

### THE WARRIOR AND THE WAR
### LES ÉGOUTS DE PARIS
### (THE SEWERS OF PARIS)
### MARCH 1983

As Deacon ran toward the door a man staggered out, blood streaming from deep crisscrossed cuts that gouged him from shoulders to hips. His belt was severed and with each step his trousers slipped down his bloody legs. But he still held an AK-47, finger jerking spasmodically on the trigger, bullets punching into the chamber beyond.

Deacon put a single .22 round into the back of his head and shoved him out of the way. Then he jumped through the doorway, pivoted as he dropped into a crouch, gun up and ready in both hands, eyes taking in the scene. He was at the end of a short tunnel that doglegged to the left and opened onto a large stone room that had been converted into a rough field lab. There were long worktables, banks of computers, and various kinds of processing machinery. Blowers pushed cool, clean air into the room and pulled dust out. Two men lay in a red tangle at the mouth of the tunnel entrance. Automatic rifles lay inches from their dead hands. Three other men—a guard with a handgun and two men in white lab coats—were down inside the room, their faces and throats slashed to ribbons.

Inside the chamber there were seven uninjured men. All of them had weapons—guns, a fire axe, and a burly man with a black T-shirt held one of Lilith's daggers. They were strung out in a wide half-circle around three figures that fought and tore at each other in the center of the room.

Lilith and two tall, pale-faced men dressed in dark clothes.

All of them were bleeding.

But Lilith was limping as she backpedaled from them. Her left arm was curled gingerly around her middle, and at first Deacon thought that the arm was broken, but then he saw the lines of bright red running down her loins and thighs—she had her arm clamped over a stomach wound. The men surrounding her were yelling and pointing weapons. Lilith coughed and there was blood on her lips.

The two men in dark clothes laughed. This had all taken seconds and it was clear that Lilith's invasion had gone horribly wrong.

Deacon took all of this in within the space of a heartbeat.

He did not pause, did not waste time processing or strategizing. He tore a grenade from his belt, pulled the pin, hurled it. It was a flash-bang, a stun grenade developed by the British SAS. Deacon dropped into a crouch and covered his head with his wrapped arms. The bang was almost unbearably loud even then. And the burst of light stabbed him through his shut eyelids.

The men in the room screamed.

Deacon immediately opened his eyes, took his guns in both hands again, and began firing as he rose. He was peripherally aware that the two men with Lilith were beyond the effective range of the flash-bang and yet they had their hands to their ears, hissing in pain.

He noted it, but it was far from a matter of first importance as he felt his gun buck in his hands.

His first shot took a scientist in the side of the face. It was not intended as a kill shot, though the bullet punched a wet hole all the way through, sending fragments of teeth flying in a spray of blood. The impact drove the man into the other men beside him. The collision took three of his opponents out in one second. Deacon swung his pistol and fired four shots, two each at guards, a center-mass shot to stop them and a headshot to close the deal. Small-caliber rounds lacked the power to exit the far side of a skull, so instead they bounced around inside and destroyed the brain. It was why the caliber was the preferred weapon of assassins.

That left two men immediately able to respond. One man had the fire axe. The other had a pistol.

Deacon shot the second man in the face and then put the axe-man down with a headshot.

He calculated his ammunition. Eight shots fired. Four dead, one wounded, two recovering from the collision with the scientist. He dropped the magazine and reached for a second, but one of the two survivors came rushing at him so fast he had no time to finish the reload.

Deacon stepped into the attack, pivoting his body as he tilted his weight onto his front leg. Both hands moved out as he simultaneously blocked with his left forearm and rammed the unloaded pistol into the attacker's face hard enough to jolt the man to a stop. Deacon recoiled his gun hand and chopped the man in the Adam's apple with the gun.

The man dropped at once.

But now the second man was up and in motion, bringing his rifle to bear. If he'd dropped the gun and used his hands, or if he'd swung the rifle's stock at Deacon, he might have had a chance. Instead he tried to aim the weapon.

Deacon stepped into him, dropping his own pistol as he intercepted the swing of the barrel and grabbed the long gun with both hands. He turned his second step into a flat-footed kick that shattered the man's knee so badly the leg buckled and bent the other way. Deacon tore the gun from his hand, reversed it, and pulled the trigger.

The gun bucked as two rounds hit the man in the chest, but then the slide locked back.

Empty.

Deacon tossed the gun aside.

Twenty feet away the two men in black and Lilith had all turned toward him. Her eyes were filled with pain and hate. Their eyes, however, were filled with a kind of pernicious delight that was appalling to behold. And those eyes were all wrong. The irises were not brown or blue or green. They were red. As red as the blood that painted this room. Instead of round pupils, theirs were slits. Like the eyes of reptiles.

The two men smiled at him.

Deacon felt the blood in his veins turn to ice.

The intelligence reports, the rumors about the killers called the Red Knights . . . So much of it had been beyond belief. Horror stories. Crazy lies.

Except . . .

Except now the truth was like a punch over the heart. It stopped the world for a terrible moment. It tore the mind open and jammed in the truth like daggers.

As their lips curled back Deacon saw their teeth. So white. So long and sharp. They had teeth like dogs, like wolves. Like monsters.

"*They're Red Knights,*" screamed Lilith. "Deacon, they'll tear you apart. For God's sake . . . *run!*"

And he could have run. He was closer to the door than the Red Knights. He could be outside, reloading as he ran, safe in darkness.

Perhaps he should have run. This was Lilith's fight. His government—even the small, clandestine groups which endorsed Deacon's personal agendas—had in no way sanctioned any contact with Arklight. The few people in the US government who even knew of Arklight considered it a borderline terrorist organization. So this was not his fight and Lilith was not his ally.

He should have run. But that would have meant that he was a different person than he was.

Instead, Deacon let the empty assault rifle clatter to the floor.

"No," he said.

The Red Knights smiled with their wicked teeth. Their red eyes flared with the joy of a coming slaughter. One of them stepped closer to Lilith. He had black fingernails, and blood dripped from them. Was that the weapon that had torn the screams from Lilith? Deacon was sure it was.

"I'll finish the whore," said that one, speaking in thickly accented French. He pointed at Deacon. "His blood is yours, my brother."

The second Red Knight began moving toward him. Not fast, not using its speed. It *stalked* him. The pleasure of anticipation twisting the smile on its face. This was what it enjoyed. The hunt. Maybe more so than the kill.

The Knight held out his hands and flexed his fingers, displaying the thick fingernails that were as sharp as bear claws. Claws for tearing the humanity from a person, claws for rending to the bone.

Deacon began backing away.

This made the Knight laugh. A low chuckle that was echoed by his companion. Lilith sagged down to her knees, blood streaming from between the fingers of the hands she pressed to her stomach.

"Run," she said weakly. "Run . . ."

Deacon turned and ran. The Knight howled with delight and ran after him. It took only six steps for the monster to catch the man. Deacon suddenly dropped to the ground, arms wrapped around his head, knees drawn up into a tight ball. The Knight paused, confused.

Not at Deacon, but at the thing that floated toward him. Something his prey had thrown as he twisted and fell.

There was only a fragment of a moment to react. The Knight said the same thing Deacon himself had said a few moments ago.

*"No."*

It meant something entirely different. The object exploded. With a flash. With a bang. Six inches from the vampire's face. The Red Knight *screamed*. He was caught point-blank inside the blast zone, and the concussive force slammed him backward. Blood burst from his nose and ears; red tears fell from its traumatized eyes as it staggered sideways, clawing at its face.

The second Knight was thirty feet away, outside of the blast zone, but even so, he staggered, too. Extraordinary hearing and eyesight were powerful tools in the quiet and in the dark, but far less so in the presence of a light-amplified concussion grenade.

Deacon rolled back to his feet and snapped a kick at the closest Red Knight's knee. The scream of pain from the flash-bang and the scream of pain from a shattered knee hit different notes. The second was sharper, higher, and it was as filled with fear and surprise as it was with agony.

Deacon hooked an uppercut into the monster's groin. That folded the creature forward and Deacon met the sudden bend by grabbing the thing's head and yanking it face-forward onto a rising knee. As the Knight rebounded from that impact, Deacon punched him in the throat three times with the extended knuckles of both fists, left, right, left. Cartilage collapsed; the hyoid bone splintered apart. But he did not stop. Deacon attacked the Knight, giving it no chance, no advantage, no mercy. He blinded it and broke its arms, he stamped again on the shattered knee, destroying the leg completely, then he used a kick-sweep to cut both legs out from under his screaming enemy. As the Knight fell, Deacon twisted and followed it to the floor so that his punch to the solar plexus landed at the same instant the monster's weight hit hard ground. The effect was to drive whatever air was trapped in the Knight's lungs upward against the wreckage of his throat. The extra force tore apart whatever was left of the structure of the throat—using the fragments of the hyoid bone as razors. Blood immediately began filling the Red Knight's lungs; it began thrashing and flopping around with hysterical force.

Deacon hurled himself backward and spun away from a dying enemy to face the other vampire. But then he froze at the spectacle before him, and he knew immediately that it would live in the darkest parts of his mind forever.

The second Red Knight was down.

Lilith sat astride him.

She had not been at the point of death from the wound in her stomach. It was immediately clear that she'd been faking, exaggerating the severity in order to find a moment to make her move. In the confusion, while Deacon killed the first Knight, Lilith had attacked the other.

Not with her hands, though. Not with her knives.

She crouched over him, her mouth buried in the side of the vampire's throat. For the oddest little fractured moment Deacon thought she was kissing the Knight.

But of course that was wrong. Everything in this moment was wrong. There was a feral snarling, tearing, ripping sound. The Red Knight thrashed beneath her, tearing at her clothing and flesh with its nails. Weakly, though.

And weaker still with each pulsing moment. Blood pooled beneath the Knight's head. Then, with a terrible spasm, the creature shivered and flopped down, where it lay utterly still. Lilith bent over him, her face still buried beside the Knight's neck, half-hidden by the corpse's profile.

"Lilith . . ." murmured Deacon.

She did not look at him. Did not react at all to him. There was only the sound of a wild animal. Wet and awful.

"Lilith," he said again.

Nothing.

He bent and picked up his fallen pistol and the second magazine he hadn't been able to use. He slapped it into place. The sound was loud, harsh. Lilith froze. The sounds she made stopped.

"Lilith," Deacon said once more as he raised the pistol and racked the slide.

Only then did she lift her head. Her face was completely covered with dark red blood. And her eyes.

Her eyes—they were entirely black. Without pupil or iris or sclera. Black within black within black. Deacon pointed the pistol at her.

"Come back," he said.

His voice was gentle. The barrel of the gun was a promise. Blood dripped from Lilith's chin and lips.

"Come back."

She blinked at him.

Once.

Twice.

And then her eyes were human again.

No, thought Deacon, that was an imprecise way of understanding what had happened. She was not human again; not even *more* human. In that moment, as Lilith stepped back from the edge of the abyss, it was simply that for now she was less of a monster.

The two of them stayed like that for a long moment. Her, kneeling astride a savaged corpse, him standing with a gun in bloody hands. The world ground on its gears around them.

Lilith spoke a single word, and it came out thick and wet and harsh. "Deacon."

His heart beat many times before he lowered his gun.

## CHAPTER 72

### PHONE CALL

Just as the lift doors closed, *he* called again.

I really almost didn't answer this time. Nicodemus was wearing me out, but because I thought that was part of what jazzed him, I wasn't about to let my frustration erase a chance to ask another question.

"Yeah," I said.

"Rumor control has it that you're now at Hadrian Tower. How are you enjoying that lovely metal castle?"

"Is knowing where I am supposed to impress me? Any of about two thousand people outside could be one of your plants."

"Or more than one," he said.

"Stop trying to show off. It's embarrassing."

He laughed, coughed, laughed some more.

"And the Deacon is in London, too," he said when he was able. "All of the chickens have fled the coop, so to speak."

I said nothing, watching the screen display tell me that the trace was bouncing all around the globe and landing nowhere.

"Question time," he said a bit breathlessly.

"Okay, this is pretty direct. Is the Red Order involved in this shit?"

"In a way," he said, and hung up. He was laughing as he did so.

"You *fucker*," I snarled and banged the wall with the flat of my palm.

# CHAPTER 73

**THE TOC**
**PHOENIX HOUSE**
**OMFORI ISLAND, GREECE**

The TOC was staffed with experts in a variety of fields, each with a great deal of professional experience. Every single one of them had been hand-selected by Church, Doc Holliday, Bug, or Scott Wilson.

As the situation in London unfolded, they applied their skills, expertise, and insights to bringing every necessary resource to bear. They were the kind of people who were not prone to missing key details, even small ones.

The crisis pulled their attention, demanding so much of them, and in turn every member of the team—led now by Major Claire Courtland—brought serious game.

How unfortunate, then, that none of them took any notice of the small metal sculpture of Dover Castle that sat on Scott Wilson's desk. There was no reason why they should. It was a piece of art Scott brought back from a recent trip to England, given to him by the head of the organization closest in structure, policy, and effect to Rogue Team International.

With all of the noise and motion in the TOC, no one noticed

when tiny panels on all four sides of the statue slid down into the base. None of them heard the nearly silent hiss this made. Nor were they aware of the completely silent signal it began transmitting.

# CHAPTER 74

## BARRIER HEADQUARTERS
## LONDON, ENGLAND

As I stepped off the elevator, I got another call and nearly bit the head off the caller, but it wasn't Nicodemus. Instead, it was Major Courtland.

"Go for Outlaw," I said. "But first . . . why are you calling on my cell and not via comms?"

"We're having some connectivity issues with comms," she said. "Could be interference from the in-house security systems there at Hadrian. Bug has someone looking into it."

"Copy that, Artemis. Does this mean you haven't been getting the feeds from the bodycams?"

"Intermittent only. Have Gator Bait place some signal boosters around. Have you had your meeting yet with Rockwell?"

"Next on my list after I check in with my team."

"He didn't come down to meet you?"

"He did not."

A beat. "That's . . . unusual. Perhaps he's making calls. No doubt there are a lot of people whose nerves he needs to soothe."

"Griffiths said Rockwell was being hit really hard by all the deaths. So, maybe he's upstairs checking his conscience. Whatever. I'll check in after I meet with him."

"Be advised that Wild Hunt is in London. Do you want them inside the building?"

"Negative, Artemis. Right now Havoc is doing an assessment. Building is nearly empty. Have the Hunt stay handy, though, with their vehicles well outside of the street crowd in case we need them to go do something fast."

"Copy that," she said. "Bedlam and Chaos are still inbound. I'll keep you posted. Artemis out."

I wrangled Havoc and had them meet me at a randomly picked spot on the second floor.

"Where are we on those boosters?" I asked.

"Signal still sucks hog dick," Remy said. "I mean, it's better but not much. This place is a big metal box and it's screwing with radio signals. Cell gets through, though."

"Can you adjust the gain?"

"I have."

"Try harder."

Remy gave me a look but nodded.

Bunny showed me his BAMS unit. "Still good, boss."

"Keep your suit on," I said.

He snorted. "You couldn't force me out of this thing at gunpoint. While you were up there with Griffiths, we got an update from Ron Coleman over at the hospital. He shared some image and video files of what's going on there."

"How bad?"

"Worse than awful."

"Shit."

"Six more casualties," said Top. "And that's since we walked in here. Some died while we were in transit. Seventeen since we left Heathrow."

"What's the full count?" I asked, though I did not want those numbers.

He looked weary. "Forty-one dead, fifty-three in ICU, and another nineteen starting to show symptoms. They're dropping like flies over there. Coleman says there's a whole bunch circling the drain and the number of deaths is likely to double or even triple over the next hour or two. It's bad, boss, and it ain't getting better."

"Jesus Christ."

"Yeah, I think Jesus took the day off."

"Here's something odd," I said. "Griffiths isn't wearing a hazmat." I explained the security director's rationale.

"Sounds stupid as balls to me," said Bunny. "This plague stuff has me so freaked I might never take this ChemRig off. Might buy one for Lydia and the baby when I get home. We can have our own show, *At Home with the Hazmats*."

"Anyone at the hospital responding to treatment?"

Top shook his head. "Ron's halfway to being freaked the hell out. They are trying every antibiotic in the locker and so far they might as well be injecting apple juice for all the good it's doing. His words."

We all stood in the heat of that furnace.

"For the record," said Belle, "I don't like Alpha Team."

I frowned. "Why? Did something happen? Did they give you any shit?"

She shook her head. "Just don't like them."

"Play nice," I said, and she made a disgusted noise.

Then Top—always the adult in the room and always a sergeant by disposition—said, "We got here in a double-damn hurry and now we're standing around like we're at a wake. What can we do to try and get in front of this?"

It was a gentle way to kick me in the ass, and I was fine with that.

"Okay, here's the play," I said as I handed out the all-access keycards. "Belle, you have the sharpest eyes, so I want you in the security video monitoring suite where all the CCTV feeds come in. Griffiths sent me the floor and room info and I forwarded it to your tac-com."

"Got it," she said, glancing at the computer on her forearm. "Will there be any problems?"

"No. The few security team members still left have been notified that we have unrestricted access. Anyone gives you problems, call me and I'll call Griffiths."

She smiled in a way that suggested she might want to handle any *problems* her own way.

"Let's all remember that these are friendlies here."

"Potential friendlies, yes?" asked Belle. "As I recall, the X-Files rule."

"What?"

"You said it yourself, Boss," said Remy. "Trust no one."

"It wasn't an *X-Files* reference," I said, but knew that it was forever going to be "X-Files" for any situation where trust is too big a risk. That, I mused, is how slang is born. Belle headed toward the elevators.

To Remy, I said, "When you're done with the boosters, go play with your drones. I want to know what's happening in every corner, under every desk, in every closet. If a mouse farts in the basement I want details."

"What am I looking for?"

"Anything that shouldn't be in this building. Anything hinky or out of place."

"So, basically anything that croaks like a frog but ain't a frog. Got it."

"How many pigeon drones do you have?"

"The ones with BAMS units? Twelve."

"Deploy them first. Program regular flybys of all AC vents but mostly do sweep patterns to air-map the room. Griffiths sent me a list of everywhere Scott went, so start there and expand out. You find so much as mold on a piece of toast, sing out. It seems pretty clear that this plague started here, so we need to find it."

"On it." He ran off, already digging his hands into one of the many small gear bags hung from his broad shoulders.

I turned to Top and Bunny. "Griffiths sent all the background data on employees to me and I forwarded that to everyone. Once we secure this building to *our* satisfaction, then we can go over the stuff, but it's also been sent to the TOC, so they'll already be digging in."

"What about me and Bunny?" asked Top. "Alpha Team's doing a floor-by-floor."

"Yeah, but I want you two to do your own check. Start with the labs. Some of the scientists are inside behind airlocks. Pay them a visit and take the pulse of things."

"And after?" asked Top.

"Then find me."

We all shared a look and a nod and went to work.

# INTERLUDE 48

**THE HANGAR**
**DEPARTMENT OF MILITARY SCIENCES HEADQUARTERS**
**FLOYD BENNETT FIELD**
**BROOKLYN, NEW YORK**
**JUNE 6, 1998**

She was not looking for what she found.

Aunt Sallie was in her office at the Hangar and in one of those rare lulls between absolute disasters, she was catching up on internal reports sent her way by the seventeen department heads. The head of Computer Sciences, Georgette Keppler, who was about to retire due to health issues, had sent several files to Auntie.

One of the files had an enigmatic label in Turkish.

**Ölümsüz Adam**

Auntie had to open it to see what the title meant.

**The Ageless Man**

Inside the file were several other Turkish words and phrases, two of which jumped out at her. One was *Gölgelerin Kitabı*—The Book of Shadows. That was something Auntie recognized from intelligence briefings left over from Deacon's days with The List.

Another was a photo of an old painting of a very tall and powerful-looking man dressed in the garments of a medieval knight. The photo's label was *Piç oğul*, meaning Bastard Son. That one was new to her, and when she zoomed in on the face of the man, her heart seemed to jolt to a stop in her chest.

The face looked so remarkably like Deacon that she began to smile, thinking that this was all some kind of joke. Georgette had a quirky sense of humor. She picked up her desk phone and hit the number for the computer office.

"Hi, Auntie," said Georgette brightly. "What can I do for ya?"

"Two words," said Aunt Sallie. "Bastard Son."

There was a significant pause. Then Georgette said, "Ah."

"Ah my ass. If it's a joke, then I do get the punch line."

"Not a joke. The image was from a batch of paintings believed stolen by the Nazis and then recovered in East Berlin by the Soviets."

"It looks like Deacon."

"Yes," said Georgette. "It does."

"What made you look at stolen art from World War II?"

"I wasn't."

"Then what?"

"I've been testing the new facial recognition software I wrote. Been using it to locate our field agents and erase them from the Net per your own directive. And that popped up."

"Oh, just a coincidence, then."

There was another long pause.

"What?" demanded Aunt Sallie.

"You didn't look through the rest of that file, did you?"

"Which? The Ageless Man thing? What's that even supposed to mean?"

"I . . . don't really want to say more. There's a folder of other pics. A lot of them. Take a look and, um . . . well . . . I'll let you decide what to do with them. I can delete them from our hard drive and launch a tapeworm to erase them from wherever they appear on the Net."

"That all sounds pretty mysterious."

"Yeah, well . . . go look."

Auntie ended the call, poured herself a fresh cup of tea, and opened the folder.

She said, "Holy shit" at least thirty times.

And then she called Georgette back and told her to delete all of them. Every single one.

Only then did she call Deacon to tell him.

All he said was, "Thank you."

And nothing else.

# CHAPTER 75

## HADRIAN TOWER
## LONDON, ENGLAND

I headed back toward the elevators, but paused to call Church.

He answered with, "Sitrep?"

I gave it to him, along with the news about the comms issue—which he already seemed to know about, likely from Courtland—and I told him my impressions of Manning, Griffiths, and the overall state of business security.

"I know you've worked with both of them before," I said, "but I have concerns."

"Understood. I trust your instincts, Outlaw. But keep me posted."

"How are things there?"

"In flux. Dr. Coleman has been working with hospital staff here to try and identify and classify the exact nature of the genetic changes imposed on the *Yersinia pestis.* They're sequencing the bacteria's DNA, but the analysis of that may take some time."

"How much time? I heard the latest casualty numbers."

"This isn't TV," said Church wearily. "Even with our best equipment some things cannot be hurried."

"That's got to hurt everyone over there who's working on it."

"Very much so."

"About the situation here," I said. "With most of the staff gone and nearly all of the security team down, the building is vulnerable. I'm on my way up now to talk with Rockwell to see what we can do about it. I know the security's supposed to be top-grade, but . . ."

"Yes," he said. "You have my endorsement to take any measures you feel are warranted."

"Copy that. I'm putting together a long-ass list of things I don't like about Hadrian Tower. First and foremost are the BSL-4 and -5 labs. What the actual fuck is that about?"

"I was both alarmed and unhappy to learn of their existence. It was kept from us."

"Even Rockwell didn't tell you?"

"He did not. When I saw him at the hospital and called him out on that, he hid behind need-to-know. As we no longer work for the

US government, that information-sharing dynamic has changed. He only admitted it now that he requested RTI be called in."

"Do we know what kind of microscopic monsters they have stored here?"

Church paused. "Apart from the usual suspects—Marburg, Ebola, and that lot—Barrier has authorized the storage of samples of two bioweapons that their government obtained without my knowledge. One is the weaponized rabies with the pertussis delivery system that we encountered during our Dogs of War case."

"Jesus. Who gave them that?"

"It was authorized at the executive level in the States."

I made no comment on that. "What's the other?"

"A more recent weapon provided to the British bioweapons research labs by the Norwegians."

I felt my blood turn to ice. "Do not fucking tell me they have Rage here."

"They do," he said.

I closed my eyes and wondered how productive it would be for me to bang my head on the wall. Rage was not a virus or bacterium, but was instead a protein, Loligo beta-microseminoprotein, found in the longfin inshore squid. In the squid world it drove competing males into rage states, with the winner earning the right to mate. When re-engineered for use as a bioweapon, it drove anyone exposed to it to extremes of shocking violence. No, not zombies . . . but alarmingly close to the "rage virus" in the film *28 Days Later* and its sequels. Mindless, unrelenting murderous insanity.

Havoc team encountered it in South Korea and then Norway, released by the Kuga criminal organization, which was originally run by Harcourt Bolton Sr.—a former top CIA agent and American hero who was thought of as being a combination of Tony Stark and Bruce Wayne, but who turned out to be a scum-sucking villain and arms dealer. The Rage releases were done to prove the effectiveness of the bioweapons he had for sale. Both Church and I were exposed to Rage, and it took a long damn time to shake it off.

My connection to that weapon ran deeper than the crisis Havoc helped stop. Bolton's right-hand man for all his wet works was a murderous Spaniard named Rafael Santoro—someone I'd first encountered during the *Sea of Hope* matter. As payback for me leading the charge to stop Rage and spoil their sales presentation, Bolton sent Santoro to my family house on Christmas Eve, and you know what happened there.

To add a layer of horror to it, we learned later that Harcourt Bolton was murdered and his identity as Kuga taken over by . . . yeah, you guessed it . . . Nicodemus.

Things were starting to come together in my head. And my own rage was beginning to boil, and that was not a good thing for anyone who wasn't at minimum safe distance.

"This is not putting me in my happy place," I said.

"There's a lot of that going around."

I ended the call, troubled, confused, and angry. I pushed the button and stepped onto the elevator.

## CHAPTER 76

### CCTV MONITORING SUITE
### HADRIAN TOWER
### LONDON, ENGLAND

Belle sat in the monitoring suite in the security office and watched the CCTV footage.

She had it queued up on three side-by-side screens, and she sat erect and looked forward, using direct and peripheral vision in exactly the same way she did when in a shooting blind watching the landscape for a target. As with many such stations, there was a foot pedal for pausing, visual rewind, and stop-start. Her right hand rested on the mouse to control viewing speed.

A security guard—one of the very few regular staff left in the Tower—sat in a chair beside and slightly behind her, watching her as she watched the videos. He was fascinated by this woman. Director Rockwell prepared him with a call to order full cooperation. When Belle arrived she said nothing and merely observed him as he ran through the system, then she jerked her head to the other chair. She'd said nothing since, either.

She held a pen in her left hand and every now and then she made a notation. When the guard tried to read her notes, Belle paused the feeds and turned toward him, rotating her head on her slender neck like a praying mantis. The guard was able to endure about three seconds of her stare and then found something fascinating on the floor between his shoes.

Belle sat like a statue and watched the images flow.

## CHAPTER 77

### RESTRICTED BIOLOGICAL RESEARCH LABORATORY H-6
### LONDON, ENGLAND

"How much do you want to go in there?" asked Bunny.

They stood at the entrance to a short hallway that ended with a massive airlock. Two guards in Hadrian Tower combat hazmat suits stood at attention at the far end, flanking the door, their eyes alert and faces showing a lot of stress.

"About as much as I want a red ant enema," said Top. "Maybe less."

"You want it more than I do," said Bunny. "I'd rather have my balls pounded flat with a hammer than go in there."

"Which can be arranged."

"So can that enema."

They grinned at each other as if the world wasn't burning down.

Then they went down the hall and into the lab.

## CHAPTER 78

### BARRIER HEADQUARTERS
### HADRIAN TOWER
### LONDON, ENGLAND

I stood outside of Rockwell's office, hand raised to knock, but I paused because I could hear him talking on the phone. Being a professional snoop, I leaned close and listened.

"I could use fifty more," he was saying. "There's nowhere near enough boots on the ground."

His call ended shortly after, with him merely saying "Very well" several times. Then I knocked.

"Come!"

I opened the door and stepped in. I'd seen photos of Rockwell and he looked like that poster boy for Iron Man competitions. My height and built, with zero visible body fat, a shaved head, and a face like a famous French movie star whose name I couldn't pull out of my memory. Manning had described him as being built like a movie superhero, and he wasn't wrong. He was in the zone somewhere between Thor and the Hulk. I'm tall and well built, but I felt like a waif next to him. Not as tall as Bunny, but built with the same science fiction parts. And as he came around the desk he did not look muscle-bound but was instead made of steel springs.

He gave my ChemRig a raised-eyebrows look. "I'm underdressed for this party," he said. Rockwell wore loose workout pants and a very tight long-sleeve Under Armour shirt. The sleeves were rolled up and he had Band-Aids on his forearm.

"You and Griffiths both," I said. He ushered me over to a long, dark brown leather couch and we sat at opposite ends.

"Same reason, I expect," he said with a sour laugh. "We were both exposed multiple times and neither of us has gotten sick."

"That's remarkable," I said flatly.

He nodded. "Odd is the word I chose. Why us and not everyone else?" Rockwell shook his head, then tapped the bandages. "Sure, the docs at St. Thomas rambled on about hereditary immunity and all that, and they juiced us up with a cocktail of antibiotics, but even so. The investigators working with Dr. Suliman grilled us on everything from recent travel to what we had for breakfast, looking for some commonality that would explain it. Your Dr. Coleman must have asked me two hundred questions. Thorough chap."

"He is."

"And he's the one that gave us the jabs before we left the hospital. Naturally we wore hazmat suits for the transport and did a full decontamination shower."

"Why come back here?"

"For exactly the reason you'd expect, Joe—may I call you Joe? I'm Jim. You know about the labs here in the Tower?"

"Know about them and am not very happy about them."

"Neither am I, quite frankly. When the Tower was built, those labs were intended for Fishing and Hunting to do research on bioweapons developed by hostile governments to infect salmon, sheep, and other key food animals. Then the PM before the last one authorized an upgrade in both facility structure and research designation. A few of the key members of Parliament who helped get him elected are from farming districts. I fought it tooth and nail and came very close to losing my job over it. Very close, actually. I may have let my mouth outrun my political caution. Lost some friends in government over that. So, I've been watchdogging everything." He paused and gestured to the door as a way of indicating the whole Tower. "When this happened, and considering what *is* stored here, I called in a few markers to clear the way for me to come back. And brought in a security team I've worked with on other projects before I took over Barrier."

"Hold on," I said, "Alpha Team *isn't* part of Barrier?"

"There were no Barrier teams in-country. Two are in Ukraine, one in Taiwan, and the other Malaysia. The timing could not be worse."

He must have read something in my expression.

"Don't let this raise your blood pressure, Joe. Alpha has been thoroughly vetted. Most of them are former SAS. If this comes down to a fight, you'll be happy to have them on our side."

I nodded. It was a reasonable explanation, but my overall trust level was running on fumes. "I'm sorry to hear about your wife," I said, and watched his eyes.

He looked away for a moment, nodding. When he turned back, there were unspilled tears in his eyes. "Life can be a real bugger at times."

"Yes it can."

"You spend your entire life trying to keep the world from blowing itself up, doing everything you can to insure that the people you love are safe, but . . . how do you protect them from disease? Cancer? Any of that?"

He launched himself from the couch and went to a sideboard and poured a healthy knock of scotch into a glass, added about a drop of water to mix it, stood looking at the wall for a moment, then knocked the whole thing back. Then he picked up a small silver statue of a castle, and I recognized it as the same kind he'd given Scott a couple of weeks back. Dover Castle, I think. Rockwell fiddled with it idly, then set it down, poured himself a less lethal glass of whisky, took a few steadying breaths, and came back to sit on the couch.

"Sorry about all that," he said. He gave a rueful smile and shook his head. "Another couple of weeks and I would have been home with my wife. The irony that poor Scott came here to interview *for* this job is not lost on me." He cut me a look. "He was the only real candidate, you know. Bright chap, ideal for the job. What a loss . . . Damn."

"We're losing too many good people, Jim," I said. "Have you been brought up to speed with what RTI has been handling lately? Things that we feel may tie into what's going on here in London?"

"Church gave me the headlines. The Red Order? The Red Knights? Nicodemus? That lab in Romania? I feel like I woke up this morning in a James Bond novel."

"Real world is scarier," I said.

"I've been read in on all of the Red Order and Book of Shadows material," said Rockwell, "and I know that Barrier helped do some cleanup here in the EU, helping the Italians and French tear down two groups of Red Knights and three Red Order cells. But that was before I even came on board with Barrier. I haven't heard a peep about them since. How sure are you that they're involved?"

I explained about Nicodemus and the Sabbatarians, and the cryptic things the dying scientist said in Corvin Castle. Rockwell sipped his whisky and stared into the middle distance for a while, then he shook his head.

"No," he said, "I'm not buying it."

"What exactly are you not buying?"

"I can see the Sabbatarian connection because you actually dealt with them. And Nicodemus seems to turn up everywhere and in everything, especially if he's still running the Kuga illegal weapons empire. But the Red Order? Excuse me, Joe, but nothing in what you said tells me that they are still in the game. Frankly, I don't believe there even *is* a Red Order anymore."

"They've gone dark before," I said, "and for long stretches of history, but they always seem to resurface."

"That's past-tense thought, isn't it? What proof do you have that they are involved in this in any way?"

I told him about the calls I'd been getting from Nicodemus, then recounted my most recent conversation.

Rockwell seemed unnerved by that. "Wait . . . he's *calling* you?"

"Yes."

"And you didn't think to mention it earlier?"

"I'm mentioning it now."

"Jesus. Tell me again exactly what you asked and he answered."

"I asked if the Red Order was involved in what was happening, and he said, '*In a way.*' That was all."

His face was flushed and he drank a bigger gulp of whisky. "That's . . . that's, well, disturbing as hell. How could he even know?"

"Is that a serious question?"

Rockwell jumped as if I'd jabbed him with a stick. "Right, right. Sorry. On top of everything else, that's really disturbing. Personally I would have thought that if any of that lot were involved it would be the Red Knights."

"Why them?"

"Because they were the ones who launched the plague back in the seventeenth century, which would have become another major pandemic had it not been for the dubious *luck* of the Great Fire of London in 1666. It pretty much burned the plague out of the picture. Oh, and there's a good chance some rogue Red Knights may have launched the original Black Death in the fourteenth century, the one that killed something like two hundred million people."

I studied his face. "What makes you think the Knights were involved in either outbreak?"

He looked surprised. "It's hinted at in the Book of Shadows. I read the transcript. Haven't you?"

"I must have missed that part," I said. "But even if that's the case, the Knights were always the militant arm of the Red Order. Everything they did was dictated by the Scriptors."

"Not everything. That Iran case was them rebelling, surely. How do we know it was the first time? And who knows—maybe they're immune to plague and wanted to reduce the human population in order to level the playing field. Or maybe they did it to send a message to the Scriptors that they could only be pushed so far. We can reasonably assume that if both the Order and the Knights are still active, then they might still be at odds."

I thought about that, and nodded. It sounded reasonable.

"Your theory is that the Upierczy obtained samples of *Yersinia pestis* and then hired a bunch of scientists in Romania to make it even more deadly and to give it resistance to the standard antibiotics, and then came here to London to release it?"

"Not sure I'd call it a 'theory,' Joe. Just a suggestion, because otherwise I'm completely in the dark. When this first happened I was building a case about it being the Russians, or ISIS—because they're making moves again."

We knocked it back and forth for a few minutes, but kept hitting walls.

"Okay," I said, standing up, "I'm going to go play cop for a while. Please advise your security teams to stay out of our way. But also have them contact us directly if they see something hinky. There are a lot of blanks to be filled in, Jim, and I'm going to do whatever is necessary to *solve* this."

He stood as well and stood looking like a sad and weary cave troll. All those shoulders and biceps and no way to use them for this kind of fight. "Call me if there is anything—and I mean anything—I can do to help."

I nodded and left.

# CHAPTER 79

## SUBBASEMENT 4
## HADRIAN TOWER
## LONDON, ENGLAND

The group of black-clad figures with their strange red goggles moved through Subbasement 4, going from room to room. There was no one down there, but even so they moved slowly and carefully so as not to set off any alarms.

When they were sure Sub-4 was empty, they moved to the stairs, deliberately bypassing the two passenger and four cargo lifts. They made no sound, moving as silently as shadows.

The leader paused, head cocked as he sniffed the air. Then he merely listened to what the building had to tell him. His team stood perfectly still, watching him and stretching out with their own senses.

After more than a minute, the leader relaxed slightly and shook his head.

They all headed for the stairs and began to climb.

# CHAPTER 80

## CCTV MONITORING SUITE
## HADRIAN TOWER
## LONDON, ENGLAND

Belle suddenly sat forward, pausing the feed on screen 2, studying it, then running it back.

"Did you find something, miss?" asked the guard, but she ignored him.

After rewatching the footage again, she consulted the data on her tac-com, scrolling through the images of each employee until she found a face that matched the one on the screen. She made a notation and then advanced the footage until she saw another clear image and checked that on her tac-com. Belle repeated this process over and over again until the notepad had a long list of checkmarks next to names.

*"Ya Allah,"* she breathed, and then looked over her shoulder at the guard. "You," she said. "Out."

"But I'm supposed to—"

"Now."

There was nothing about her expression that invited discussion but quite a lot that promised consequences. The guard cleared his throat, rose, and left. As soon as the door clicked shut, Belle called Joe Ledger.

# CHAPTER 81

## RESTRICTED BIOLOGICAL RESEARCH LABORATORY H-6
## LONDON, ENGLAND

Top and Bunny met with the senior researchers and were given a tour. The suite was composed of ten medium-sized rooms, four of which were dedicated for the study of dangerous pathogens. Each of these labs had their own restricted-access sample storage cabinets, and central to the block of four was a larger and far more sophisticated main hot room.

The senior research scientist in charge was a woman named Dr. Regina Byrd. She was short, slender, bookish, and visibly terrified. She was also not wearing a hazmat suit.

"We've been in here since before the breakout," she explained. "When Mr. Wilson fell ill and the symptoms reported, our protocols called for an immediate soft-seal. Doors are locked, access codes changed hourly, and staff ordered to shelter in place. We have two staff rooms with pull-down cots, showers, the lot; and we have our own water purification system and stores of emergency rations. We can remain in quarantine for a fortnight without required resupply."

"Has anyone from your staff been outside of this lab?" asked Top.

"God no," she said. "You gentlemen are the very first people to enter here since lockdown."

Bunny grunted. "Wait, no one's been in here to check on you?"

"Not in person, no," said Byrd. "We've videoconferenced with Mr. Griffiths and Mr. Manning, and we have had hourly updates from the hospital. In fact, right before you got here I was on a video call with Dr. Coleman."

Bunny and Top exchanged a look but made no further comment.

Byrd, looking awkward and tiny in her immaculate white lab coat and oversized glasses, fidgeted for a bit, then offered to give them a tour, which they accepted. She showed them everything, explaining even the most basic functions and procedures as if they were unfamiliar with the place. Top and Bunny had agreed before coming in that it was best to keep what they actually knew about all of this to themselves for now.

The chief researcher showed them different kinds of storage setups.

"Some samples," she said outside of one medium-sized room, "like skin and tissue that are fixed with preservatives, and those we store at room temperature."

The next room had windows fogged with condensation.

"We have a variety of temperature-controlled rooms," she said. "Special systems, of course, because conventional refrigeration is not suitable for proper sample storage. Different containers inside are set to temperatures appropriate for what's stored in them. And over here we have ultra-low freezers, set anywhere between minus 40° Celsius all the way down to minus 80°. Such freezers are a common choice for long-term storage because they prevent the degradation of biological molecules."

Another cold room.

"This is our cryogenic storage," she said. "That allows for freezing samples at extremely low temperatures down to minus 196° Celsius. We use liquid nitrogen or other cooling agents for that. Frankly, this method is considered the gold standard for long-term storage."

She paused to explain some basics.

"When storing biological samples, it's important to consider the Freeze-Thaw protocols. How key samples are frozen and thawed can affect how long they remain viable. For example, cells are typically preserved best when frozen slowly and thawed quickly. With each new sample we receive, we develop a storage plan to ensure the value and viability of samples. It's fair to say that the quality of stored samples depends on the storage environment, equipment, and maintenance."

Byrd gestured to the rows of research rooms, some of which were as small as an accountant's office while others were quite large. "Cleanrooms are classified by their cleanliness," she explained. "That level of cleanliness is determined by the number and size of particles in the air. The International Organization for Standardization—ISO, for short—established a classification system for cleanrooms called ISO 14644–1. This ISO system has nine subordinate classifications, with Class 1 being the cleanest and Class 9 being the least clean."

"Want to break that down for us?" asked Top.

"Oh, sure. Let's see . . . ISO 14644–1 is a nongovernmental standard applied to all cleanrooms in general. ISO 14698 are cleanrooms where biocontamination may be an issue, and there are many of them in all of the labs here in the Tower. Then there's EU GMP, a standard that applies to pharmaceutical products and requires cleanrooms to meet particle counts while operating and at rest."

The lecture went on and they absorbed it, mentally transferring the American safety standards with which they were more familiar with the British standards used locally.

"Now," said Top, "where do you store your samples of *Yersinia pestis*?"

"Yeah," said Bunny, "and Rage."

# CHAPTER 82

## HADRIAN TOWER
## LONDON, ENGLAND

Playing cop was what Church wanted from me, and it was my favorite gear.

I spent the next few hours going through the building, using the data and diagrams on my tactical computer to guide me. I checked every spot where known infected had worked, including their workstations and break rooms. Each workstation was a copy of the others in terms of structure—a sectional deck in three parts that formed an arc around a comfortable chair. A big desktop computer and, in many cases, smaller subordinate screens for working complex projects.

Like most offices, employees were allowed to personalize their spaces. The photos, tchotchkes, Post-it notes, and pop culture souvenirs made them real people, but matching each desk to the lists of healthy, infected, and deceased was emotionally corrosive.

Ron Coleman called me with an update on the drama at the hospital.

"God damn, Outlaw," he said, "people are dropping so fast. We've lost another thirteen since you last spoke with the Big Man."

"Isn't *anything* working?"

"Only kind of. We're trying different combinations of antibiotics and some are helping slow it, but that's as far as we've gotten. Adding two to three hours to the process of system collapse."

"Is there even a smidgeon of optimism here?"

He was a very long time in answering that.

"Please, for the love of baby goats, tell me there's some good news."

"Hold on . . . I'm thinking. Look, how much do you know about immunity?"

"A lot more about the legal kind than medical. So, use small words."

"Okay, of the people brought here from Barrier, we're seeing a percentage who, based on data collected, appear to have some natural immunity. Understand, about ten percent of Europeans were immune or somewhat immune to *Yersinia pestis* and survived the plague."

"How?"

"The primary source of immunity is a mutation called CCR5-Delta32," explained Coleman. "This is a seemingly spontaneous rare mutation, but during the Black Death so many people died that this mutation was enriched in the population, you follow?"

"Sure . . . by the time the plague ran its course there was a higher percentage of the population with immunity. Question is, were they able to pass that immunity on to their kids?"

"Yes. You're talking about someone who is CCR5-Delta32 homozygous—someone with hereditary immunity. The math is in the favor of those who survived, and anyone who lived through fourteenth-century Europe might have a higher chance of having CCR5-Delta32. And anyone who got the plague and recovered from it would probably have neutralizing antibodies in their blood. It's one of the reasons that when the plague came back in the middle of the seventeenth century, fewer people died per capita because the existing population had a higher proportion of CCR-Delta32 homozygous descendants."

"Damn . . ." I breathed. "If the plague jumps the quarantine around the Tower and the hospital, will that immunity protect a good chunk of England?"

"Joe, that immunity is in the DNA of anyone descended from a survivor. But go walk around outside. Britain was an empire. There are so many people here from Jamaica, South Africa, India, and Pakistan . . . you name it. The population demographics of modern London are a hodgepodge. If someone from one of the former colonies married into a family with immunity, then their kids may get the

CCR5-Delta32 protection, but there are so many families here that wouldn't have it. Weirdly, a higher percentage would have survived if the plague hit in, say, 1800 than right now."

"Fuck me up and down."

"But look," said Coleman, "here's the exciting part . . . well, maybe just promising, 'cause I have to do a crap-ton of lab work on it. But you know that I was pretty deeply involved in HIV research before coming onboard with RTI. That same receptor CCR5 is important for HIV to get into cells. So people with this current mutation can be virtually immune to HIV as well. Three of the Barrier staff are HIV positive but it's not active. All three of them are immune to the plague."

"Can something in their blood or DNA be used to create a cure?"

"Cure is a tricky word. Right now we're hoping for a treatment to slow the spread and lessen the severity of symptoms. That said, we're looking into what's called 'recovered plasma donation.'"

"You lost me."

"You actually can sort of transfer it but it is difficult and dangerous," said Coleman. "The transfer may only work for HIV. But if you transfer the bone marrow from someone with the mutation it *might* work. This one patient had leukemia and HIV. So they irradiated his bone marrow and transferred in the marrow of someone with the mutation and it cured both. It looks like at this point this has been done with only seven people, though. It's not something we can do for the nearly nine million people living in London."

"Could recovered plasma donations be used as the basis for a treatment if this thing goes on for a while?" I asked.

"That and the CCR5 antagonist drugs, maraviroc and aplaviroc."

"Are they some kind of antibiotics?"

"No," he said. "Maraviroc and aplaviroc are in a class of medications called HIV entry and fusion inhibitors. Those would be the stopgap, and for otherwise healthy people it might be enough. But I'm also considering making a semisynthetic form of gentamicin."

"Which is . . . ?"

"Gentamicin—gent for short—works by binding to a specific part of the bacterial ribosome. Ribosomes are the parts of the cells that make new protein. If cells can't make new proteins they die. So, a way that cells can become resistant to gentamicin is to have a mutation in the gene that codes for the amino acid of the ribosome where gentamicin binds. Following me?"

"Clinging on by my fingernails, but . . . yeah."

"Okay, so this mutation slightly changes the shape and then the antibiotic can't bind and therefore can't stop the bacteria from making new proteins. Think of it like a lock and key. The ribosome is the lock and gentamicin is the key that can lock it down. By mutating the ribosome the old key doesn't fit. So I made a new key that does. The nice thing is we use gent as the starting material and it is a chemical reaction so it is fast. The CCR5 antagonists could be that stabilizing factor."

"In that old movie *Outbreak,* they mass-produce the cures or treatments overnight. How far from the truth is that?"

"It's never as easy as that, but then again science—and cooperation within the science community—has come a long way. For the antagonists it would simply be a matter of shipping them from all over the world. Say twenty-four to forty-eight hours, because there are protocols in place thanks to HIV, COVID, and other pandemics that have speeded the process up. For the novel antibiotics I think we could talk a week or so."

I thought about that. "Given the speed with which people are dying today, Ron, a week sounds like an awfully long time."

"Given how aggressive this is, Joe, an *hour* feels like the apocalypse."

# CHAPTER 83

**CCTV MONITORING SUITE**
**HADRIAN TOWER**
**LONDON, ENGLAND**

I hauled ass to the monitoring suite.

A confused and disgruntled guard stood outside, looking like a very sad Stay Puft marshmallow man in his hazmat suit. He gave me a hopeful look, maybe expecting me to reestablish his relevance, but quickly realized I wasn't there for that, so he leaned back against the wall and looked at the inside of his hood's visor.

I used my keycard to enter and when I saw Belle's face I knew she had something.

"Hit me," I said.

Belle had some video clips ready for me, and as I sat she prefaced them by pointing to one of the monitors. "This camera is located outside of the bathroom Scott used while waiting for his interview."

The clip ran and moved at high speed. People came and went, but Belle paused frequently to showcase different faces. All men, of course, going into that particular bathroom. Then she ran a second clip for the corresponding women's restroom on the other side of a short side corridor. When both clips were done she turned to me.

"I checked facial recognition using MindReader," she said, touching her tac-com. "Then matched them against the most recent list from Coleman as to who was sick, who died, and who has no symptoms. Now, look how many people who were taken to the hospital used that same bathroom." She handed me a clipboard.

I took the clipboard and scanned the numbers, and felt another wave of nausea at seeing that there were now 117 dead, and nearly as many sick.

"Those are the totals," she explained, then handed me a second clipboard with a shorter list. "These are the people who used the executive washrooms on the same floor where Scott had his interview."

Of the forty-three men who used the same men's room, forty-one were either sick or had already died. For the women's room, there were fifty-eight sick or dead.

"Shit. This is it," I cried. "Excellent work, but keep at it. Let's find out which bathrooms were used by the rest of the people who got sick."

"I'm running a search algorithm," she said. "I used one of Bug's programs to tag each person, not just in and out of the bathroom, but as they moved into the fields of other cameras."

"You're mapping each person?"

"Yes."

"You're a bloody genius, Belle."

She said nothing, but looked pleased and intense as she sat back down.

"I'm going to call this into Church," I said, "then I'm going to take a close look at those bathrooms."

## CHAPTER 84

### DISUSED ARM OF SEWER SYSTEM
### LONDON, ENGLAND

They moved through the darkness, moving like living shadows.

A line of figures dressed all in black except for goggles that glowed with a faint, eerie red. Like rat's eyes made larger and stranger. Their equipment—knives, guns, explosives, electronic devices—were in cloth holsters padded to prevent rattling and squeaking.

They walked along the ledges above the running water, each of them sure-footed even on the mossy stone. Water dripped and rats scurried and spiders watched from inside their complex webs.

There was a tube station down there that had been abandoned nearly as soon as it was built, the engineers fearing that the cracks in the ceiling foretold imminent collapse. Even when that disaster never occurred, by then the network of subway lines had been rethought and history moved on. Only a handful of clerks in obscure offices even knew of that otherwise forgotten series of tunnels. Them, and one or two other people who made it their business to know what everyone else had forgotten about.

There were several iron doors rusted shut so thoroughly that the walls would have to be demolished to remove them.

All except one.

It looked as rusted and unusable as the others. What drew the intruders to it was a mark left on the lower left corner. A small thing that had to be looked for to be seen at all. A tiny cross painted in dark red.

The leader of the group raised a fist, and they all stopped, kneeling at once with rifles pointed forward and back and up at the ceiling, covering all possible angles of threat. The leader bent to peer at the mark, nodded to himself, then began counting the tiles on the right side. When he reached twenty, he moved two tiles away from the doorframe and pressed the corners of that tile in an anticlockwise sequence. A panel opened above it, and it was so cleverly hidden, even to its covering of moss and slime, that not even the leader could have found it without using the trigger device hidden behind the brick.

As the cover swung open it revealed something never made by the nineteenth-century engineers who built the London Underground. There was an ultrasophisticated scanner with sensors for retina scan, breath, and left-hand little finger. He held his hand out and one of the others handed him three items in succession. The first was a human eye in a sanitized clear container that preserved the chemicals that kept the eye fresh and prevented separation of the lens. The leader held that to the retina scanner and waited for a small green light to snap on.

The second item was a small, pressurized cylinder about the size of a breath spray, which in truth it was, though instead of something minty it shot out the stored breath of the person who had once owned the eye. A second green light appeared.

The third was a little finger, also preserved to retain freshness and fingerprint integrity. The final light flared and there was a somewhat louder, deeper *click* as the main lock disengaged. It did not release that rusted door, but instead hidden hydraulics pushed a section out and then rolled it sideways to reveal a short corridor that led to a second door with similar scanners.

The line of intruders checked their weapons and moved up to follow their leader inside. The doors hissed shut behind them, sealing them inside the deepest subbasement below Hadrian Tower.

## CHAPTER 85

### HADRIAN TOWER
### LONDON, ENGLAND

I ran from the monitoring suite and took the first elevator I found, riding it up to the Barrier floors. Excitement was sparking inside me and it was making me jittery. I used some tricks to calm myself, including box breathing—inhaling for a four-count, holding for four, exhaling for four, and again pausing. While I did that, I played a game of solo patty-cake by tapping every pocket, pouch, sheath, and holster while mentally naming the contents. Sounds silly, but isn't.

When I stepped off the elevator I was calmer.

The bathroom used by Scott Wilson was on the lowest level, so I hurried that way, slowing, though, as four of the Alpha Team members saw me and moved to intercept. It was the first time I'd seen them, and began to consider them ghosts for all the presence they had. Of course, eighty-six floors is a lot of real estate to patrol.

One of them, a woman, came directly to me. "You are Colonel Ledger?" she asked.

"Guess we're not using those pesky combat call signs," I said.

"Excuse me, sir, but we were not provided with your call signs," she said. "I'm Bess Turner, late of the SAS. I'm second-in-command for Alpha."

"Turner? I know the name."

"I was a friend of Grace Courtland."

"Ah," I said.

Grace seemed to be everywhere lately. Busy for a ghost.

"If I remember right," I said, "you were part of that first group of women who qualified for the SAS."

"I was. Grace broke the glass ceiling on that and allowed the rest of us to move upward."

The face behind the clear visor of her Hammer Suit was blunt, hard, and unsmiling. Her eyes were that shade of blue that was almost black. Not at all a friendly face, but then again this wasn't summer camp.

"You find anything of interest in your sweeps?" I asked.

"A lot of empty rooms and corridors," she said. "Nothing where it's not supposed to be, and nothing missing from where it should."

"Where are your teams right now?"

"Patrolling the building."

"I asked *where*." She seemed to turn to stone inside her hazmat suit, but I was in no mood to be stonewalled. "Maybe you didn't get the memo, Turner, but I'm actually in charge of the investigation. That means everyone in this building reports to me, starting with

Director Rockwell on down to the cockroaches in the walls, are we clear on that?"

"We're private contractors," she countered.

"How does that matter? You were hired to patrol. The people who hired you went to the prime minister and asked for me and my team to take charge here. What part of that arithmetic is fuzzy?"

"I need to check in."

If we were closer to the balcony rail I might have tossed her over.

"Go ahead," I said. "Make the call right now. I'll wait. No . . . make the call right here. I want to eavesdrop."

Turner did not like that one little bit, but she tapped her comms and got Bedwyr Griffiths on the call. I could only hear her part of it, though.

"Sir," she said, "I'm on eighty-four with Colonel Ledger and . . . yes, sir, I mean Outlaw. I . . . yes sir . . . no, sir, I . . . yes, sir. Yes, sir. I . . . yes, sir, I understand. Of course, sir."

She tapped out of the call. I waited. I wasn't feeling petty enough to gloat, though. Cooperation in a crisis is the preferred pathway, even when someone was being an ass. Her face was three shades paler and it was clear Griffiths had read her the riot act. I was fine with that. She came slowly to attention and it looked like the process caused her actual physical pain.

"Please accept my apologies, Outlaw," she said crisply. "Mr. Griffiths explained things. Whatever you need from me and my team will be provided at once."

It cost her, but she said it, so I decided to take her off the hook.

"Let's start over again, shall we? Clean slate? Tensions are high and to say that this is a stressful situation qualifies as the understatement of the century."

She studied me, trying to decide her best course of action. Then, by slow degrees, her rigid posture softened and she gave me her first smile. Not exactly a friendly one, but with no evident hostility.

"That sounds like a good plan, sir."

"You can skip the sir stuff with me. Outlaw works just fine. And your call sign is . . . ?"

"Harrier." She almost said *sir,* but managed to edit it out.

"Very well, Harrier. Please check in with your teams and then contact my guys. Your comms seem to be working but ours, for some reason, suck, so here's my cell number." I gave it to her and watched her tap it into her phone. Then, unasked, she texted me so I had her number. "Give me names and call signs for everyone. My cell is heavily encrypted, so the data is safe. I'll send you the call signs for Havoc Team. And please update me every hour as to your patrol status. That work for you?"

"It does."

"Good. Then I'll let you get back to it and I'll do the same."

"I doubt you'll find much in the toilets," she said. "Good hunting, though."

We exchanged a nod and she moved off. If she walked a bit stiffly, it was understandable. I watched them go.

Then I turned and headed down the hall toward the bathrooms.

## CHAPTER 86

### BARRIER HEADQUARTERS
### HADRIAN TOWER
### LONDON, ENGLAND

The two bathrooms were on 84, the lowest of the three levels occupied by Barrier.

I could see why Rockwell and Griffiths asked for out-of-town talent. They *worked* there and didn't figure this out. To be fair, the old DMS was compromised a couple of times, and it was a real bitch figuring out who the bad guy was among all the people we thought we knew and trusted. When Church built the RTI he went to some pretty extreme lengths to make sure that would never happen again.

On the other hand, everyone at Barrier was in the covert ops end of the spy game. They were exactly the kind of people who *could* pull something like this off, just as they had the skills and knowledge to build false identities and play the long game of doing the day-to-day job and earning trust. About the only people who weren't way at the top of my Maybe-it's-them list were Rockwell and Griffiths. They asked for outside help even at the risk of trashing their own careers.

Not saying I trusted them completely—my personal circle of trust is about the size of a kid's hula hoop—but they had the most to lose because of this. Well . . . apart from the people who were dying or dead.

# CHAPTER 87

## HADRIAN TOWER
## LONDON, ENGLAND

Even with a ChemRig, stepping into that bathroom was creepy. This was where the plague began its cruel work. I fancied I could almost see Scott Wilson's ghost standing at the sink straightening his tie and looking for any hair out of place. That caused a pang of grief that surprised me.

He and I never got along, not from day one. He came on board RTI when Church started it, and the chemistry was bad between us. He was all about structure and patterns, and I tend to improvise because structure leads to predictability. Sure, Scott had been in the field and earned his stripes, but we were entirely different kinds of people.

Now, though, I could feel his loss. Despite our mutual dislike we'd done important work together. We stopped terrorist plots that would have resulted in millions of civilian deaths, and he played his part in that. And did it well.

I looked into the mirror where I'd imagined him standing and called up a memory of his face. "Sorry this happened to you, brother. You didn't deserve this."

There was no one in there but me, and Scott was in a morgue, yet somehow I think he heard me.

As I turned around, I forced all emotional thoughts back and let the cynical, pragmatic, hyper-observant Cop personality step forward and take possession of me. It sounds creepy, and to anyone else that might be weird. For me, though, it was like becoming more fully myself.

The answer was in this room. I *felt* that.

Scott Wilson became the patient zero of this outbreak of plague right here. Belle logged such a high percentage of infected using this bathroom that this had to be ground zero. So, I unclipped my BAMS unit and held it up.

The light was green, but not intense. More of a yellowish green. I tapped the data button and sure enough, there was *Yersinia pestis*. However, the parts per million was low, and that didn't seem to make sense. So I walked around, holding the BAMS out in front of me as I moved along the row of a dozen sinks. The yellow went orange a few times but came back to yellow-green. When I poked it into corners I got the same color shift. The orange was a little more distinct in eight of the twelve toilet stalls. The green was most intense around the door and sink drains.

Once I'd completed a circuit of the whole room I left there and repeated the process in the ladies' room, and got nearly identical results, minus the absent urinals.

After that I stood in the gap between the bathrooms and thought it through for several minutes. There was a pattern now. Stronger in some of the toilet stalls, a little stronger in corners. And upticks with drop-offs while I walked along the sinks.

A pattern for sure.

The question was what to infer from the pattern.

I walked back inside the men's room and stood very still, my back to the closed door. Crime scenes are a story told, but like all good stories they are waiting to be retold.

A picture was starting to form, but as so often happens it was fuzzy and indistinct, needing action to support cognition. So I pushed off the door and did a likely path through the room, following an assumptive reconstruction of what Scott might have done.

He is—*was*—a fastidious man and according to the video Belle showed me, there were at least four other men in the bathroom at the same time. There was a natural curving path the average man takes when approaching the urinals, based either on observation or past knowledge of where the urinals are located. The timetable of his visit suggested he had to pee, and he wasn't so insecure that he would lock himself in a toilet stall to take a whizz.

So, yes, urinals.

There were twelve and the first in the row would have required a sharp left because it was positioned by the wall that was shared with the hall. No reason for so sharp a turn. Urinals four and five were at the end of a natural, gradual turn. I went to them first and waved the BAMS around. Weak green light. Not a heavy bacterial load in the air.

I went to the next two most natural urinals and got about the same reading. Then I stepped back and looked at the wall. Standard white subway tile, with the urinals and sinks made by Victorian Plumbing, a well-known company. Higher on the wall was a room sanitizer and a box with an emergency light, both standard.

I stood again at the urinal I estimated as most likely, then turned toward the sinks. From the few times Scott and I were in the bathroom at Phoenix House at the same time, I knew he preferred an end sink, closer to the paper towel dispenser and trash can. He was right-handed, so he would turn that way in most cases. If there was a man to his right, he might go left out of politeness. If flanked on both sides—which I deemed unlikely with five men in a lavatory with twelve urinals—he would back up a step and again likely turn right. Which meant that as he turned, the sink farthest to the left would be in line-of-sight.

I went over to that sink and studied it. Normal automatic hand soap dispenser, a single lift-tap that could be adjusted for hot, cold, or a mix. I considered that for a moment, but there were several reasons I discounted it as the source of the bacteria. First, whether Scott turned the tap on first and then soaped his hands, or soap first and then tap, the washing process would eliminate any bacteria left on the fixtures. And it would require someone coming in to reapply bacteria frequently throughout the day to up the odds of catching Scott.

But when I waved the BAMS unit around the sink, the light shifted into the orange.

The soap dispenser didn't trigger the shift, nor did the tap, or the paper towel dispenser.

It was the trash can.

I squatted down and examined it. There was still some paper debris in there, left over from the second day of Scott's interview process. I took a paper towel, scanned it with the BAMS to make sure it was green and clear, and used that to tip the trash can over and spill the paper onto the floor. Then I removed the clear plastic liner and set it aside. When I ran the BAMS over the lineup of trash, liner, and can, the light shifted back and forth, wobbling in the lower settings of the orange.

Here's the thing, though. The liner was green, the trash was a faint orange. The can, though, was more solidly orange. Not the inside, but the outside.

"Hmmm," I murmured.

What this told me was that it was highly unlikely anything directly around the sink carried the disease, but the *outside* of the can did.

I straightened and repeated this process with all the sinks. There were three trash cans—one at either end of the row of sinks, and a third in the middle, between sinks six and seven. The can that triggered the strongest orange was the middle one.

I stood and turned around and looked at the room again, setting the scene in my head from that angle.

Then I went into each toilet stall and ran the BAMS units. The seats glowed faint orange. The inside of the tanks was green. But as I straightened from scanning those, the BAMS light went from green to orange and then slightly into the red. This sliding scale of intensity was weakest at the lower part of one inside stall wall and strongest near the top.

Of the two metal cubicle divider walls, the rear tiled wall, and the metal door, the bacterial load was heaviest on the tiles above the stall, the upper part of the right-hand wall, and the upper inside right of the door.

I backed out of the stall and went down the line repeating the test.

About midway along, the orange/red intensity changed as to which parts of the divider walls were affected. In the two centermost stalls there was a moderate red light behind the toilets and on the upper section of both divider walls. Then, as I moved down the line, the intensity shifted from upper right divider to upper left. And as I exited each stall the toilets auto-flushed. The incoming water registered as green and clean, eliminating the water as the source.

I exited the stalls and walked backward, looking at the walls.

I saw it around the same time I heard it.

There was a second of the automatic air sanitizers, and I realized that it was either on a timer, or synced to discharge spray with each auto flush. I tried it a few times and listened through the noise of the gurgling water, and each time there was a tiny electronic buzz and a puff of something I assumed was perfumed. Couldn't smell it with the ChemRig on, and was glad of that because with the last three sprays I held the BAMS up and saw the green flash with an intense, furious red.

The device was one of two in the room. One centered over the urinals and the other over the toilets. I stepped up onto a toilet seat and looked at the device. There was a small sticker on each that read: Fresh-N-Clean Systems.

"Got you, you sneaky bastard," I said.

## CHAPTER 88

### HADRIAN TOWER
### LONDON, ENGLAND

I went across the hall and repeated the process with the ladies' room and got the same results.

Back in the hall, I typed Fresh-N-Clean Systems into my tac-com. The piss-poor signal strength was still playing games with connectivity, so I tried a Google search on my cell and that went straight through and brought up the webpage for a company located in the town of Ilford.

Then I called Top, Bunny, and Remy and told them to meet me in the monitoring suite. By the time they got there, I was already seated next to Belle and we went over everything she found and what I'd discovered.

"Weird," said Remy. "They're even listed as currently open for business."

"I know," I said. "I made a call as a potential customer and asked if I could swing by next Tuesday and talk to a salesman. They were very accommodating."

"Don't suppose they had sinister hold-music and answered with a maniacal laugh."

"No."

Remy shook his head. "People just don't know how to be supervillains."

Bunny frowned. "It's almost like they didn't care if we found out."

"If they're even the bad guys," said Top. "We know the plague's in the sanitizers but we don't know who put it in there. If it is these folks, then Farm Boy here is right and they don't give a shit."

"Either way, we need eyes on them," I said, and took out my cell.

Toys answered with, "I don't suppose you're calling to say you have the plague and are at death's door."

"Sorry to disappoint."

"Life is full of regrets," said Toys. "Why *are* you calling? Me and the lads have been out here for eleven hours."

"How quickly can you get to Ilford?"

"It's close, but why would I *want* to go to Ilford?"

I explained it to him and gave him the address.

"You're sending a crack team of former thugs and criminals to harass a vendor of urinals? Under any other circumstances I'd ask if you were taking the piss, but you're not clever enough for that."

"Just fucking go."

I heard a heavy SUV engine start.

"Go and do what, exactly?"

"Play detective."

"Mmm. Fun. And if the bad guys are all there in a back room plotting the downfall of the free world?"

"Disabuse them of that notion."

"First intelligent thing you've said," laughed Toys, and rang off.

"Dick," I muttered, then called Church.

# CHAPTER 89

## ST THOMAS' HOSPITAL
## WESTMINSTER BRIDGE ROAD
## LONDON, ENGLAND

Mr. Church was in a meeting with the medical team, all of them focused on what Dr. Coleman was saying about potential shortcuts in developing a treatment for the outbreak, when Joe Ledger called.

"Excuse me," he said, rising. "I have to take this."

He stepped into the hall and closed the door. The silence, however brief, was a comfort.

Church thumbed the button. "Outlaw."

"Boss," said Ledger, "I think we have our first strong lead. Not an answer, but a starting place."

"Tell me," said Church, forcing the sound of desperation from his voice.

Ledger told him, concluding with, "The Wild Hunt's already on their way."

"This is excellent work. I'll contact Toys and Bird Dog to make sure the Hunt has all the protective gear they need."

"Good. Is there news from the hospital?"

"Death toll is rising, but the number of casualties is dropping."

"That's good."

"No, it's just that all of the Barrier employees from the Tower are here, and there are only a handful left. Six with inherited immunity who have not presented with any symptoms. Twenty-two infected who are not yet critical. The rest are either in ICU or have already passed."

"Jesus."

"The only good news so far is that the infection appears to have been contained within Barrier. No one else got sick except for the EMTs who transported the first victims from the Tower to the hospital, and five police officers who were among the first responders."

"As much as I absolutely do not want the answer to this . . . how many have died in all?"

"As of ten minutes ago, two hundred sixty-seven."

There was a long silence at the other end of the call.

Finally, Ledger said, "I've got some leads to follow up here. I need to talk to Manning about the company who provided the sanitizers. Belle checked the earlier CCTV and that company did its usual maintenance check two days before Scott arrived for his interviews. I want to know who hired Fresh-N-Clean Systems. Then I want to grill Griffiths about their security vetting and clearance."

"Don't be gentle about it, Colonel. We're losing this fight."

"I intend to win the war," growled Ledger and disconnected.

Church stood looking at his phone, smiling faintly at the optimism of that last statement. It brought back memories of so many friends and allies along the way who believed that the war could be won and not merely fought.

He sighed, and went back inside.

# CHAPTER 90

## SUBBASEMENT 3
## HADRIAN TOWER
## LONDON, ENGLAND

The leader of the black-clad figures stopped at the top of the stairs, gesturing for his team to freeze in place. Then he placed his ear to the door and listened.

A male voice speaking Russian with a distinctly Volga accent was arguing with someone else.

"We'll damn well stay here until he calls us," he growled. "That was the agreement. When and if he needs us, he will call. Until then, Vassily, shut up and eat your stew. We have to be fed and ready. The rest of you, make sure you're all ready to go at a moment's notice. That means you, too, Popovitch."

There was more, but what he heard was enough. Beneath his mask, the leader of the infiltrators smiled.

He touched his various weapons, considering his choices, and decided on an Akinak double-edged combat dagger with a matte black finish. He shifted this to his left hand and drew a throwing spike with his right. Behind him the first four of his fighters drew their own steel and a fifth slid a matched pair of combat hatchets from their holsters. The rest of the team screwed sound suppressors onto their Fort-12 pistols, each of which was loaded with a 24-round box magazine.

The door was locked, but the leader shifted to one side and let his lieutenant bypass it with a set of flexible lockpicks. There was the faintest of clicks.

*"Lăsați-l pe unul dintre ei în viață,"* murmured the leader.

*Leave one of them alive.*

He opened the door and peered through the narrow gap.

The room was clearly set aside for the storage of paper records. Hundreds of banker's boxes stacked ten high stood in neat rows that created a maze. There were dim yellow security lights on, but a brighter glow blossomed up from the other side of the closest line of boxes.

The leader slipped into the room and crouched down. When his five senior fighters were inside, they crept to the end of the row. The lieutenant handed the leader a dentist's mirror, which he used to study the scene on the other side. Twelve people stood or sat around a camping lantern. There were two camp stoves on which cans of stew were heating. Bedrolls and other supplies told the story that these men were living in that space and had been doing so for at least a few days.

He frowned, wondering why they were there at all.

Then he sniffed the air and smelled that horrid scent.

Garlic.

*Sabbatarians.*

But why were they here? And what were they waiting for?

He glanced back at his team. A dozen Sabbatarians and six of his own currently in the room. Those odds made him smile.

They moved like a dark storm, going from stillness into action all at once. No hesitation, no sound.

Then the slaughter began.

# CHAPTER 91

## SUBBASEMENT 3
## HADRIAN TOWER
## LONDON, ENGLAND

Smirnov, the leader of the Sabbatarians, was a red-haired giant from the Volga region of Russia. He was bending over to pour a cup of coffee when he caught movement out of the corner of his eye. A cloud of blackness as if the shadows of the storeroom had suddenly and inexplicably come alive.

Then Smirnov saw the glowing red goggles and knew that doom

had come upon him and his people. He flung himself sideways, knocking two others back as black darts filled the room. There was a meaty *thunk-thunk* as throwing spikes found flesh and buried themselves deep in muscle tissue. He tore at the heavy pistol holstered at his hip as he cried a warning.

*"Upierczy!"*

It became a melee.

The attackers flooded the room, throwing spikes and slashing with knives; and the Sabbatarians rallied to meet them. All of the Sabbatarians—the Saturday People—were armed and guns appeared with the same appearance of magic as the platoon of Upierczy. Gunfire boomed but screams of rage and hate and pain rose above that noise.

Smirnov rolled to his feet as the leader of the infiltrators came at him, and he brought up his pistol at the same instant the attacker slashed with a black blade. The bullet hit the Upierczy in the center of his chest, staggering him but for a moment. The attacker whirled away from it, letting the impact push and turn him and he dropped into a cross-ankle crouch, spinning like a dancer as he corkscrewed upright again and slashed down with his blade. The big Russian screeched as the thin blade sliced like a razor through the tendons of his wrist. His pistol fired once more, but the bullet hit another Sabbatarian, catching the man above his ear and blowing out the far side of his skull, spraying a third of their group in the face with blood and brains.

The leader of the Upierczy closed with the Russian giant and wove a net of black agony around him, ducking to slash ankle tendons, shearing through biceps, cutting a deep line through the meat on the tops of both thighs. Smirnov cried out in helpless agony and fell, unable to stand, unable to use either hand.

Then the Upierczy whirled away from him and joined his brothers in their butchery, forcing Smirnov to lie there, helpless and weeping with pain and horror as the figures in black tore his strike team apart.

## CHAPTER 92

### ST THOMAS' HOSPITAL
### WESTMINSTER BRIDGE ROAD
### LONDON, ENGLAND

"I'm going down to the morgue," announced Coleman as the meeting wrapped. "I want to take my own set of samples from Wilson and certain others."

"To what end?" asked Dr. Suliman.

Coleman smiled crookedly. "Following a hunch."

With that he hurried out, his hazmat suit rustling like autumn leaves as he went.

Church fell into step and waited with him at the elevator.

"I have people flying in from all over the globe," he said. "And, at your request, I've passed along the request for emergency shipments of the CCR5 antagonists as well as the list of antibiotics you prepared."

"Shipped how?" asked Coleman.

"We're mostly relying on standard international shipping companies because they have the infrastructure for this. DHL and others," explained Church. "In some cases, military flights will be used."

Coleman nodded. "I don't know if any of the infected will be alive by the time that stuff gets here."

"We have to prepare for the possibility of a containment failure somewhere. I've also put in a request with the home secretary to order police to clear all streets within four blocks in every direction."

"That's smart."

"It might also be too late. It's the third time I've asked, but there are—as always—breaks in the chain of efficiency."

"Jeeeez, people are weird," said Coleman as the elevator car arrived. "I know that's not news, but . . ."

He left it hanging as he stepped inside.

"Keep me posted," said Church.

The doors closed. Coleman hit the button for the lower ground floor, and once the door opened again he hurried to the North Wing to find the mortuary.

Two people, both in hospital-issued hazmats, waited for him. A man and a woman, though he did not know either.

"Dr. Coleman," said the woman, rushing forward to meet him, "we heard you were coming down here. I'm Phelps and this is Lefèbvre. We're here to help in any way we can."

"That's great, but where's Dr. Markham and his nurse? What's her name? Amy something."

"Amy Cooper. They're both inside," said Phelps, half-turning to allow him to enter the mortuary first.

Coleman stepped inside and immediately slipped on something wet. His feet went out from under him and he fell hard on the poured-linoleum floor. He'd had just enough martial arts training in his teens and twenties to know how to land, and so did not crack his head on the floor, but the impact knocked the wind out of him.

Oddly, neither Phelps nor Lefèbvre made a move to help him. With great effort, a gasping, aching Coleman sat up. That was when he saw what made him slip.

The blood.

All that blood.

He gaped at it and then at the two sprawled things that lay in a pool of it not ten feet away. Dr. Colin Markham and nurse Amy Cooper stared at him with open eyes. So did two soldiers. All of them wore hazmat suits. Each of those suits was slashed to ribbons. They all seemed to scream at him with gaping mouths. Yet they saw nothing and said nothing because everything that defined them as human beings had been hacked or slashed or torn.

He swiveled his head around and looked up at Phelps as she unfastened the hood of her protective overgarment. As she pulled the hood off, he saw that she wore a huge smile of triumph and dark joy.

"This is going to be fun," she said. "Granted, more so for us."

Lefèbvre closed and locked the mortuary door.

# CHAPTER 93
## BARRIER HEADQUARTERS
## HADRIAN TOWER
## LONDON, ENGLAND

I called Manning and told him to meet me in the lobby.

While I waited for the elevator, I called the TOC and got Major Courtland and Bug on a conference call. I brought them up to speed about my discovery and then had to bark at them to stop congratulating me.

"Listen, damn it. The Hunt is heading to Ilford to check things out, and I'm heading down to ask Manning what he knows about the company providing and servicing the sprayers. But I need some MindReader action and our Wi-Fi is as wonky as our comms. Not sure why cell reception is still working, though."

"What do you need?" asked Bug.

"First," I said as I got into the lift, "are you any closer to repairing the Corvin Castle data?"

"A lot closer," he said. "Doc Holliday's reviewing the stuff we decrypted now. She says it's definitely part of the research and development protocols for the weaponized plague. So far it's the wrong *part* of that material, though. Stuff Ron would already know. He sent us a new set of keywords to look for, and that's helping."

"Anything in there about the Red Order or Red Knights?"

"Not so far."

"Shit."

"Doing our best, Outlaw," said Bug, sounding a little hurt.

"I know you are. I'm just frustrated. Look, can you put someone on deep background searches?"

"Sure. Nikki Bloom just got here. She was on vacation in—"

"Good, put Nikki on it," I said, cutting in. "I want everything on Griffiths, Manning, Rockwell, and everyone in Alpha Team. Can she handle that?"

"Nikki? You kidding?"

"Good. When she has anything at all, have her email it to me or text. Use my phone because the last couple of data downloads through our tac-coms were gibberish."

"Sure."

"Also, check out Griffiths's niece. The one who's sick. My gut tells me that there's something there, but I don't know what. Nikki's the genius with patterns, so if there is anything . . ."

". . . she'll find it," Bug finished. "We're on it."

He dropped off the call, leaving me with Courtland.

"Bedlam and Chaos Teams are in England," she told me. "I'm sending Chaos to you and Bedlam to St. Thomas."

The elevators reached the ground floor.

"Keep me posted," I told her and hung up.

The doors opened and I saw Ken Manning there, looking anxious, waiting for me.

"Listen, Manning," I began, but he raised a pistol and fired point-blank. The rounds hit me center-mass and slammed me back against the edge of the elevator door. I spun and dropped and the floor rushed up at me.

And all my lights went out.

# ASHES, ASHES, WE ALL FALL DOWN

# PART 5

"And one by one dropped the revelers in the blood-bedewed halls of their revel, and died each in the despairing posture of his fall. And the life of the ebony clock went out with that of the last of the gay. And the flames of the tripods expired. And Darkness and Decay and the Red Death held illimitable dominion over all."

—EDGAR ALLAN POE, "THE MASQUE OF THE RED DEATH"

"Everybody knows that pestilences have a way of recurring in the world, yet somehow we find it hard to believe in ones that crash down on our heads from a blue sky. There have been as many plagues as wars in history, yet always plagues and wars take people equally by surprise."

—ALBERT CAMUS, *THE PLAGUE*

## CHAPTER 94

**ST THOMAS' HOSPITAL**
**WESTMINSTER BRIDGE ROAD**
**LONDON, ENGLAND**

Coleman tried to get up, slipped again in the blood, and then frantically kicked backward to slide away from Lefèbvre and Phelps as fast and as far as he could. Within ten feet his back thumped up against the tiled wall.

The two killers stood there, still grinning, looking confident and happy.

"You're quite the catch, Doc," said Lefèbvre. "The American rock-star molecular biologist who wants to ride to everyone's rescue and stop the Black Death in its tracks."

"Oh, aye," said Phelps. "It would have made a great scene in a summer blockbuster. The unassuming nerd who levels up to be a hero."

Lefèbvre opened his lab coat and removed a long, slender knife from a hidden sheath. The silver blade gleamed but its length was still smeared in places with dark red. "Shame it won't work out that way," he said.

"Wh-who are you?" stammered Coleman.

"She's Little Red Riding Hood and I'm the Big Bad Wolf," said Lefèbvre, and both of them laughed as if that was the funniest thing anyone ever said.

"What . . . what do you want?"

"Three guesses."

"Why are you people doing this?"

Lefèbvre approached slowly, crouching a little as he did so, moving the bloody knife back and forth in front of the scientist's face. "Oh, it's simple really, Doc. We're working to make a better world. That's what we've always done. Though, admittedly, we've moved on from licking the blood from the foot of the cross. Now we're a sight more practical."

"I don't even know what that means."

"I know," said Lefèbvre, now almost within cutting range. "Thought it'd be fun to fuck with your head. Let you die with no sodding clue as to what's going on."

"Much more fun that way," said Phelps.

Coleman looked back and forth from one to the other. "This is funny to you?"

"Rather a lot, actually," said Lefèbvre, then he darted forward and slashed with the knife.

Coleman was waiting for that, and as the tall man lunged, the scientist braced hard against the wall, twisting onto his side, and kicked the knife man just below the knee.

It was a good kick, too. Fast, hard, and aimed with the precision of an anatomist. The shin jerked to an immovable stop but the man's mass was already committed to an irrevocable forward motion. Coleman was short but not light, and he put all of his fear, his anger, and several years of martial arts back in his younger years into the kick. The anterior cruciate ligament tore, ripping parts of the meniscus and medial collateral ligament. All in a blinding second of white-hot agony.

Lefèbvre screamed.

Coleman chambered his leg and kicked again, this time hitting above the patella, mashing the quadriceps tendon and ripping the entire femur back nearly a full inch. The tall man's leg bent backward into impossibility; his body weight was jerked downward by the inexorability of gravity. His scream rose to a shriek.

The woman, Phelps, shrieked as loudly as if she had been kicked, and stood staring in shock for a full second. Coleman used that time to get to his feet. It was sloppy, and he slipped a bit in the blood, but he managed it. The indecision caught him for a moment and he froze halfway between her and the door.

Then the woman ran three steps and launched herself into the air, slamming into him like a missile, driving him back against the wall, and the two of them fell into a snarling, thrashing tangle right atop Lefèbvre, whose screams now reached the ultrasonic.

# CHAPTER 95

## BARRIER HEADQUARTERS
## HADRIAN TOWER
## LONDON, ENGLAND

I woke up feeling like my head had been cracked open with a hammer, my brains carved out and run through a food processor before being poured back in and my skull stapled back together.

No, let me correct that. It hurt a fuck ton worse than that.

My senses were dulled from pain but my brain was so sluggish it took me way too long to determine what hurt, where it hurt, and how bad it was. The worst by a long mile was my face. I sort of remember falling face-forward but don't recall hitting anything. However, my cheek hurt like hell and the right half of my face felt like a wad of cotton candy wrapped with barbed wire. I also had the taste of blood in my mouth. The nausea hinted that maybe I had a concussion.

There were other points of pain that were less intense, though collectively they hurt one hell of a lot. I was not entertained.

I tried to open my eyes but something brushed against my eyelids. With my dulled senses it took a few seconds to work out that there was a blindfold tied around my head.

Which is when I became aware of the sharp edges of flex-cuffs around my wrists and ankles. My hands were behind my back and the cuffs were slowly cutting off the circulation.

I never saw the slap.

Felt it sure enough. Son of a bitch must have wound that one up like an outfielder throwing to first. Slaps and concussions are not a happy combination.

*"Fuck,"* I snarled.

"He's awake," said a voice. Male. Vaguely familiar. British?

Of course.

Things started coming back to me. I was in London. In an office building. Was it Barrier? The offices near Downing Street?

No.

No, that was wrong. Or partly wrong.

Hadrian?

The word swam up from the depths. Hadrian what? Hadrian's

Wall? But, why was I up there? The Romans built that wall like two thousand years ago in the North of England. I couldn't recall exactly why. Picts, maybe?

How did I get to Northern England?

Wait . . . no. I was in . . .

London.

Hadrian was . . . what? Ah . . . right. An office building. And it *was* Barrier HQ. The new place with all the fancy security and . . .

Then it all came flooding back. Hadrian Tower. The building locked down like a steel tomb. Scott Wilson. Pneumonic Plague. Air Fresheners. Church and Coleman at the hospital. Alpha Team . . . and . . . a lot of people dead or dying.

"Manning, you miserable cock-sucking dog-fucking shit-eating son of a whore."

"Yeah," said the same voice. "Definitely awake."

Who was that? Maybe . . . Bedwyr Griffiths? Sounded right but I now had a hazy memory of Ken Manning, building director, shooting me. And, apologizing . . . ?

A hand grabbed the blindfold and tore it from my head.

There was Griffiths and next to him, looking sheepish, scared, and confused, was Ken Manning. He was no longer holding a gun. Griffiths, however, was.

"Wakey, wakey," said the director of security.

I tried to summon a smart-ass remark, but nothing came to mind. My brain was way too busy screaming inside my skull because I realized that I was no longer wearing my ChemRig. It lay nearby, with my weapons and gear dumped atop it.

And me?

I was exposed to the air inside the sealed and hardened Hadrian Tower. Where the plague started.

# CHAPTER 96

## FRESH-N-CLEAN
## CRANBROOK ROAD
## ILFORD, ENGLAND

"Well, there it is," said Rugger.

"You sure that's the place?" asked Muppet.

Toys gave him three seconds of icy silence. "The name Fresh-N-Clean is literally painted on the outside wall."

"Well, I—"

"We drove past a billboard that said Welcome to Fresh-N-Clean."

"True, but—"

"And there are half a dozen lorries parked outside with Fresh-N-Clean painted in bright, highly visible colors on them. So, maybe—just *maybe*—this might be . . . oh, what's the name I'm looking for . . . ?"

"Fresh-N-Clean," suggested Rent Boy sotto voce.

"Ah yes, Fresh-N-Clean," said Toys.

Muppet colored. "Well, I was only asking," he mumbled sulkily.

"Do shut up."

Muppet and Rent Boy were new, and there were two more back on Omfori Island being trained. Rugger and Zombie were the only survivors of the original Wild Hunt, the rest having been wiped out on their first mission as part of the Cave 13 matter in Israel.

Toys enjoyed having a team, and enjoyed a bit of bashing now and then. Like himself, every member of the Hunt was a former criminal of one stripe or another. Rugger had been a securities manipulator and scam artist. Zombie broke legs for the crime families in Birmingham. Rent Boy pulled triggers for three different private military companies whose agendas had nothing to do with protecting the innocent and everything to do with helping to keep heroin flowing into Australia, Canada, and England. And Muppet committed more than eighty armed robberies from age fifteen to twenty-two.

As for Toys, his crimes were far too numerous to count. He spent a part of every night alone in his room writing out all the names of every person he killed, either directly while working for Sebastian Gault, or while apprenticing to Hugo Vox. After the Assassins Code matter in Iran, when Church executed Vox, the Big Man gave him a chance to redeem himself. Why Church believed that someone with that much blood on his hands *could* be redeemed, or why—out of all the criminals in the world—he picked Toys, was something the young man could never work out. He gave Toys access to a bank account with most of the billions looted from Hugo Vox's many criminal enterprises, and challenged Toys to do something worthwhile with it. Toys partnered with Junie Flynn to found FreeTech, the corporation that took some of the most terrifying technologies Ledger and the other team leaders acquired from the bad guys and then together Toys and Junie repurposed them for humanitarian application.

Despite the hundreds of thousands of lives saved by those technologies, including new medicines, free medical care in Third World countries, and clean water for countless villages; and despite the millions who would benefit from FreeTech's ongoing work, Toys did not care a whit about his own redemption. He knew that he had been evil too long and transgressed so profoundly that he deserved no grace in heaven. His Catholicism had returned with terrible force, and he believed with his whole heart that hell waited for him, and that this punishment was just.

Church often brought him out of his *retirement* to provide special services during some of Joe Ledger's more dangerous missions. This often meant pulling a trigger or slitting a throat.

Toys finally challenged Church and begged to be removed from FreeTech and allowed to use his own skills and many of the contacts he developed while working for Gault, Vox, and the Seven Kings. Church agreed and the Wild Hunt was born.

As Rugger parked, Toys studied the building. Fresh-N-Clean was in a small industrial park shared with several other businesses that did not require walk-in trade. The target building was a squat two-story place with the name painted in a tacky and nearly eye-hurting luminous yellow-green.

"Lot of cars in the parking lot," observed Rugger. "But isn't it after hours for a concern like that?"

"You would think," mused Toys. He took a small but powerful pair of binoculars and studied the lot. They were still at the near end, just inside the shared entrance, and Rugger had found a shadowy spot between two industrial dumpsters—one for trash and the other for recycling.

Muppet pointed to the recycle bin. "Nice to know that even terrorists have gone green."

"From what Bug gave us," replied Rugger, "that business has a long list of legitimate clients." To Toys he added, "Might mean that most of the employees are innocents and don't know what the owners have gotten up to."

"Let's go find out for ourselves," Toys said. "Everyone kit up. Three minutes."

# CHAPTER 97

## HADRIAN TOWER
## LONDON, ENGLAND

Griffiths came over and stood inches in front of me.

"Take a sniff, Ledger," he said. "The scent you're smelling is called 'fuck you, you're dead.'"

I looked up at him, forcing myself to see past the terror that was rising like a tsunami inside me. I refused to let my face show what I was feeling, and believe me I was feeling every goddamn bit of it. The fear of the plague. My pulse was playing backbeat to the symphony of my own impending demise, but I wasn't going to let them know how completely I knew I was fucked.

"You two assholes are part of the group that's trying to kill everyone in London? Maybe all of England? The hell's that all about?"

"You wouldn't begin to understand," sneered Griffiths.

"I might. Try me," I said. "After all, if a pair of short-bus dipshits like you can understand it, I like my own odds."

"Says the genius zip-tied and with his bollocks in a mangle."

"No, seriously. What's this all about? Domestic terrorism? Are you working for a foreign power? Maybe in bed with ISIS? Give a fella a clue here."

"Ha!" laughed Griffiths. "And here we all were worried that the big bad Yank psychopath was a real danger. And what are you? A helpless sheep-shagging twat who is going to be coughing up blood anytime now while we sit around and watch."

I shoved my inner Cop to one side and let the Killer in my head construct the smile I showed him. It was the kind of smile you would never want to show anyone you ever wanted to like you afterward. It was a monster smile, a werewolf grin, a demon's leer. That's what people have told me. A lot of those people are dead. I didn't say a word. Just smiled.

Ken Manning took an actual step back, even though I was bound ankles and wrists. His face went dead pale and his eyes kept blinking as if trying to clear his vision of even the afterimage of that grin.

Even Griffiths's smile flickered for a moment, but he recovered with visible effort.

So, while I still had control of the moment, I said, "I'm going to kill you first, Griffiths. It'll be ugly and you'll scream like a butchered hog."

"Sh-shut up," said Manning, tripping over it.

Without turning to him, I said, "And I'll kill you next, Manning. Maybe I'll make it quick because you aren't worth shit. Or maybe I'll just break your neck—there's a way to do it so you don't die. Maybe I'll leave you like that . . . a living head on a dead body, shitting in your pants."

"You talk pretty bold for a bloke with a dent in his head and no options," said Griffiths.

I kept smiling, and his eyes slid away. Without being obvious about it I slowly flexed my wrists and ankles, hoping to find some slack in the plastic cuffs. I wasn't actually secured to the chair, though if I stood all I'd be able to do is hop. But a little slack in the wrists held a smidge of promise. And all the while I was listening inside my body for the first signs that I was infected. Maybe these assholes had natural immunity and maybe—more likely, I figured—they'd been given some kind of inoculation. Either way, they thought they were safe and I was screwed.

Manning said, "This is madness, Bedwyr."

The security chief ignored him and stepped close, cocking a threatening fist. "I bet I can knock that stupid smile off your face."

"Feel free to try," I said.

Griffiths's whole body was so tense that his raised fist visibly trembled with fear, anger, and desire to prove to himself he could hurt me. Then he made a disgusted sound and threw the punch, but deliberately missed. He wanted to see me flinch, but I've been in enough fights to be able to judge distance, arc, and angle. I knew he was faking me and all I did was smile.

"Stop playing around," cried Manning. His nerves were really bad, and I wondered if he was a full part of this or acting under duress. My guess was the latter.

Griffiths used his reaction to Manning as his opportunity to step out of his bully mode. He flipped a dismissive hand to me as he turned to the building director.

"Whatever," he muttered.

"You the assholes who sicced those Sabbatarian idiots on me?"

Griffiths looked momentarily blank, then laughed. "The Saturday People? Those tossers? Please give us a measure of credit. We wouldn't trust them to wash piss off their own shoes. Besides . . . we have God's Warriors."

"Wow, could you be more pretentious?" I laughed. "If not them, how about the fang gang? Did you all kiss and make up?"

"The Red Knights are dead or scattered," said Manning. "Grigor was the last of them. Well, except for the Vampir—"

"Shut the fuck up," snapped Griffiths and emphasized it with a slap across Manning's face. It spun the man halfway around.

"It's not like he can bloody well tell anyone," protested Manning, a hand clamped to his reddening face.

I heard the beginning of the word, and the pronunciation was telling. He wasn't starting to say vampire. The "I" wasn't long. He said vam-*peer* before he was cut off, and that rang a very recent bell. I thought I knew what he was going to say, but left it for now because something more important popped into my head. I grunted. "Ah . . . that's who Alpha Team is, right? They're your new foot soldiers."

"And each and every one of them is worth ten of you or your so-called Havoc team," said Griffiths.

Manning looked almost apologetically at me. "I guess you realize this whole thing was a setup?"

“It’s occurred to me, yes,” I said, showing him the flex cuffs. “But tell me why.”

He licked his lips. “That’s . . . um . . . not for me to say.”

“Then who should I be talking to? Who’s in charge here?” I nodded to Griffiths. “It’s not this piece of discount monkey shit. So, who’s the big bad? Is it Nicodemus?”

“Who? Oh . . . him. No, of course not.”

“Will you shut up, Manning,” snapped Griffiths. “He’s pumping you for information.”

“What does it matter if he knows or doesn’t?” demanded Manning. “He’s exposed to the air, and he’s tied up. He’ll never be able to say anything.”

“The Scr . . .” began Griffiths and caught himself, though, like Manning, he was just a little too late.

“The Scriptor of the Red Order,” I said. “Well, well, isn’t that interesting as all hell. Though, I seem to recall that we shoved a Hellfire missile up his ass in Iran. But Sir Charles LaRoque didn’t have kids and the Scriptor is an inherited title . . . so, is there someone else dumb enough to take up the mantle? Love child? Pet chihuahua?”

Griffiths wheeled on me. “Ha! Shows how much *you* know, you. There *is* no Red Order. It died in Iran, thanks to you and your team of wankers.”

“So, what is it now? The Red Roosters? Red Robin, Red Robin? Ninety-nine Red Balloons?”

Griffiths straightened with obvious pride. He held his arms out to indicate the building or maybe the world. “This is the dawn of the Red *Empire*.”

I said, “Yawn.”

And he punched me.

One of those big haymakers that start down near the floor and are intended to send the target into low Earth orbit. Had he actually *hit* the target—the left side of my jaw—he’d have shattered it and maybe knocked half my teeth out. He really screwed himself into the floor for it and threw all of his torque and body weight into the blow.

But . . . they should have lashed me to the chair. No joke.

As the punch whistled toward me I shot to my feet, hunched and shoved the petrous part my temporal bone in the flight path. That’s the hardest part of the skull, and the human fist is made up of a bunch of little bones—knuckles, carpals, metacarpals, cartilage. The punch hurt. Of course it hurt, and I already had a concussion, but I did it exactly right and his fist exploded.

You could hear the bones break. Pieces of shattered carpal ripped up through the back of his hand, his wrist buckled in the way it does when cartilage and tendons are ripped to shit.

I sagged back to my chair and then fell out of it, but Griffiths froze for one incendiary moment, caught between the Scylla and Charybdis of crushing impact and the full fanfare of white-hot agony. All the color drained from his face and then the scream ripped itself from way down deep in his chest. He whirled away, tucking the ruined fist between his thighs as his shriek dwindled down to a thin, high, piercing keening sound.

Standing was possible, but so what? Even as the world spun around me I rolled onto my hip, cocked my knees, and stamped out with the flats of both heels. The lashing around my ankles actually helped concentrate and focus the PSI of that kick as I caught him on the outside of his left knee. This time the bone break was as loud as a gunshot.

There was no second to lose, so I rolled over onto my back, pulled my knees up to my chest, and looped my bound hands over my butt and heels and then pulled them up in front. Then I turned, got my feet under me and rose to a crouch. Then I pressed my knees together, tensed, drew a deep lungful of air, and with a snap pulled my arms down past my hips. The flex cuffs snapped. Manning saw this and began backpedaling, wanting no part of what was about to happen.

I staggered over to where my weapons lay in an untidy pile. I snatched up my knife, slashed the ankle restraints, and chased Manning. He ran with panic and I ran like a concussed man who just took a real bastard of a punch to the head. Before I made a dozen sloppy steps, he was gone.

But I stopped running, paused, dropped the knife, bent over with my palms on my knees, and threw up everything I've eaten since my first year of college. I swear I puked stuff I never even ate. It was awful, but what kept it from being as bad as it otherwise might have been were the agonized whimpers coming from Bedwyr Griffiths.

When I could stand I picked up the knife and walked in a crooked line over to the director of security for Hadrian Tower. I knelt in front of him and showed him the knife.

"I'll ask this only one time," I said, my voice a bit creaky. "Who is the Scriptor of this Red Empire bullshit?"

He stared at me through a dozen overlapping filters of pain and tried—really tried, I have to give him that—to look tough. In this he failed. I held the knife up so that it caught the light in interesting ways.

"For God and the Red Empire," he wheezed, and then snapped his jaws shut. I heard the crunch and knew what it was even before I caught the whiff of almonds. A hollow tooth filled with cyanide. I watched him die and felt deeply cheated.

He died quickly and badly, and I wished he lasted longer to feel more of it.

Then I got up and stumbled to where my weapons lay. The first thing I picked up, though, was my BAMS unit. No, I did not want to turn it on. No way in hell.

I did anyway.

And I stood there for a long time staring dumbly at the burning red light.

## CHAPTER 98

**ST THOMAS' HOSPITAL**
**WESTMINSTER BRIDGE ROAD**
**LONDON, ENGLAND**

The woman was Coleman's height, but slimmer and possessed of a shocking amount of wiry strength. She clambered atop Coleman and seemed to grow six extra arms and legs, trying to immobilize him with mixed martial arts grappling. And she was dishearteningly good.

Coleman gave up trying to buck her off and instead built a cage of shoulders, elbows, and fists around his head. Even with this, the woman tore at the thin fabric of his hazmat suit, trying to rip it open. His wire-frame glasses were gone, knocked askew so that the world was a disjointed madhouse blur. Phelps grabbed handfuls of his hood and began knocking his head against the floor, even as

Lefèbvre continued to thrash and scream. Then she kneed Coleman in the crotch, head-butted his nose, and tried to bite his face through the material. It was like fighting five wildcats all at once. And she had absolutely no regard for all the infected bodies in the cold drawers, on gurneys, or laid in a row in the back in black body bags. It was like she did not care about the bacteria.

Or . . . like she was immune to it.

Coleman fought back with desperate force, knowing that to lose this fight was to lose his life and, far worse, to lose the best chance they had of getting in front of the plague. Stopping him was why these two were here—whoever the hell they were.

Coleman slapped her hands away from his hair and buried his chin down on his chest in the hopes she would break her hands trying to hit him. Instead she used palm-heel shots to his cheek and temple, rocking him and igniting a firefall of sparks in his eyes.

As she fought, Phelps began yelling. "Mercer, Pierce . . . where the fuck are you assholes?"

A man's voice from out in the hall yelled back, "The hell's going on?" There was the sound of feet running.

Coleman knew he was out of time. He took a risk and swung a big circular elbow smash that caught Phelps on the side right below her armpit and knocked her hard to his left. She had to use her right hand as a brace to keep from falling on Lefèbvre's face, and Coleman took that moment to use the balled fist of the same arm he'd just struck with to deliver four very fast punches to the side of her head. It staggered her, and Coleman bucked his hips and scrambled backward.

Just as the door burst open and two men barged into the room. Both were dressed in the benign scrubs of hospital orderlies. No hazmat suits. No weapons. But a lot of fury and muscle.

They rushed forward, grinning at the prospect of an easy kill.

# CHAPTER 99

## BARRIER HEADQUARTERS
## HADRIAN TOWER
## LONDON, ENGLAND

It took about a thousand years for me to sort my shit out.

When I could think past the fact that I actually *had Yersinia pestis,* I began scrambling through my gear to find my cell phone and my comms unit. The comms—earbud, tiny mic, and signal booster—were in a little pile of smashed bits, all of the wires and computer chips spilled like guts on the floor.

"Shit," I said, and it came out as half a sob.

Here's the thing—yes, I was scared of being sick with the plague, but it wasn't actually a fear of dying. I always assumed that this line of work was going to kill me one of these days. Working for Church didn't make one believe in the concept of a peaceful retirement. So, no, that wasn't what had me so upset.

It was failure.

Hadrian Tower was a tomb. Locked-down, hardened from electronic intrusion, and with alloy walls that would require hours of steady work with acetylene torches or maybe some well-placed RPGs. And it's not like Ron Coleman would be first through the breach with a hypo of a wonder cure.

I was also pretty badly hurt. A concussion, maybe a crack in my sternum, dizziness, nausea, and I was nowhere close to figuring this out, let alone solving it. I also had intel the rest of the team needed, and that was why I dug through my stuff so frantically, looking for my cell. Which I found. It wasn't with my gear. Someone had thrown it against a wall and it was as dead as my long-term life plans.

My knees wanted to buckle, and my heart wanted to break. This was failure. This was proof that I should have left the game before I lost my edge.

Then a tiny spark of hope flared when I realized that there was one other means of communication—my tactical computer. But Manning and Griffiths had been thorough. The tac-com was smashed.

As quickly as trembling hands could manage, I buckled on my gun belt and slid my other weapons into their pouches. No need for the full ChemRig now, though I detached the torso shell and slipped that on because it was bulletproof. Then I tottered awkwardly over to Griffiths in the hope of finding his cell. It was there, but the lockscreen was on and he was way past giving me the password. I tried using his fingerprint, but no joy. It was a burner and he must have had it set for a number code, and he was past being able to tell me what it was.

"Well fuck me with a chain saw."

I looked around the empty lobby and saw exactly no one. No Havoc Team, no Mr. Church magically appearing out of nowhere, no Seventh Cavalry riding in with banners flying and horns blowing. None of Remy's video-drones swept into view.

There was nothing else to do, so I made my swaying, drunken way to the elevators. Top and Bunny were in one of the labs. Belle was still in the monitoring suites. They had comms, and what I needed most was a way to talk to the medical team at St. Thomas. And tell Mr. Church, the TOC, and every-damn-body else to cowboy up and come a'running.

While I waited for the elevator, I realized how cold the room was. I was shivering.

Then I put the back of my wrist to my forehead. My very sweaty and clammy forehead. My skin was hot as open flames.

God damn.

## CHAPTER 100

### ST THOMAS' HOSPITAL
### WESTMINSTER BRIDGE ROAD
### LONDON, ENGLAND

Mr. Church decided to head down to the morgue to see if he could provide any assistance to Coleman. There was not much else he could do at the moment. The dozens of calls he'd made set so many wheels in motion that the system was virtually running on autopilot.

Although he showed outward calm as a matter of habit, he felt doubt and worry churning in his stomach.

It gnawed at him that he had been so completely unaware of this threat. The first inkling had been a tipoff about the lab in Corvin

Castle, and that was days ago. The strange encounter Ledger had with a curiously ill Nicodemus and the Sabbatarian bunglers had to be connected, but how was still a question. Was this the return of the Red Order? If so, with who running it?

And why? The Order had always been at war with Islam, not with England. Launching the plague centuries before was the working of a Red Knight splinter group after they discovered that they were immune to the bacteria. The Great Fire of London stopped that threat, and resulted in the splinter group's extermination.

Now someone in the extended sphere of the Holy Agreement was likely behind this outbreak. But who? And to what end?

He had made some calls to allies in various Muslim communities around the world, but none of them knew of any plot like this that could have come from even the most radical groups. He believed that intelligence, and moved extremist Islamic sects far down on his list.

Sir Charles LaRoque, last Scriptor of the Red Order, was dead and he had no sons. So, who might have picked up the reins of that group? If, in fact, that was what happened. Or did the last surviving Red Knights—scattered, leaderless, in hiding—regroup and resurrect an old biological attack strategy. If so, why aim it at London? And why Barrier? Yes, they had participated in the global hunt for the Red Order and Red Knights following the Iran matter, but so had virtually every government and police organization in the world.

So, again, why London? Why Barrier? Did the power represented by Hadrian Tower epitomize something loathsome to the Knights? If so, what?

With these and other questions swirling in his thoughts he headed for the elevator. Just as he reached for the button his cell rang. Since he and the other professionals there at the hospital all wore some kind of hazmat suit, he had a burner cell hung on a lanyard around his neck. The call was from Bug.

"Tell me something good," said Church.

"Might actually have something," said Bug. "I brought Nikki in on the repair job and right away she said that the damage is wrong."

"Wrong in what way?"

"It's too orderly. Now that she saw the pattern I can't unsee it. It's like if you stained the outside of a roll of paper towels . . . just a dot, but enough for it to sink through layer after layer, which you'd see as you unrolled the roll. Though it's maybe more like if you stabbed it. An ink stain fades the deeper it goes, but Miss Pattern Recognition Queen saw that the breaks are too regular and too often the same size."

"It was my understanding that accessing the data triggered a self-destruct."

"Yeah, well, this is now looking like the guy who designed this knew enough about MindReader to install software that would encrypt key data but do it in a way that looks like data corruption. That's sophisticated. It's elegant."

"Where does it leave us?"

"At the rate we're going? Maybe four to six hours before we can read it."

"That is remarkable news, Bug. If the developmental science is in that data, then Coleman and Doc can walk it back and find a fix."

"That's what Doc said. She . . . um . . . kissed Nikki on the mouth. Me, um, too."

"Feel free to file sexual harassment charges."

"Actually Nikki kind of liked it. And, maybe I did, too."

Bug got off the line to go back to work, leaving Church smiling and amused. He once more reached for the button and again his cell rang. He recognized the incoming number, though, as that of Major Claire Courtland.

"Artemis," he said by way of a greeting. "What's the sitrep?"

"A quick catch-up, sir," said Courtland. "Bedlam Team will be at St. Thomas in under fifteen minutes. Chaos Team is ready to breach their way into the Tower now. Waiting on your go order."

"Consider it given."

He then gave her the latest updates. The alarming body count, but also Coleman's theories on how to make an emergency treatment and plans for a long-term nationwide program. It would cost many billions of dollars and take months, but the plan was workable.

"Understood," she said, and ended the call.

Church pushed the button and stepped onto the elevator, frowning in thought as he considered how someone who was as close to being a twin to Grace Courtland was going to work out as chief of operations for RTI. It could be an easy transition or it could be fraught with emotional complexities, and he rather thought the latter was more likely.

The door closed and he rode down to the basement where Coleman was at work in the morgue.

## CHAPTER 101

### FRESH-N-CLEAN
### CRANBROOK ROAD
### ILFORD, ENGLAND

The Hunt crouched behind the SUV and in near total darkness they pulled on the ChemRigs supplied by Bird Dog. It was the first time the team rolled out in that gear and none of them were happy about it.

"There's no room for me meat and two veg," complained Rent Boy, who—as they had since discovered—was built like a champion porn star. He admitted that he had made quite a few reels during his college days.

"Next time you see Bird Dog, lad," said Toys, "tell him to his face that he packed the wrong trousers for you. He'll like that."

"And we'll make sure to send flowers to your folks," mused Zombie. "Now shove that overinflated plonker out of sight before I toss my cookies."

"Gormless twat," said Rent Boy under his breath.

Rugger handed out gun belts with two holstered sidearms—Sig Sauer P226 and Snellig A-385 Supershot, the latter being the latest version of the high-powered dart guns developed exclusively for Rogue Team. Everyone had identical weapons to allow for easy magazine sharing. The Hunt each had personal weapons of choice for backup, including throwdown pieces with no serial numbers, strangle wires, explosives, and knives.

Toys tapped his comms. "Wild Hunt actual to TOC."

"Go for Artemis," said Claire Courtland.

"On-site and ready."

"Proceed with caution."

Then they approached the building. The parking lot was nicely landscaped with bushy shrubs and beech trees, and with the sun well down, they provided plenty of cover. Rugger, who served as tech man for the team, deployed some pigeon drones but all the images showed was a quiet building with the standard security cameras and infrequent exterior lights.

When they reached the east side wall, they paused by a utility door that emptied out to a small patio for staff cigarette breaks. A keycard reader was mounted beside the door, but Rugger bypassed it using a blank master keycard uplinked to MindReader. The door unlocked itself and MindReader rewrote the target software to erase any record of the entry.

Toys drew his Snellig and went in first, moving only as fast as caution allowed. Beyond the door was a hallway that ran for ten meters and had closed doors on either side. No alarms rang as the team entered, following Toys and taking turns listening at each door. They all had Nosy Nells, one of Doc Holliday's inventions, which looked like half a tennis ball with a sugar-cube-sized device attached. The open end of the device was placed against each door and the ultrasensitive listening device sent any sounds from the room beyond to their earbuds.

Only one room had any sound at all, and it was the low hum of some kind of machine. Rugger waved Toys back and they both listened.

"Bypass the lock," ordered Toys, and Muppet produced a sophisticated set of lockpicks, using them with a deftness at odds with his cloddish personality. The door opened in seconds.

Toys eased it open and stepped inside and discovered a glass wall with a vault-door-style airlock, with decontamination cubicles on either side. On the other side of the window was some very impressive machinery, with stainless steel tanks, pumps, heat exchangers, filters, valves, pipes, meters, and other devices he recognized from his days as personal assistant to Sebastian Gault, a corrupt pharmaceutical magnate.

He said, "Bloody hell . . ."

He knew what that machinery was. Sweat burst from his pores and he tapped into the command channel again. In a tense, hushed voice he requested Major Courtland and Doc Holliday to get on the line at once.

They were waiting for his call.

"What've you found, sweet-cheeks?" asked Doc.

"This place is supposed to manufacture air and hand sanitizers for commercial companies, yes?"

"That's what their website says."

"So, why am I here pissing my pants staring at a high-performance pharmaceutical bioreactor?"

Doc Holliday said, "Oh dear."

Courtland snapped, "Is the unit compromised?"

Zombie held a BAMS unit out so Toys could see the display.

"We're on the thank-Jesus side of the glass wall and the air is clear," Toys said. "Lights are green. Do you want us to do something daft like go in there and obtain samples?"

"That is a hard negative," snapped Courtland. "Leave everything intact. Search the building and, if possible, retrieve computers, drives, and anything with a hard drive, then exfil."

"There are a lot of vehicles in the car park and it's after hours," he said.

"What is your estimate of possible hostile numbers?"

"If every car had a single occupant, then count forty-two."

A pause at the other end.

"This is your call, Toys," said Courtland. "If you feel that you can complete the mission and retrieve the drives without a fight, do so. Otherwise, exfil now and wait for the locals. I can have police and CBRN on-site in thirty minutes."

Toys debated for a long moment, aware of his team watching him. They were on the same command channel and heard the options.

"I'm going to try for the hardware," Toys said. "But if this gets nasty then we are getting the hell out of here."

"Listen to me, Toys," said Courtland. "You've already established that this is the likely source of the plague. Your job is done. You can fall back."

"No," he said, "and I want Doc to hear this, too."

"Go on, honeybunch," Doc said.

"They have one bioreactor, and it isn't one of the bigger ones. There are options. One is that this is one of many sites where they are mass-producing the plague. I don't think that's likely, though, because of the expense in setting up that kind of machinery and the inherent dangers."

"Agreed," said Doc.

"Or they could be ambitious enough to believe that an outbreak in London will be enough to start a new Black Death."

"Not buying it," said Doc. "Too many ways that could fail."

"Quite," said Courtland. "We already have it contained at the Tower and inside the hospital."

"Option three is that this is window dressing for a trap," Toys said.

"All the more reason to get out of there," argued Courtland.

"Even so," Toys told them, "I'm going for the hardware."

Which is exactly when all the alarms in the building began to scream.

## CHAPTER 102

### ST THOMAS' HOSPITAL
### WESTMINSTER BRIDGE ROAD
### LONDON, ENGLAND

Coleman snatched at the knife Lefèbvre had dropped and staggered to his feet, trying to assume a combat fighting crouch like Joe Ledger once showed him. His martial arts classes were a very long time ago and he wished he'd kept at it.

The bigger of the two men swung a piledriver of a fist at him, and Coleman tried to duck it. If the attacker had been less skilled, the scientist would have managed it, but the man corrected the angle of his swing and chased Coleman down, tagging him hard on the back of the neck. Coleman splatted down onto the bloody floor. His nose—cracked by Phelps's head-butt—now broke completely, filling his visor with blood and blinding him. The pain was exquisite, and he tried to fight through it.

Then hands grabbed him and hauled him to his feet as punches struck like a storm of rocks. Coleman tried to block with his elbow frame, tried to twist away and let them hit his shoulders and hips and thighs, but they knew what they were doing and he was mostly blind from his own blood.

Smaller rocks—or what felt like them—began hammering his back, and he knew that Phelps had joined the fight. He was in the center of a tornado of savage blows. The knife he picked up was gone and he didn't remember dropping it. Coleman lashed out with blindingly fast punches and kicks, but he had no way to aim anything. He felt a few lucky shots strike home and heard a few grunts of pain, but it was three to one and they could see.

His knees buckled and as he fell he tried to hammer down with his closed fist on top of a foot—any foot—but his hand bounced off the bloody linoleum floor.

Suddenly there was a piercing screech of shocked agony and two of those pounding fists were gone. The other blows paused as another scream tore the air. Phelps that time.

A man—Pierce or Mercer—cried out, "Oh God! It's *him*."

And then his next sound was a bloody, wet, choked gurgle.

Abruptly it was all over.

Just like that.

Coleman fell once more, and sat there, shaking his head to try and clear his eyes and face mask. He blinked away his own blood and saw a single figure standing there now, and all around him were bodies. Two of them writhing in pain; two of them sprawled with the kind of slackness that only comes from death.

"Ronald," said the figure. "How badly are you hurt?"

Ron Coleman got to his knees, feeling his hazmat suit to make sure it was undamaged, and he looked up into the face of Mr. Church.

"I . . . I . . ." he began and then his words died on his tongue.

His fingers touched the material just below his chin . . . and he felt his own beard. It was soaked with blood and completely exposed to the air.

His hazmat suit was ripped open.

# CHAPTER 103

## THE SS *ARCHANGEL*
## PORT OF REGISTRY, CYPRESS
## THE IONIAN SEA

The ship was an old one that had undergone several reincarnations while still wearing the same durable steel skin. It was born as a minesweeper during the Vietnam War, then sold out of the service in the mid-1990s. A Saudi prince bought it and turned it into a luxury yacht, but covert fratricide put him in the dirt before the renovations were complete. A Greek tycoon bought it at auction, but when his fortunes plummeted during one of the many dips in that nation's economy, he sold it to a company that converted it into a cargo vessel. This alteration took away every trace of elegance and extravagance in favor of pure function. The deck was leveled out and much of the interior repurposed into roomy holds big enough to hold farm tractors and harvesters.

When COVID struck and international sales of heavy farm equipment faltered, it was bought for pennies on the dollar in a foreclosure auction. The buyer was an off-book purchasing agent for the Kuga organization and spent two years moving top-quality used military equipment from the wars in Iraq and Afghanistan. One year ago, the ship was sold again to an unknown buyer.

Now it moved slowly through the night-dark waters of the Ionian Sea. The ship's hull was rusted and pitted from years of hard use, though much of that rust was cosmetic, painted on to sell the fiction that the ship was a junker transporting the lower-end goods of those manufacturers who couldn't afford something better.

Looks are often deceiving. Aft of the lumpy bridge were the two sets of big cargo doors. The captain was on comms with the deck officer, waiting for a go-order from far away. They waited with as much patience as nerves permitted, each of them feeling the tension of being poised but stalled.

Then the screen of the captain's cell phone lit up with a four-word text.

***As God Wills It***

"About bloody time," breathed the captain. He tapped into the shipboard channel and said, "Go."

The deck officer exhaled the lungfuls of air that had begun to burn in his chest. He gave the orders that resulted in the iron doors on both cargo bays to rise with a metallic groan. As the doors yawned wide, powerful hydraulics lifted two platforms out of the shadows and up into starlight.

Upon each was a silent monster made of metal and polymers and fiberglass. They squatted on the platforms, each with a fuselage that was forty-nine feet long and—with pilots, crew, and armaments—weighed more than 22,000 pounds. Once the decks were up and locked, crewmen ran around to unleash the four main-rotor blades and position them; then did the same with the smaller tail rotors. This was done very quickly and efficiently and soon the heavy General Electric T700-GE-701 turboshaft engines roared to life, sounding hungry and angry.

When the blades were spinning, the crew faded back and watched as the two Boeing AH-64 Apache attack helicopters rose into the night sky and turned east.

# CHAPTER 104

## RESTRICTED BIOLOGICAL RESEARCH LABORATORY H-6
## LONDON, ENGLAND

"Do you want to see where Rage is stored?" asked Dr. Byrd.

"Oh yes," said Bunny.

She gave one of those half-frown/half-smiles. "If I may ask, why that one in particular?"

"Call it an emotional attachment."

Byrd glanced at Top for clarification but only got a stony-faced nod. She nodded. "Well, of course we have that locked up inside the Special Projects lab."

"Where's that?" asked Bunny.

"It's at the very back of the facility," explained Byrd. "With several levels of added protection. Come with me and I'll show you."

They went through the entire facility, through some areas they had already seen, and stopped at a set of reinforced glass security doors with a decontamination cubicle between them. A wall-mounted BAMS unit scanned them and gave a green light, and they watched as Dr. Byrd entered the codes for access. Once inside they followed her down a corridor with offices and small labs on either side dedicated to different aspects of the most sensitive research. There were people in those labs, though no one seemed to be doing anything but sitting or standing.

"Who are they?" asked Top.

"The staff that work in this wing," said Byrd. "When the shelter-in-place order came down, many staff members preferred to stay in the areas and with the people most familiar to them. A comfort, I suppose. And maybe some optimism because, given what we do here, we feel we're amply suited to help with a crisis of this kind. I said as much to Dr. Coleman."

At the end of the hall was another set of glass doors with a security guard standing there, one hand resting on his sidearm. He had a 20-gauge shotgun slung, and Top nodded at it, understanding why a small-bore weapon would be used instead of an automatic rifle. Even reinforced glass could shatter if hit with enough rounds. The 20-gauge was almost certainly loaded with either beanbag rounds or compacted clay beads that would hurt any person but lacked the penetrating power to damage the glass.

The guard nodded to Byrd but gave Top and Bunny close scrutiny.

"It's okay, Trevor," said Dr. Byrd. "These men are with Havoc Team. They have full authority from the PM and Director Griffiths. Please assist them in any way."

"Ma'am," said the guard crisply and he stood to one side as Byrd went through another round of scans and codes.

As she did so, she spoke over her shoulder. "Most of the Special Projects team are in here. I already put them to work on *Yersinia pestis*. While we don't have actual samples of the weaponized version, we have enough of a sense of the situation to hopefully partner with the team at St. Thomas and help to find useful treatments. We've done some work in the past with CCR5 antagonist drugs and our lab here is more sophisticated for this kind of research than what they have at St. Thomas."

"That's good to know," Top said.

The door opened and they stepped into a large space that served as foyer and cleanroom prep area. Trevor, the guard, came with them but lingered at the door, explaining that with comms out and cell phones acting wonky, he wanted to keep an eye on Dr. Byrd in case she needed any help.

"We can handle that," said Top.

"My job, sir."

Top let it go.

Dr. Byrd paused to pull on a high-end protective garment. While she dressed, Top and Bunny walked the foyer and peered through small windows in the two interior doors.

"Clear over here," said Top.

"I can see the staff," Bunny said. "Couple of them, anyway. Looks like one of them dropped a binder and they're picking up papers or something."

"Nerves," suggested Byrd, joining them. "Let's go see if we can help."

She used a keycard to open the door, and they stepped inside. Bunny went first, his Cloudburst shotgun swung forward—not pointing at anything, but ready to hand. Top was next and then Byrd.

Bunny heard her speaking and turned to see Byrd talking to Trevor. "Tell the Scriptor that they're inside. As God wills it."

The guard immediately faded back and slammed the heavy outer door. Bunny stared at Byrd, who smiled back.

"What the hell was—?" began Bunny, but Top suddenly cried, "Watch out!"

Something hit Bunny in the small of the back with such force that he was slammed against the wall. He tried to turn fast enough to shake off whatever hit him, but the whole thing was too fast and too hard. Behind him there was a burst of gunfire, and he saw Top stagger as bullets hammered his chest.

Dr. Byrd stood fifteen feet away and had an automatic pistol in her hand. There was no time for Bunny to help in any way, because the person who hit him with that sneak attack was clawing at the flexible reinforced material around his throat—tearing with cracked and broken fingernails and snapping at his visor with bloody teeth. It was a man, one of the two people who had been kneeling on the floor. In a flash moment of horrifying reality, Bunny saw that the other person was getting up, too. The spilled papers were splashed with blood because part of an arm lay there, and the second person was still chewing as she stood.

Then he understood.

This was a setup, a trap.

And worse, Rage was loose in these labs.

Byrd kept firing at Top even though he was down, and as the second infected leapt at him, Bunny went down beneath the weight of two Rage-maddened maniacs.

# CHAPTER 105

## HADRIAN TOWER
## LONDON, ENGLAND

The elevator seemed to crawl upward by slow inches.

I lay back against the wall, conserving what energy I had. These symptoms were coming on fast, and they weren't being nice about it. My clothes, already soaked from having worn the full ChemRig, offered no warmth as the fever burned its way through me with cold fire. Even the torso shell didn't provide much comfort.

I needed to call Church and Coleman.

I wanted to tell my team what I'd learned. It wasn't much but it was something.

I wished I could call Junie.

I wished all sorts of things, including romantically dying in her arms like a crusading knight back from the wars in some nineteenth-century epic poem. Bryon or Tennyson would have loved it. In my more lucid moments, I realized what a horrible parting gift it would be for poor Junie. The dying can be dramatic and in doing so forget that the living have to go on.

To try and get my head in the game, I drew my sidearm and checked the action, made sure there was a round chambered and a full magazine. I reholstered it and patted myself down to make sure everything nasty was where it should be and ready to use. Despite the fear I felt, there was an anger building up inside to critical mass. They did this to me, but they *killed* Scott Wilson and a couple hundred other people. If we couldn't stop them there was no telling how many were going to die.

Was James Rockwell part of it? Hard to imagine he wasn't, but then again he was the chief of Barrier and an old "friend in the industry" of Mr. Church. Most likely he was a pawn or a dupe. Or maybe already dead.

The elevator reached the floor where Belle was working. As the car settled, I realized I needed to be more ready than I was, and redrew my pistol. That itself scared me because I very nearly made a rookie mistake. And I seldom make those kinds of errors.

I raised the pistol and shifted off-center of the door as it slid open. The hallway was empty. Small mercies.

With my first step I tripped and almost fell, caught myself in a hunch with fingertips on the floor. Then straightened slowly, hissing at new and sudden pain in my lower back. And my guts felt like I'd swallowed a bag of razor blades.

"You miserable bastards," I groaned and staggered down the hall to the monitoring suite. The door was open. The guard who'd been twiddling his fingers while Belle worked sat on a roller-chair in front of the array of screens.

Most of him, anyway.

The front of his skull, a chunk of his face, and a lot of blood and brains were splashed across the screens. I saw that his sidearm was half-drawn from his belt holster, his dead fingers curled around the butt.

Had Belle done this as the guard said or did something to announce that he was *not* playing for the angels? Or, conversely, was this the corpse of an innocent caught up in the treachery of his bosses?

I searched the suite and found only a small utility room filled with replacement parts for the monitoring equipment, a card table and two folding chairs, and a toilet cubicle. There was no one else in there.

Returning to the console, I gently pushed the dead man away, hooked another chair with my foot and dragged it over. Sitting was oddly painful, or maybe it's more precise that it was painful in odd places. My kidneys and liver were pretty unhappy, and my lungs felt wet and sluggish.

With the gore on several monitors, and a big bullet hole in one of them, I had to find the controls that gave me access to the other screens. With my head getting fuzzy, that took more time than it should have, but I got there just as the coughing began.

I suddenly had a memory of Nicodemus coughing and looking sickly. Had that evil little bastard been sick with plague? There was no way to tell unless he called me again and I asked.

With the console controls, one of the problems I had was that the station was meant for monitoring but it was not a communications center. There were no mics anywhere. I looked and looked, but it simply wasn't made for broadcasting. There wasn't even an intercom. So . . . how did the dead guy talk to his superiors?

I kick-swiveled my chair and pulled myself close to the dead man. "Sorry, pal," I said as I picked his pockets. He had a cell phone that was password protected . . . which they all are unless it's plot-convenient on a TV show. I couldn't use facial recognition because the guard had no face.

Would it accept a fingerprint? The cell wasn't a burner like Griffiths's had been, so it was worth a try. I used the dead man's index finger, and there was still enough warmth and softness left in the skin allowing the print to work. Thank Jesus and all twelve of his drinking buddies.

It was an Apple cell, this year's model, and the first thing I did was to go into *Settings, Display & Brightness,* then *Auto-lock* and changed it to *Never.* Then found the *Turn Passcode Off.* Only then did I start making calls.

I tried calling Top and got no answer. The call rang through to voicemail. Same with Bunny and Belle and Remy. That made my heart sink. I had been ambushed and infected. Had they? I sat there, coughing, shivering, blotting my streaming eyes, and wiping my nose. Dying by degrees and feeling fear grow in my heart.

I called Church and his rang through to voicemail, too. Same with Coleman. Was this some kind of cell blocking? If so, why could I hear the phones ring and the voicemail messages? It made no sense to me, and it was getting really hard to think straight.

"Rockwell will know how to reach people," I told myself. It took so much of the little energy I had left just to stand, I had to hold on to the doorway to get out, and lean on the wall all the way back to the elevator. Thirty feet away. A journey of months.

I was about to call Church, when the phone rang. I glanced at the screen, but it wasn't Top calling back and the display read *Unknown Caller.* What the hell, I thought, and answered it.

"Yes," I gasped.

"Have I caught you at a bad time?" asked Nicodemus.

## CHAPTER 106

### ST THOMAS' HOSPITAL
### WESTMINSTER BRIDGE ROAD
### LONDON, ENGLAND

Church rushed forward and grabbed Coleman, pulling and turning him, pushing him out into the hall and up against the closest wall. He ripped the torn and bloody hood from Coleman with a screech of no-leak Velcro, then tore his own off and pulled it down over the scientist's head.

"Fasten it," he snapped.

"What about you? The air in there could be filled with—"

"I'm immune," Church barked. "Seal the suit. Do it right now."

Coleman's fingers were shaking so badly that Church had to help him.

"How badly are you hurt?"

"I'm not . . . I . . . my nose," said Coleman, but he paused to spit a mouthful of blood down into the lower part of the hood. "She broke my nose."

"Clearly. Who are they?"

"I don't know. They gave names. Lefèbvre and Phelps were the first two, and the guys you just . . . um . . . fought . . . are Mercer and Pierce. No way to know if they're real names. But, listen . . . how are you immune?"

"Does it matter?"

"It might. Scientifically, yes . . . it might."

But Church shook his head. "It's not a transferable quality."

"But, I—"

"Believe me," said Church firmly. "You do not want to give my blood, plasma, or bone marrow to anyone. That's the truth and the discussion ends right now."

He stepped away to look up and down the hallway, but it was empty. "There should have been guards here."

"They're inside," said Coleman weakly. "Colin Markham and the nurse, too. God . . . they . . . Jesus I need to throw up."

"Don't," snapped Church. "Wait here."

He went back inside. Coleman turned and leaned his face against the picture window. Although the blinds were drawn, the slats were not so tight that he couldn't see. What he saw made his heart lurch in his chest.

Church bent down and took Lefèbvre by the throat and lifted him off the ground. The killer was over six feet tall and had to weigh at least one-ninety, and yet Church lifted him one-handed as if he hoisted a scarecrow made of straw and rags. It was a feat of strength that even with all of Coleman's deep knowledge of physics and physiology he could not make sense of. It simply was not possible and yet Church raised the man to his feet and then onto tiptoes before slamming him against the wall. Lefèbvre screamed in pain, but the sound was muffled both by the closed door and the constricting hand.

Coleman watched as Church leaned so close that his lips nearly brushed the wounded killer's ear. It looked intimate in all the wrong ways. He saw Church's mouth work as he spoke, but none of it was audible to the scientist. Then he saw Lefèbvre begin talking. The man began slowly, with obvious reluctance, but then his jaw and mouth worked furiously as if he could not answer Church's questions quickly enough. It was as impressive as it was horrible.

There was more back-and-forth, and then Church exhaled and let the man fall. When Lefèbvre dropped, it was with a boneless finality, and his head lolled on a clearly broken neck.

With a face as expressionless as a statue, Church turned toward the three bodies on the floor. The woman was the only one still alive, still on the wrong side of consciousness, able to see what reached for her. Even through the closed door, Coleman heard her cries.

"Please! Oh, God, please . . ."

She was lifted off the ground and that terrible process of interrogation began again. And ended the same way. And again, Coleman did not hear either questions or answers.

When it was over, Church looked around the room. He unclipped a BAMS unit from his belt and waved it around, grunted, nodded, then walked over to the door, opened it, and stepped into the hall.

"The room is clean," he said. "Markham and Cooper were thorough in maintaining protocols. You're safe, Doctor. You can take off your hood."

Coleman did that with fingers that shook so much Church once more had to help him. The hood fluttered to the floor. They stared at each other for several appalling moments.

"If you have any questions, Doctor," said Church quietly, "ask them now. You will not get another opportunity."

Coleman began to ask. There were a thousand questions elbowing each other to be asked; there were so many things he wanted—needed—to know. When he finally managed to speak, what he said was, "What did they tell you?"

"All they knew," said Church. "Hard to say if it's enough."

"No . . . what did they say? Please, tell me."

Church considered, then nodded. "They are not mercenaries. They are not hired guns. All four of them belong to a group that calls itself God's Warriors."

"Never heard of them."

"I heard only rumors but until today hadn't spoken with anyone who knew anything of substance."

"Pardon me for saying this, boss," said Coleman, "but you look upset. I mean, about what you heard just now. Am I out of line by saying that?"

Church shook his head. "The name—God's Warriors—has a very old meaning for me, and in . . . my younger days . . . a certain group referred to me by that name. I was never sure if it was a term of respect or mockery. Now I'm even less certain because these thugs are connected to a group born from the ashes of the older one."

Coleman stood there, wanting more but not comfortable asking.

Church seemed to notice and there was the ghost of a small, tolerant smile.

"Long ago," he said, "that nickname was hung on me by a Scriptor of the Red Order."

"Because of your, um, name? Or names. Church, Deacon, and so on."

"I suppose so."

"The Red Order, as a functional organization, is no more, or am I wrong? The DMS and RTI tore them down. Them and their Red Knights." Coleman paused, then snapped his fingers. "Wait, Nicodemus had Sabbatarians attack Joe, and they're tied to the Red Order, right?"

"Not exactly. The Sabbatarians are a large group of very dangerous but not particularly effective radicalized and militant religious fanatics. Killers who believe they are fighting God's war against earthly evil. They have been manipulated by a raft of individuals who are either with the Church or pretend to be. Nicodemus has a foot on both sides of that line. They have often been tricked into doing grunt work for the Red Order, but were never inside their circle of trust." He walked over and looked down at the corpses. "However, these four are of a better caliber. I'm impressed that you were able to handle two of them. Perhaps I should give you a field team."

He was smiling as he said that, but Coleman held up his hands, palms out. "On behalf of my lower back, my common sense, and my dreams of retiring to Aruba, thank you but no."

They stood for a moment in silence, surrounded by death and horror.

In a distant tone, Church said, "They told me that they are ordained priests and a nun whose lives are dedicated to the Red Empire and their war against Islam."

"A . . . nun . . . ?" Coleman's face turned the color of old cottage cheese. Then he shook his head like a dog just out of the rain. "Wait . . . Red Empire?"

"Call it the Red Order 2.0," said Church. "And, yes, they are behind the plague."

"How does a pandemic of a lethal bioweapon serve God?"

"It doesn't, of course. That's the nature of cults . . . all that matters is what they have been convinced is the truth. And few things fuel murderous zeal more effectively than hatred. Race, religion, nationality, whatever. Story of mankind." Church shook his head in obvious disgust. "Humanity is a savage species and, despite our technological and artistic advancements, most of us are one bad day away from barbarism."

"Most," echoed Coleman. "Not all."

The harsh lines on Church's face softened. "No," he said, "not all."

The room lights flickered for a moment and they both paused to look up.

After a moment, Church said, "I need to call all of this into the TOC and bring Colonel Ledger up to speed. Then we—"

And all of the lights in St. Thomas' Hospital immediately winked out.

## CHAPTER 107

### HADRIAN TOWER
### LONDON, ENGLAND

"Fuck you," I said.

"Always so polite," said Nicodemus. "Tell me, Joe, how are you feeling?"

"*Kisama,*" I said, translating my greeting into Japanese. Then Greek. "*As to thialo.*"

"Now now."

"*Javla, fick dich, cao ni,*" I said in Swedish, German, and Mandarin.

"Impressive, but isn't all this a waste of a dying man's breath?"

"You're calling to gloat. That's what's wasting my time. Hanging up now."

"Hold on," he said, chuckling. Then he coughed for a few moments. That deep kind of cough that sounds like a wood rasp on knotty hardwood. "You haven't asked me a question in a while."

"Eat a bag of dicks."

"You get cranky when you have man-flu. Go on, play the game, Ledger. Ask your question."

The truth was that I didn't have one already in the chamber and my head felt like it was full of drunken bees. Even so, the opportunity was one I couldn't pass up. After all, he had answered my imprecise question with an equally imprecise yet truthful reply. When I asked if the Red Order was involved, he told me *"In a way."*

That now made sense because the Red Order had reinvented itself as the Red Empire. Fifty new questions crowded into my brain, each one elbowing and kicking the others to be noticed. I asked the one that might help me shortcut the process of getting in front of this thing while I was still on this side of the dirt. The elevator pinged and the door opened. I all but fell into the carriage and pawed at the buttons.

"Who is the Scriptor of the Red Empire?" I asked.

And, after a long fit of wet coughing, Nicodemus told me.

# CHAPTER 108

## FRESH-N-CLEAN
## CRANBROOK ROAD
## ILFORD, ENGLAND

Toys and his team dropped into crouches, guns up and out in a rough defensive circle. The alarms were blaring from everywhere in the building, but they had no idea yet from which direction responders would come.

"What's the call, boss?" yelled Zombie, trying to be heard above the din. "Rules of engagement?"

"Yeah," said Rent Boy, "there could be civilians in here. Not looking forward to killing innocent bystanders here."

Toys gave them such a withering look that they recoiled from it.

"No one in this sodding building is innocent," he snarled. "No one gets a pass."

The others—each a career criminal who was fighting for every forward step on the path of redemption—stared at him. Rugger and Zombie nodded. The others merely looked uncertain.

"Here they come," said Muppet.

They turned to see figures clustering at the far end of the hallway.

They were in riot gear, with ballistic helmets, high-density plastic shields, and automatic weapons.

"Moaning Myrtle," snapped Toys, and without pause Muppet rose up and hurled a hand grenade. It was one of Doc Holliday's toys, named after the deeply depressed ghost haunting the bathroom at Hogwarts. The reality of the weapon was that it combined the massive sound-burst and terrible light of a flash-bang with the obfuscation of a standard gas grenade. Muppet threw it with all the speed and precision of a demon bowler on a cricket pitch and it took a single bounce five meters from the end of the hall and burst in the air.

The Wild Hunt covered their ears and ducked to avoid the light-burst, then immediately rose up and opened fire. They burned through whole magazines to turn the far end of the hall into a kill-box. Screams rose higher than the alarms and the clouds of gas were instantly tinged a dark red.

"That'll show the buggers," Rent Boy growled.

Rugger pivoted to look back the way the Hunt had come. "There's more coming."

And that fast they were caught between two forces while pinned down in a hallway. Toys realized that he had made a critical tactical error.

He whirled toward the second team, straightened, and hosed the newcomers. They were closer and they were dressed more like building security—gray jackets and trousers with black seams down the legs, and old-fashioned eight-point caps with patent leather visors. There had been eight of them, but now three lay dead or screaming on the floor, and one other leaned against the wall, one hand clamped to a spurting wound in his thigh.

"Rugger and Rent Boy," he bellowed. "The rest of you lads deal with the commandos."

They ducked into the questionable shelter of shallow entrances to locked rooms, with Toys standing right outside the processing plant for the plague. Bullets filled the air with the angry intensity of a locust swarm.

*We're bloody well going to die here,* he thought as he swapped a new magazine into his gun. *And it's all my fault.*

He leaned out to fire, but a barrage drove him back. Two of the incoming rounds struck the reinforced glass window, and he turned in horror as spiderweb cracks whipsawed out from each impact point.

## CHAPTER 109

### ST THOMAS' HOSPITAL
### WESTMINSTER BRIDGE ROAD
### LONDON, ENGLAND

"Down and back," snapped Church as he used one hand to push Coleman behind him. With his other, he produced a Snellig dart pistol. Coleman didn't need to ask why that instead of a more lethal nine-millimeter because the answer was obvious—if this meant there were more Red Empire killers here, Church wanted to be able to interrogate them.

The thought disgusted Coleman on one level—on his personal level of what Joe Ledger called his Modern Man—but he felt a shift inside him. He had fought two people and now they were dead. It did not matter if he had actually killed anyone—his actions were part of the process of them being killed. He could feel the wound of that gouge itself into the flesh of his soul.

All that flashed through his thoughts in a microsecond as he hunkered down behind the steel table used for autopsies. It was heavy and anchored to the floor.

"Stay here," said Church as he stepped toward the door. Emergency lights flashed on, dim but not murky.

"I have to get my samples and get to work on treatments and a cure," Coleman said sharply. "People are upstairs dying right now that maybe we can save."

Church nodded. He bent and patted the corpses down for weapons and took several handguns and spare magazines. "Very well. Are you comfortable with these?"

"Joe taught me how to shoot. Top, too."

"Then use them if you need to. No risks and no hesitation. If anyone comes in here that you don't know, put them down. Tell me you understand."

"I do. And there's a backup generator down here. They use it for the cold storage, but I can tap into it enough to give me light and juice to run my tests."

"Good. Lock yourself in when I leave."

And then he was gone.

Coleman locked the door, then as an afterthought took a gurney from against one wall and shoved it against the door, then locked the wheels. Satisfied, he turned and went to work.

# CHAPTER 110

## HADRIAN TOWER
## LONDON, ENGLAND

I reached the 86th floor and stepped out. My knees buckled but I caught myself.

The information Nicodemus gave me was questionable. I did not, in fact, believe him. I tried to call Church to share the info anyway, but this time the call did not go through at all. I tried the TOC, too, and got the same results.

Uh-oh.

I was already shivering from fever and this made me feel positively frozen down to my DNA. Someone was being very clever, first jamming the comms and now cell calls. And right after I spoke with Nicodemus, and he planted a mind worm in my brain with his answer to my question.

I went over to the balcony rail and used that for support while I headed to Rockwell's office. When I glanced down the hall, I saw that his door was ajar and the lights on. Getting there took a lot of effort and I was sweating bullets. Cold, icy bullets. I kept having to wipe sweat from my eyes, but I made it and lumbered across the hall to grab the doorframe for support.

Not sure what I expected to find. Maybe him strangling Ken Manning. Maybe him gearing up to try and take back his building.

"Rockwell," I croaked. "Cowboy up, 'cause we're in deep shit."

Then I all but fell into his office.

Rockwell caught me with his powerful hands and steadied me. "I know," he said, looking concerned.

"You know about the Red Empire . . . ?"

His look of concern slowly transformed into a smile of pure happiness. "Of course I do," he said. "I'd be a sorry excuse for Scriptor if I didn't."

And then he plucked me off the floor like I was a rag doll and hurled me across the room as easily as if I were a lightweight piece of trash.

# CHAPTER 111

**BARRIER HEADQUARTERS**
**HADRIAN TOWER**
**LONDON, ENGLAND**

Captain Luis Salazar—combat call sign Sinbad—looked up and down the alley that ran alongside Hadrian Tower. Both ends of the alley were protected by heavy security gates, but with all the rubberneckers swarming around the tower, he wanted to make sure no one had scaled a fence to watch. The coast was clear, though.

He turned and touched the shoulder of his tech operative, Hazi Gafford—call sign Coati. "Blow it."

Coati, a short Mexican-American woman with a sturdy build and wild red hair, nodded, picked up her detonator, and began walking backward, shooing everyone else behind a huge steel dumpster. "Fire in the hole," she said with a happy arsonist's grin.

The blast was not huge because of acoustic material she'd draped over the steel grate snugged up against the wall. In lockdown mode the building was basically a steel spike. But every facility in the City of London needed services from the local utility companies. In this case the feeds ran under two meters of reinforced concrete paving. Except the hatch. This was triple locked, and made from complex alloys that could not easily be cut with a torch. The charge Coati set was packed over the two hinges that anchored the cover to the steel inner frame. It was a minor vulnerability backed up by an unusually complex series of countermeasures overseen by a tactical computer.

The blast tore the hinges out and buckled the hatch.

Before the smoke even cleared, the team's biggest operator, Anders Strøm—call sign Iceman—stepped up with a long pry bar. Even so, Coati and Rosemary Wyman—Fangirl—had to lend their muscle and even Sinbad threw his bulk against it. The hatch did not bend, but the weight of four strong people provided the leverage to rip the screws from the frame and up it came.

Coati quickly attached MindReader clip-links to every exposed wire and fiber-optic tube. With seconds MindReader Q1 stole its way into the Tower's security mainframe.

"Would've been nice if Ken Manning or Bedwyr Griffiths would just open the back door for us," Hazi said.

"They have their own crap to deal with inside," said Sinbad. "But Director Rockwell told the Big Man that this was the best and fastest way in without compromising the biohazard protocols. Speaking of which, before we go down in that access tunnel, everybody buddy-check ChemRigs. If you have so much as a nick, you're benched. And I don't want to hear anyone bitch and moan about it."

They did their check while waiting for MindReader to finish its job. It took three minutes, which was more than two minutes longer than Bug said it would require.

"That's some badass security," mused Hazi. "Jeez."

Relays clicked and locks disengaged, and the network of wires slid away to reveal a narrow entrance at the top of a metal ladder.

"Coati, take point," said Sinbad. "I'm next. Fangirl, watch our asses."

She pointed at Iceman. "I'll watch his ass for sure."

One by one they climbed down to the first basement level. Above them the panel slid back and a second panel of pure titanium quietly slid out a hidden compartment and sealed them in.

## CHAPTER 112

### ST THOMAS' HOSPITAL
### WESTMINSTER BRIDGE ROAD
### LONDON, ENGLAND

Mr. Church took his cell out of his pocket and studied the screen. During the fight in the morgue he thought he heard the phone ringing but momentarily forgot about it. Now he looked at the last incoming call and didn't recognize it. The number configuration was in keeping with burner phones, which meant it could be anyone. He paused and hit redial, but the call would not go through. He tucked the phone away and moved along the hallway, avoiding the shallow pools of light spilled by the battery-powered emergency lights.

The elevator stood with open doors, its default setting when there was an interruption in main power.

Letting his dart gun lead the way, he used one foot to push open the stairway fire door. The hinges were in good order and made no sound at all. Church stood at the base of the stairs, pistol pointed up to the next landing as he stretched out with his senses to listen to what the situation had to tell him.

There were some muffled shouts and cries of alarm, but they were distant and not from within the stairwell itself.

Moving with the silent efficiency of a hunting cat, he began to climb.

# CHAPTER 113

**SUBBASEMENT 3**
**HADRIAN TOWER**
**LONDON, ENGLAND**

The leader of the Upierczy knelt beside Smirnov, and all around them were the remains of what had been the Sabbatarian strike team. Only Smirnov yet lived, though the deep wounds on his leg continued to bleed freely.

"You are dying," said the leader of the team of killers. "I do not know if your soul will rise to heaven or fall down to hell. You can help steer that course."

Smirnov tried to spit at him, but his mouth was too dry. Instead, he growled out a prayer against evil.

The leader reached up and removed the black balaclava and red goggles he wore and set them on the floor. This revealed a face that did not look at all monstrous. There were no pointed ears, no saturnine features with a ghoul's hungry grin. There was no outrageous array of fangs. Instead, what Smirnov saw was a thin, ascetic countenance that looked more like a nineteenth-century poet. A Percy Shelley, perhaps, born to a different era. Or Gerard Manley Hopkins as a young man. A long face, with graceful brows over large and lustrous eyes. A full-lipped mouth below an aquiline nose.

"Listen to me," he said in a voice that was surprisingly gentle and refined. "You have called us Upierczy, and so we are. My brothers and I are all from that thorn on the vine of human evolution. But we are not Red Knights. My name is Michael."

"Satan is the Prince of Lies."

"Satan is not here," said Michael, then he smiled sadly as he glanced briefly at the ceiling. "He is in this building, however. Satan or his pawn."

"You are fiends of hell."

"Not that, either."

Smirnov looked confused. "And yet you come here to kill."

"As have you. As has everyone who is in this Tower." Michael shook his head. "You are Sabbatarians. I have read your tracts and heard your propaganda. The false priest Nicodemus has warped you. All of you. You have been lied to, made to serve false prophets, and been tricked into committing many acts that have blackened your soul. Had it been you who surprised my team, you would have butchered us without pause or remorse."

Smirnov looked around and sneered. "You are the butchers."

"Oh yes," said Michael. "We are. We are killers and we will go on killing as long as this war lasts. My wish, though, would be for you Sabbatarians to pause and question the truth of your mission. You blunder through this world, shoved in the direction of anyone the Scriptor or Nicodemus tells you are the enemies of God. Have you never questioned if *they*—the ones who aim you like a gun—serve heaven? Truly serve it? Or are sanctity and holiness merely disguises of convenience?"

"I . . . I do not understand."

Michael nodded slowly. "I know. Nor do we have time to discuss theology, propaganda, or justice. I just wanted you to know that I do not hold hate in my heart for you. I pity you, for you have been badly used. And it breaks my heart that we, who did not start this war, are forced to kill others who were equally duped."

Smirnov winced but his eyes were drooping. He had lost too much blood and as it continued to flow, the whole scene took on the unfocused qualities of a dream.

"I bless you and forgive you," said Michael. "I hope you find the grace that in your truest heart you believe you deserve. Be at peace."

The last words were spoken to ears that could no longer hear.

Michael bowed over the corpse and prayed. Around him, the others of his kind were doing the same.

## CHAPTER 114

### IN FLIGHT OVER THE IONIAN SEA

The two Apache attack helicopters flew low and fast, their metal bellies barely thirty meters above the moon-kissed wave-tops.

In the cockpits, each pilot was intent on his task, flying through darkness with no exterior lights. A display on the console showed a GPS map and one small, slowly pulsing light. A signal that drew the choppers toward their destination. The signal was transmitted on a special frequency from a small, decorative model of Dover Castle.

The copilots read from Deuteronomy 9:3.

*"Know, then, today that the Lord your God is the one who crosses over before you as a devouring fire; he will defeat them and subdue them before you, so that you may dispossess and destroy them quickly, as the Lord has promised you."*

Over and over and over again.

## CHAPTER 115

### HADRIAN TOWER
### LONDON, ENGLAND

I hit the back of the leather couch and sent it crashing over. I landed hard and the couch toppled over me. It was big and heavy, and I was weaker than a three-day-old kitten.

For a moment I lay there, pinned by the sofa, most of the breath knocked out of me, my battered head spinning and black poppies blooming in front of my eyes. My brain was mush and the only clear thought I had was this: *Nicodemus told me the truth.*

Hardly a consolation. Any hope I had that Rockwell and I would have a good laugh over an obvious lie and then he'd find a way to medevac me over to St. Thomas evaporated.

Shit.

Then the couch that lay atop me seemed to vanish. It took me a few seconds to process the bizarre truth that Rockwell simply grabbed it by one hand, stood it up, and shoved the thing ten feet behind him, where it smashed into a trophy case and shattered the glass. Trophies, awards, and medals fell onto the floor.

Rockwell towered over me, not red-faced from throwing a two-hundred-pound man or a three-hundred-pound leather couch. Both actions should have been impossible.

"Surprise, surprise," he said.

He then bent, grabbed me, jerked me to my feet, and slapped my face sideways and back again. What little balance and coordination I had went way the hell out the window. I sagged in his absurdly powerful one-handed grip while he took away both guns and my combat knife, tossing them onto the floor like toys.

Then he dragged me over and shoved me down into one of the visitor chairs that faced his desk. I nearly slid out onto the floor but managed not to further humiliate myself or entertain him. But, damn, I was nearly done. I hurt in so many places that my whole being felt like one vast, all-encompassing bruise.

Rockwell walked over to the wet bar and poured Bell's scotch into two glasses. Hefty shots. He placed one on the edge of the desk within easy reach of my trembling hands, and took small sips of his as he strolled around and sat down with a relaxed sigh.

"Joseph Edwin Ledger," he said amiably. "Have to say, you don't live up to your billing. Every Tier One operator I know whispers your name like you're John Wick on steroids. Hell, even the Red Knights were afraid of you. A couple of them said so before I cut their throats. And yet, look at you. Jesus, you couldn't win a wrestling match with Dame Maggie Smith and she's been dead for years. Tsk, tsk, tsk. How the mighty have fallen."

"Yeah, well," I wheezed, "if we had this same conversation an hour ago the math would have been a little different."

"Maybe. Though, frankly, I don't think we're in the same league anymore."

"I guess this is why Manning said you were scary strong."

"He has no clue," said Rockwell. He licked the rim of his glass. "Honestly, Joe, Manning is so damn dumb he'd starve to death if he was locked in a grocery store overnight. I think his spirit animal is a rocking horse."

"So, he doesn't know how strong you really are?"

"Hardly."

"Pretty curious myself, though."

He looked at me. "Stalling for time? Waiting on the cavalry?"

"Looking to upgrade my fitness plan."

Rockwell chuckled. "Sure, why not?"

He reached over and picked up a metal stapler, showed it to me, then closed his hand around it. It was a heavy Swingline office model and I sat there in ugly astonishment as he crumpled it like tinfoil. Okay, maybe he struggled a little. Then he tossed the mangled device onto the desktop.

"A very long time ago the Red Order gathered a bunch of alchemists together to try and create an elixir that accomplished two things. The first was the one you'd expect from that crowd—the philosopher's stone."

"Isn't that a Harry Potter novel?"

"It's a substance made from a variety of rare minerals and ground so finely that it could be used in chemical compounds. The goal was an *elixir vitae,* a potion to extend human life indefinitely. Not sure if it was immortality precisely, more like a slowdown on aging. Something like aging one year for every sixteen years lived. That was the plan. But they screwed something up because nearly everyone who drank it went bonkers. Stark raving, in point of fact. Had to be put down."

"Give me a moment to process my grief," I said and pretended to sponge away tears. He chuckled.

"They gave up on that and instead focused on finding a way to imbue normal humans with the physical strength, healing qualities, and stamina of the Upierczy."

"And that's why you're able to bench-press leather furniture?"

"To a degree. But that's cart before the horse," he said. "Truth is a few decades ago, some scientists working for the old Red Order invested a lot of cash into the development of a new generation of nootropic compounds to increase and regulate the hypothalamic histamine levels. The goal was to treat sweatshop workers with it so they could work shifts four or five times longer than normal, and without fatigue or loss of useful motor control. Then your boss, the Deacon, came in with that witch from Arklight—the one he's now shagging, by the by—and tore down the lab. It's my understanding that you and the witch's daughter had to come back and finish that job a few years ago."

"We did."

Rockwell shook his head. "Nope. The Deacon and Lilith hurt the program, and we shifted it out of Paris and into labs in Malaysia, and from there into workshops. That's how the Ordo Ruber was funded over the last few decades. We even reopened the lab in the Paris sewers, though that was a lure to try and trap Deacon, but instead you and Violin showed up and it was like watching a movie remake of Deacon and Lilith. Fun and informative, but really that whole thing—your part, at least—was a red herring. You thought you destroyed the samples and the research and went smugly on your way. But both you *and* the Deacon were wrong. God, you both believe so much in your own press that you think that once you've smashed your way through something then that thing is dead. That, my friend, is the kind of hopeful naïveté people like me find very useful." Sipped his scotch. "As for the research, one of the Red Order historians found the notes left over from a group of alchemists called the Quinque Patre—the Five Fathers. They had been very close to solving the superhuman upgrade issue, but because of their failures with the main plan—longevity—their work was shut down. So, the new science team went through those notes and found some things that solved problems with the nootropic drug therapy. And bang! We had our super-soldier formula. Yeah, yeah, I know, *everyone* wants to create Captain America. Though our goals were a bit closer to the Winter Soldier. Oh, don't look so surprised that I know pop culture references."

"You used yourself as a test subject?"

"Me? No. A few thousand homeless people scooped up in the right cities—those that don't care what happened to the unsheltered just as long as they go away—and *they* were the test subjects." He pursed his lip and contrived to look rueful. "There was a fairly high attrition rate, but who cares?"

"What happened to the test subjects?"

He shrugged. "Disposed of. I didn't ask for details because who gives a fuck? Homeless twats. What are they worth?"

"You're a real saint."

"Cry me a river." He sipped his drink. "Anyway . . . once the process was proven to be both effective and safe, then I started getting the shots. And . . . well, you have seen and felt the result."

"Did it make your balls shrivel up and your dick turn to a piece of limp rigatoni?"

He shrugged. "Drugs have their side effects. You have to give to get. Besides, I have plenty of sperm on ice and a whole facility of breeders waiting for IVF."

"Breeders? Jesus H Fucking Christ."

"I will add that blasphemy to the list of reasons why I will enjoy watching you die from our lovely new version of the plague. How is it, by the way? Have you started shitting your pants yet?"

"Maybe I need more fiber in my diet," I said, all the time wondering where the hell Havoc was. I could have really used Top and Bunny right about now. Bunny may not be as strong as Rockwell, but he was an advanced judo player and one of the most experienced hand-to-hand fighters I've ever known. Top was an expert in karate. Both of them also had a lot of damn guns. I could die happy watching them use Rockwell's balls for target practice.

Keeping the conversation going gave me focus and a little bit of hope. The more Rockwell told me—and he seemed chatty because he held so many winning cards—the better the chance of sharing that intel with Havoc and Church if the opportunity presented itself.

"So," I said. "Red Empire. Catchy."

"Empire Rouge. Yeah," he said. "We like it."

"Is there a point to it?"

"The Empire? Sure. As a cop you should already have that sorted out. It's money and power, what else is there?"

I wiped fever sweat off my face and flicked it at him. None of the drops reached him, alas. "How exactly is launching a new Black Plague getting you paid? You're locked in this tower with me. Someone will figure it out and then you're cooked. Or do you think that once the plague spreads far enough there won't be enough MI5 guys and cops left to arrest you?"

Rockwell looked genuinely perplexed. "Let it spread? Good Lord, Ledger, why on Earth would I want to do that?"

# CHAPTER 116

## FRESH-N-CLEAN
## CRANBROOK ROAD
## ILFORD, ENGLAND

Zombie staggered and fell back into the doorway from which he'd been leaning to fire. His back hit the locked office door and he slid down and landed hard on his rump. Everyone was wearing ChemRig body armor—the high-end kind designed by Doc Holliday—and it had saved them all multiple times already in this firefight, but a stray shot found the vulnerable gap at the armhole. The bullet-resistant material was thinnest there to allow for combat movement, but the heavily armored team at the far end of the hall were firing armor-piercing rounds.

Blood pumped from the wound and Toys saw the agony on Zombie's suddenly ashen face. There was nothing that could be done. Not now, and maybe not at all. There was so much blood. Far too much for a muscle wound, and Toys knew that a major bleeder had been clipped, likely the axillary artery.

He spun, aimed, and killed an armored fighter with a double-tap to the face. It snapped the man's head back and likely broke his neck, and the shooter crumpled in the path of the men behind him.

"Rugger," he roared, "get Zombie's bag. We need some drones. Killer Bees or RugRats."

"We're too close for the RugRats, Boss."

"Fuck it and send them!"

Rugger dove across the hall and crammed himself into the doorway where Zombie lay. He scooped up the bag and pressed himself flat as he dug around for drones. There were a dozen Killer Bees and he worked like a maniac to arm each one and toss them left and right, sending most toward the armored killers and the rest at the guards. Then he took four larger drones that were made to look like overfed rats. The bodies were natural-looking, but their insides were packed with C-4. He sent one scuttling toward the guards and the other three toward the greater threat.

"Fire in the hole," he cried and tried to melt into the door. Everyone else did the same in each of the doorways where they stood to make their stand.

The Killer Bees fired first. They were multipurpose single-use drones that could carry and discharge four Sandman darts or one shotgun shell, each with a tiny explosive charge acting as a firing pin. Rugger hadn't even checked to see which version he deployed. There were several big bangs—the ten-gauge shotgun shells—while the dart payloads fired much too quietly to be heard over the alarms and automatic gunfire. Figures staggered and some fell, but the return fire intensified from the others.

Until the RugRats detonated. It happened at both ends of the hall less than a second apart and the densely packed high-explosives did terrible work. Fireballs punched up and down the hallway. Rent Boy's sleeve began to burn, and he had to slap at the flames even as cracks ran along the upper walls. Acoustic ceiling tiles fell flaming to the floor, and dozens of electrical wires hissed and sparked like furious snakes.

The blasts killed the gunfire and the alarms there in the hall.

Toys reeled, his head ringing with the thunder of those explosions. When he could force his eyes open and bully his mind into useful thought, he leaned out to look and saw bloody carnage everywhere. Zombie lay slumped half into the hall, much of his body covered with debris. His eyes were open and there was a light film of dust on them.

It was as if someone slipped a stiletto between Toys's ribs and twisted it. He was as hard on Zombie as he was on all the lads, but they knew that it was humor. There was no animus among the Hunt. And Zombie had been with him from the beginning.

"I'm sorry, mate," he murmured.

When he looked down the hall toward the armored soldiers, he saw one or two stirring almost drunkenly, and he stepped out, raised his gun, and killed them both. Then he turned, nearly falling over as he did so because the shock waves were playing merry hob with his balance. None of the security guards were moving, and none of them even looked human anymore. Behind them, the smoke was funneling out, pulled by winds, and it took Toys a moment to realize that the blast had ripped the rear door off its hinges. The light values down there were different, showing the distinctive glow of the sodium vapor lamps in the parking lot.

The line of escape was open.

"Lads, bring Zombie and let's get the hell out of—"

Which was as far as he got because through the thinning smoke he saw two large SUVs screeched to a stop right outside the ruin of the door. Each vehicle disgorged half a dozen men and women dressed in loose black clothes—and yet clearly civilian attire—and all of them had guns except for one tall, ascetic-looking man who held a rubber-headed mallet in one hand and a length of tapered wood in the other. A hammer and stake.

Sabbatarians. A dozen of them, and they rushed into the building, firing as they came.

## CHAPTER 117

### ST THOMAS' HOSPITAL
### WESTMINSTER BRIDGE ROAD
### LONDON, ENGLAND

At each landing Church paused to listen at the fire door and then open it enough to peer out.

The first floor was filled with confused people, all of them in hazmat suits, mostly Level D types, which had been provided to ambulatory patients, visitors stuck in the building during the lockdown, and staff whose duties would not take them to the two floors under hard quarantine. He saw hospital security guards wearing modified Level C suits.

There was no panic and no violence, and so he continued up.

Outside the second-floor door he paused to call Major Mun Ji-Woo—call sign Leopard—top-kick of Bedlam Team. When she answered he asked, “What’s your twenty?”

“We are outside the quarantine zone on Level 33 of the Tower Wing.”

There was a burst of static on the line and the call dropped. Church called right back. “Cell signal is bad here in the fire tower.”

“No,” said Mun, “ours keep going out now and then. And all comms are down. Wi-Fi, too.”

“Now isn’t that interesting? No jammer affects both, so either something here in the physical structure of the hospital is interfering, or our enemies have very sophisticated tech. I rather think it’s the latter, because the other would be a suspicious coincidence.”

“And you don’t believe in coincidences,” she said.

“No. So, tell me, Leopard, have you encountered any hostiles?”

“Negative, Merlin. Why?”

He quickly told her about the attack in the morgue and ordered that one of her team go down to provide protection. He heard her give that order to Billy Robinette—call sign Kingsnake.

Church then brought her up to speed on the Red Empire, the Sabbatarians, and the likelihood of other hostiles at large in the hospital.

“Everyone’s wearing a hazmat,” she said. “How are we supposed to know good guys from bad?”

“Switch to Snelligs and when in doubt use Sandman and flex cuffs on anyone about whom you’re uncertain. We can make all necessary apologies and reparations when this is done.”

Major Mun paused for a moment. “Is Wooley Bear going to solve this?”

The call sign for Coleman—hung on him by Doc Holliday—seemed so wildly out of place given the horrors of the situation that it was almost absurd. Church made a mental note to ask Coleman to pick his own combat name for future use.

“He thinks so,” he told Mun. “I’m coming up the stairs. Send someone to meet me so there’s no surprises. I’m on two now.”

"I'll send Smoker," she said, using the combat call sign for veteran RTI operative Felix Rhineheart. "With the power out, let's use a call and response."

"Agreed," said Church. "Call is *Sweater*, reply is *Jumper*."

"Copy that."

He dropped the cell and let it hang on its lanyard, and he continued to climb.

# CHAPTER 118

## HADRIAN TOWER
## LONDON, ENGLAND

"Why let it spread?" I said, echoing my own question. "To start a pandemic . . . ? That's kind of the obvious takeaway given your whole global domination master plan. Am I wrong? Did I miss something?"

James Rockwell laughed. "Dear Lord, I guess there must be a certain measure of comfort in being that clueless. You really do fail to live up to expectations, Ledger."

"Oh, stop showing off. Anyone can be blindsided. And if they hadn't dosed me with this shit then this meeting would be playing out a whole lot different."

"So you say," said Rockwell, then gestured to the crumpled stapler. "Opinions differ."

I shook my head. "You could have killed me just now. You could have had Griffiths and Manning cut my throat before I woke up. You're keeping me alive for some reason, and I assume it's for some kind of big reveal. Or do you just like to brag? Is that it? You want to be seen as clever, as some kind of evil mastermind. And then what? You let a lot of people die, maybe hundreds of thousands, maybe most of Europe, and you waltz away during the outbreak and set yourself up as Dr. Evil, British edition?"

"Ah, you think this is all about me," he said, nodding. "You think this is me being actually insane. That's dim. Two things—I'm neither mad nor a scientist. So, no, you twit, this isn't about me. Well, not entirely, at least. No, my friend, this is about *revenge*."

That gave me a moment's pause.

"Revenge . . . ? For *what*? You want payback for what happened in Iran a few years ago? The Red Order and the Red Knights picked that fight. What were we supposed to do? Sit back and let them turn the entire Middle East into a radioactive wasteland?"

"God, no," he said and sounded like he meant it. "Are you still unclear that it was the Knights and *only* the Knights who wanted to detonate the nukes under the oil fields? The Red Order was totally against that. It's why we helped steer the Sabbatarians at the Knights in an attempt to stop it."

"You also sicced them on me."

Rockwell shook his head. "That was a happy accident, but the truth is that we had nothing to do with it."

"*And* your pal Nicodemus sicced them on me in Maryland."

He raised his eyebrows. "Did he, indeed? When? Where?"

"A few days ago and where doesn't matter." I studied his face. "You're saying you had nothing to do with it?"

"Nothing at all."

"Or with Nicodemus calling me all the time like I was his BFF?"

"First I'm hearing about it." The frown that clouded his face looked entirely genuine. "He calls you? Now, why would he do that?" He said it as much to himself as to me.

I said nothing, because if he was really as surprised as he looked, then a big chunk of my assumptions about what the hell was happening just fell off the table.

Rockwell spent a few long moments staring into the amber depths of his whisky. "Nicodemus helped form the Red Order, you know."

"You mean one of his ancestors did," I countered.

His smile was small and enigmatic. "Sure. That's what I must have meant. In any case, he led Sir Guy, the first Scriptor, down a path that did not really serve God in the way he said it would. The Holy Agreement was all about perpetuating chaos. Don't believe it? Look around. Islam is still the enemy of all God-fearing Christians, but what percentage of the population actually goes to church anymore? Fewer and fewer every year, even while hostilities with Islam burn hotter than ever. And the, um, *current* Nicodemus was responsible for conning Hugo Vox into helping the Red Knights with their insane fucking plan. It's because of all of those wheels within wheels that

Sir Charles LaRoque was killed. Blown to pieces by a Hellfire missile that the Deacon ordered."

"Boo-fucking-hoo. Bad guy gets comeuppance. Life is so unfair."

His smile remained, but grew colder. "Life isn't unfair, but loyalty and trust in a creature like Nicodemus has brought nothing but pain to the LaRoque family."

A coughing fit took me for a bit. As it was happening, I fought the urge to look over my shoulder to see if Top was creeping down the hall with all of Havoc Team behind him. This would be a really damn good time. And where the hell was Chaos Team? They should be here by now.

"Is that what you mean by this being about revenge?" I asked, wiping spit from my lips and chin.

I think he knew I was stretching this out, but Rockwell seemed to be enjoying it. Rubbing my nose in it. "It is," he said. "And it's a damn fine plan, too. Quite proud of it."

"Mass murder looks great on a résumé."

"The right kind of murder does, to be sure," he corrected, taking no obvious offense. "But it's not about the body count, Ledger. That's the part you and Deacon and all of you missed. It's about the *choreography*."

"You lost me. Are we talking about a flash-mob dance routine with Sabbatarians, Red Order freaks, and the dying population of London? If so, I don't see an MTV award anytime soon."

He chuckled. Glad I was able to amuse him. "You see, Ledger, I managed to choreograph this so that all the people I want dead are in separate and specific locations. You and Havoc Team are here in the Tower, and I am reliably informed that Chaos Team just blew a hole in a basement wall in order to infiltrate. Nice. At St. Thomas' Hospital I have Deacon, Dr. Coleman, and Bedlam Team, which just arrived. Then there's the RTI version of the Suicide Squad out in Ilford, and by now things should be getting pretty dicey for them. Pity. And . . . there's one or two other locations I'll keep to myself for now, awaiting confirmation of certain players on the chessboard. All nicely corralled and right on schedule. Everyone *contained* within the sensible security protocols at each location. St. Thomas is on lockdown with half the police in London making sure no one gets in or out, and Hadrian's

Tower is locked up tighter than a nun's chastity. That means I have the famous Joe Ledger and Havoc Team along with forty of my best—all here for the party."

"Your best? God's Warriors," I said. "Adorable nickname. Sounds like a Christian hard rock band."

"It's truth in advertising," said Rockwell. "Every single one of them has taken holy orders. Ordained soldiers of God. Granted, they're a bit more Old Testament than New, but these are troubled times." He finished his drink, fetched a refill, and sat back down.

Still no Top.

Still no Havoc.

And now I was getting worried that something very bad was happening. My fluttering pulse began to jump.

"And at the hospital," continued Rockwell, "I have the Deacon himself and some of the top epidemiologists in the world that *he* brought in. His *friends in the industry.* Always a trademark of his."

He leaned forward and gave me a very intense stare.

"He's the real prize, Joe. No doubt about that. The Scriptors of the Red Order, the Sabbatarians, and the Red Knights have been trying to kill him for a long time. A very, *very* long time. You have no idea."

The image of that old painting flashed through my mind, but I said nothing.

"Tell me," said Rockwell, "how deep into his confidence are you? Do you know about Sir John the Bastard Knight? Do you know about his son? Do you know the names Jonah Tabernacle, the Nameless Man, Jean Ardeaglais, Iain Kirk, Michael Bethel, Simon Chapel? No? Le Comte de Saint Germain?"

I said nothing.

Rockwell gave me a knowing smile, then he got up and went to a wall safe that he opened with a punch-code and fingerprint scan. He opened the heavy door and removed a thick book bound in ancient and cracked brown leather. The book was wrapped with thick red braided cord and tied with a complex knot. Rockwell hefted it in his hands for a moment, nodding in agreement with his own thoughts, and then tossed it onto his desk. It landed with a *whup,* and the resulting air pressure knocked over a pencil jar, spilling pens and pencils everywhere. By reflex I caught two as they rolled off the edge. I tossed one back onto the desk but secreted the other under my thigh. Rockwell did not appear to notice.

"What's that?" I asked, nodding to the book. "The latest Danielle Steel novel?"

"That, my lad, is the *Scriptor's Diary.* It is the personal record kept by the unbroken line dating back the first Scriptor, Sir Guy LaRoque, and passed down father to son for nearly a thousand years all the way to Sir Charles."

"Hope he had time to write *The End* before that Hellfire missile blew him into orbit."

Rockwell did not smile at that. "Sir Charles was, admittedly, not among the best or boldest of the Scriptors. No. But his notes and insights are quite valuable."

"Speaking of which, how did *you* get it if the book was handed down from father to son? Sir Charles didn't have any kids."

"He did not," said Rockwell, sitting down once more behind his desk. He took a thoughtful sip of his scotch. "He did, however, have a brother, Andrew, who died twenty years ago."

"Ah," I said, getting it. "And you're Andrew's son."

"Took you a while, but yes."

"And your last name . . . Rockwell. Rock . . . LaRoque. English branch of the family?"

"Obviously."

"Which means you regard yourself as the visionary who will rebuild the Red Order. Excuse me . . . Red Empire."

"You speak as if that hasn't already happened." Rockwell shook his head. "As much as I loved my uncle Charles, we had fundamental differences in how we viewed the best path forward for the Order. I made my case to him that the Ordo Ruber had long outlived its usefulness, at least in that form. It needed to get its head out of the Middle Ages and embrace the potential for growth in the twenty-first century. Even before the Red Knights rebelled, I recommended he cut ties with them. Give them their freedom and look elsewhere for more reliable and—dare I say *controllable*—military assets. That's why I steered my career toward the position I'm in now. You wouldn't believe how useful it is, in terms of recruitment, to run Barrier. I have files on *thousands* of official military and private soldiers—not just from the UK but globally. Barrier's resources allowed me to hide all of my actions."

"Should I applaud now or weave you a crown of laurels?"

He ignored that and reached out to pat the diary. "Wouldn't you like to browse this tome? It has so many interesting bits of data, including the most comprehensive biography of Mr. Church."

"No thanks," I said. "I'm halfway through a Scott Sigler novel and can't wait to see how it ends."

"Oh, come now, Ledger, you can't tell me you're not intrigued."

"Not even a little," I lied.

"I think you're making a mistake," said Rockwell. "If I were you I'd be very damned interested to know what kind of monster you've been working for all this time."

## CHAPTER 119

### ST THOMAS' HOSPITAL
### WESTMINSTER BRIDGE ROAD
### LONDON, ENGLAND

"Sweater!"

The word seemed to spiral downward from the shadows three landings above him. Church paused and replied, "Jumper."

"Come ahead, Merlin," called Smoker. "Kingsnake's with me. The way's clear."

Pistol in hand, Church ran up the stairs until he saw the hulking figure of Billy Robinette, who was the size of a defensive fullback and had a faceful of freckles and scars. He sketched a salute and hurried past Church to head down to the morgue to act as Coleman's bodyguard. Robinette had been Marine Force Recon for eight years and had been on Bedlam Team through nine tough missions.

Church watched him go, nodding to himself. Good choice.

Then he turned to Smoker, a former SEAL with the kindly face of a schoolteacher but the eyes of a pit viper.

"What's going on, boss?" he asked as Church joined him on the landing of floor 26. "I mean, Leopard told me about the Red Empire and Sabbatarians and all, but who's in the building with us? And what's the enemy strength?"

"Unknown on both counts. But we have to be ready for whatever they throw at us."

There was the slightest flicker of doubt in Smoker's eyes. "They sent four people after Wooley Bear, right?"

"Yes."

"How come?"

"Likely to prevent him from doing exactly what he is doing."

"Okay, but how'd they know he was even going down there?"

"It means there is at least one of their spies among the people on the quarantine floors. Once we're up there, we will need to impose a little order on the situation."

"People are under stress," said Smoker. "They won't like us bossing them around."

Church gave him a steely look. "Try to imagine how much I care."

They ran up the rest of the way to floor 33.

## CHAPTER 120

### FRESH-N-CLEAN
### CRANBROOK ROAD
### ILFORD, ENGLAND

"Who are these wankers?" demanded Rent Boy.

"Sodding Sabbatarians?" snarled Toys. "They're not on our side. Kill the bastards."

He punctuated his order by taking his pistol in both hands and firing as he ran toward the newcomers. The two men leading the pack stumbled and went down. One of the pair had been running with finger on the trigger and as the agony of the bullet impacts tore through him and he collapsed, he burned through an entire magazine. The bullets went everywhere, ricocheting like mad in the concrete hall. Some of the office windows blew inward. Other rounds whinged and panged off the walls around the Hunt, and Muppet cried out as blood exploded on both sides of his thigh. A through-and-through wound. Rugger caught him under one armpit and Rent Boy the other as they dragged him forward. Muppet was even more furious than hurt—or was able to turn pain into useful rage. He cut down two more of the Sabbatarians, and his helpers took one each.

This meant leaving Zombie's body behind, which Toys was loath to do. He plucked a grenade from his belt and lobbed it. It was another of the gas-filled flash-bangs. The Sabbatarians saw it and dove for cover, thinking it was a fragmentation grenade. Toys emptied a magazine into the lot of them as soon as the flash-bang detonated.

It was a total cock-up.

"Rent Boy, help Muppet. Rugger, drag Zombie. We're not leaving his sorry ass behind."

*So much for being an unsentimental git,* he thought as he slapped a new magazine into place.

Then the Sabbatarians made a fresh surge, the uninjured ones in back shoving the others forward into the teeth of the Wild Hunt's guns. In one of those bizarre combat moments that looks like bad theater, a ricochet hit the side of Toys's pistol, ripping it from his hand. It hurt like hell, but Toys was used to pain. He felt something change in him, a sudden and chilling shift from the leader of the Wild Hunt and a sinner on the redemption road, and in the space of a heartbeat became the *old* Toys. Brutal, vicious, and efficient. As the nearest Sabbatarians swung a rifle around toward him, Toys drew his two fighting knives—a double-edged British commando dagger and a U.S. Marine Corps Ka-Bar. And then he was among them.

He bashed the rifle aside and drove the dagger into the side of the lead Sabbatarian's neck, neatly severing the subclavian artery, then gave it a harder turn and tore it free. As blood shot upward from the wound, he used a Muay Thai sliding knee kick to knock the dying man into the oncoming swarm. But he followed the man, knocking him down into the knees of two running killers. They went down and Toys leapt over them, leaving the killing to his men. He put a foot on the wall, kicked off, turning lithe as a danseur so that his midair turn created torque for the downward slash that took half a face off. As he landed he drove the dagger forward in a corkscrew motion, destroying the left eye of the next man; he tore the knife free, checked his withdraw and chopped with the steel butt of the knife into the shrieking Sabbatarian's cheek, sending him into the others, who were still trying to regain their balance from their first fallen comrade. Bullets hammered the Sabbatarians as Muppet, Rent Boy, and Rugger made them pay for what happened to Zombie.

A brawny man with a double-barrel shotgun swung the weapon toward Toys, but it was too slow and the wrong weapon for close-quarters fighting. Without hesitation, Toys dropped the dagger, grabbed the shotgun a few centimeters behind the double black barrel mouths, jerked it around and then shoved it forward, forcing the man's trapped finger to pull both triggers. The combined blast of buckshot caught the lone female Sabbatarian and another man at a level equal to the man's chest and the woman's face, and both disintegrated into red grotesquery.

Rent Boy cried out and Toys risked a look to see him stagger forward as bullets hit him between the shoulder blades. The ChemRig saved his life, but the impact knocked him flat. The shots had not come from the Sabbatarians, though, and Toys gaped in horror as more of the armored fighters came climbing over the bodies of their friends.

Once more it was a trap between hammer and anvil.

"Fuck it," said Toys. He was in the wrong mood to die. There was still too much red fun to be had and he was in the mood for it. If this was how he was going to die, then he'd slide down to hell on a water slide of blood. That was the thought in his mind as he ducked to grab his dagger and drove into the Sabbatarians.

He waded into them the way he had learned years back, using flourishes borrowed from both Rafael Santoro and Joe Ledger, the two best knife fighters he'd ever met. The fact that he detested them both, and one had killed the other, did not matter. He had the skills and the complete and utter disregard for human life that maximized everything he did. His blades moved with the speed of his hate.

His men had turned to face the renewed threat from behind, and each of them sought cover in a doorway. Half of the Sabbatarians were firing past the Hunt at the armored killers, and that made little sense to Toys. He did not care. If he lived, then answers would be found. If he died, then fuck it all.

He stabbed and slashed, kicked and chopped, and laughed as he did it.

More figures began crowding in through the exit, and he felt the first flicker of despair. They were not the armored soldiers, though. More Sabbatarians? How many of them were there, Toys wondered as panic and despair fought within for control.

But the Sabbatarians whirled toward these newcomers. The Saturday People shouted, some even screamed—not merely in fear, but with a kind of outrage that crossed over into frenzy.

*"Upierczy!"* they yelled. One of them dug a small glass globe from his pocket and hurled it against the wall beside the door, showering the newcomers with a beige powder. Even through the blood and gun smoke, Toys could smell it.

*Garlic.*

"Red Knights, for fuck's sake," he said. Then he heard a change in the timbre of the gunfire. When he turned it was clear his men had stopped firing, because the armored soldiers were now firing past them at both Sabbatarians and Red Knights.

"What in the fucking hell?" he demanded.

# CHAPTER 121

## HADRIAN TOWER ATRIUM
## LONDON, ENGLAND

Remy Neddo wanted very much to throw his cell phone onto the floor and line-dance over it until he felt better. The same with the comms units.

"Can't *both* be out at the same time," he told himself. "Getting me a bad feeling up in here."

Yet they were both out.

The comms had begun malfunctioning as soon as Havoc began their investigation, and that Remy had ascribed to the building's unusually hardened safety features. It was like being inside a Faraday cage, except that the jackasses on Alpha Team seemed to have no trouble at all. Bastards. Remy wanted to knock one of them out, drag him out of sight, and take a real close look at their tech. It offended him that anything could interfere with the communications systems codesigned by Bug and Doc Holliday, and which was powered by MindReader Q1.

How did the Tower's security allow Alpha Team to chatter and not any other tech?

That not only pissed him off but it made him suspicious, and Remy was raised in New Orleans, where everyone he knew was always playing some kind of game or working some kind of angle.

Back when his cell was still sort of working he had called Bug to complain and ask for advice, but the big brain who ran Computer Sciences was too busy with the Corvin Castle decryption to offer much help. Instead, Remy's requests had to go through the new COO, Major Courtland, whom Remy had only met once and didn't know. Or trust.

Halfway through his most recent call to the TOC, the line got all staticky and then went totally dead. No signal at all, not even enough to call the colonel or the rest of Havoc.

Which left Remy standing in the big atrium on the first floor, feeling like he was a castaway on a desert island way out in the middle of the ocean. When he tried the wall-mounted intercom there was no signal at all and the service light was red.

"Well, hell," he growled. "How the hell am I supposed to do anything when I don't know where anyone is or what's happening?"

The intercom lights glowed and offered no other response.

Remy tried his tac-com to the drones and that worked after a fashion. He could locate the drones but not recall them. Or access their cameras. And, after a few minutes of fiddling with the controls, the sensors went offline. Bing-bang-boom. Dead.

He stepped back from the intercom, a dozen vulgarities warring with one another to be screamed at the dumb machine. Remy managed to swallow them as he turned to a building directory mounted on the wall. He had no idea where Outlaw was, but located the biological research lab Top and Bunny said they were going to check out. And then he found the floor with the monitoring suite. Maybe someone else on Havoc would have answers . . . or some bars on their cell.

He stepped back from the wall and gave the vast atrium a final look, saw the same nothing he'd seen a moment ago, and he turned toward the closest bank of elevators. The hit, when it came, was like being struck by a Ben Joyce hundred-mile-per-hour fastball. He staggered and dropped to his knees, sliding on the polished marble for two or three feet. Remy fell forward and lay there, breathless and hurt, listening to the echoes of that shot bounce off the walls.

One of Top Sims's many training aphorisms seemed to ignite in big burning letters inside his mind. *If you're shot, you're dead. So be dead.*

Remy did not move.

He knew he was hurt but not actually injured. The ChemRigs were lined with graphene and spider silk as well as a new Kevlar blend, and nothing short of an armor-piercing round from a GE Six-Pak could penetrate it. And even with the impact-dampening nano-tubes inside the armor, he was sure he'd been knocked down by a high-powered sniper rifle. The kind of shot that would cause hydrostatic shock on a level that a bullet in the arm could be as lethal as one through the heart. So, it was reasonable for the shooter to assume that a bullet striking between the shoulder blades was a guaranteed kill shot.

So, he was dead.

There was no follow-up shot. One bullet, one kill. The sniper's goal. Nothing as precise as a headshot was needed since this shot had come from a balcony, and not a high one. The angle of impact told him that much. The shooter was no more than two flights up, and likely one, and was positioned behind where he lay. A straight shot at a slightly depressed angle to a target that was within a hundred yards. Easy. No one could survive it.

He figured the shooter thought he was wearing a Saratoga Hammer Suit which, though flexible enough for full combat use, was not bulletproof.

The point of impact hurt like hell and with each very slow, very shallow breath there was a spike of pain that told him at least one rib was broken.

Remy Neddo lay there, praying to the Holy Mother, playing dead until he felt safe enough to be alive.

# CHAPTER 122

## ST THOMAS' HOSPITAL
## WESTMINSTER BRIDGE ROAD
## LONDON, ENGLAND

Church and Smoker found Amy Neal—call sign Pond—at the top of the stairs. She held one of the new Snellig FA-100 assault rifles, the barrel aimed down the steps, but to one side. "Sweater," she called.

"Jumper," said Smoker.

Pond stepped back and pulled the door open for them.

Church found Major Mun in close discussion with Dr. Suliman, and they both turned expectantly toward him.

"Do we know how the power went out?" Church asked.

"Not yet," said Mun. "I sent Mountain Man with three security guards and a building engineer to check it out. He has a Cloudburst shotgun, and I gave Snellig handguns to the guards."

Mountain Man—George Yazzie—was a burly Navajo who was wider than Bunny though not as tall.

"My comms are out," said Church. "Cell still works."

"Same with us," agreed Mun. "Everyone on Bedlam has burners."

She looked around for a moment, and Church did, too, latching on to what she looked at as a way of aligning with her probable thoughts.

"They sent those guys after Wooley Bear, but why didn't they send a team up here? If their goal is to disrupt the treatment and research plans, this would have been the better move. And why start a fight with Wooley Bear rather than put two center-mass? This strategy is weird bordering on unsound. And from what I've read of the Red Order they weren't as clumsy as the Sabbatarians."

Church studied her and then glanced back toward the stairs.

"Yes," he said slowly. "It is very strange."

## CHAPTER 123

### BARRIER HEADQUARTERS
### HADRIAN TOWER
### LONDON, ENGLAND

I looked at the *Scriptor's Diary* on the desk and fished for something clever to say, but came up dry. While I tried to conjure a response that was at least reasonably useful, Rockwell's phone rang. He snatched it up, looked at the display for a moment, then took the call.

"Is it done?" he asked, then listened. I saw his look of expectant optimism change slowly into disappointment and anger. "The hell do you mean *Red Knights*? There are no sodding Red Knights anymore. How far up your ass is your head? What . . . ?" He listened some more. "And Sabbatarians? What the hell's happening over there? It was a simple job. Kill that faggot Toys and his group of thugs and then close up shop. Tell me how you managed to complicate that easy math."

He listened some more, and I thought I could hear the sound of screams and gunfire from the cell caller. I'd sent the Wild Hunt to the sanitizer company, but it was pretty clear that was another of Rockwell's traps. Like the Tower and the hospital. I'd sent them into that trap. And now there were God's Warriors in ambush and both Sabbatarians and Red Knights? How? Not for the first time in this job I felt like I walked onto a stage armed with the wrong script and laryngitis.

My fever was so high now that I was seeing fireworks of white and yellow and red in my eyes. My scalp felt like it was covered with ants and if I had anything left in my stomach, I'd have puked it up.

*This is what dying feels like,* I thought. A wave of sadness slammed into me. Not because my life was ending, and ending badly, but because I knew how much this would hurt Junie. God, how I wanted to say goodbye. To tell her how sorry I was for coming into her life and polluting her blue skies. I wanted to apologize for not being a better soldier, a better fighter. A better man.

As happens sometimes at the edge of delirium, I had a flash of something unconnected to this moment, yet somehow apt. It was a snatch of lyrics. Couldn't tell you the band or when it was released, or even where I heard it. Just the lines.

*This is no place for a better man.*

*This is no place for heroes.*

Something like that. Close enough for an epitaph.

And yet . . .

I had the pen still tucked under my thigh. I had a knife Rockwell hadn't found because it was inside my trouser pocket, clipped there with a spring release.

What, though, could I do with a knife and a pen against a guy who wasn't sick, wasn't weak as a newborn kitten, and could probably break me in half with his bare hands?

I leaned back in my chair and put one foot against the edge of his desk as if trying to brace myself from falling. Looking wasted and sick and helpless took no acting chops. I was so close to complete collapse that the weight of my own weak hopes of survival was too heavy a burden. I began coughing again and used a lot of strength I couldn't spare to stay in that chair and keep my foot braced.

Rockwell finished the call and tossed the phone onto the desk in disgust. "Christ on the Cross."

"Isn't that blasphemy?"

His scowl creased with a rueful smile. "Fair. I'll do a few Hail Marys later."

He said it as a joke, but I think he actually meant it. Then he looked at his wristwatch and the tension on his face melted away and he looked oddly calm. Or relieved. He was hard to read.

"Fun time," he said in exactly the way that let me know that there was nothing fun about to happen.

## CHAPTER 124

### ST THOMAS' HOSPITAL
### WESTMINSTER BRIDGE ROAD
### LONDON, ENGLAND

Church stood apart from Major Mun, Dr. Suliman, and all the others while he thought about what Mun said.

*This strategy is weird bordering on unsound. And from what I've read of the Red Order they weren't as clumsy as the Sabbatarians.*

She was, of course, correct, but Church had been so busy helping to manage the influx of infection, arranging for some of the world's top specialists to fly in or consult via video, coordinating with the TOC, and checking in on the field teams that he had not had the time to pause and analyze the strategy employed by the enemy.

With a few minutes of silent inactivity, he let his logical mind step out of active gear and become passive, receptive. That had always been his best tactic—to allow each bit of information to find its way toward its place as a link in a chain of logic.

The current image was awkward, clunky, and inefficient. Which told him, on reflection, that he was not seeing the whole picture. But even that wasn't quite the right diagnosis. The truth was that this felt like stage management. Alarums and excursions, as Shakespeare would have put it. As he contemplated the details, he applied another tool of understanding to the problem by stepping out of the role of opponent and into a borrowed role of villain. If *he* was doing this deliberately and with calculated precision, then would what was happening at Hadrian Tower and here at St. Thomas make sense? Moreover, in what way would these actions and steps be so logical as to be imperative?

An idea began to take form in his mind, and it was one that sent small waves of icy chills through him.

He snatched up his cell and called Joe Ledger.

There was no answer.

He tried three times, and got nothing each time.

He called Top Sims and Bunny, Remy, and Belle. No answer. Then he tried Captain Salazar of Chaos Team.

Nothing.

To assure himself that the call blockage was not on his end, he punched in Coleman's number. The scientist answered on the third ring.

"Checking the line. Talk soon."

Church hung up and tried one more number. Major Claire Courtland answered.

"Go for Artemis," she said.

Church explained that the comms were out at the hospital, as was the power, and that both comms and cell service to the Tower were out.

Although she was not Grace Courtland, Claire was every bit as sharp. "They're about to make their move," she said. "We have to—"

The call died right there. Redialing got no answer, but instead a recorded message said, *This call cannot be completed as dialed.*

Church felt his heart turn to ice.

Whatever was happening, was happening now.

# CHAPTER 125

**BARRIER HEADQUARTERS**
**HADRIAN TOWER**
**LONDON, ENGLAND**

"Okay," Rockwell said, "so I have a couple of things to say."

"I'm all ears," I said, trying to sound offhand, but I wound up coughing afterward and that spoiled the effect. My stomach was beginning to churn and I prayed to every celestial deity I could think of not to let explosive diarrhea be the next symptom to present. If that happened, I might actually *ask* Rockwell to shoot me.

"First," he said, "I'll be up front about some things. Only fair. You know the expression that no plan ever survives contact with the enemy? Of course you do. It probably crossed your mind after Griffiths and Manning ambushed you. But it cuts both ways. Your Wild Hunt guys should have been an easy target, but they're making my guys earn it. And now a rogue Sabbatarian team and another group that the idiot who called me swears are Red Knights are in a four-way gun battle. That wasn't anticipated." He paused for a sigh. A bit dramatic, but he had that vibe. He was showing off and enjoying himself. "You see, what separates average good soldiers from bad ones is built-in contingencies. But, the building is wired nine ways from Sunday, so if we lose too much ground—ka-boooom."

I said nothing. My teeth were chattering from the deep chills.

"Second," he said brightly, "this building is also wired. There's enough explosives in the basement and packed into the walls to blow the Tower and four city blocks all the way to Jupiter."

"Unless someone puts a bullet in your brain pan," I managed to say.

But Rockwell shook his head. He opened his shirt to show me a surgical scar above his heart. "Had a pacemaker put in six years ago. But four months ago I had my docs give it an upgrade. If my heart stops beating, a little signal gets sent and bang-o, bang-o. Cool, huh? A *literal* dead man's switch."

"That's dedication for you."

"Insurance plan. Even my enemies have to keep me alive."

I said nothing.

"Third thing, Ledger, is that as of right now, *all* of the people on Santa's naughty list—that's you, Havoc, Chaos, Bedlam, the Wild Hunt, and Mr. Church—are exactly where I want and need you to be. Everyone is in my playground."

"Hooray for you," I said weakly, "though that might bite you in the ass."

"Anything's possible, but I tend to rely on contingency plans. And on misdirection."

"Meaning . . . ?"

He opened a laptop on his desk and tapped a few keys. Then he turned it so we could both see the screen.

"Meaning, that like any good stage magician, I let you look into my hat and up my sleeves and everywhere but where the real trick was hiding. Watch."

He tapped a key and the image showed a mass of men in black armor running through the halls in the Tower. Some broke off and headed toward the monitoring suites.

He tapped the key again. Another group followed a drone that buzzed overhead and then went over a balcony and down to where Remy waited for it.

Another tap and I saw Top and Bunny in what was clearly one of the high-security labs here in the Tower, and they were trapped between two groups of ordinary people in lab coats . . . except all of those people had vacant eyes and snarling mouths and they screamed with unfiltered rage as they charged my men.

Tap. The gun battle at the sanitizer plant, showing the Wild Hunt caught in a no-win fight with three sets of armed combatants.

Tap. More of the fighters in black armor—God's Warriors—running up a set of stairs, doing it right, checking the corners, covering each other, checking doors on every landing as they headed up to the quarantine floors. There were a *lot* of them. Too many to count as they swarmed past.

"And now," said a radiant and triumphant Rockwell, "the real crowning glory of God's plan. The jewel in the crown of my plan to wipe the Deacon and everything he spent his life building from the face of the Earth. Watch, Ledger. This will be a real showstopper."

Tap.

The view was from a camera mounted forward on a helicopter. I could hear the rotors chopping the air. The view showed the rolling waters below and the shadows of two attack helicopters. Then the camera panned up to show a shadowy shape painted against the star-field sky. It was an island created ages ago by a volcano. Sitting atop the island's highest point was a building. A castle.

My heart tore loose from its moorings and dropped inside my chest.

It was Mr. Church's transplanted and rebuilt Transylvanian castle. It was Phoenix House there on Omfori Island.

"As God wills it," said Rockwell.

Fire erupted from both helicopters as wave after wave of Hellfire missiles tore through the night, their gasses dark as shadows. I watched in absolute horror as the missiles screamed through the air and slammed, one by one, into the castle.

The pilots kept firing, sending all of their missiles at the target.

The night bloomed with dreadful fires that rose up into the sky, spreading out, showing me as true a vision of hell as I have ever seen.

## CHAPTER 126

### PHOENIX HOUSE
### OMFORI ISLAND, GREECE

The two helicopters fired their complete complement of Hellfire missiles. Sixteen each, thirty-two in all.

The pilots watched them hit.

They leaned forward with awed fascination as the towers of the ancient castle bowed down and vanished into the fury of smoke and flame. Huge chunks of debris were flung high into the sky and far out to sea. There were small figures hurled into the air as well—burning as they arched toward the rocky shores, their flesh turned black inside the shrouds of fire. The sculptured gardens and lush trees that surrounded the building became bonfires. Fissures cracked open from the base of the mount on which the castle had been meticulously reconstructed.

"God almighty," breathed the pilot of the first Apache.

His copilot gave him a stern look and in a reproving tone said, "God's will be *done*."

The pilot turned slowly toward him and almost snapped at him, but controlled himself. Instead, he nodded and murmured, "As God wills it."

The two choppers turned in the smoky air and flew back to their waiting ship.

## CHAPTER 127

### ST THOMAS' HOSPITAL
### WESTMINSTER BRIDGE ROAD
### LONDON, ENGLAND

Mr. Church staggered and almost fell. Major Mun rushed over and caught him by the arm, steadying him. Her leg, though mostly healed, was still weak and she sagged under his weight.

"What's wrong?" she cried.

He pushed her gently back and forced his legs to hold himself upright, but stayed there, shaking his head slowly from side to side.

"I . . ." he began, but faltered.

Dr. Suliman came hurrying over, too, but Church waved him away.

"Leave me be," Church said weakly. He closed his eyes and searched inside his mind for some clue as to what it was that hit him like this. Few things ever affected him so suddenly or profoundly. There was a pain deep in his chest that felt real and not born of emotions.

He remained standing for several seconds, searching for answers as the intensity of the feeling began to ebb. The pain faded, faded, and was gone, leaving behind only the certainty that something dreadful had occurred.

When he trusted himself to speak, he turned to Mun and the doctor. "Excuse me. I am recovered."

Even to his own ears the words sounded overly formal and emotionless. Like stilted dialogue badly read.

"I'll go get Coleman," said Pond, and left at a dead run.

"Perhaps you should sit down for a—" began Dr. Suliman, but whatever else he planned to say was lost forever as a hail of bullets punched into him and tore the life from him. And then a swarm of soldiers dressed all in black poured out of the stairwell and onto the quarantine floor. All of them were armed and every single gun was firing.

Church saw Major Mun stagger as she was hit by a fuselage of rounds that danced her back against the nurses' station. She had her guns out and returned fire, teeth gritted against the pain. Her ChemRig stopped the rounds . . . until it didn't. Bullets stitched across her body, finding those weaker areas at joints and waist and throat. Her last shots struck the ceiling because by then she was falling backward, mouth open as if in dreadful surprise.

Two other Bedlam agents rushed forward, one trying to protect Mun and the other putting himself between Church and the killers. They burned through whole magazines, cutting down some of the invaders. But there were simply too many, and some of God's Warriors were firing armor-piercing rounds. The RTI agents died with snarks of hate on their mouths, fingers tight on their triggers.

Bullets hit Church in the chest and stomach and he went down, too. He lay there, covered in blood, as still as death.

## CHAPTER 128

### HADRIAN TOWER
### LONDON, ENGLAND

I stared in absolute horror at the nightmare images on Rockwell's laptop.

Phoenix House.

Gone.

Utterly destroyed.

Church's apartment, his collection of priceless art and literature. Gone. His staff, gone. The apartments of the senior staff. Gone.

And what else?

The TOC, the training center, the main staff quarters, the mess hall, the kennels for the combat dogs—where Ghost waited for me. They were all down inside the cone of the old volcano. Had the force of that blast and the millions of tons of rock and stone from the castle come crashing down through the floors?

Were they gone, too?

Bug, Doc Holliday, Mustapha, Yoda, Nikki.

Ghost.

Did they see it coming and have time to get down into the bunkers below Phoenix House? Had some managed to get outside? Or . . . God help me, had I just witnessed the mass slaughter of everyone who was not here in London?

There was a pain in my heart so huge, so intense that I thought I was having cardiac arrest. It felt that bad, that real.

And part of me wanted to die, too.

Part of me.

The Modern Man. Maybe even the Cop.

Part of me. But not all of me. The Killer screamed in rage and hate and need. And behind him, swirling in a cage of my own willpower, the Darkness howled to be let out.

# AS GOD WILLS IT

# PART 6

**In 345 BCE, Philip of Macedon sent a message to the Spartan army:**

**"You are advised to submit without further delay,**

**for if I bring my army into your land,**

**I will destroy your farms, slay your people,**

**and raze your city."**

**The Spartans sent back a reply: *"If."***

**—PLUTARCH**

**"I don't know what your destiny will be,**
**but one thing I know:**
**the only ones among you who will be really happy**
**are those who will have sought and found how to serve."**

**—ALBERT SCHWEITZER**

# CHAPTER 129

## THE TOC
## OMFORI ISLAND, GREECE

**He Was Dying.**

He was sure of it.

It took him a long time to remember his name, or where he was. Or why he was there. Or anything specific.

The name came first. Someone had . . . had what?

Said it?

**Called it?**

Just before whatever happened . . . happened.

The name on the air in that last moment.

"Hey, Bug, can you—?"

A piece of a sentence. Not even a full question.

But the name was there.

Bug.

He knew that much, and the more he clung to the name, the more pieces of his identity crept into the mess that was his mind.

Computers. Always computers first. Mind . . . something.

. . . MindReader . . .

God, it was so hard to think.

He woke, not realizing he'd fallen asleep.

No.

Not . . .

. . . sleep.

Unconsciousness.

This time his mind was clearer. Less . . .

. . . jangled. Dusty. Broken.

He had been in the . . .

. . . tick-tock, hickory dock . . .

TOC.

Yes. He made himself deconstruct the acronym. Imposing order onto chaos.

Tactical.

Operations.

Center.

Yes.

Yes.

Why had he been there? It had been something important. That was immediately certain. Something very important. About the . . .

He woke up again and had to claw back the thread of his last remembered thought.

He had come to the TOC to say that he'd . . .

"I solved it," Bug said to the darkness that seemed to define everything about him. Solved what, though?

It was right there.

The . . . data files.

The damage. No, *fake* damage. It was hidden there. Then a big chunk of understanding burst in his mind.

It wasn't damaged. Nikki was right about that. Once Bug grasped what she saw, he could not unsee it. He threw everything he had, all of his insight into computers and software and structure and language differences and . . . and . . .

"I solved it."

The entire research logs, detailing every step of weaponizing *Yersinia pestis* so that the infection/symptom presentation cycle started within minutes of exposure. But that was only part of it.

The other thing . . .

That was what Bug had come to the TOC to announce. To share.

To say that . . .

. . . we just *won* this.

The cure was detailed in the computer records, hidden behind the fake data corruption.

That, and one short line that was so anomalous that he thought it was some fragment of software left over from a previously overwritten drive. But, no . . .

It was a statement. He knew that now.

*As God Wills It.*

As soon as he remembered that, he remembered who was in the TOC when he came running in.

Doc Holliday, looking outrageous in tight pink jeans and a sequined cowgirl blouse. Nikki Bloom, Bug's second-in-command and the pattern recognition genius. Major Claire Courtland.

Courtland was on a cell call and the others were leaning close to hear. Bug heard her, too, but his eyes snapped over to one of the screens on the big wall at the front of the TOC. It showed an exterior view of Omfori Island and the velvety night sky. A technician was rising in alarm, one hand stabbing a finger toward the screen as he began to shout. On the screen there were flashes of fire and then a confusion of smoky vapor trails as something—a *lot* of somethings—came flying toward Phoenix House. Just as Major Courtland said, "They're about to make their move. We have to—"

Then a whiteness. A redness. And then blackness.

Bug tried to open his eyes, but they felt pasted shut. When he tried to raise a hand to wipe whatever it was away, his left hand moved, but his right did not. He could feel his right hand. It would not move. He couldn't feel his fingers or anything on his right arm.

Or on his entire right side.

Or his legs.

Only his left was able to move and it took a long time to figure out how to raise it to his face and use his fingertips to clear his eyes. He blinked a lot, seeing brightness of a kind. It was yellow and it flickered.

When he looked at his fingertips, he was only slightly surprised to see how red and wet they were. He tasted it, then. That salty, coppery nastiness of blood in his mouth.

He did not start screaming then.

No.

The scream began as a gasp trapped in his chest. He turned and saw debris. Stone and brick and lath and beam. He saw pieces of machinery so badly mangled that he could not recognize or grasp what it could have been. He saw small fires flickering here and there. He saw severed wires sparking and dancing like electric snakes. They made him gasp as he realized what had happened—the flashes of fire were missiles being launched. The island had been attacked. That was obvious.

The gasp began a cry of alarm when he saw the technician who had gotten out of his chair to shout a warning. His name was Roger. Had *been* Roger. Now he lay on his back with the corner of the two-ton main viewscreen atop him. Roger looked flattened and his swollen tongue bulged from his open mouth.

Bug looked away, unable to bear the horror of that . . . and looked into the wide, beautiful brown eyes of Nikki Bloom. He stared into those eyes and saw that they were thin window glass behind which was an empty house from which all light and warmth and presence had fled. Bug could not see the injury that killed his best friend. That wasn't a mercy. There was no mercy to be found.

Not here.

Not anymore.

And Bug threw back his head and screamed.

## CHAPTER 130

### HADRIAN TOWER ATRIUM
### LONDON, ENGLAND

Remy heard them coming down the stairs from the balcony and continued to play dead. He could not actually feel the laser site, but knew there had to be one on him. The sniper wouldn't be the one coming down to take his pulse for proof of death. No. The shooter would be up there, watching and waiting, a round chambered and supple finger laid along the curve of the trigger guard.

He lay at an angle where he could see the stairs with extreme peripheral vision. His shoulder and the structure of his ChemRig hood would hide his eyes, but the sniper would see any other movement. And so he played dead.

When the people on the stairs came into view, he saw two sets of legs. Black trousers with limb-pads. Definitely Alpha Team.

Which meant what?

Was Alpha Team part of the bad guys? Or did they somehow

think *he* was with the assholes who released the plague? He didn't know. However, they had shot him down without any kind of warning. Was that outraged patriotism against someone they thought was endangering England?

He wanted to believe that, because then this situation might step back from a really bad brink.

"Yeah, he's down for the count," said a voice. "Those fancy rigs are trash."

"Be careful, though," said another. "I'm not seeing much blood."

"Bullet probably punched through the outer layer but lost too much force to come out. Like a .22 round to the head."

He watched them approach. He could see them more clearly now. Two men, both about average height, both wearing Alpha Team rigs. Both training their rifles at him. They stopped and looked down at him.

"Thought these Yanks were supposed to be tough," said the first one.

"No one's tough enough to go against the will of God," said his companion.

Which is when Remy understood.

"Wait," said the second one as he knelt to try and turn Remy over. "I'm not seeing an entry wound. Is this bloke—"

And Remy rolled over and shot him in the throat. Two rounds through the thinnest part of the tough armor, and then he shot the other in the face. As they fell, a bullet slammed into the floor where his head had been, but Remy was up, running like crazy to get out of range in that half a second as the sniper worked the bolt on the rifle. The next round caught him in the shoulder and pitched him face-first into a decorative shrubbery in a big tub. He fell twisting and rolled behind the pot as a third shot rang out.

He frowned, because the blast signature was wrong. Different. A higher caliber with a different tone. And no bullet struck either him or the tub. A moment later there was a heavy *thud* as something fell from the balcony.

Remy risked leaning out, doing so with his gun barrel pointing. A figure lay in an awkward and bloody sprawl on the floor twenty feet away. It was a man in black armor, but most of his head was gone, destroyed by a high-powered explosive round. He looked up sharply and saw a slim figure standing up there with a rifle in one hand, the barrel laid casually across her shoulders.

Belle.

Remy burst out laughing with relief, then he threw back his head and yelled, *"I love you!"*

Up above, Belle merely shook her head.

Then there was the distant but distinctive roar of automatic gunfire. Remy ran for the stairs, then together he and Belle went looking for another fight.

## CHAPTER 131

### SUBBASEMENT 3
### HADRIAN TOWER
### LONDON, ENGLAND

"Michael," said one of the Upierczy, "someone is coming."

Michael rose at once from where he had been kneeling to pray. The bodies of the Sabbatarians had been moved to one side of the big room, laid out in a row and with shirts or jackets placed with reverence over their faces. He crossed to meet Antoni, the soldier who had returned from a scouting mission in the other basement rooms.

"What have you found?"

"The outer wall was breached two levels up," said Antoni. "A group of heavily armed soldiers is searching that level."

"Describe them."

Antoni did and Michael nodded thoughtfully. "One of *his* teams. Bedlam or Chaos Teams."

"What should we do?"

Michael reached for his balaclava and pulled it on, then ordered everyone to check their weapons and prepare for battle.

"Let us go meet them," he said.

# CHAPTER 132

## ST THOMAS' HOSPITAL
## WESTMINSTER BRIDGE ROAD
## LONDON, ENGLAND

God's Warriors swarmed into the halls between the nurses' station and the row of isolation rooms where the victims of the plague suffered and died. Dr. Suliman lay in a tangle of limbs, his lab coat ripped apart by automatic gunfire, and his flesh torn to rags. He stared at the ceiling with fixed eyes that seemed to behold wonders no living person could perceive.

Several nurses were down, too—some as still as Suliman, others screaming from levels of pain that transcended anything they had ever experienced firsthand. Attending to the sick and injured and dying was in no way a preparation for what they now felt. The warriors began gathering everyone else up and shoving them into the corner of the solarium that faced the curved desk where nursing was overseen. There were more than a dozen people still uninjured, and these were the ones pushed and kicked and bellowed at until they all huddled in a cluster. Three men with machine guns stood in a line, smoking weapons aimed at them. A fourth man, tall and slender, stood near them with a drawn pistol held loosely in one hand, the barrel pointed at the floor.

"You lot are going to sit down here and shut the fuck up," he told the prisoners. "And before anyone gets any stray thoughts about being a hero then know this—if even *one* of you gives us shit, then we will kill that person and three others. That's the math. You can work out your own risk-reward ratios."

"Please," begged a radiologist, "who are you and what is this all about?"

The man with the pistol—Ames—walked over to him and spoke in a thick Cockney accent. "Do you have any family, mate? Wife? Some kids at home?"

"I . . . yes . . ."

"What's your wife's name?"

The doctor licked his lips. "Constance."

"Kids . . . ?"

"Colin and Liz."

"And your name?"

"Blake. Malcolm Blake."

"Nice," said Ames, and then he shot him in the face.

Everyone screamed as blood and tissue spattered them and Dr. Malcolm Blake slumped backward into death. The leader of the God's Warriors team glared at them all, then bellowed for them all to shut up. They did, though they cowered and tried to make themselves small and invisible.

"Anyone else here have a question for me?" Ames demanded, pointing at Blake's corpse with his gun. "No? Good. Now shut the fuck up and follow my goddamn rules."

They cringed and wept and none of them dared utter a word.

"Jinx, Powell, Edderly," he said to the three guards. "Stay here. Anyone so much as farts too loud then everyone dies. Am I clear?"

"As God wills it," they replied crisply.

"Damn right."

Ames signaled for several other warriors and a sergeant, and they came at the run. "Gather up the bodies and drag them into one of the rooms."

"Even him?" asked the sergeant, nodding to the sprawled body of Mr. Church.

"Especially 'im, but leave 'is body on top the pile. The man upstairs wants a photo of the legendary Mr. Church with all the people he failed."

"Why?" asked the sergeant. "It's not like he can put it on the Net."

"'Ow the fuck should I know? Maybe he wants your mother to tape it to her ass while the boss fucks her. What do I know? 'Ell, what do I care? Get it done. Clock's ticking."

"As God wills it." The sergeant turned to call some of the bigger men over to help. While they began their work, the soldier stood looking down at Church, who was covered with blood. "Big fucking scary man," he said. He kicked Church in the ribs twice. Very hard. All the body did was rock back and forth. "Not so fucking scary now, are ya?"

His men came and dragged the body away.

## CHAPTER 133

### BARRIER HEADQUARTERS
### HADRIAN TOWER
### LONDON, ENGLAND

James Rockwell watched me as I stared in horror at the devastation on the screen. I don't know for how long. It was probably no more than a full minute, though it felt like forever.

Phoenix House was gone. Not a stone of it still stood. Most of the main structure had been vaporized within the conflagration of those thirty-two Hellfire missiles. Battlements and towers and even the iron portcullis had been torn away, mangled, and hurled into the sea. Flaming pieces landed on the grounds, amplifying the roaring blaze that spread outward until every blade of grass, every tree, every flowering plant was dying in a firestorm of flames.

I sagged back against my chair, my foot still braced against the desk, and let the shock and hurt and loss have their way with me. Rockwell was not smiling at the moment. Instead, he seemed acutely interested in whatever he read on my face.

"Hurts, doesn't it?" he asked.

I said nothing.

"I thought it was poetic justice to use Hellfire missiles," he said conversationally. "After all, it's what the Deacon used against my uncle. I bet he thought there was poetry in that, too."

"You . . . you . . ." I began, but coughing took me and I let it.

He waited me out.

"That was why we've had this lovely chat, Ledger," Rockwell said. "Partly to stall long enough for the helos to get into place. Since Church is over at St. Thomas, I couldn't as easily give him a ticket for the show. But you . . . ah, you were here with me. And, yes, I'll admit that I wanted a witness. I wanted an audience, and there's justice in that, too. There should be witnesses to history. There should be witnesses for anything done *truly* in God's name."

"God . . . ?" I croaked.

"Like I said, I lean more Old Testament than New. God was angry back then. He said it himself, he's jealous. Sure, he allows free will, but that's like free speech—you can say whatever you want, but in some cases there are consequences. Yell 'fire' in a cinema and the coppers will trot you off to jail. God allows for other religions, but he doesn't like them. Exodus 20:3–5. *Thou shalt have no other gods before me*. And yet there's Allah and Muhammad."

"There are older religions, you assbag."

He shrugged. "I'll grant that some religions have been around for a while. The Hindus, Buddhists, whatever the hell those sand niggers in Australia believe in. Doesn't matter. We *know* what the true religion is and why it's the dominant one on this planet, and why true believers need to do whatever they have to in order to knock down those golden idols. God doesn't play well with others, and if you ever bothered to read the Old Testament you'll know how many times he told his people to make war on the pagans and followers of false gods."

"Stop with the fucking sermons," I growled. "If you are so religious, then what about everything Jesus said?"

"Oh sure, Jesus," said Rockwell with a dismissive wave of his hand. "God, talk about being a victim of bad reporting. His apostles didn't write the gospels. The whole New Testament was written after the Messiah died. We barely know what Jesus actually said and did. All that do-goody bullshit was propaganda ascribed to Jesus. The Church is as guilty as the Muslims. They twisted the holy truths into whatever was convenient for them. It's all public relations to sell a point of view that is so far away from the Old Testament that for any serious scholar—one who is devoted to God's truth—it's easy to discount. No, Ledger, the Red Empire respects and loves Jesus, but we don't believe we've ever gotten the straight story about him. The fact that the Romans crucified him is the key takeaway there. They were afraid of him, don't you get that? Jesus was probably a hell of a lot closer in temperament to his father, and there are ancient documents that say he was secretly working with Zealots in order to overthrow Herod and toss out the Romans. So, they trumped up a bunch of lies about him, discredited him, and nailed him up."

I stared at him. It was clear that beneath his cynicism and modernity, he believed what he was saying. He was a fanatic and clearly a murderous and radical one. There was no common ground left for us to stand on for a debate.

And I was dying.

I said, "You infected me. You killed Scott Wilson and most of the Barrier staff. You . . . destroyed . . . Phoenix House. And you have Church locked up in the hospital and my guys trapped here. Now what?"

"Now?" He looked mildly surprised at the question. "Now the war begins, Ledger."

## CHAPTER 134

### ST THOMAS' HOSPITAL
### WESTMINSTER BRIDGE ROAD
### LONDON, ENGLAND

Coleman worked faster than he had on other projects. Never had each tick of a wall clock sounded more like an accusation. Or a challenge.

Kingsnake hovered nearby, ready to fetch anything the doctor needed.

As Coleman worked, he narrated the process. Ostensibly for Kingsnake's benefit, but he actually worked best when he talked aloud.

"So," he said, "the normal antibiotic for use against *Yersinia pestis* is gentamicin. But this weaponized strain of the bacteria is resistant to that because of a mutation in a specific ribosomal protein, which means the antibiotic cannot fit where it needs to in order to stop the bacteria. That's our challenge."

"Can you do anything about that?" asked Kingsnake.

Coleman blinked as if surprised to discover the Chaos operative was still in the room. "Hmm? What? Oh . . . well we're not without options."

"Like what?"

Coleman went back to work. "It's my plan to take that antibiotic and, with the magic of organic chemistry, change gentamicin's *nature* so it would work."

"So . . . you're kind of weaponizing an antibiotic to kick the ass of a weaponized version of the plague bacteria."

"Pretty much. Though, obviously I left the deoxystreptamine core alone."

"Um, yeah. Sure. Obviously."

"But," continued Coleman, talking once more to himself, "I realized that a simple substitution in the C1a group would allow it to fit. Honestly, once I figured out what to do the chemistry is pretty straightforward. I'm using a pretty standard Hofmann elimination to reshape an unprotected amine and it fit."

"Amine? Isn't that those Japanese cartoons with all the robots and such?"

Coleman laughed, but shook his head. "Amine is a nitrogen connected to a carbon and two hydrogens."

"Ah. That would have been my, um, second guess."

Coleman went back to work.

# CHAPTER 135

## RESTRICTED BIOLOGICAL RESEARCH LABORATORY H-6
## LONDON, ENGLAND

Bunny roared with fear and fury and shook off the two infected who clung to his back, rising up to his feet as he did so. They landed hard but immediately began scrabbling to their feet, hissing and spitting with naked hate.

Both of them were lab techs in white lab coats. Both were spattered with blood and had mouths slick with gore from some awful feast. Bunny did not know whom they'd attacked, but with all that blood it must have been murderous. He fumbled for his Cloudburst shotgun, but it was gone, lost when he fell. He drew his two pistols—the Snellig dart gun in his left and a nine mil in his right.

Dr. Byrd swung her gun barrel toward him. She was not infected and she was not innocent and he shot her in the chest and face, blowing her eyes forever dark and sending her spinning to the floor. No Sandman for her. No mercy for her, either.

Then he pivoted and used the Snellig on the infected techs. They were not contagious, and the Rage itself would wear off in hours. Because they were infected and used as weapons, he had to go on the assumption that they were victims and not part of the Red Empire. He shot them with Sandman.

Rage was a powerful bioweapon that turned everyone into a mindless murder machine. But it did not change overall blood chemistry, and the Sandman tore into their flesh and pumped the cocktail of chemicals into their bloodstreams.

They went right down. There was no hesitation, no struggle against the effects. Both of them dropped as bonelessly as if he had killed them.

Bunny looked around and saw other figures milling in agitated confusion at the end of the hall. More of them were clawing at the doorknobs and crash-bars of different adjoining rooms.

"Christ," he growled and ran over to where Top lay. "Tell me you ain't dead, Old Man. If you are I swear to God I will have séances and resurrect your sorry ass."

Top blinked up at him. He licked his lips and coughed, steaming up the inside of his visor. "Ow," he said. "And I really fuckin' mean that."

"Don't scare me like that."

"Stop acting like my mother and help me up, Farm Boy."

Bunny bent and pulled his friend up. Top was a solid one-eighty, but Bunny lifted him easily and then stood with hands on the outside of Top's arms, holding him steady. Top pushed the hands away.

"I can stand on my own, damn it."

"You took a lot of hits. She put half a damn magazine into you."

Top touched the front of his ChemRig. "When I get back to the island, I'm going to bring Doc Holliday about six dozen red roses."

They looked around.

"How much shit are we in here?" asked Top.

The infected at the far end of the hall had stopped milling and were looking their way, each of them trembling as the impulses of the squid protein that was the heart of the Rage weapon began exerting its unbreakable imperatives. They threw back their heads and howled like demons, and then ran forward. It was not a slow acceleration but abrupt, going from idleness to shockingly fast movement.

Top reached for his Snellig but it was gone, and he had to look around to see where it went. Somehow it had fallen from its holster and skidded under the edge of a shared printer set near the corridor entrance. He dove for that while Bunny spotted his Cloudburst and flung himself toward that. Both of them scooped up their weapons and rose—Bunny on one knee and Top standing in a combat crouch.

As the howling infected raced toward them, the two men opened fire.

## CHAPTER 136

### THE TOC
### PHOENIX HOUSE
### OMFORI ISLAND, GREECE

Bug screamed himself raw and then fell into a silence and a stillness that frightened him.

He became more acutely aware of how little of his body he could feel. At first it was almost a comfort because he knew he should be in pain, but there wasn't much of it anywhere. Some bruises on his face and cuts on his scalp.

Now the absence of pain became as alarming as he knew it should be. There was no feeling at all below his chest. Nothing. It was as if he and his body were orbiting different stars in a vast darkness. He did not dare put names to what he thought might be happening beneath the pile of cracked stone and mangled machinery that covered him.

That same rubble covered most of Nikki, too. He kept telling himself he would not look into her dead eyes again, and each time he looked. Again and again. Bug worked for Mr. Church and he had seen all manner of violent death on field operation live feed. His own mother had been killed by a terrorist drone a few years ago. He had been right there when some terrible things happened. Death was known to him.

But this . . .

His encyclopedic mind replayed what happened. The missiles came from moving targets. Helicopters, then. The elevation was too high for an attack by boat. Air-to-surface missiles. Maybe HARM or Javelins or Hellfires. There were a lot of possible weapons, though given that they came from choppers, Hellfire seemed most likely.

They were ubiquitous and carried a lot of destructive form, living up to their name.

The trajectory intrigued him. The flight path—what he saw off it in those few seconds—suggested they were aimed at Phoenix House, the castle Church owned. There, but not at the base of the old volcano. Did they think that RTI was inside the castle?

Of course they did. *All* of the missiles were aimed at Phoenix House. Okay, but what did that tell him? What was the inference?

They had some knowledge but not enough. They didn't know about the RTI base being built in levels inside the heart of the island. The TOC was Sublevel 2. Sub-1 was the gym, armory, and training centers. The senior trainers and rangemaster had apartments on that level. That jabbed him again with the pain of likely loss.

The TOC took up most of Sub-1, and below that were five other levels with all the labs, the cold rooms where the rows of supercomputers lived—MindReader's heart and soul. His own suite of offices was on Sub-3. If Nikki had been in her office, would she be okay? Would she still be . . . ?

He started to cry. Softly.

And in the ruins of the TOC he felt more completely alone than he had ever felt.

## CHAPTER 137

**BARRIER HEADQUARTERS**
**HADRIAN TOWER**
**LONDON, ENGLAND**

"War . . . ?" I asked.

"You really must be so sick you're losing your ability to reason," Rockwell said as he went over to the wet bar and poured himself a fresh glass of whisky. By now he had to be buzzed, unless his newly enhanced physical condition buffered him from inebriation. He sat down heavily behind the desk, sipped his scotch, and smiled contentedly. "Here's the short version. You all get to die now."

"Me, maybe, but my guys are going to tear you apart for what you've done."

"Your guys? That's rich. Do you want to know about your group of misfit toys? Church is about to get buried in an avalanche of God's Warriors. I have fifty of them at the hospital now. Some in full battle kit, and some seeded among the staff. This isn't like fighting towelheads in the Middle East. My people look like ordinary folks. Even some dark-skinned folks working for us; people who—despite their skin color and background—have come to embrace our truth."

He sipped.

"Toys and his lot are probably dead by now. Your Chaos Team came in through the basement, and I have a shitload of Sabbatarians down there lying in wait."

"You think your crew of participation-trophy terrorists have a chance against a full RTI team?"

He laughed at that. "Participation-trophy terrorists. Man, that's brilliant. I'll have to use that. And, yes, there are a *lot* of Sabbatarians down there. One-to-one they suck, but in large numbers and in a confined space, I like the odds. Oh, and Top, Bunny, the lesbian nigger, and that jackass from New Orleans are probably dead by now, too."

"I'll let Belle know you said that." I tried to grin, but he snorted.

"Go ahead. If she lives long enough to take a run at me, then fine. I'll bust her up just enough so she's got to lie there and take what *else* I might choose to do."

Keeping my voice under control was a bigger labor than anything Hercules ever did.

"And then what?"

"Then we go to Phase Two," he said. "Which is already set up. A few assassinations here and there, some faux terrorist bombings with the blame directed at Islam, the Jews, and anyone else who stands in opposition to the righteous path laid down by the Red Empire."

He studied my face for a few moments.

"How are you feeling? You certainly look like something the cat would never have dragged in. This new plague variant works fast."

He looked at his watch.

"In about five minutes I'll give the word to detonate the hospital. Yes, we mined that place as well. Every bomb is made from parts sourced in Iran, Syria, Iraq, Egypt, and Qatar. Then, while all eyes are turned that way, me and my team will make our exits from the Tower and then we'll blow it, too. Couple of big bangs that collectively match the World Trade Center hits. Which is the point. Everything points to Islamic extremists. And, since both buildings are wired with incendiaries, not only will it destroy the plague, thereby saving London—cue the applause of a grateful nation—but it will hide my disappearance. It'll take months or years—if ever—for them to realize I'm not in the rubble. And by then . . . well, let's just say the shit would already have hit the fan. We've seeded evidence out on the Net to support this. What a *shame* that MindReader no longer exists because that's about the only thing that could have gotten in our way. Damn good thing I'm a forward-thinking kind of chap."

"So am I," I said, and used my braced foot and every ounce of rage I possess to shove his desk back against him. The heavy oak top slammed into him, catching Rockwell in the stomach as he was taking another sip of whisky.

And then I launched myself from my chair. Sick or not, dying or not, the Killer surged over the desk and I tackled him, stabbing at his face with the pen I'd hidden under my leg.

# CHAPTER 138

## RESTRICTED BIOLOGICAL RESEARCH LABORATORY H-6
## LONDON, ENGLAND

The Cloudburst did the greatest work. It was the first field test of a shotgun loaded with shells packed with cellulose flechettes filled with Sandman. The greater power of the weapon caused the darts to damage exposed flesh, and several of the infected reeled away with gashes in their faces and throats and their reaching hands. One dart caught a middle-aged Indian woman in the eye. She fell just as quickly and surely as the others.

Bunny felt a pang about it, though, knowing this woman was an innocent victim of the pathogen released by the traitorous Dr. Byrd. She would likely lose that eye, but there was no way to un-ring the bell of this unfolding violence. He tried to console himself with the knowledge that a lost eye was far better than the spray of lead pellets from a standard shotgun. He felt like a coward and a bully.

Even so, he fired the weapon until every single infected was down. Top did the same, opening doors to the adjoining rooms and darting the people in there. He lost count after the first dozen.

The Snelligs were quiet weapons, even the shotgun, and so the battle unfolded inside an envelope of eerie quiet, with the guns whispering and the screams of the infected dwindling one by one.

Until Top and Bunny stood there, guns out, chests heaving, icy sweat running down their faces and bodies inside their ChemRigs. When there was no more movement, they remained standing, even as their arms began to tremble from holding the guns out.

Then, moving very slowly, they lowered their guns. Bodies lay all around them. Only one was truly lifeless—Dr. Byrd—but everyone else *looked* so damn dead.

"God in heaven," breathed Bunny.

Top shook his head. "God sure as shit ain't here."

He tapped his comms and got nothing. Tried his cell and got the same result. Bunny gave him a hard look. "Communications are completely down and then this happens? How deep is the shit we're standing in?"

Top dropped the spent magazine from his Snellig and slapped in a new one. "I don't know, Farm Boy, but we need to find the colonel and the others and see about getting ahead of this shit."

They turned and ran for the airlock to get the hell out of there.

## CHAPTER 139

**THE TOC**
**PHOENIX HOUSE**
**OMFORI ISLAND, GREECE**

Bug heard a sound and it made him go still to listen.

It was soft.

Dust falling from the ceiling?

Was it a loose bit of debris tumbling down from one of the many mountains of rubble?

He heard it again. No. Not a random noise. It was definite. A step? And . . . a grunt?

He strained to hear, not wanting this to be a hallucination.

Another step, this time with a scuffing noise as if the foot slipped on a dusty surface. Not a grunt this time. A curse. Low. *Female.*

*Was it Nikki? God, please, let it be her. Was he wrong about her being . . . about . . .*

His thoughts raced ahead of logic and what he knew was the truth. No. It wasn't ever going to be Nikki Bloom again.

"Wh-who's . . . there . . . ?" His voice was barely a voice at all. Thin and weak, sounding far away even to his own ears.

The sounds stopped so suddenly that Bug thought his words did nothing more than chase a delusion away.

Then . . .

"Bug . . . ?"

He knew the voice, but it was as impossible as if he'd heard Nikki's voice. This was a woman, but the voice was another woman Bug had known and cared about, had been close with, but who died. Years ago. It couldn't be her.

"Here . . . I'm over here . . ." he called.

"Hang on, mate," said the voice. "Keep talking so I can find you."

"I'm here . . ." he said, and sobbed again. He was here with the dead, and one of the dead was coming for him. Why?

Why else?

To take him with her down to death's kingdom.

That was okay. He could accept that. He had fought in Mr. Church's war for all of his adult life. He believed in the war and knew that no matter how many battles they won the war would go on. The war was, after all, the war. But not everyone had to keep fighting the war forever. People were allowed to do their part and then lay down their swords and shields and find a peaceful place on which to lie down and rest.

That's what this was, he was sure of it. What was it called when a ghost came to escort the soul of a dying person away from the ruins of life? A psychopomp? He thought that was the right word.

The steps were getting closer. More dust fell from the cracked ceiling. The only light was from the fires, but those did not seem to be spreading. Merely burning.

"I'm here," he said. "I'm ready to go . . ."

A shadow moved across his vision, but in silhouette against a burning leather chair. It paused there, but try as he might, Bug could not make out the face. He knew her, though. He mourned for her for years.

The figure bent and grasped the corners of something and straightened, lifting it off of him. It was heavy, and she grunted with effort, cursing a little as she struggled to move it.

Bug almost smiled. Even ghosts have to really put some elbow grease into things. How strange.

The big object fell away and rolled heavily down the pile of debris on which he lay. With it gone he felt pain—*real pain*—for the first time. His entire body seemed to explode into a million separate and burning points of searing white-hot agony. He felt every nerve ending in his chest, his ribs, his waist, his stomach, his hips, his . . . legs.

Bug screamed again. So loud that he felt the force of it tearing the flesh of his throat.

The ghost kept working, lifting pieces of metal and stone, levering some and pushing some, and deconstructing the tomb of junk in which his body was buried. With each piece removed he felt more of his body. More of the damage. Leg and hips. His right arm. His stomach. The pain was so big that he nearly passed out again.

"Stay with me, Bug," said the ghost.

He reached up for her. He wanted to touch her. To tell her how much he missed her all these years. The ghost paused and took his hand. She squeezed it and her flesh was not as cold as he expected. Not like he thought a ghost's should be.

"I . . . missed you, Grace," he said. The words were broken by a sob. "I missed you so much."

The specter knelt by him, holding his hand in one of her own. With the other, she caressed Bug's cheek.

"I missed you," he said again. "Do you remember how we used to laugh at the goofy things Joe would say?"

"Yes," said Major Claire Courtland. "Of course I remember."

He smiled at her then. Even as his eyes closed and darkness took him, he smiled.

# CHAPTER 140

### HADRIAN TOWER
### LONDON, ENGLAND

"Havoc coming in," called Remy, and at the far end of a hallway they saw Top and Bunny standing amid a cluster of Alpha Team soldiers. The black-armored killers were down and gun smoke drifted slowly away from them.

Bunny waved them on.

"We're in deep shit, kids," he said.

"You're a little late with that news," Remy said and quickly told them what happened in the atrium.

"You're sure the shooters belonged to Alpha Team?"

"One hundred percent," Remy affirmed, and nodded to the ones who lay on the floor. "Same as those. When I was on the atrium floor playing possum, I heard them talking. They call themselves God's Warriors."

Top and Bunny exchanged a look.

"Really, 'God's Warriors'? Are we talking Sabbatarians with an upgrade?"

Top thought about it, then shook his head. "Don't think so. Else they would have sent guys like these after Outlaw when they confronted him at the cemetery. No, I think this is something else."

He knelt between two corpses and removed their helmets and visors, then thumbed their upper lips up to examine their teeth. He straightened.

"They ain't next-gen Red Knights, either."

"Yeah," said Bunny, "but who's that leave?"

"Maybe the Red Order?" he suggested. "The Knights used to be their SpecOps team, but we pretty much shut that shit down. And, besides, they turned on the Order anyway."

"You lost me, Pappy," said Remy. "I mean, I get who the Red Order are, and who the Sabbatarians are, and the Knights. What's that make these God's Warriors?"

"Makes them bad guys," Top said. "All I need to know right now."

"Yeah, but there's like forty of them in here."

"Closer to thirty," Bunny corrected. "Between the ones here and the ones you and Belle spanked downstairs."

"Okay, thirty, but there's four of us."

"Five counting Outlaw," said Bunny.

"And we don't know where he is," Top said angrily. "Comms and cells are still out."

Belle nodded. "There were more of these shooters upstairs. They came for me in the monitoring suite. Too many for me to handle, so I ran and hid. I think they killed the guard who was with me. I heard him screaming and then there was a shot."

"Listen," Remy said, looking stressed. "I found the building security director, Griffiths, dead downstairs, too. Somebody fucked him but real good. And there was a ChemRig near his body. I think it was Outlaw's. Torso armor was gone, though."

Bunny shook his head. "Why would he take his rig off? The air here is poison soup."

Top didn't answer but he looked deeply troubled.

"I found Ken Manning in a stairwell," said Belle.

"Where is he now?" Top demanded.

"Where I found him. He was already dead. Ate his gun."

Top said, "He must have been involved. Guilty conscience, maybe. Fuck him. Where's Outlaw?"

No one had an answer.

"Where do we look?" Belle asked.

"Barrier?" said Top and Bunny at the same time. "Maybe this whole thing was an attack on Barrier, which means that Rockwell and the colonel are up there like it's the Alamo."

"Wasn't the Alamo a massacre?" asked Belle, then immediately looked sorry she'd brought it up.

Top went to the balcony rail and pointed up. Hadrian Tower was hollow, with all of the offices wrapping around the great central shaft. "Let's start there."

They ran for the elevators.

Two of the cars opened when they were still forty feet away. A second car reached their floor a moment later. Both were crammed with figures in black armor.

# CHAPTER 141

## BARRIER HEADQUARTERS
## HADRIAN TOWER
## LONDON, ENGLAND

I stabbed him as hard as I could, hoping to drive the pen into one eye and then into the cesspit that he called his brain.

Rockwell was quick, though. He turned his head and the penpoint dug into his ear. Blood welled and I leaned in, trying to push it deeper. But Rockwell got a hand between us, palm flat on my sternum, and shoved. It was like being hit by a car. I flew backward across the desk, slid, and fell onto the floor near where I'd started.

Winded and sick as I was, I immediately shoved my full weight against the desk, hoping to keep him pinned, or maybe exacerbate any damage already inflicted. Then another shove drove the desk—and me—away. I rolled sideways, ignoring the broken glass on the floor from the destroyed trophy case.

Rockwell stood swaying, his face screwed up in terrible pain as he took hold of the pen and pulled it out of his ear. Blood poured down his shirt. He looked at the pen and then threw it at me with such shocking force that it stuck into the wall like a knife, its end vibrating. Then he gripped the edge of the desk and spun it halfway around. When he took a step toward me he nearly fell, and had to grab that desk to steady himself.

I knew it wasn't merely pain that made him so unsteady. The pen had gone deep enough to rupture an eardrum and disrupt the vestibular system that controlled balance.

"You fucking bastard," he snarled. Then he banged his fist on the desktop. "I'm going to literally rip you limb from limb. Think that's just something people say? Let me show you the real deal."

He pushed off the desk and took a step toward me. I scooped up a trophy—no idea what it was for—and slid it fast as I could along the floor so that it was right where his foot landed. His foot shot out and up and he went down hard. So I threw four more trophies at him, hitting him in the crotch and chest and twice in the face. One of the trophies was all spikes and it slashed him from the side of his mouth to the lobe of one ear.

We both tried to get up. I slipped on glass, cutting my palms and my knee. His balance was for shit and he fell once getting up.

I knew I hadn't hurt him bad enough. Not yet. And God, how I wanted to ruin everything that defined him as a human being. The room was spinning like a top and I could feel my pulse in my ears, hammering at me like a deranged monkey using a steel pot as a drum.

Rockwell pawed the blood from his face, looked at it on his palm, and flicked the drops at me as he charged. I ducked and threw my weight forward, hitting him in the gut while his reaching arms grabbed air above me. Then I tried to punch his floating ribs into breadcrumbs, and even landed a couple of good ones, but Rockwell was recovering and he brought an uppercut up from the basement and drove it all the way to my backbone. It lifted me off the floor and folded me in half. As I dropped, he kicked me, but that, at least, was weaker because his balance was still bad.

I took the force of the kick and used it to roll away from him and allow myself time to drag a teaspoonful of air into my lungs. That punch definitely did some damage and when I coughed, blood sprayed the floor.

Half the lights in my brain were flickering and the other half were out. So, it took me that long to remember how quickly and badly he'd searched me. He took my guns and my combat knife, but he hadn't dug into my pockets. He was either too confident in his newfound power or he assumed that he'd gotten everything of use. In my head I could hear my mom scolding me after I'd made an assumption about how well an umbrella would work as a parachute. I'd conned Sean into trying it by jumping off the shed roof. The umbrella turned inside out and Sean bruised his tailbone. This was when I was eight and Sean was little. I told her that I thought it would work. And she said that was an assumption. "When you assume, Joey, it makes an ass of U and me."

If I felt better, or if this was a good moment for sarcastic wit, I might have said it to him in the same singsong voice. Or maybe not.

Instead, I reached halfway into my pants pocket, hooked fingers around the handle, and pulled. The spring released it into my hand and with a snap of my wrist the blade snapped into place. All of that took about half a second and him charging me took maybe a quarter. He hit me like the 20th Century Limited, driving me backward toward the closed office door.

He slammed me against the oak door, pinned me with a flat palm on my chest, and began throwing punches. I saw the first one coming and drove the four-inch blade into his body. Not sure where the first hit struck. My brain was going dark. Then the fist hit me in the face and I felt my cheekbone crack.

My arm kept moving, almost of its own accord. Tearing the knife free and stabbing. Again and again.

And it did not seem to stop him at all.

Another big punch floated my way and I knew that this was it. This was the end.

Then the whole world seemed to explode.

## CHAPTER 142

### BARRIER HEADQUARTERS
### HADRIAN TOWER
### LONDON, ENGLAND

The four members of Havoc Team scattered, each of them diving for what little cover was available as God's Warriors piled out of the elevator cars, guns blazing.

It was immediately and overwhelmingly intense.

Belle tucked herself behind a trash can in a decorative stone base. It wouldn't stand up to persistent fire, but it was a haven for the moment. She unslung her sniper rifle. Like most of the better rifles in that class, hers was bolt-action because the design allowed for superior accuracy, reduced weight, and overall reliability. In that moment, however, she wished she had one of the HK automatic rifles, or even a good old-fashioned AK-47. This fight was so close-range that volume of ammunition was likely to play a bigger role than shot-by-shot accuracy.

Across the hall, Remy had flattened out behind a mail delivery cart heavy with boxes that had been abandoned during the forced evacuation. He was busy digging through his pouch for drones that could work autonomously rather than via radio-control. With the jammers still operating, the more sophisticated drones were so much deadweight.

Top and Bunny had ducked into recessed office doorways. Both of them had been carrying Snelligs, but now they switched back to standard firearms.

By the elevators, the armored warriors were scattering. They had greater numbers but less cover. A few backpedaled into the elevator cars, while some flattened out on the floor. Three of the slower soldiers went down in the first few seconds, because Havoc was loaded with armor-piercing rounds.

Remy found two RoadRunner drones that were little more than wind-up toys, but designed to move fast. There were Velcro straps on the bag that allowed the devices to carry anything from extra magazines to first-aid supplies during a firefight. He turned them on and waited until the motors were humming, then he took two fragmentation grenades from his chest harness, strapped them in, pulled the pins, and set them down.

"Fire in the hole," he called as the RoadRunners raced toward the elevators.

The shooters at the end of that hall fired at the devices, hitting one and causing it to race toward the balcony. The other made it to within fifteen feet of the prone shooters. By then the Warriors saw what the payload was and tried to rise and run. Havoc poured on the suppressing fire and the grenades detonated.

The bomb on the wayward drone blew out a chunk of the balcony rail big enough to drive a compact car through. The one closer to God's Warriors tore four of them to rags and flung meat and burning pieces of body armor against the walls.

In the confusion, Bunny plucked off one of his grenades, stepped out of hiding, and hurled it overhand. It flew right into one of the elevator cars and exploded. Pieces of things that no longer even vaguely resembled the men they had been were hurled out onto the floor.

The rest of the ambush team scrambled to their feet, firing continuously as they backed up to the bank of elevators and then cut right down the hall.

"Get the bastards," growled Top, and he was off running, with the other three in close pursuit. But they all skidded to a stop when fresh gunfire erupted out of sight around the corner. Two of the Warriors fell back into view, their helmets pieced by rounds and blood painting the walls.

Havoc flattened out on the wall and, with Top leading, edged quickly to the T-juncture. The firing was intense for a few moments and then faded out into an eerie silence. Top risked a quick look, pulling back at once and letting his mind process what his eyes had seen.

"What the fuck?" he breathed.

Then a voice rang out. "Friendlies. Chaos to Havoc, we are friendlies."

Top knew that voice. Knew it very well. It was Captain Luis Salazar, top-kick of Chaos.

"Sinbad, that you?"

"All's clear here, Pappy."

"You ain't alone," Top called back. "Who's that with you? And I better like the answer."

There was a brief pause. Then Salazar walked slowly into view, holding his rifle over his head with one hand. Hazi Gafford was with him, her face streaked with dust and blood, but she was smiling a strange little smile.

"It's me, Top," said Salazer. "And I brought some friends."

With all of Havoc in a shooting line, they watched as Chaos Team walked up, guns lowered. And with them were several men dressed all in black. Not in God's Warriors body armor, but simpler black clothing. They also wore balaclavas and goggles with unusual red lenses.

One of them, taller than the others, reached up and pulled off his mask, to reveal a thin, ascetic face and eyes that were as red as those of a sewer rat. Top swiveled his gun barrel to point directly at that pale face.

"What the fuck is this shit?" he demanded.

Salazar took two careful steps forward so that he stood between Top and the stranger. He reached up and slowly, gently pushed Top's gun down.

"We have a lot to talk about," he said.

## CHAPTER 143

### ST THOMAS' HOSPITAL
### WESTMINSTER BRIDGE ROAD
### LONDON, ENGLAND

"You want me to stand here and guard a bunch of bloody stiffs?" The soldier was a thick-bodied lowland Scot. He looked imploringly at his sergeant, but all he got was a shake of the head. "Seriously, Sarge? I'm going to miss all the fun."

"Fun's nearly over, mate," said the sergeant. "Soon as we get that Coleman asshole added to the pile then we can take the pics and get the hell out of here."

The Scotsman sighed. "All this for a photo? How's that make any sense?"

The sergeant stepped close and tapped the man on the forehead with the pad of one thick finger. "This is what the Scriptor wants done. Or should I pass along your request to his suggestion box? Bet he'd love to hear that you're dissatisfied with his orders."

The soldier's face went dead pale. "No, wait . . . I was just taking the piss. Just joking about. I didn't mean nothing by it."

"Just do your job, Ferguson."

"As . . . um . . . God wills it. Yes, Sergeant."

The sergeant left the room and Ferguson was left with the bodies of the murdered dead. He closed the door and tried not to look at the corpses. The bullets had torn them apart, revealing internal organs and broken shards of bone. And, typical of people who died violent deaths, some of them had shit themselves as sphincter muscles relaxed. The room smelled worse than a construction site portaloo.

The bodies were heaped in what had been an office shared by specialists called in for temporary matters. There was a desk and chair, a single visitor's chair, a locked file cabinet, and a worktable. The desk had been pushed out of the way to allow for the stacking of the corpses. The floor had bloody drag-tracks and the soldier had to be careful not to slip. He was sure there was some shit mixed in with the blood in those trails.

Ferguson dragged the visitor chair to the farthest point in the room and sat, laying his rifle across his thighs, and the chair angled mostly away from the dead bodies. He was told to guard them, but no one said he had to watch them.

However, before he turned away to look at the blank and bloodless wall, he paused to study the slack face of the man he and all of his fellow soldiers had been taught to fear. Mr. Church. The Deacon. The Nameless Man. The one that people said even Father Nicodemus was afraid of.

Dead now. Dead as all hell. His clothes were torn and he was painted red with blood.

Ferguson began to say something. A bit of trash talk, like what the sergeant had said. Maybe kick him as the sergeant had done. Just so he could say he did it. But the more he looked into those dark, dead, unblinking eyes, the more he wanted—needed—to look absolutely anywhere else.

He touched his chest, where a small tattoo of a red crown surrounded by a circle lay. All of them had that tattoo. Every foot soldier, all of God's Warriors were blessed with the symbol of the Red Empire. It was there as a sign of having been ordained as a warrior monk. It was a talisman against evil.

At that moment, though, he felt no comfort from it. Not at all.

## CHAPTER 144

### ST THOMAS' HOSPITAL
### WESTMINSTER BRIDGE ROAD
### LONDON, ENGLAND

"We got incoming," yelled a sergeant as he came running from the closest stairwell.

All of God's Warriors whipped around, raising their weapons.

"Where and how many?" demanded Ames as he drew his pistol.

The sergeant jerked to a stop. "What's left of Bedlam Team is coming up the stairs. I think they picked up some hospital security guys, too. There's eight of them total on the stairs, three floors down and coming fast."

Ames went into action, detailing shooters to set up an ambush on the top landing, and had others gather the hostages in case they needed a barrier that the RTI team would never shoot through.

Then he took out a device about the size of a cell phone and carefully opened the cover. There was a keypad for a code, and he punched it in with utmost care. A light turned green at the top of the screen and a small symbol—the red circle around a regal crown—appeared on the touchpad.

The code activated the explosives throughout the hospital. With more than a dozen operatives seeded into the hospital's maintenance staff over the last eighteen months, it was fairly easy to bring the bombs in. They were a mix of two kinds of high explosives. One was an industrial type that would destroy the building's structural supports in a way that would blow out the ground floor first, forcing the upper floors to pancake down. The rest of the mix was a special blend of thermite and other substances that would burn with ferocious intensity. The goal—destroy the building and everyone inside of it, while incinerating every last trace of the plague.

If this was truly Bedlam Team, then the last of Ames's goals was being met—killing Mr. Church, ensuring that Dr. Coleman and the other specialists Church brought in were in-house, and trapping Bedlam inside. He knew that his counterpart over at Hadrian Tower would be doing the same thing as soon as his goals were achieved. Over there, Joe Ledger, along with Havoc and Chaos teams, would be trapped inside, and when those bombs blew, every bit of evidence that Mr. Rockwell was ever involved with would be blown to bits and burned to ash. The same was true for Fresh-N-Clean. He'd already gotten word that the RTI headquarters on that Greek island was destroyed.

Everything was going according to plan, and this would be a total clean sweep, leaving the world without any version—any *piece*—of what Church had built. He was the real prize, and Ames could not be more proud that his team had taken out the man even Rockwell feared. Ames had avenged the murder of the last Scriptor of the Red Order, and he had done it to please the first Scriptor of the Red Empire.

Two last details remained.

Killing Bedlam Team and getting the hell out of the hospital alive. One was easy, because he had the numbers. Eight of them to twenty-nine of God's Warriors. He loved that kind of math.

The timer was running now, and it was all going to work.

He punched the sergeant's shoulder lightly. "Tell you what, Jimmy, I'm going to let you take care of those twats. Toss some grenades down or whatever. Do it fast, though. Clock's ticking."

Jimmy, the sergeant, grinned like a shark and spun away, calling for the shooters he knew best. They ran in a pack toward the stairwell, passing the room where the corpses lay.

## CHAPTER 145

### FRESH-N-CLEAN
### CRANBROOK ROAD
### ILFORD, ENGLAND

The battle raged and raged and then . . . stopped.

Toys and his remaining team members played almost no part in it, but instead crouched in their shallow hiding places and watched with amazement as the Sabbatarians, God's Warriors, and the newcomers with their red goggles filled the hallway with more ammunition than Toys had ever seen discharged in a single battle. A ricochet hit Rugger and he collapsed, clutching a bleeding thigh with both hands. Rent Boy had his shoulder clipped twice and while neither was a mortal wound, they bled with disheartening enthusiasm. Muppet took a splinter as long as a steak knife in his left buttock and had to jam a fist into his mouth to keep from screaming.

The gunfire was so intense at times that Toys actually *did* scream.

Then it was done.

It dwindled to sporadic shots and then nothing at all.

Toys was afraid to look, but knew he had to. He leaned out only as far as necessary and was shocked by what he saw. The far end of the hall was a slaughterhouse in which nothing moved except gun smoke that was tinted red. The walls were so heavily pocked with bullet holes that it looked like an art installation showcasing the horrors of war.

When he turned the other way to see if the exit door was clear, he ducked back at once.

There were three of the men in black suits and red goggles standing there. All of them had guns, and he knew that they saw him. Toys had no grenades left and only half a magazine for his pistol. Everyone else was injured.

He began to steel himself for what was almost certainly going to be a suicide run—to lean out and try to take those three before they cut him down. If he could manage it, then at least the rest of his Wild Hunt would be able to escape.

A voice, heavily accented with what sounded like Romanian, spoke out clear and, oddly, calm.

"Are you Colonel Joseph Ledger?"

Toys almost laughed at the absurdity and randomness of the question.

"Oh *hell* no, and thank God for that," he yelled back.

"Who are you?" asked the speaker.

"Who the fuck are *you*?"

"A friend."

"We don't seem to have any friends here, or haven't you noticed."

"Perhaps 'enemy of your enemy' might be more apt," said the man. There was a pause, then a rifle came sliding along the floor. Toys could hear the scuff of footfalls that were so clear he knew that the man was announcing his approach. "We need to talk. I am unarmed."

Toys braced himself, ready to take the shot.

A moment later a figure stepped into view. He held no weapon and had his hands raised. He had removed his black balaclava and the face Toys looked into was entirely unknown to him. Toys aimed the pistol at the man's forehead.

"Who in the effing hell are you?" he demanded.

The man actually smiled. "My name is Nakir," he said quietly. "I am a team leader for the *Vampirii Lui Dumnezeu*. And we are here to help you save London from the Black Death."

# CHAPTER 146

**BARRIER HEADQUARTERS**
**HADRIAN TOWER**
**LONDON, ENGLAND**

I fell to my knees then toppled onto my face.

What was left of my face.

There was blood in my eyes, and more of it leaked from my nose and mouth. Rockwell's last punch was the hardest blow I had ever felt. More powerful than the blows that Grigor, the king of the Red Knights, used on me during the Assassins Code case in Iran.

It was freakishly strong and my real surprise was why I was still alive. It should have smashed my head to pulp and broken my neck. I should be lying there dead.

So . . . why wasn't I?

Why had Rockwell stopped hitting me? There was too much blood in my eyes to see anything. I could feel the knife handle in my hand. Its structure and how it fit into my hand was a kind of anchor to the real world. A tether to life in some odd way.

It took me forever to get to my feet and I immediately vomited. Mostly liquid and bile, and it burned the hell out of my throat. Literal insult to injury. My balance faltered and I fell sideways, but hit shoulder and hip against the remains of the trophy case. A few little pieces of glass jabbed me, but that level of pain was so minor compared to the overwhelming universe of agony I was in that I didn't much care.

I rested there, gasping in what air I could while I tried to sponge the blood out of my eyes. Even with the return of vision, things were still out of focus and distorted. I knew that the concussion I'd gotten earlier was now much worse. I had no illusions about my being able to get out of this. I wanted to, because I wanted to kill every one of these Red Empire sons of bitches, and I wanted to pet Ghost again, and I wanted to hold Junie in my arms in some place where no one hated me and tried to hurt those I love.

But, I thought if I just could manage to kill James Rockwell then at least there would be some closure. Some sense of justice.

That's when my vision returned by slow degrees and I looked around the ruin of the office but didn't see him. Then I noticed that a section of wall was at a wrong angle and realized it was the concealed opening to his executive bathroom.

Knife in hand, I staggered along the wall using it as a crutch to keep me from falling, leaving bloody footprints behind me, feeling my whole body wanting to just simply collapse in on itself. No one was built for the kind of stuff that had been happening to me. I'm a strong and very fit individual, but I was way past any pretense at combat readiness.

When I reached that door, I held the knife between my teeth and tried to dry the blood off my palm and fingers so I had a decent grip. Then I took the weapon in my right, grabbed the edge of the door with my left, and pulled it open.

And Rockwell was right there. He sat on the closed lid of the toilet seat and there was a widening pool of blood around his feet. A syringe with a few drops of some reddish gold liquid lay on the floor next to an empty vial. The door to the medicine chest stood open, and a whole row of little bottles identical to that one stood there. Didn't take a fully functioning brain to grasp that this was the concoction that gave him his incredible strength. Would it also help him heal from the stab wounds I'd given him?

Maybe I would never get the answer to that question because he held a pistol in one bloody hand and the barrel was pointing right at me.

## CHAPTER 147

### ST THOMAS' HOSPITAL
### WESTMINSTER BRIDGE ROAD
### LONDON, ENGLAND

Jimmy Howell was a former SAS operative who had seen action during three tours in Afghanistan. When he left the service, a recruiter for the Red Empire bought him his first beer as a civilian.

Three weeks later Howell was on a plane to the nation of Georgia where an Empire training center was in full swing. He was a natural leader of men and his lads all liked and respected him. When he called for volunteers, even for the more dangerous gigs, he always got takers. Now he had a full dozen of God's Warriors with him, some of whom he had personally trained. Smart, strong, and brave, and he loved them all.

He entered the stair tower and took a quick look over the pipe rail. But with the hospital lights out and only dim safety lights on each landing he couldn't see a thing. He backed out, and at the entrance to the fire tower he told his corporal to drop some party favors. The corporal pulled the pins on two fragmentation grenades and tossed them down to where he could hear feet moving carefully on the concrete steps.

Everyone faded back as the grenades exploded, sending a tornado of fiery smoke funneling up.

Then Howell had four of his men enter the fire tower and empty a couple of magazines down into the smoke. In the confines of the tower, the guns made a deafening thunder. Howell signaled them to stop and then he stepped up to the rail and listened. The smoke was thick and it was utterly black down there, the grenade shrapnel having put paid to the emergency lights.

"Yep, that's about done it." He turned to the corporal. "I surely do love it when a plan comes together."

Behind him he heard a commotion and turned to see something large and round come flying at him. Howell got a hand up in time to bash it away. It hit a wall, bounced onto the ground, and rolled right up to the sergeant's booted feet.

He looked down into the face of Ferguson, the Scottish soldier left to guard the corpses.

Howell said, "What . . . ?"

And then the shadows took him.

## CHAPTER 148

### THE TOC
### PHOENIX HOUSE
### OMFORI ISLAND, GREECE

Major Courtland seemed to be everywhere. Pulling people out of the wreckage. Covering bodies with whatever cloth they could find. Dressing wounds. Administering jabs of painkillers. Finding work lights and turning them on. Helping others get themselves together enough to help.

The TOC was a total ruin, and there were far too many silent forms under makeshift shrouds. Twenty-six so far.

The survivors were a smaller community. Eight awake. Five unconscious.

Now she knelt by someone who hovered on the edge of life and death. Courtland had applied compression bandages to the deep cuts, but there were two pieces of metal strutting from a destroyed worktable that were buried deep—one in the woman's stomach and the other in her chest. The struts were plugging the wounds they caused, but their placement was dreadful, especially the one that was shockingly close to her heart. The victim would need surgery and a lot of it. Soon.

Even so, the woman was awake. Sometimes it happens that way—shock that manifests as a kind of precise, nearly calm clarity. Bright blue eyes looked up from a bloody face, watching Courtland work.

"Pack it tighter around the entry point of the wound," suggested the victim. "It'll help keep that thing from banging around and trying to break my heart."

Courtland did that, being as quick as care would permit. When she was done she sat back on her heels and wiped her own dark hair from a sweaty forehead. "Best I can do for now."

Doc Holliday looked down at the shaft of metal that rose from her chest. "Stake through the heart and I'm still ready to kick ass and take names."

"I have to go find some kind of working phone or radio," said Courtland. "We need—"

"I know what we need, sugar. You go do what you gotta do. I'll just stay here and contemplate my list of personal sins. That should take a while and it'll be wildly entertaining."

They smiled at each other, neither willing to yield to the presence of death, which loomed above them.

"Hold on, Doc," said Courtland. "I'll be as fast as I can."

She rose reluctantly from the scientist's side and looked around. Some of the less injured survivors had shaken off enough of their shock to be moving around, doing for others what she had done for them. Courtland nodded.

Then she climbed over the devastation of the room toward the exit that led to the lower levels where, she hoped, there was something she could use as a lifeline.

# CHAPTER 149

## BARRIER HEADQUARTERS
## HADRIAN TOWER
## LONDON, ENGLAND

"At least I get to take you out," said Rockwell. There was blood on his lips and some ran from the corners of his mouth.

"Church will find you and tear your heart out," I said.

Rockwell laughed, then winced. But his smile remained despite the pain. "Mr. Church is dead. By now so is Coleman and Bedlam Team."

"You're a lying sack of shit."

"I have the gun," he said. "Why would I lie? Why would I need to? Don't you get it, Ledger? I won. Phoenix House is gone. I have teams at every other location where any member of your group is in play, and if they're not already dead they will be in a few minutes. The timer is already running at the hospital, and I just started the clock here."

He nodded past me to his desk chair and I saw that on it was a cell phone with a screen display of a crown surrounded by a red circle. There was a digital timer counting down from 20. And it was now at 17:32.

"And don't get any stupid ideas about taking the trigger device and stamping on it or shutting it off. It doesn't have an off switch. There's a counter code, of course, and guess who's the only person who knows it?"

"You're stuck in here with me, asshole. You get to go boom, too."

"Yeah," he said, "and I have my own way out. And I have this gun. And you're not going to do fuck-all to stop me. And, hell, even if you were the one with the gun what could you do? I could stall you long enough for the bombs to go off or you could kill me and the bombs would go off." He tapped his chest as he had before to indicate where the trigger device was attached to his pacemaker. "You cannot win this. When I heard you starting to get up off the floor in there I was about to take my stage-right exit, but I waited because I really wanted you to know just how big a failure you are. You've accomplished nothing since coming here to this tower. Nothing. Everything that has happened to you since you went to Corvin Castle has been because I've been moving you all round the chess board in exactly the way I want. I did the same with Mr. Church, all of your RTI field teams, and everyone else who matters in this situation. All of the people who in one way or another were part of the death of my uncle and the fall of the Red Order. And when I'm done here, as soon as this wonderful elixir patches me up, I'm going to make some little day trips to Greece and other places. I'm going to go visit Rudy Sanchez and Circe O'Tree and their wee ones. I'm going to visit Junie Flynn and see how many different ways I can make her scream. Then maybe I'll go to Maryland and take a healthy shit on your family's graves. Oh, the places I will go and the things I will do. I could come in my pants just thinking about it. And when all that is done, I will build the Red Empire up and turn it into the most powerful political force this world has seen since Rome."

He began to raise the pistol.

The Killer in me stepped aside and let the Darkness have its way.

The gun fired.

Twice.

One bullet hit the wall. The other hit me somewhere low on the side. I didn't care. I was enveloped in a level of rage that doesn't care about pain. Doesn't fear death. A level of hatred that had no definition in any human language.

I knocked the gun aside and began cutting.

# CHAPTER 150

## FRESH-N-CLEAN
## CRANBROOK ROAD
## ILFORD, ENGLAND

Toys stood in the parking lot and watched the building burn.

His men sat or lay against the car in which they had come. Except for Zombie, who had been placed in the back of the SUV with his coat over him.

The man who had identified himself as Nakir stood next to Toys, and the firelight dancing on his face made goblin shapes. The man's eyes were dark and quiet, though.

"Frankly, mate," said Toys with an affectation of his own insouciance, "I don't have the slightest bloody clue how I'm going to explain this in my after-action report."

Nakir turned to him. "You haven't heard, then?"

"Heard what?"

"About Phoenix House."

"What about it? And how do you even know that name? It's literally a secret hideout."

Nakir looked sad, and he gave a slow shake of his head.

"Why? What's happened?"

The team leader for the *Vampirii Lui Dumnezeu* told him.

Toys felt the ground tilt under his feet. He pressed his hands to his head and slowly, like a diseased tree, he crumpled down to the ground and wept.

## CHAPTER 151

### ST THOMAS' HOSPITAL
### WESTMINSTER BRIDGE ROAD
### LONDON, ENGLAND

The screams that came from the fire tower froze everyone to silence. The hostages, the patients dying in their beds, and every member of God's Warriors.

Then Ames began bellowing orders as he and his men rushed forward, leaving only one guard standing over the hostages. Everyone else ran with their guns ready.

"Kill them all," bellowed Ames. "Kill the bloody bastards."

Men began firing as soon as they entered the tower, shooting into smoke, into darkness. Emptying magazines down the stairs.

"Cease firing," snapped Ames. There was no return fire at all.

He heard one of his men gag and he turned to see Sergeant Howell and his corporal tangled together in a heap in a corner. Their heads were twisted around behind them, and on the ground between them was a third head, that of Ferguson.

"What happened?" he demanded. "Who fucking did this?"

Even the soldiers who had followed Howell to the stairwell looked blank.

"I didn't see nothing, Sarge," said one of the men, scared and defensive.

The stairwell was totally black, without even a glimmer from emergency lights. The hospital floor itself was dark, but there were lanterns. As Ames backed out of the stairwell, he became aware that there were not as *many* lanterns glowing as there had been.

He stopped, stunned.

Four of his men lay on the floor.

"What the fuck is happening here?" he demanded.

His men clustered around him, guns out, but there was nothing to be seen. The hostages still cowered, the patients were all in their beds and wired to machines. Ames hurried over to the room where the corpses were kept. Ferguson's headless corpse sat splay-legged against the wall.

And the body of Mr. Church was missing.

"No . . ." breathed Ames. "No, no, no."

Behind him a cold voice whispered, "Yes."

## CHAPTER 152

### BARRIER HEADQUARTERS
### HADRIAN TOWER
### LONDON, ENGLAND

I didn't kill him.

Of course I didn't.

The Darkness wanted to.

The Killer wanted to.

Even the Cop and the Modern Man wanted to.

But I didn't.

Top and Bunny and the rest of Havoc and maybe all of Chaos Team were somewhere in the tower. I could hear gunfire, and the distinctive tones of each kind of gun. I knew my friends—what was left of my *family*—were down there fighting for their lives.

So, no, I didn't kill James Rockwell. But oh how he begged me to.

Even after he gave me the cancel code, he begged for it. What was left of him screamed for me to end it. To end him.

I left him there and staggered out of the bathroom. Tripped. Fell.

Crawled to the chair. Took the device.

Prayed that Rockwell hadn't lied. Though, by that point, I don't think lying was something he was even capable of.

No.

I slumped against the wall and with every last ounce of willpower I had left, I forced my finger to be steady as I punched in the code. It was two numbers, then two more, then four. The month, day, and date that Sir Charles LaRoque was killed by a Hellfire missile.

The digital readout stopped at 5:12.

"Not even that close," I said. Then I started coughing, and the coughs would not stop. I fell over, coughing up blood, feeling my body collapse under the weight of damage and disease and grief.

"Junie," I managed to say as the darkness closed around me, "I'm so sorry."

Then, not wanting an apology to be the last thing I said, I spat my mouth clear of blood and said what really mattered.

"Junie . . . I love you."

She would never hear those words but somehow I believed she knew me well enough to guess that's what I said as I left the stage.

I lay there, looking at the broken glass and the blood on the floor. I could hear Rockwell's inarticulate mewling noises. Now he could die if he wanted to. And no furnace in hell would be hot enough.

The lights dimmed.

Even the gunfire downstairs seemed to dwindle and fade.

My eyes closed and my mind settled into a kind of peace. My war was over. Someone else would have to pick up my battered sword and shield and carry on the fight. The war, after all, was the war.

Then I heard a sound. For a crazy moment I thought it was Rockwell, even though I knew that he could not be on his feet. That was impossible.

My eyes were so dim but I saw a figure standing in the doorway. He was all in shadows or . . . maybe dressed in black. I could no longer distinguish one from the other. He stood there, watching me watch him.

Then, moving without haste, he entered the ruined office. His shoes crunched quietly on the glass. He passed me and stood for maybe a whole minute with his hands on the bathroom doorframe. Looking in.

My eyelids were closing despite all of my efforts to keep them open. I settled back, feeling myself die.

I imagined that I was leaving my body. My soul, maybe. Rising out of the broken, torn, bloody, infected wreck.

But . . .

It wasn't that.

There were arms under me. Lifting me as if I were a little child. I saw a face above me, looking down, a brow furrowed with concern, and dark eyes filled with strange lights.

I tried to ask him his name for he was a stranger. No one I had ever known or met. My lips formed words but there was no sound beyond the desperate wheezing of my failing lungs.

When he spoke, his voice was oddly gentle.

He said, "My name is Michael."

And then the darkness closed around me and extinguished all light.

# EPILOGUE

## -1-

The first time I woke up I wished I was still asleep.

Or dead. That would have hurt less.

My body was a horror show of lingering effects, unnamable pains, and remembered grief.

My mind . . . well . . .

Being dead would make that hurt less, too.

## -2-

The second time I woke up, Junie was there.

Tall, blue-eyed, with masses of wavy blond hair, all kinds of jewelry made from crystals and chunky stones and bits of copper. And lines on her face I didn't remember seeing before.

She sat there and held my hand, and for a long time neither of us said a word. Neither of us could.

The list of people we lost was so long. So many people we cared about. Friends of mine. Friends of ours. People who were important to us, to RTI, to each other, and to the world.

Nikki Bloom. Nearly half of Bug's computer team. Two-thirds of the staff at the TOC. Mrs. Karasu, the older Japanese woman who served as housekeeper for Church. Three entire teams in training who had been on Sub-1, the practice hall. A total of 111 members of Rogue Team International, ranging from Aldus the head of maintenance to Isaac Breslau, who had been one of the most senior scientists working for Doc Holliday. Most of Chaos Team, half of Bedlam. And, of course, Scott Wilson.

Gone.

How do you calculate that level of loss?

And for the survivors . . . many will have a long, slow, painful road to recovery. Bug had seventeen broken bones, including both femurs.

Doc Holliday needed extensive surgery to repair a kidney, her liver, and her pancreas. No one at the TOC or on any of the lower levels inside the volcano escaped without injuries. A few had minor cuts and bruising, but others were more badly hurt. Apparently, there were a dozen medevac choppers working for a whole day to bring the wounded to mainland hospitals.

Actually, one person got through it all with barely a scratch. Major Claire Courtland. She was in the TOC, standing with Doc and Nikki when part of the roof came down. She led the rescue operation. She saved a lot of lives. But she wasn't hurt. People joked that it was a miracle. Who knows, maybe it was. For me, though, it added another layer of mystery over our new chief of operations.

If there even *was* any RTI left after this to continue the fight. The war was still out there, waiting to be fought.

Junie, always able to read my emotions, kissed my hand. "It's okay, love," she said. "It'll all be okay."

It was a lie, of course. A kind one.

But the truth hurt too much and sometimes lies are the best drug.

**-3-**

People came to see me in shifts.

Ron Coleman came by but couldn't stay long because he was the acting head of the Integrated Sciences Division while Doc was recovering. It would be weeks or maybe months before she was able to return. If she returned at all. Ron sat in a guest chair next to me and told me all about gentamicin and a lot of very sciency things. Rudy and Junie had already told me about how Church arranged for a chopper to bring Ron's cure to me at the Tower. When he realized I was barely listening, he put a movie on his laptop. Nothing with guns. Nothing with monsters or war or violence. We watched a Pixar thing, and I fell asleep during it, and he left because there was still a lot of work left for him to do. We had not spoken of our shared losses. The time wasn't ready for that.

Major Claire Courtland came by, though she seemed nervous about it. She told me about what happened, and gave me information about all the funerals. She told me that Church had already set up trusts for the families of everyone who died—with amounts big enough to pay off mortgages, provide first-class perpetual health care, fund college tuitions, and more. Telling me all that made her cry.

Before she left, Claire said, "I'm not Grace."

"I know."

"I can't change how much I look like her."

"I know."

"Will . . . you be able to work alongside me?"

It seemed like a silly question, but wasn't. I looked at her for a while, then smiled. "Of course, Major."

"Claire," she prompted.

"Of course, Claire."

She studied my face, then nodded. Then she patted my shoulder and left.

Rudy came and brought Circe with him. They showed me pictures of the kids, and videos of the little ones saying they hoped I got better soon. Then we lapsed into one of those conversations where we all three needed to discuss something but none of us wanted to.

Finally, Circe said, "The *Scriptor's Diary*."

"Yes," I said.

"Did you read it?"

I looked at her for a very long time. "Does it matter to you either way?"

"He's my father," she said.

"I know."

She studied the lines on my face and maybe the ghosts in my eyes. "You kept the book?"

I shrugged. "For now. If your dad wants it back, he can have it."

Her face hardened and she looked away. After a minute she got up and walked out of my room, leaving Rudy there with me. We both stared at the door long after it had closed.

"She might never forgive you for that, Cowboy," he said.

"It isn't mine to keep," I said. "And it's not mine to share."

Rudy nodded. "I know," he said.

**-4-**

I did not see Church again until I was home.

Not home in Greece, where Junie and I had a place. For now, for what I needed in body and soul, *home* was in Robinwood, Maryland. Junie, Ghost, and I moved back there. Five weeks after London, on a cloudy day with a warm rain that promised an early spring, a car drove up our drive and parked in front of the house. A figure got out wearing a heavy soot-gray overcoat, hat, sunglasses, and gloves. He walked through the rain but stopped at the foot of my porch stairs. I was alone there, except for Ghost, and my dog got to his feet and showed the visitor a lot of titanium teeth.

The man removed his glove and held his hand out so Ghost could take his scent. I watched Ghost's reaction. He did not bark or snarl or wag his tail. All he did was sit down between me and the visitor.

"I came to pay my respects," said Michael.

I nodded. "Thanks for helping me back there."

Michael shook his head. Then he said, "I really came here to tell you three things."

I waited.

"First," he said, "on behalf of my people, I offer my sincerest condolences for your many losses. I know the pain of loss. Of great loss. I know that you must be suffering at this time."

He bowed to me.

I said, "There would have been more losses if you hadn't been there."

"That was kind of you to say." He paused, looking sad and uncomfortable. "What I did—what my brothers and I did—was not for you, you understand that, yes? Of course you do. I was born a monster, into a family of monsters. I cannot stop being what I am. I'm not sure I would do so even if I could. I am what God made me."

"God gets the blame for a lot of what happens in this world. Makes me wonder if he was ever involved at all."

Michael nodded. "I also wonder. Perhaps the future will tell each of us."

"You said there were three things," I prompted.

"The second is that neither you nor any of your allies need ever fear from the Upierczy again."

"Can you really make that kind of promise? Aren't there rogues left over from the fall of the Red Knights?"

"Fewer every day," said Michael. "My intelligence agents have been scouring the world for them. They can try to hide, but we know how to hunt."

"Monsters hunting monsters," I said. "I know that dance."

But Michael shook his head. "We have allies in this hunt, Colonel. I have been having talks with Lilith and the Mothers of the Fallen."

"Well, well," I said. "That sounds dangerous."

"It is, of course. The Mothers have scant reason to trust me or my kind. But my half sister intervened and is brokering a truce. A working arrangement."

"Your half sister?"

He almost smiled. "I am the last of Grigor's sons. My only living blood relative now is the woman you call Violin."

"Jesus."

"She understands me," said Michael. "She, like me, is not entirely human."

"If you put one foot wrong—" I began, but he cut me off.

"She will kill me, yes I know. And if that is her desire, or if Lilith orders my death, I will do nothing to prevent it. The blood debt we owe to the Mothers can never be repaid. My life means less than nothing compared to what those women have endured."

I reached out and scratched Ghost between the ears. "Good luck with that. What's the third thing?"

He suddenly looked hesitant, even embarrassed. "I . . ."

"Whatever it is, just say it."

Michael nodded and held out his hand. "I wanted the honor of shaking your hand."

I sat there and stared at him. At this Upierczy, this monster. I had fought and killed his father and helped tear down the Upierczy culture. I've lost count of how many of his kind—of his *brothers*—I'd killed. And here he was, offering me his hand.

Ghost growled ever so faintly.

Michael stood in the rain with his hand out and did not move.

After a long time, I got up and walked down to face him. We stood in the rain. And shook hands. Then he stepped back, bowed again, and walked back to his car. He got in and started the engine, and began edging along the edge of the turnaround. But as he passed me, he paused and gave me a single, silent nod.

I nodded back.

One monster to another.

**-5-**

**VICTORY LAKE CAMPGROUND**
**COUNTY RD 542**
**EGG HARBOR CITY, NEW JERSEY**

Nicodemus sat on the bank of a grassy hill that led down to a cedar-water creek. The water burbled contentedly and birds sang in all the trees. Butterflies and bees went about their business. Tree frogs croaked like rusty hinges. And a deer peered at him from the shadows between the pines.

He was very thin now. Wasted to a caricature of who he had been. His flesh was sallow and dry as parchment, accentuating his cheekbones and brows so that the shadows cast by the sun made his face look like a skull.

Nicodemus was well satisfied, having played ambassador for all of the groups, steering them together in conflict. One last game before bedtime. But he felt old and tired. Used up and glutted with his own games.

He dug his cell phone out of his pocket and considered calling Joe Ledger. Or Church. But as he held the phone his eyes focused more on the hand. He stared at it for a long while. The skin was so thin that he could see through it to the bones. And farther still.

"I can see right through into nowhere at all," he said, then tossed the cell phone into the creek.

Nicodemus leaned back against the grass and closed his eyes.

Hours later, when a pair of hikers passed that same spot, they both shivered without knowing why, and moved on. They saw nothing because, of course, there was nothing left to see.

**-6-**

Two days later a black Escalade pulled up in front of my house.

The sun was edging toward the horizon and I was sitting in an Adirondack chair in front of a firepit placed in the lee of an ancient oak. The only tree this close to the house that had survived the blast that killed my family. I had swung from a tire hung from that oak when I was a kid. So had Sean. So had his kids.

I knew Church was coming. I didn't get up and just waited until he walked over. I saw Luke standing by the Escalade, and we traded nods. He was now Church's valet, bodyguard, and—quite possibly—his only real friend.

Church sat down across from me, and for a while we watched the first fireflies of the season flashing their love lights among the tall stalks of grass.

Without preamble, I said, "Phoenix House?"

Church shook his head. "RTI doesn't live there anymore."

"Where, then?"

"That is still a question. But I am exploring a number of interesting options. By the time you are well enough to come back, we will have that answer. And in the meantime, we are set up on a deep-sea research platform in the North Sea."

"As guests of the crown?"

He shook his head. "Something I bought some years back. It'll be our home for now, and who knows, maybe forever. It's current code name is Avalon."

I nodded.

Ghost came over from where he'd been sprawled in the last of the day's patches of good sunlight. He brushed me as he passed and then went over to Church, bushy tail wagging. Church reached into an inner pocket and brought out a package of Ghost's favorite dried goat snacks. We sat there as Church broke off little pieces and let Ghost eat them out of his hand.

Then Church nodded to the parcel that sat on the arm of my chair. It was wrapped in brown butcher's paper and tied with hairy twine.

"The diary?" he asked.

"Yes."

A crow cawed softly from a nearby tree.

"Have you read it?" he asked.

"No."

He looked surprised. "Aren't you curious? About what's in it? All the secrets? All of the mysteries explained?"

I picked up the book and weighed it. The thing was old and heavy and ugly and I'm glad I'd taken the time to wrap it.

Church studied me. "You have the right to ask. You have more than earned my trust. You have the right to know who and what I am."

I took the book in both hands.

Then I leaned forward and set it atop the blazing logs. The paper caught at once but the book did not, almost as if it did not want to be burned. As if it didn't want to die without revealing all of its secrets. But then I saw the moment where the flames took hold. It burned slowly, but it burned.

I looked at Mr. Church. "I already know who and what you are," I said.

He said nothing. But as the book was consumed down to coals and the last of the daylight fled from our skies, I thought I saw the silvery sheen of wetness on his cheek.

We sat there until the stars came out, and then long, long into the evening.

# ACKNOWLEDGMENTS

The Joe Ledger novels could not be undertaken without the help of a lot of talented and generous people. In no particular order, then . . .

Thanks to my literary agent, Sara Crowe of Sara Crowe Literary; my stalwart editor at St. Martin's Griffin, Michael Homler; Robert Allen and the crew at Macmillan Audio; and my film agent, Dana Spector of Creative Artists Agency. And special thanks to my brilliant audiobook reader, Ray Porter. As always, thanks to Dana Fredsti, my superhero of an assistant.

Many thanks to Dr. Ronald Coleman, Principal Scientist at International Stem Cell Corporation. Thanks to my friends in the International Thriller Writers, International Association of Media Tie-In Writers, the Mystery Writers of America, The Writers Coffeehouse, and the Horror Writers Association.

# ABOUT THE AUTHOR

Sara Jo West

**Jonathan Maberry** is a *New York Times* bestselling, Inkpot-winning, five-time Bram Stoker Award–winning author of *Relentless, Ink, Patient Zero, Rot & Ruin, Dead of Night,* the Pine Deep Trilogy, *The Wolfman, Zombie CSU,* and *They Bite,* among others. His V-Wars series has been adapted by Netflix, and his work for Marvel Comics includes *The Punisher, Wolverine, Doomwar, Marvel Zombies Return,* and *Black Panther.* He is the editor of *Weird Tales* magazine and also edits anthologies such as *Aliens vs. Predators, Nights of the Living Dead* (with George A. Romero), *Don't Turn Out the Lights,* and others. His Joe Ledger series was optioned for television by Chad Stahelski (*John Wick*).